D0423962

THE PEARL OF
ORR'S ISLAND

The PEARL
of ORR'S ISLAND

A Story of the Coast of Maine

HARRIET BEECHER STOWE

With a new foreword by Joan D. Hedrick

HOUGHTON MIFFLIN COMPANY

Boston   New York

First Houghton Mifflin paperback edition 2001
Foreword © 2001 by Joan D. Hedrick
Copyright, 1862 and 1890, by Harriet Beecher Stowe
Copyright, 1896, by Houghton Mifflin Company

All rights reserved

For information about permission to reproduce selections from
this book, write to Permissions, Houghton Mifflin Company,
215 Park Avenue South, New York, New York 10003.

Visit our Web site: www.houghtonmifflinbooks.com.

Library of Congress Cataloging-in-Publication Data

Stowe, Harriet Beecher, 1811–1896.
The pearl of Orr's Island : a story of the coast of Maine /
Harriet Beecher Stowe ; with a new foreword by Joan D. Hedrick.
          p.   cm.
Originally published: Boston : Houghton Mifflin, 1862.
ISBN 0-618-08347-2
1. Girls—Fiction. 2. Islands—Fiction. 3. Maine—Fiction.
I. Title.

PS2954.P4   2001
813'.3—dc21   00-053877

Book design by Anne Chalmers
Typeface: Hoefler Text

Printed in the United States of America

QUM 10 9 8 7 6 5 4 3 2 1

CONTENTS

CONTENTS

FOREWORD

BY JOAN D. HEDRICK

Stowe began writing *The Pearl of Orr's Island* in the summer of 1852, flush with the extraordinary success of *Uncle Tom's Cabin,* which sold 10,000 copies in its first week of publication and required six printing presses running day and night to keep up with the demand. At the end of the first year *Uncle Tom's Cabin* had sold 300,000 copies in the United States and a million and a half in Great Britain. The book generated plays, songs, figurines, and handkerchiefs and was translated into more than sixty-three languages. It is striking that, having written a book outsold only by the Bible, Stowe should immediately turn to this haunting and beautiful story about the limits of an ordinary woman's life.

It may have been the extraordinariness of her public success that led her to reflect on the more ordinary course of life for a nineteenth-century woman. Yet Stowe's heroine, Mara Lincoln, is not typical. That role more nearly suits her foil, the sprightly Sally Kittridge, who, while bright and energetic, is better suited to the domestic and wifely duties that marked the limits of what was commonly referred to in the nineteenth century as the "woman's sphere." In *The Pearl of Orr's Island* Stowe explores the inner life of a reticent, daydreaming, imaginative woman as she attempts to conform to conventional expectations.

Nineteenth-century gender roles were strongly marked in Stowe's childhood models. Stowe's father, Lyman Beecher, was one of the most famous evangelical preachers of the pre–Civil War era. His public persona overshadowed that of his literary and artistic wife, Roxana Foote Beecher, who was so shy that even the duties of a minister's wife were difficult for her. She bore nine children and died in 1816 at the age of forty-one, when Harriet was five. After her death the Beecher family eulogized her as the perfect wife and mother, the embodiment of "true womanhood."

Harriet, a precocious child with a quick memory, received an unusually rigorous education for a girl of her time. At age eight she entered the Litchfield Female Academy, an excellent school founded to "vindicate the equality of the female intellect." An eager writer, she volunteered at age nine to write weekly essays. Her first assignment was an essay on "The Difference between the Natural and Moral Sublime"—a topic, Stowe noted, "not trashy or sentimental, such as are often supposed to be the style for female schools." At age thirteen she won the honor of having her composition read aloud at the annual school exhibit, where her father sat up and asked who the author was. When the answer came, "Your daughter, sir," Stowe experienced what she later called "the proudest moment of my life."

In 1824 Stowe entered her sister Catharine Beecher's Hartford Female Seminary, where she studied the most difficult subjects in the male college curriculum, including Latin and moral philosophy. In 1832, after teaching composition at the seminary for three years, she moved with her family to Cincinnati, Ohio, where her father had accepted the presidency of Lane Seminary. Stowe observed new customs and relished the dialects spoken at the Cincinnati landing, a center of commerce for the booming West. Her literary career blossomed. She published a widely adopted *Primary Geography* (1833) and participated in the social and literary gatherings of the Semi-Colon Club, for which she wrote many of her early sketches and stories, pioneering the use of dialect and reflecting on customs in her native New England.

Stowe moved back to New England in 1850 when her husband, Calvin Stowe, a Biblical scholar, accepted a position at Bowdoin College in Brunswick, Maine. Her eighteen years in Cincinnati had broadened her horizons and her grasp of the regions that made up the nation. In 1851, the year of the "American renaissance," when many now-classic American books were written, she began writing *Uncle Tom's Cabin,* a novel bristling with regional speech and social types.

The Pearl of Orr's Island similarly bears a strong stamp of place. Like *Uncle Tom's Cabin,* it is enlivened by garrulous characters with distinctive voices. The practical Miss Roxy Toothacre undercuts the sentimentality of the opening scene, in which Mara Lincoln's mother dies shortly after giving birth to her, by remarking, "she'll make a beautiful corpse." At the end of chapter 2, Stowe describes Mara as having struck her roots "in the salt, bitter waters of our mortal life," a phrase that concisely recalls the shipwreck of her parents and her own orphaning at the moment of her birth. Spare, crisp descriptions of the wild and bare scenery of coastal Maine create a world apart.

Typically Stowe's New England novels are set not in her lifetime but in that of her mother, when women's domestic power was more visible and distinct than it would become in the age of the sewing machine. *The Pearl of Orr's Island* takes place before the invention of stoves, during "the days of the genial open kitchen-fire." The reigning priestesses of the domestic hearth are Miss Roxy and Miss Ruey Toothacre, "two brisk old bodies of the feminine gender and singular number." These women represent a familiar institution in Stowe's fiction, the unmarried "aunt" who travels from household to household rendering herself useful. They are also, like Katy Scudder in Stowe's *The Minister's Wooing* (1859), women of "faculty."

> It was impossible to say what they could not do: they could make dresses, and make shirts and vests and pantaloons, and cut out boys' jackets, and braid straw, and bleach and trim bonnets, and cook and wash, and iron and mend, could upholster and quilt, could nurse all kinds of sicknesses, and in default of a doctor, who was often miles away, were supposed to be infallible medical oracles.

Stowe had a great appreciation for the energy, talent, creativity, and resourcefulness involved in such domestic arts, and through these activities women emerge in her fiction as significant subjects. But if women's "faculty" was more evident when women turned silk dresses and nursed the sick and built kitchen fires, so too were the limits of a woman's sphere. Even Sally Kittridge is shown to rebel against the neat cross-stitches of a New England daughter's education. Set to hemming a sheet, the six-year-old girl looks "surly and wrathful." "In old times," Stowe comments, "turning sheets was thought a most especial and wholesome discipline for young girls; in the first place, because it took off the hands of their betters a very uninteresting and monotonous labor; . . . a dull child took it tolerably well; but to a lively, energetic one, it was a perfect torture."

Stowe's heroine, Mara, longs for a wider sphere in a world in which men represent ambition and adventure. When Moses, her male counterpart, goes on his first fishing expedition, Mara is left at home to dream dreams for him, her "glorious knight." Moses comes back full of his own importance, and Mara's response is to resent "the continual disparaging tone in which Moses spoke of her girlhood." Mara's adventures are all inward; like the young Harriet Beecher, she finds a fragmentary copy of Shakespeare's *The Tempest* and reads it with the conviction that it transpired in a place much like Orr's Island. The "beautiful young Prince Ferdinand" is "much like what Moses would be when he grew up," and Mara imagines herself his Miranda. While Moses has the advantage in outdoor exploits, Mara surpasses him in imagination and learning. The readiness with which she acquires Latin by overhearing Moses struggling unsuccessfully with it leads the minister, Mr. Sewell, to teach her along with him. This strange, sensitive, extraordinary young girl, all nerve and spirit, causes Mr. Sewell to reflect: "'If she were a boy, and you would take her away cod-fishing, as you have Moses, the sea-winds would blow away some of the thinking, and her little body would grow stout, and her mind less delicate and sensitive. But she's a woman,' he said, with a sigh, 'and they are all alike. We can't do much for them, but let them come up as they will and make the best of it.'" The point, of course, is that women are not all alike. They are individuals with unique temperaments and longings, some of which get ironed out when they conform to their domestic role.

Mara tries very hard to be a conventional woman—though, significantly, we never see her engaged in domestic work. She always has a book in her hand and a dream in her head. But she does fall in love with Moses and tries very hard to suit herself to his needs. Through this traditional plot, Stowe does something very untraditional. As Judith Fetterley argues, Stowe systematically unravels the romance plot. In Fetterley's apt formulation, having experienced the world as his oyster, Moses has no qualms about appropriating its "pearl" for his exclusive use.

Stowe was reading *Jane Eyre* while she wrote *The Pearl of Orr's Island,* and one can see both Brontë and Stowe probing what it means to marry, to be the possession of another. Brontë evened the playing field by having Rochester blinded in a fire before he married Jane. Stowe has her heroine escape through a sublimely sentimental death.

Critics have generally been unhappy with Stowe's resolution of her plot. Sarah Orne Jewett, who drew much inspiration in her own work from Stowe's New England novels, praised the originality and strength of the beginning and lamented "that she couldn't finish it in the same noble key of simplicity and harmony. You must throw everything and everybody aside at times, but a woman made like Mrs. Stowe cannot bring herself to that cold selfishness of the moment for one's work's sake."

Stowe started and stopped the novel several times, but not because she was attending to her large family. Immediately after the publication of *Uncle Tom's Cabin* she was threatened with a lawsuit by a Protestant minister whom she had quoted as a defender of slavery. Her reply to him and other critics blossomed into *A Key to Uncle Tom's Cabin* (1853), both a defense of her novel and an antislavery polemic in its own right. Upon finishing the *Key* she went on a triumphal tour of Great Britain, where she was celebrated at large soirees and showered with money. Now considered one of the world's foremost antislavery voices, Stowe responded to the bloodshed in Kansas by writing *Dred* (1856)—her second antislavery novel—instead of finishing *Pearl.* As *Dred* was going to press she made her second tour of Europe. Soon after her return in 1857, her nineteen-year-old son Henry drowned while swimming in the Connecticut River. Stowe turned her grief into the first of her New England novels, *The Minister's Wooing* (1859), which attacked the Calvinist theology of predestination for the pain it caused parents who had lost children. In 1860 she made another tour of Europe, this time going to France, Switzerland, and Italy. She returned to writing *The Pearl of Orr's Island* later that year and contracted with the *Independent* to publish it serially. At the same time she contracted with *Cornhill* magazine in London for an Italian novel, *Agnes of Sorrento*. Realizing too late that she could not keep two novels going at once, she brought *Pearl* to a halt at the end of chapter 17. A card inserted in the April 4, 1861, issue of the *Independent* explained to her readers that she would continue her story in the fall.

Stowe's dilatory approach to writing *Pearl* is due in part to her riding out the phenomenon of *Uncle Tom's Cabin*. It is likely that an even larger deterrent to bringing *The Pearl of Orr's Island* to an end was the author's inability to resolve the intractable gender issues she had engaged. It is instructive to examine the point in the plot where Stowe got stuck. At the end of chapter 17, Mara's education is complete. She knows how to read Virgil and "to paint partridge, and checkerberry, and trailing arbutus." That is to say, Stowe leaves her heroine on the verge of adulthood, prepared with the education of a young man and the "accomplishments" of a young woman. What can Mara do?

Stowe's difficulties can be compared to the difficulty that Mark Twain had in ending *Huckleberry Finn*. *Huckleberry Finn* is also a story about growing up, and particularly about the psychic pressure to conform to society's rules. Like Stowe, Twain got stuck at a crossroads. At the end of chapter 16, the raft on which Huck flees from "civilization" and Jim flees from slavery floats past Cairo in the fog. Instead of finding the Ohio River and freedom, the boy and the man are drifting further into bondage. At this point in his story, begun in 1876 shortly after Twain moved into the mansion he built next door to Stowe's house in Hartford, Twain put it down, and he did not finish it for seven years. He could not see how to write an emancipation plot in a world of frauds, thieves, and murderers. The so-called evasion chapters with which the novel ends, in which Huck colludes with Tom Sawyer in playing humiliating tricks on Jim, have led critics to lament that Twain could not finish the book with the same wit and moral vision with which he began it.

In their stories of growing up, Twain and Stowe faced intractable realities that constrained the development of their protagonists. Both chose to have them escape. As writers and social critics, they had several choices: to portray the reality unvarnished, to deny and cover up that reality, or to portray it in such a way as to point toward social transformation. It is tempting to equate the first option with what we have learned to call "realism" and the second with what we have learned to call "sentimentalism." This leaves us, however, with no name for the third category, which in fact combines the first and third choices in the prophetic manner of *Uncle Tom's Cabin*. In her study of the nineteenth-century French novel, Margaret Cohen has suggested "sentimental social novel" to describe works that utilized "the novel's power to intervene in public life," works that combine the descriptive power of realism with the transformative power of idealism. Both *Huckleberry Finn* and *The Pearl of Orr's Island* promise the transforming power of the sentimental social novel but fail to deliver it, and both retreat into sentimental evasions. This is because both, as Jane Smiley has observed of *Huckleberry Finn*, engage social issues at the level of individuals rather than institutions.

Yet at this level Stowe provides a penetrating analysis of gender dynamics. In the last half of the novel, all Mara asks for is a suitable mate with whom to share her rich inner life. This is a modest enough desire, considering that she might have wanted to be an artist like Prospero rather than a helper like Miranda.

But even this proves difficult, as Stowe reveals. Mara's incompatibility with Moses is suggested early on, when she works up the courage to share with him her delight in *The Tempest*. He listens in a matter-of-fact way, astounding Mara with his apparent indifference to correspondences with his own stormy history. He even "interrupted her once in the middle of the celebrated 'Full fathom five thy father lies,' by asking her to hold up the mast a minute, while he drove in a peg to make it rake a little more." Moses is less a Prince Ferdinand than a cloddish Caliban. Mara gives up when she understands that Moses can never enter into her most intimate concerns. The novel ultimately suggests that it is impossible for men and women to truly understand each other:

> No man—especially one that is living a rough, busy, out-of-doors life—can form the slightest conception of that veiled and secluded life which exists in the heart of a sensitive woman, whose sphere is narrow, whose external diversions are few, and whose mind, therefore, acts by a continual introversion upon itself . . . Man's utter ignorance of woman's nature is a cause of a great deal of unsuspected cruelty which he practices toward her.

This incompatibility sets women up for a double contradiction: unable to be active in the world, restricted to the private sphere and marriage, women are bound to men with whom true intimacy is impossible. This is the reality that leaves Stowe with no option better than the sentimental death she accords her heroine. The beauty and texture of this interesting novel arise from Stowe's clear-eyed probing of a social problem to which she could envision no solution.

Works Cited

Cohen, Margaret. *The Sentimental Education of the Novel.* Princeton, N.J.: Princeton University Press, 1999.

Cross, Barbara M. ed., Vol. 1, *The Autobiography of Lyman Beecher.* Cambridge, Mass.: Harvard University Press, 1961.

Fetterley, Judith. *Provisions: A Reader from 19th-Century American Women.* Bloomington: Indiana University Press, 1985.

Hedrick, Joan D. *Harriet Beecher Stowe: A Life.* New York: Oxford University Press, 1994.

Smiley, Jane. "Say It Ain't So, Huck: Second Thoughts on Mark Twain's Masterpiece," *Harper's* (January, 1996): 61–67.

JOAN D. HEDRICK is the Charles A. Dana Professor of History at Trinity College in Hartford, Connecticut. She is the author of *The Oxford Harriet Beecher Stowe Reader* and the Pulitzer Prize–winning *Harriet Beecher Stowe: A Life.*

INTRODUCTORY
NOTE

The publication of *Uncle Tom's Cabin,* though much more than an incident in an author's career, seems to have determined Mrs. Stowe more surely in her purpose to devote herself to literature. During the summer following its appearance, she was in Andover, making over the house which she and her husband were to occupy upon leaving Brunswick; and yet, busy as she was, she was writing articles for *The Independent* and *The National Era.* The following extract from a letter written at that time, July 29, 1852, intimates that she already was sketching the outline of the story which later grew into *The Pearl of Orr's Island:* —

"I seem to have so much to fill my time, and yet there is my Maine story waiting. However, I am composing it every day, only I greatly need living studies for the filling in of my sketches. There is old Jonas, my "fish father," a sturdy, independent fisherman farmer, who in his youth sailed all over the world and made up his mind about everything. In his old age he attends prayer-meetings and reads the *Missionary Herald.* He also has plenty of money in an old brown sea-chest. He is a great heart with an inflexible will and iron muscles. I must go to Orr's Island and see him again." The story seems to have remained in her mind, for we are told by her son that she worked upon it by turns with *The Minister's Wooing*.

It was not, however, until eight years later, after *The Minister's Wooing* had been published and *Agnes of Sorrento* was well begun, that she took up her old story in earnest and set about making it into a short serial. It would seem that her first intention was to confine herself to a sketch of the childhood of her chief characters, with a view to delineating the influences at work upon them; but, as she herself expressed it, "Out of the simple history of the little Pearl of Orr's Island as it had shaped itself in her mind, rose up a Captain Kittridge with his garrulous yarns, and Misses Roxy and Ruey, given to talk, and a whole pigeon roost of yet undreamed of fancies and dreams which would insist on being written." So it came about that the story as originally planned came to a stopping place at the end of chapter 17, as the reader may see when he reaches that place. The childish life of her characters ended there, and a lapse of ten years was assumed before their story was taken up again in the next chapter. The book when published had no chapter headings. These have been supplied in the present edition.

THE PEARL OF
ORR'S ISLAND

I

NAOMI

On the road to the Kennebec, below the town of Bath, in the State of Maine, might have been seen, on a certain autumnal afternoon, a one-horse wagon, in which two persons were sitting. One was an old man, with the peculiarly hard but expressive physiognomy which characterizes the seafaring population of the New England shores. A clear blue eye, evidently practiced in habits of keen observation, white hair, bronzed, weather-beaten cheeks, and a face deeply lined with the furrows of shrewd thought and anxious care, were points of the portrait that made themselves felt at a glance.

By his side sat a young woman of two-and-twenty, of a marked and peculiar personal appearance. Her hair was black, and smoothly parted on a broad forehead, to which a pair of penciled dark eyebrows gave a striking and definite outline. Beneath, lay a pair of large black eyes, remarkable for tremulous expression of melancholy and timidity. The cheek was white and bloodless as a snowberry, though with the clear and perfect oval of good health; the mouth was delicately formed, with a certain sad quiet in its lines, which indicated a habitually repressed and sensitive nature.

The dress of this young person, as often happens in New England, was, in refinement and even elegance, a marked contrast to that of her male companion and to the humble vehicle in which she rode. There was not only the most fastidious neatness, but a delicacy in the choice of colors, an indication of elegant tastes in the whole arrangement, and the quietest suggestion in the world of an acquaintance with the usages of fashion, which struck one oddly in those wild and dreary surroundings. On the whole, she impressed one like those fragile wild-flowers which in April cast their fluttering shadows from the mossy crevices of the old New England granite,—an existence in which colorless delicacy is united to a sort of elastic hardihood of life, fit for the rocky soil and harsh winds it is born to encounter.

The scenery of the road along which the two were riding was wild and bare. Only savins and mulleins, with their dark pyramids or white spires of velvet leaves, diversified the sandy wayside; but out at sea was a wide sweep of blue, reaching far to the open ocean, which lay rolling, tossing, and breaking into white caps of foam in the bright sunshine. For two or three days a northeast storm had been raging, and the sea was in all the commotion which such a general upturning creates.

The two travelers reached a point of elevated land, where they paused a moment, and the man drew up the jogging, stiff-jointed old farm-horse, and raised himself upon his feet to look out at the prospect.

There might be seen in the distance the blue Kennebec sweeping out toward the ocean through its picturesque rocky shores, decked with cedars and other dusky evergreens, which were illuminated by the orange and flame-colored trees of Indian summer. Here and there scarlet creepers swung long trailing garlands over the faces of the dark rock, and fringes of goldenrod above swayed with the brisk blowing wind that was driving the blue waters seaward, in face of the up-coming ocean tide,—a conflict which caused them to rise in great foam-crested waves. There are two channels into this river from the open sea, navigable for ships which are coming in to the city of Bath; one is broad and shallow, the other narrow and deep, and these are divided by a steep ledge of rocks.

Where the spectators of this scene were sitting, they could see in the distance a ship borne with tremendous force by the rising tide into the mouth of the river, and encountering a northwest wind which had succeeded the gale, as northwest winds often do on this coast. The ship, from what might be observed in the distance, seemed struggling to make the wider channel, but was constantly driven off by the baffling force of the wind.

"There she is, Naomi," said the old fisherman, eagerly, to his companion, "coming right in." The young woman was one of the sort that never start, and never exclaim, but with all deeper emotions grow still. The color slowly mounted into her cheek, her lips parted, and her eyes dilated with a wide, bright expression; her breathing came in thick gasps, but she said nothing.

The old fisherman stood up in the wagon, his coarse, butter-nut-colored coat-flaps fluttering and snapping in the breeze, while his interest seemed to be so intense in the efforts of the ship that he made involuntary and eager movements as if to direct her course. A moment passed, and his keen, practiced eye discovered a change in her movements, for he cried out involuntarily,—

"*Don't* take the narrow channel to-day!" and a moment after, "O Lord! O Lord! have mercy,—there they go! Look! look! look!"

And, in fact, the ship rose on a great wave clear out of the water, and the next second seemed to leap with a desperate plunge into the narrow passage; for a moment there was a shivering of the masts and the rigging, and she went down and was gone.

"They 're split to pieces!" cried the fisherman. "Oh, my poor girl—my poor girl—they 're gone! O Lord, have mercy!"

The woman lifted up no voice, but, as one who has been shot through the heart falls with no cry, she fell back,—a mist rose up over her great mournful eyes,—she had fainted.

The story of this wreck of a home-bound ship just entering the harbor is yet told in many a family on this coast. A few hours after, the unfortunate crew were washed ashore in all the joyous holiday rig in which they had attired themselves that morning to go to their sisters, wives, and mothers.

This is the first scene in our story.

II

MARA

Down near the end of Orr's Island, facing the open ocean, stands a brown house of the kind that the natives call "lean-to," or "linter,"—one of those large, comfortable structures, barren in the ideal, but rich in the practical, which the workingman of New England can always command. The waters of the ocean came up within a rod of this house, and the sound of its moaning waves was even now filling the clear autumn starlight. Evidently something was going on within, for candles fluttered and winked from window to window, like fireflies in a dark meadow, and sounds as of quick footsteps, and the flutter of brushing garments, might be heard.

Something unusual is certainly going on within the dwelling of Zephaniah Pennel to-night.

Let us enter the dark front-door. We feel our way to the right, where a solitary ray of light comes from the chink of a half-opened door. Here is the front room of the house, set apart as its place of especial social hilarity and sanctity,—the "best room," with its low studded walls, white dimity window-curtains, rag carpet, and polished wood chairs. It is now lit by the dim gleam of a solitary tallow candle, which seems in the gloom to make only a feeble circle of light around itself, leaving all the rest of the apartment in shadow.

In the centre of the room, stretched upon a table, and covered partially by a sea-cloak, lies the body of a man of twenty-five,—lies, too, evidently as one of whom it is written, "He shall return to his house no more, neither shall his place know him any more." A splendid manhood has suddenly been called to forsake that lifeless form, leaving it, like a deserted palace, beautiful in its desolation. The hair, dripping with the salt wave, curled in glossy abundance on the finely-formed head; the flat, broad brow; the closed eye, with its long black lashes; the firm, manly mouth; the strongly-moulded chin,—all, all were sealed with that seal which is never to be broken till the great resurrection day.

He was lying in a full suit of broadcloth, with a white vest and smart blue neck-tie, fastened with a pin, in which was some braided hair under a crystal. All his clothing, as well as his hair, was saturated with sea-water, which trickled from time to time, and struck with a leaden and dropping sound into a sullen pool which lay under the table.

This was the body of James Lincoln, ship-master of the brig Flying Scud, who that morning had dressed himself gayly in his state-room to go on shore and meet his wife,—singing and jesting as he did so.

This is all that you have to learn in the room below; but as we stand there, we hear a trampling of feet in the apartment above,—the quick yet careful opening and shutting of doors,— and voices come and go about the house, and whisper consultations on the stairs. Now comes the roll of wheels, and the Doctor's gig drives up to the door; and, as he goes creaking up with his heavy boots, we will follow and gain admission to the dimly-lighted chamber.

Two gossips are sitting in earnest, whispering conversation over a small bundle done up in an old flannel petticoat. To them the doctor is about to address himself cheerily, but is repelled by sundry signs and sounds which warn him not to speak. Moderating his heavy boots as well as he is able to a pace of quiet, he advances for a moment, and the petticoat is unfolded for him to glance at its contents; while a low, eager, whispered conversation, attended with much head-shaking, warns him that his first duty is with somebody behind the checked curtains of a bed in the farther corner of the room. He steps on tiptoe, and draws the curtain; and there, with closed eye, and cheek as white as wintry snow, lies the same face over which passed the shadow of death when that ill-fated ship went down.

This woman was wife to him who lies below, and within the hour has been made mother to a frail little human existence, which the storm of a great anguish has driven untimely on the shores of life,—a precious pearl cast up from the past eternity upon the wet, wave-ribbed sand of the present. Now, weary with her moanings, and beaten out with the wrench of a double anguish, she lies with closed eyes in that passive apathy which precedes deeper shadows and longer rest.

Over against her, on the other side of the bed, sits an aged woman in an attitude of deep dejection, and the old man we saw with her in the morning is standing with an anxious, awestruck face at the foot of the bed.

The doctor feels the pulse of the woman, or rather lays an inquiring finger where the slightest thread of vital current is scarcely throbbing, and shakes his head mournfully. The touch of his hand rouses her,—her large wild, melancholy eyes fix themselves on him with an inquiring glance, then she shivers and moans,—

"Oh, Doctor, Doctor!—Jamie, Jamie!"

"Come, come!" said the doctor, "cheer up, my girl, you've got a fine little daughter,—the Lord mingles mercies with his afflictions."

Her eyes closed, her head moved with a mournful but decided dissent.

A moment after she spoke in the sad old words of the Hebrew Scripture,—

"Call her not Naomi; call her Mara, for the Almighty hath dealt very bitterly with me."

And as she spoke, there passed over her face the sharp frost of the last winter; but even as it passed there broke out a smile, as if a flower had been thrown down from Paradise, and she said,—

"Not my will, but thy will," and so was gone.

Aunt Roxy and Aunt Ruey were soon left alone in the chamber of death.

"She'll make a beautiful corpse," said Aunt Roxy, surveying the still, white form contemplatively, with her head in an artistic attitude.

"She was a pretty girl," said Aunt Ruey; "dear me, what a Providence! I 'member the wedd'n down in that lower room, and what a handsome couple they were."

"They were lovely and pleasant in their lives, and in their deaths they were not divided," said Aunt Roxy, sententiously.

"What was it she said, did ye hear?" said Aunt Ruey.

"She called the baby 'Mary.'"

"Ah! sure enough, her mother's name afore her. What a still, softly-spoken thing she always was!"

"A pity the poor baby did n't go with her," said Aunt Roxy; "seven-months' children are so hard to raise."

"'Tis a pity," said the other.

But babies will live, and all the more when everybody says

that it is a pity they should. Life goes on as inexorably in this world as death. It was ordered by THE WILL above that out of these two graves should spring one frail, trembling autumn flower,—the "Mara" whose poor little roots first struck deep in the salt, bitter waters of our mortal life.

III

THE BAPTISM
AND THE BURIAL

Now, I cannot think of anything more unlikely and uninteresting to make a story of than that old brown "linter" house of Captain Zephaniah Pennel, down on the south end of Orr's Island.

Zephaniah and Mary Pennel, like Zacharias and Elizabeth, are a pair of worthy, God-fearing people, walking in all the commandments and ordinances of the Lord blameless; but that is no great recommendation to a world gaping for sensation and calling for something stimulating. This worthy couple never read anything but the Bible, the "Missionary Herald," and the "Christian Mirror,"—never went anywhere except in the round of daily business. He owned a fishing-smack, in which he labored after the apostolic fashion; and she washed, and ironed, and scrubbed, and brewed, and baked, in her contented round, week in and out. The only recreation they ever enjoyed was the going once a week, in good weather, to a prayer-meeting in a little old brown school-house, about a mile from their dwelling; and making a weekly excursion every Sunday, in their fishing craft, to the church opposite, on Harpswell Neck.

To be sure, Zephaniah had read many wide leaves of God's great book of Nature, for, like most Maine sea-captains, he had been wherever ship can go,—to all usual and unusual ports. His hard, shrewd, weather-beaten visage had been seen looking over the railings of his brig in the port of Genoa, swept round by its splendid crescent of palaces and its snow-crested Apennines. It had looked out in the Lagoons of Venice at that wavy floor which in evening seems a sea of glass mingled with fire, and out of which rise temples, and palaces, and churches, and distant silvery Alps, like so many fabrics of dream-land. He had been through the Skagerrack and Cattegat,—into the Baltic, and away round to Archangel, and there chewed a bit of chip, and considered and calculated what bargains it was best to make. He had walked the streets of Calcutta in his shirt-sleeves, with his best Sunday vest, backed with black glazed cambric, which six months before came from the hands of Miss Roxy, and was pronounced by her to be as good as any tailor could make; and in all these places he was just Zephaniah Pennel,—a chip of old Maine,—thrifty, careful, shrewd, honest, God-fearing, and carrying an instinctive knowledge of men and things under a face of rustic simplicity.

It was once, returning from one of his voyages, that he found his wife with a black-eyed, curly-headed little creature, who called him papa, and climbed on his knee, nestled under his coat, rifled his pockets, and woke him every morning by pulling open his eyes with little fingers, and jabbering unintelligible dialects in his ears.

"We will call this child Naomi, wife," he said, after consulting his old Bible; "for that means pleasant, and I'm sure I never see anything beat her for pleasantness. I never knew as children was so engagin'!"

It was to be remarked that Zephaniah after this made shorter and shorter voyages, being somehow conscious of a string around his heart which pulled him harder and harder, till one Sunday, when the little Naomi was five years old, he said to his wife,—

"I hope I ain't a-pervertin' Scriptur' nor nuthin', but I can't help thinkin' of one passage, 'The kingdom of heaven is like a merchantman seeking goodly pearls, and when he hath found one pearl of great price, for joy thereof he goeth and selleth all that he hath, and buyeth that pearl.' Well, Mary, I 've been and sold my brig last week," he said, folding his daughter's little quiet head under his coat, "'cause it seems to me the Lord's given us this pearl of great price, and it 's enough for us. I don't want to be rambling round the world after riches. We 'll have a little farm down on Orr's Island, and I 'll have a little fishing-smack, and we 'll live and be happy together."

And so Mary, who in those days was a pretty young married woman, felt herself rich and happy,—no duchess richer or happier. The two contentedly delved and toiled, and the little Naomi was their princess. The wise men of the East at the feet of an infant, offering gifts, gold, frankincense, and myrrh, is just a parable of what goes on in every house where there is a young child. All the hard and the harsh, and the common and the disagreeable, is for the parents,—all the bright and beautiful for their child.

When the fishing-smack went to Portland to sell mackerel, there came home in Zephaniah's fishy coat pocket strings of coral beads, tiny gaiter boots, brilliant silks and ribbons for the little fairy princess,—his Pearl of the Island; and sometimes, when a stray party from the neighboring town of Brunswick came down to explore the romantic scenery of the solitary island, they would be startled by the apparition of this still, graceful, dark-eyed child exquisitely dressed in the best and brightest that the shops of a neighboring city could afford,—sitting like some tropical bird on a lonely rock, where the sea came dashing up into the edges of arbor vitæ, or tripping along the wet sands for shells and sea-weed.

Many children would have been spoiled by such unlimited indulgence; but there are natures sent down into this harsh world so timorous, and sensitive, and helpless in themselves, that the utmost stretch of indulgence and kindness is needed for their development,—like plants which the warmest shelf of the green-house and the most careful watch of the gardener alone can bring into flower. The pale child, with her large, lustrous, dark eyes, and sensitive organization, was nursed and brooded into a beautiful womanhood, and then found a protector in a high-spirited, manly young shipmaster, and she became his wife.

And now we see in the best room—the walls lined with serious faces—men, women, and children, that have come to pay the last tribute of sympathy to the living and the dead. The house looked so utterly alone and solitary in that wild, sea-girt island, that one would have as soon expected the sea-waves to rise and walk in, as so many neighbors; but they had come from neighboring points, crossing the glassy sea in their little crafts, whose white sails looked like millers' wings, or walking miles from distant parts of the island.

Some writer calls a funeral one of the amusements of a New England population. Must we call it an amusement to go and see the acted despair of Medea? or the dying agonies of poor Adrienne Lecouvreur? It is something of the same awful interest in life's tragedy, which makes an untaught and primitive people gather to a funeral,—a tragedy where there is no acting,—and one which each one feels must come at some time to his own dwelling.

Be that as it may, here was a roomful. Not only Aunt Roxy and Aunt Ruey, who by a prescriptive right presided over all the births, deaths, and marriages of the neighborhood, but there was Captain Kittridge, a long, dry, weather-beaten old sea-captain, who sat as if tied in a double bow-knot, with his little fussy old wife, with a great Leghorn bonnet, and eyes like black glass beads shining through the bows of her horn spectacles, and her hymn-book in her hand ready to lead the psalm. There were aunts, uncles, cousins, and brethren of the deceased; and in the midst stood two coffins, where the two united in death lay sleeping tenderly, as those to whom rest is good. All was still as death, except a chance whisper from some busy neighbor, or a creak of an old lady's great black fan, or the fizz of a _fly_ down the window-pane, and then a stifled sound of deep-drawn breath and weeping from under a cloud of heavy black crape veils, that were together in the group which country-people call the mourners.

A gleam of autumn sunlight streamed through the white curtains, and fell on a silver baptismal vase that stood on the mother's coffin, as the minister rose and said, "The ordinance of baptism will now be administered." A few moments more, and on a baby brow had fallen a few drops of water, and the little pilgrim of a new life had been called Mara in the name of the Father, Son, and Holy Ghost,—the minister slowly repeating thereafter those beautiful words of Holy Writ, "A father of the fatherless is God in his holy habitation,"—as if the baptism of that bereaved one had been a solemn adoption into the infinite heart of the Lord.

With something of the quaint pathos which distinguishes the primitive and Biblical people of that lonely shore, the minister read the passage in Ruth from which the name of the little stranger was drawn, and which describes the return of the bereaved Naomi to her native land. His voice trembled, and there were tears in many eyes as he read, "And it came to pass as she came to Bethlehem, all the city was moved about them; and they said, Is this Naomi? And she said unto them, Call me not Naomi; call me Mara; for the Almighty hath dealt very bitterly with me. I went out full, and the Lord hath brought me home again empty: why then call ye me Naomi, seeing the Lord hath testified against me, and the Almighty hath afflicted me?"

Deep, heavy sobs from the mourners were for a few moments the only answer to these sad words, till the minister raised the old funeral psalm of New England, —

> "Why do we mourn departing friends,
>   Or shake at Death's alarms?
> 'Tis but the voice that Jesus sends
>   To call them to his arms.
>
> "Are we not tending upward too,
>   As fast as time can move?
> And should we wish the hours more slow
>   That bear us to our love?"

The words rose in old "China," — that strange, wild warble, whose quaintly blended harmonies might have been learned of moaning seas or wailing winds, so strange and grand they rose, full of that intense pathos which rises over every defect of execution; and as they sung, Zephaniah Pennel straightened his tall form, before bowed on his hands, and looked heavenward, his cheeks wet with tears, but something sublime and immortal shining upward through his blue eyes; and at the last verse he came forward involuntarily, and stood by his dead, and his voice rose over all the others as he sung, —

"Then let the last loud trumpet sound,
   And bid the dead arise!
Awake, ye nations under ground!
   Ye saints, ascend the skies!"

The sunbeam through the window-curtain fell on his silver hair, and they that looked beheld his face as it were the face of an angel; he had gotten a sight of the city whose foundation is jasper, and whose every gate is a separate pearl.

IV

AUNT ROXY
AND AUNT RUEY

The sea lay like an unbroken mirror all around the pine-girt, lonely shores of Orr's Island. Tall, kingly spruces wore their regal crowns of cones high in air, sparkling with diamonds of clear exuded gum; vast old hemlocks of primeval growth stood darkling in their forest shadows, their branches hung with long hoary moss; while feathery larches, turned to brilliant gold by autumn frosts, lighted up the darker shadows of the evergreens. It was one of those hazy, calm, dissolving days of Indian summer, when everything is so quiet that the faintest kiss of the wave on the beach can be heard, and white clouds seem to faint into the blue of the sky, and soft swathing bands of violet vapor make all earth look dreamy, and give to the sharp, clear-cut outlines of the northern landscape all those mysteries of light and shade which impart such tenderness to Italian scenery.

The funeral was over; the tread of many feet, bearing the heavy burden of two broken lives, had been to the lonely graveyard, and had come back again,—each footstep lighter and more unconstrained as each one went his way from the great old tragedy of Death to the common cheerful walks of Life.

The solemn black clock stood swaying with its eternal "tick-tock, tick-tock," in the kitchen of the brown house on Orr's Island. There was there that sense of a stillness that can be felt,—such as settles down on a dwelling when any of its inmates have passed through its doors for the last time, to go whence they shall not return. The best room was shut up and darkened, with only so much light as could fall through a little heart-shaped hole in the window-shutter,—for except on solemn visits, or prayer meetings, or weddings, or funerals, that room formed no part of the daily family scenery.

The kitchen was clean and ample, with a great open fireplace and wide stone hearth, and oven on one side, and rows of old-fashioned splint-bottomed chairs against the wall. A table scoured to snowy whiteness, and a little work-stand whereon lay the Bible, the "Missionary Herald" and the "Weekly Christian Mirror," before named, formed the principal furniture. One feature, however, must not be forgotten,—a great sea-chest, which had been the companion of Zephaniah through all the countries of the earth. Old, and battered, and unsightly it looked, yet report said that there was good store within of that which men for the most part respect more than anything else; and, indeed, it proved often when a deed of grace was to be done,—when a woman was suddenly made a widow in a coast gale, or a fishing-smack was run down in the fogs off the banks, leaving in some neighboring cottage a family of orphans,—in all such cases, the opening of this sea-chest was an event of good omen to the bereaved; for Zephaniah had a large heart and a large hand, and was apt to take it out full of silver dollars when once it went in. So the ark of the covenant could not have been looked on with more reverence than the neighbors usually showed to Captain Pennel's sea-chest.

The afternoon sun is shining in a square of light through the open kitchen-door, whence one dreamily disposed might look far out to sea, and behold ships coming and going in every variety of shape and size.

But Aunt Roxy and Aunt Ruey, who for the present were sole occupants of the premises, were not people of the dreamy kind, and consequently were not gazing off to sea, but attending to very terrestrial matters that in all cases somebody must attend to. The afternoon was warm and balmy, but a few smouldering sticks were kept in the great chimney, and thrust deep into the embers was a mongrel species of snub-nosed tea-pot, which fumed strongly of catnip-tea, a little of which gracious beverage Miss Roxy was preparing in an old-fashioned cracked India china tea-cup, tasting it as she did so with the air of a connoisseur.

Apparently this was for the benefit of a small something in long white clothes, that lay face downward under a little blanket of very blue new flannel, and which something Aunt Roxy, when not otherwise engaged, constantly patted with a gentle tattoo, in tune to the steady trot of her knee. All babies knew Miss Roxy's tattoo on their backs, and never thought of taking it in ill part. On the contrary, it had a vital and mesmeric effect of sovereign force against colic, and all other disturbers of the nursery; and never was infant known so pressed with those internal troubles which infants cry about, as not speedily to give over and sink to slumber at this soothing appliance.

At a little distance sat Aunt Ruey, with a quantity of black crape strewed on two chairs about her, very busily employed in getting up a mourning-bonnet, at which she snipped, and clipped, and worked, zealously singing, in a high cracked voice, from time to time, certain verses of a funeral psalm.

Miss Roxy and Miss Ruey Toothacre were two brisk old bodies of the feminine gender and singular number, well known in all the region of Harpswell Neck and Middle Bay, and such was their fame that it had even reached the town of Brunswick, eighteen miles away.

They were of that class of females who might be denominated, in the Old Testament language, "cunning women,"—that is, gifted with an infinite diversity of practical "faculty," which made them an essential requisite in every family for miles and miles around. It was impossible to say what they could not do: they could make dresses, and make shirts and vests and pantaloons, and cut out boys' jackets, and braid straw, and bleach and trim bonnets, and cook and wash, and iron and mend, could upholster and quilt, could nurse all kinds of sicknesses, and in default of a doctor, who was often miles away, were supposed to be infallible medical oracles. Many a human being had been ushered into life under their auspices,—trotted, chirruped in babyhood on their knees, clothed by their handiwork in garments gradually enlarging from year to year, watched by them in the last sickness, and finally arrayed for the long repose by their hands.

These universally useful persons receive among us the title of "aunt" by a sort of general consent, showing the strong ties of relationship which bind them to the whole human family. They are nobody's aunts in particular, but aunts to human nature generally. The idea of restricting their usefulness to any one family, would strike dismay through a whole community. Nobody would be so unprincipled as to think of such a thing as having their services more than a week or two at most. Your country factotum knows better than anybody else how absurd it would be

"To give to a part what was meant for mankind."

Nobody knew very well the ages of these useful sisters. In that cold, clear, severe climate of the North, the roots of human existence are hard to strike; but, if once people do take to living, they come in time to a place where they seem never to grow any older, but can always be found, like last year's mullein stalks, upright, dry, and seedy, warranted to last for any length of time.

Miss Roxy Toothacre, who sits trotting the baby, is a tall, thin, angular woman, with sharp black eyes, and hair once black, but now well streaked with gray. These ravages of time, however, were concealed by an ample mohair frisette of glossy blackness woven on each side into a heap of stiff little curls, which pushed up her cap border in rather a bristling and decisive way. In all her movements and personal habits, even to her tone of voice and manner of speaking, Miss Roxy was vigorous, spicy, and decided. Her mind on all subjects was made up, and she spoke generally as one having authority; and who should, if she should not? Was she not a sort of priestess and sibyl in all the most awful straits and mysteries of life? How many births, and weddings, and deaths had come and gone under her jurisdiction! And amid weeping or rejoicing, was not Miss Roxy still the master-spirit,—consulted, referred to by all?—was not her word law and precedent? Her younger sister, Miss Ruey, a pliant, cozy, easy-to-be-entreated personage, plump and cushiony, revolved around her as a humble satellite. Miss Roxy looked on Miss Ruey as quite a frisky young thing, though under her ample frisette of carroty hair her head might be seen white with the same snow that had powdered that of her sister. Aunt Ruey had a face much resembling the kind of one you may see, reader, by looking at yourself in the convex side of a silver milk-pitcher. If you try the experiment, this description will need no further amplification.

The two almost always went together, for the variety of talent comprised in their stock could always find employment in the varying wants of a family. While one nursed the sick, the other made clothes for the well; and thus they were always chippering and chatting to each other, like a pair of antiquated house-sparrows, retailing over harmless gossips, and moralizing in that gentle jog-trot which befits serious old women. In fact, they had talked over everything in Nature, and said everything they could think of to each other so often, that the opinions of one were as like those of the other as two sides of a pea-pod. But as often happens in cases of the sort, this was not because the two were in all respects exactly alike, but because the stronger one had mesmerized the weaker into consent.

Miss Roxy was the master-spirit of the two, and, like the great coining machine of a mint, came down with her own sharp, heavy stamp on every opinion her sister put out. She was matter-of-fact, positive, and declarative to the highest degree, while her sister was naturally inclined to the elegiac and the pathetic, indulging herself in sentimental poetry, and keeping a store thereof in her threadcase, which she had cut from the "Christian Mirror." Miss Roxy sometimes, in her brusque way, popped out observations on life and things, with a droll, hard quaintness that took one's breath a little, yet never failed to have a sharp crystallization of truth,—frosty though it were. She was one of those sensible, practical creatures who tear every veil, and lay their fingers on every spot in pure business-like good-will; and if we shiver at them at times, as at the first plunge of a cold bath, we confess to an invigorating power in them after all.

"Well, now," said Miss Roxy, giving a decisive push to the tea-pot, which buried it yet deeper in the embers, "ain't it all a strange kind o' providence that this 'ere little thing is left behind so; and then their callin' on her by such a strange, mournful kind of name,—Mara. I thought sure as could be 'twas Mary, till the minister read the passage from Scriptur'. Seems to me it 's kind o' odd. I 'd call it Maria, or I 'd put an Ann on to it. Mara-ann, now, would n't sound so strange."

"It 's a Scriptur' name, sister," said Aunt Ruey, "and that ought to be enough for us."

"Well, I don't know," said Aunt Roxy. "Now there was Miss Jones down on Mure P'int called her twins Tiglath-Pileser and Shalmaneser,—Scriptur' names both, but I never liked 'em. The boys used to call 'em, Tiggy and Shally, so no mortal could guess they was Scriptur'."

"Well," said Aunt Ruey, drawing a sigh which caused her plump proportions to be agitated in gentle waves, "'t ain't much matter, after all, *what* they call the little thing, for 't ain't 't all likely it 's goin' to live,—cried and worried all night, and kep' a-suckin' my cheek and my night-gown, poor little thing! This 'ere 's a baby that won't get along without its mother. What Mis' Pennel 's a-goin' to do with it when we is gone, I'm sure I don't know. It comes kind o' hard on old people to be broke o' their rest. If it 's goin' to be called home, it 's a pity, as I said, it did n't go with its mother"—

"And save the expense of another funeral," said Aunt Roxy. "Now when Mis' Pennel's sister asked her what she was going to do with Naomi's clothes, I could n't help wonderin' when she said she should keep 'em for the child."

"She had a sight of things, Naomi did," said Aunt Ruey. "Nothin' was never too much for her. I don't believe that Cap'n Pennel ever went to Bath or Portland without havin' it in his mind to bring Naomi somethin'."

"Yes, and she had a faculty of puttin' of 'em on," said Miss Roxy, with a decisive shake of the head. "Naomi was a still girl, but her faculty was uncommon; and I tell you, Ruey, 't ain't everybody hes faculty as hes things."

"The poor Cap'n," said Miss Ruey, "he seemed greatly supported at the funeral, but he 's dreadful broke down since. I went into Naomi's room this morning, and there the old man was a-sittin' by her bed, and he had a pair of her shoes in his hand,—you know what a leetle bit of a foot she had. I never saw nothin' look so kind o' solitary as that poor old man did!"

"Well," said Miss Roxy, "she was a master-hand for keepin' things, Naomi was; her drawers is just a sight; she 's got all the little presents and things they ever give her since she was a baby, in one drawer. There 's a little pair of red shoes there that she had when she wa'n't more 'n five year old. You 'member, Ruey, the Cap'n brought 'em over from Portland when we was to the house a-makin' Mis' Pennel's figured black silk that he brought from Calcutty. You 'member they cost just five and six-pence, but, law! the Cap'n he never grudged the money when 't was for Naomi. And so she 's got all her husband's keepsakes and things just as nice as when he giv' 'em to her."

"It's real affectin'," said Miss Ruey, "I can't all the while help a-thinkin' of the Psalm,—

> " 'So fades the lovely blooming flower,—
> Frail, smiling solace of an hour;
> So quick our transient comforts fly,
> And pleasure only blooms to die.' "

"Yes," said Miss Roxy; "and, Ruey, I was a-thinkin' whether or no it wa'n't best to pack away them things, 'cause Naomi had n't fixed no baby drawers, and we seem to want some."

"I was kind o' hintin' that to Mis' Pennel this morning," said Ruey, "but she can't seem to want to have 'em touched."

"Well, we may just as well come to such things first as last," said Aunt Roxy; " 'cause if the Lord takes our friends, he does take 'em; and we can't lose 'em and have 'em too, and we may as well give right up at first, and done with it, that they are gone, and we 've got to do without 'em, and not to be hangin' on to keep things just as they was."

"So I was a-tellin' Mis' Pennel," said Miss Ruey, "but she 'll come to it by and by. I wish the baby might live, and kind o' grow up into her mother's place."

"Well," said Miss Roxy, "I wish it might, but there 'd be a sight o' trouble fetchin' on it up. Folks can do pretty well with children when they 're young and spry, if they do get 'em up nights; but come to grandchildren, it 's pretty tough."

"I 'm a-thinkin', sister," said Miss Ruey, taking off her spectacles and rubbing her nose thoughtfully, "whether or no cow's milk ain't goin' to be too hearty for it, it 's such a pindlin' little thing. Now, Mis' Badger she brought up a seven-months' child, and she told me she gave it nothin' but these 'ere little seed cookies, wet in water, and it throve nicely,—and the seed is good for wind."

"Oh, don't tell me none of Mis' Badger's stories," said Miss Roxy, "I don't believe in 'em. Cows is the Lord's ordinances for bringing up babies that 's lost their mothers; it stands to reason they should be,—and babies that can't eat milk, why they can't be fetched up; but babies can eat milk, and this un will if it lives, and if it can't it won't live." So saying, Miss Roxy drummed away on the little back of the party in question, authoritatively, as if to pound in a wholesome conviction at the outset.

"I hope," said Miss Ruey, holding up a strip of black crape, and looking through it from end to end so as to test its capabilities, "I hope the Cap'n and Mis' Pennel 'll get some support at the prayer-meetin' this afternoon."

"It 's the right place to go to," said Miss Roxy, with decision.

"Mis' Pennel said this mornin' that she was just beat out tryin' to submit; and the more she said, 'Thy will be done,' the more she did n't seem to feel it."

"Them 's common feelin's among mourners, Ruey. These 'ere forty years that I 've been round nussin', and layin'-out, and tendin' funerals, I 've watched people's exercises. People 's sometimes supported wonderfully just at the time, and maybe at the funeral; but the three or four weeks after, most everybody, if they 's to say what they feel, is <u>unreconciled.</u>"

"The Cap'n, he don't say nothin'," said Miss Ruey.

"No, he don't, but he looks it in his eyes," said Miss Roxy; "he 's one of the kind o' mourners as takes it deep; that kind don't cry; it 's a kind o' dry, deep pain; them 's the worst to get over it,—sometimes they just says nothin', and in about six months they send for you to nuss 'em in consumption or somethin'. Now, Mis' Pennel, she can cry and she can talk,—well, she 'll get over it; but *he* won't get no support unless the Lord reaches right down and lifts him up over the world. I 've seen that happen sometimes, and I tell you, Ruey, that sort makes powerful Christians."

At that moment the old pair entered the door. Zephaniah Pennel came and stood quietly by the pillow where the little form was laid, and lifted a corner of the blanket. The tiny head was turned to one side, showing the soft, warm cheek, and the little hand was holding tightly a morsel of the flannel blanket. He stood swallowing hard for a few moments. At last he said, with deep humility, to the wise and mighty woman who held her, "I 'll tell you what it is, Miss Roxy, I 'll give all there is in my old chest yonder if you 'll only make her—live."

V

THE KITTRIDGES

It did live. The little life, so frail, so unprofitable in every mere material view, so precious in the eyes of love, expanded and flowered at last into fair childhood. Not without much watching and weariness. Many a night the old fisherman walked the floor with the little thing in his arms, talking to it that jargon of tender nonsense which fairies bring as love-gifts to all who tend a cradle. Many a day the good little old grandmother called the aid of gossips about her, trying various experiments of catnip, and sweet fern, and bayberry, and other teas of rustic reputation for baby frailties.

At the end of three years, the two graves in the lonely grave-yard were sodded and cemented down by smooth velvet turf, and playing round the door of the brown houses was a slender child, with ways and manners so still and singular as often to re-mind the neighbors that she was not like other children,—a bud of hope and joy,—but the outcome of a great sorrow,—a pearl washed ashore by a mighty, uprooting tempest. They that looked at her remembered that her father's eye had never be-held her, and her baptismal cup had rested on her mother's cof-fin.

She was small of stature, beyond the wont of children of her age, and moulded with a fine waxen delicacy that won admiration from all eyes. Her hair was curly and golden, but her eyes were dark like her mother's, and the lids drooped over them in that manner which gives a peculiar expression of dreamy wistfulness. Every one of us must remember eyes that have a strange, peculiar expression of pathos and desire, as if the spirit that looked out of them were pressed with vague remembrances of a past, or but dimly comprehended the mystery of its present life. Even when the baby lay in its cradle, and its dark, inquiring eyes would follow now one object and now another, the gossips would say the child was longing for something, and Miss Roxy would still further venture to predict that that child always would long and never would know exactly what she was after.

That dignitary sits at this minute enthroned in the kitchen corner, looking majestically over the press-board on her knee, where she is pressing the next year's Sunday vest of Zephaniah Pennel. As she makes her heavy tailor's goose squeak on the work, her eyes follow the little delicate fairy form which trips about the kitchen, busily and silently arranging a little grotto of gold and silver shells and seaweed. The child sings to herself as she works in a low chant, like the prattle of a brook, but ever and anon she rests her little arms on a chair and looks through the open kitchen-door far, far off where the horizon line of the blue sea dissolves in the blue sky.

"See that child now, Roxy," said Miss Ruey, who sat stitching beside her; "do look at her eyes. She 's as handsome as a pictur', but 't ain't an ordinary look she has neither; she seems a contented little thing; but what makes her eyes always look so kind o' wishful?"

"Wa'n't her mother always a-longin' and a-lookin' to sea, and watchin' the ships, afore she was born?" said Miss Roxy; "and did n't her heart break afore she was born? Babies like that is marked always. They don't know what ails 'em, nor nobody."

"It's her mother she 's after," said Miss Ruey.

"The Lord only knows," said Miss Roxy; "but them kind o' children always seem homesick to go back where they come from. They 're mostly grave and old-fashioned like this 'un. If they gets past seven years, why they live; but it 's always in 'em to long; they don't seem to be really unhappy neither, but if anything 's ever the matter with 'em, it seems a great deal easier for 'em to die than to live. Some say it 's the mothers longin' after 'em makes 'em feel so, and some say it 's them longin' after their mothers; but dear knows, Ruey, what anything is or what makes anything. Children 's mysterious, that 's my mind."

"Mara, dear," said Miss Ruey, interrupting the child's steady look-out, "what you thinking of?"

"Me want somefin'," said the little one.

"That 's what she 's always sayin'," said Miss Roxy.

"Me want somebody to pay wis'," continued the little one.

"Want somebody to play with," said old Dame Pennel, as she came in from the back-room with her hands yet floury with kneading bread; "sure enough, she does. Our house stands in such a lonesome place, and there ain't any children. But I never saw such a quiet little thing—always still and always busy."

"I 'll take her down with me to Cap'n Kittridge's," said Miss Roxy, "and let her play with their little girl; she 'll chirk her up, I 'll warrant. She 's a regular little witch, Sally is, but she 'll chirk her up. It ain't good for children to be so still and old-fashioned; children ought to be children. Sally takes to Mara just 'cause she 's so different."

"Well, now, you may," said Dame Pennel; "to be sure *he* can't bear her out of his sight a minute after he comes in; but after all, old folks can't be company for children."

Accordingly, that afternoon, the little Mara was arrayed in a little blue flounced dress, which stood out like a balloon, made by Miss Roxy in first-rate style, from a French fashion-plate; her golden hair was twined in manifold curls by Dame Pennel, who, restricted in her ideas of ornamentation, spared, nevertheless, neither time nor money to enhance the charms of this single ornament to her dwelling. Mara was her picture-gallery, who gave her in the twenty-four hours as many Murillos or Greuzes as a lover of art could desire; and as she tied over the child's golden curls a little flat hat, and saw her go dancing off along the sea-sands, holding to Miss Roxy's bony finger, she felt she had in her what galleries of pictures could not buy.

It was a good mile to the one story, gambrel-roofed cottage where lived Captain Kittridge,—the long, lean, brown man, with his good wife of the great Leghorn bonnet, round, black bead eyes, and psalm-book, whom we told you of at the funeral. The Captain, too, had followed the sea in his early life, but being not, as he expressed it, "very rugged," in time changed his ship for a tight little cottage on the sea-shore, and devoted himself to boat-building, which he found sufficiently lucrative to furnish his brown cottage with all that his wife's heart desired, besides extra money for knick-knacks when she chose to go up to Brunswick or over to Portland to shop.

The Captain himself was a welcome guest at all the firesides round, being a chatty body, and disposed to make the most of his foreign experiences, in which he took the usual advantages of a traveler. In fact, it was said, whether slanderously or not, that the Captain's yarns were spun to order; and as, when pressed to relate his foreign adventures, he always responded with, "What would you like to hear?" it was thought that he fabricated his article to suit his market. In short, there was no species of experience, finny, fishy, or aquatic,—no legend of strange and unaccountable incident of fire or flood,—no ro-

mance of foreign scenery and productions, to which his tongue
was not competent, when he had once seated himself in a double bow-knot at a neighbor's evening fireside.

His good wife, a sharp-eyed, literal body, and a vigorous
church-member, felt some concern of conscience on the score
of these narrations; for, being their constant auditor, she, better
than any one else, could perceive the variations and discrepan-
cies of text which showed their mythical character, and often-
times her black eyes would snap and her knitting-needles rattle
with an admonitory vigor as he went on, and sometimes she
would unmercifully come in at the end of a narrative with,—

"Well, now, the Cap'n 's told them ar stories till he begins to
b'lieve 'em himself, I think."

But works of fiction, as we all know, if only well gotten up,
have always their advantages in the hearts of listeners over
plain, homely truth; and so Captain Kittridge's yarns were mar-
ketable fireside commodities still, despite the skepticisms
which attended them.

The afternoon sunbeams at this moment are painting the
gambrel-roof with a golden brown. It is September again, as it
was three years ago when our story commenced, and the sea
and sky are purple and amethystine with its Italian haziness of
atmosphere.

The brown house stands on a little knoll, about a hundred
yards from the open ocean. Behind it rises a ledge of rocks,
where cedars and hemlocks make deep shadows into which the
sun shoots golden shafts of light, illuminating the scarlet feathers of the sumach, which throw themselves jauntily forth from
the crevices; while down below, in deep, damp, mossy recesses,
rise ferns which autumn has just begun to tinge with yellow and
brown. The little knoll where the cottage stood had on its right
hand a tiny bay, where the ocean water made up amid pic-

turesque rocks — shaggy and solemn. Here trees of the primeval forest, grand and lordly, looked down silently into the waters which ebbed and flowed daily into this little pool. Every variety of those beautiful evergreens which feather the coast of Maine, and dip their wings in the very spray of its ocean foam, found here a representative. There were aspiring black spruces, crowned on the very top with heavy coronets of cones; there were balsamic firs, whose young buds breathe the scent of strawberries; there were cedars, black as midnight clouds, and white pines with their swaying plumage of needle-like leaves, strewing the ground beneath with a golden, fragrant matting; and there were the gigantic, wide-winged hemlocks, hundreds of years old, and with long, swaying, gray beards of moss, looking white and ghostly under the deep shadows of their boughs. And beneath, creeping round trunk and matting over stones, were many and many of those wild, beautiful things which embellish the shadows of these northern forests. Long, feathery wreaths of what are called ground-pines ran here and there in little ruffles of green, and the prince's pine raised its oriental feather, with a mimic cone on the top, as if it conceived itself to be a grown-up tree. Whole patches of partridge-berry wove their evergreen matting, dotted plentifully with brilliant scarlet berries. Here and there, the rocks were covered with a curiously inwoven tapestry of moss, overshot with the exquisite vine of the Linnea borealis, which in early spring rings its two fairy bells on the end of every spray; while elsewhere the wrinkled leaves of the mayflower wove themselves through and through deep beds of moss, meditating silently thoughts of the thousand little cups of pink shell which they had it in hand to make when the time of miracles should come round next spring.

Nothing, in short, could be more quaintly fresh, wild, and

beautiful than the surroundings of this little cove which Captain Kittridge had thought fit to dedicate to his boat-building operations,—where he had set up his tar-kettle between two great rocks above the highest tide-mark, and where, at the present moment, he had a boat upon the stocks.

Mrs. Kittridge, at this hour, was sitting in her clean kitchen, very busily engaged in ripping up a silk dress, which Miss Roxy had engaged to come and make into a new one; and, as she ripped, she cast now and then an eye at the face of a tall, black clock, whose solemn tick-tock was the only sound that could be heard in the kitchen.

By her side, on a low stool, sat a vigorous, healthy girl of six years, whose employment evidently did not please her, for her well-marked black eyebrows were bent in a frown, and her large black eyes looked surly and wrathful, and one versed in children's grievances could easily see what the matter was,—she was turning a sheet! Perhaps, happy young female reader, you don't know what that is,—most likely not; for in these degenerate days the strait and narrow ways of self-denial, formerly thought so wholesome for little feet, are quite grass-grown with neglect. Childhood nowadays is unceasingly fêted and caressed, the principal difficulty of the grown people seeming to be to discover what the little dears want,—a thing not always clear to the little dears themselves. But in old times, turning sheets was thought a most especial and wholesome discipline for young girls; in the first place, because it took off the hands of their betters a very uninteresting and monotonous labor; and in the second place, because it was such a long, straight, unending turnpike, that the youthful travelers, once started thereupon, could go on indefinitely, without requiring guidance and direction of their elders. For these reasons, also, the task was held in special detestation by children in direct proportion to their amount of life, and their ingenuity and love of variety. A dull child took it tolerably well; but to a lively, energetic one, it was a perfect torture.

"I don't see the use of sewing up sheets one side, and ripping up the other," at last said Sally, breaking the monotonous tick-tock of the clock by an observation which has probably occurred to every child in similar circumstances.

"Sally Kittridge, if you say another word about that ar sheet, I 'll whip you," was the very explicit rejoinder; and there was a snap of Mrs. Kittridge's black eyes, that seemed to make it likely that she would keep her word. It was answered by another snap from the six-year-old eyes, as Sally comforted herself with thinking that when she was a woman she 'd speak her mind out in pay for all this.

At this moment a burst of silvery child-laughter rang out, and there appeared in the doorway, illuminated by the afternoon sunbeams, the vision of Miss Roxy's tall, lank figure, with the little golden-haired, blue-robed fairy, hanging like a gay butterfly upon the tip of a thorn-bush. Sally dropped the sheet and clapped her hands, unnoticed by her mother, who rose to pay her respects to the "cunning woman" of the neighborhood.

"Well, now, Miss Roxy, I was 'mazin' afraid you wer' n't a-comin'. I 'd just been an' got my silk ripped up, and did n't know how to get a step farther without you."

"Well, I was finishin' up Cap'n Pennel's best pantaloons," said Miss Roxy; "and I 've got 'em along so, Ruey can go on with 'em; and I told Mis' Pennel I must come to you, if 't was only for a day; and I fetched the little girl down, 'cause the little thing's so kind o' lonesome like. I thought Sally could play with her, and chirk her up a little."

"Well, Sally," said Mrs. Kittridge, "stick in your needle, fold up your sheet, put your thimble in your work-pocket, and then you may take the little Mara down to the cove to play; but be sure you don't let her go near the tar, nor wet her shoes. D 'ye hear?"

"Yes, ma'am," said Sally, who had sprung up in light and radiance, like a translated creature, at this unexpected turn of fortune, and performed the welcome orders with a celerity which showed how agreeable they were; and then, stooping and catching the little one in her arms, disappeared through the door, with the golden curls fluttering over her own crow-black hair.

The fact was, that Sally, at that moment, was as happy as human creature could be, with a keenness of happiness that children who have never been made to turn sheets of a bright afternoon can never realize. The sun was yet an hour high, as she saw, by the flash of her shrewd, time-keeping eye, and she could bear her little prize down to the cove, and collect unknown quantities of gold and silver shells, and starfish, and salad-dish shells, and white pebbles for her, besides quantities of well turned shavings, brown and white, from the pile which constantly was falling under her father's joiner's bench, and with which she would make long extemporaneous tresses, so that they might play at being mermaids, like those that she had heard her father tell about in some of his sea-stories.

"Now, railly, Sally, what you got there?" said Captain Kittridge, as he stood in his shirt-sleeves peering over his joiner's bench, to watch the little one whom Sally had dumped down into a nest of clean white shavings. "Wal', wal', I should think you 'd a-stolen the big doll I see in a shop-window the last time I was to Portland. So this is Pennel's little girl?—poor child!"

"Yes, father, and we want some nice shavings."

"Stay a bit, I 'll make ye a few a-purpose," said the old man, reaching his long, bony arm, with the greatest ease, to the farther part of his bench, and bringing up a board, from which he proceeded to roll off shavings in fine satin rings, which perfectly delighted the hearts of the children, and made them dance with glee; and, truth to say, reader, there are coarser and homelier things in the world than a well turned shaving.

"There, go now," he said, when both of them stood with both hands full; "go now and play; and mind you don't let the baby wet her feet, Sally; them shoes o' hern must have cost five-and-sixpence at the very least."

That sunny hour before sundown seemed as long to Sally as the whole seam of the sheet; for childhood's joys are all pure gold; and as she ran up and down the white sands, shouting at every shell she found, or darted up into the overhanging forest for checkerberries and ground-pine, all the sorrows of the morning came no more into her remembrance.

The little Mara had one of those sensitive, excitable natures, on which every external influence acts with immediate power. Stimulated by the society of her energetic, buoyant little neighbor, she no longer seemed wishful or pensive, but kindled into a perfect flame of wild delight, and gamboled about the shore like a blue and gold-winged fly; while her bursts of laughter made the squirrels and blue jays look out inquisitively from their fastnesses in the old evergreens. Gradually the sunbeams faded from the pines, and the waves of the tide in the little cove came in, solemnly tinted with purple, flaked with orange and crimson, borne in from a great rippling sea of fire, into which the sun had just sunk.

"Mercy on us—them children!" said Miss Roxy.

"*He's* bringin' 'em along," said Mrs. Kittridge, as she looked out of the window and saw the tall, lank form of the Captain, with one child seated on either shoulder, and holding on by his head.

The two children were both in the highest state of excitement, but never was there a more marked contrast of nature. The one seemed a perfect type of well-developed childish health and vigor, good solid flesh and bones, with glowing skin, brilliant eyes, shining teeth, well-knit, supple limbs,—vigorously and healthily beautiful; while the other appeared one of those aerial mixtures of cloud and fire, whose radiance seems scarcely earthly. A physiologist, looking at the child, would shake his head, seeing one of those perilous organizations, all nerve and brain, which come to life under the clear, stimulating skies of America, and, burning with the intensity of lighted phosphorus, waste themselves too early.

The little Mara seemed like a fairy sprite, possessed with a wild spirit of glee. She laughed and clapped her hands incessantly, and when set down on the kitchen-floor spun round like a little elf; and that night it was late and long before her wide, wakeful eyes could be veiled in sleep.

"Company jist sets this 'ere child crazy," said Miss Roxy; "it's jist her lonely way of livin'; a pity Mis' Pennel had n't another child to keep company along with her."

"Mis' Pennel oughter be trainin' of her up to work," said Mrs. Kittridge. "Sally could oversew and hem when she wa'n't more 'n three years old; nothin' straightens out children like work. Mis' Pennel she just keeps that ar child to look at."

"All children ain't alike, Mis' Kittridge," said Miss Roxy, sententiously. "This 'un ain't like your Sally. 'A hen and a bumblebee can't be fetched up alike, fix it how you will!'"

VI

🌲🌲🌲🌲

GRANDPARENTS

Zephaniah Pennel came back to his house in the evening, after Miss Roxy had taken the little Mara away. He looked for the flowery face and golden hair as he came towards the door, and put his hand in his vest-pocket, where he had deposited a small store of very choice shells and sea curiosities, thinking of the widening of those dark, soft eyes when he should present them.

"Where 's Mara?" was the first inquiry after he had crossed the threshold.

"Why, Roxy 's been an' taken her down to Cap'n Kittridge's to spend the night," said Miss Ruey. "Roxy 's gone to help Mis' Kittridge to turn her spotted gray and black silk. We was talking this mornin' whether 'no 't would turn, 'cause *I* thought the spot was overshot, and would n't make up on the wrong side; but Roxy she says it 's one of them ar Calcutty silks that has two sides to 'em, like the one you bought Miss Pennel, that we made up for her, you know;" and Miss Ruey arose and gave a finishing snap to the Sunday pantaloons, which she had been left to "finish off,"—which snap said, as plainly as words could say, that there was a good job disposed of.

Zephaniah stood looking as helpless as animals of the male kind generally do when appealed to with such prolixity on feminine details; in reply to it all, only he asked meekly,—

"Where 's Mary?"

"Mis' Pennel? Why, she 's up chamber. She 'll be down in a minute, she said; she thought she 'd have time afore supper to get to the bottom of the big chist, and see if that 'ere vest pattern ain't there, and them sticks o' twist for the button-holes, 'cause Roxy she says she never see nothin' so rotten as that 'ere twist we 've been a-workin' with, that Mis' Pennel got over to Portland; it 's a clear cheat, and Mis' Pennel she give more 'n half a cent a stick more for 't than what Roxy got for her up to Brunswick; so you see these 'ere Portland stores charge up, and their things want lookin' after."

Here Mrs. Pennel entered the room, "the Captain" addressing her eagerly,—

"How came you to let Aunt Roxy take Mara off so far, and be gone so long?"

"Why, law me, Captain Pennel! the little thing seems kind o' lonesome. Chil'en want chil'en; Miss Roxy says she 's altogether too sort o' still and old-fashioned, and must have child's company to chirk her up, and so she took her down to play with Sally Kittridge; there 's no manner of danger or harm in it, and she 'll be back to-morrow afternoon, and Mara will have a real good time."

"Wal', now, really," said the good man, "but it 's 'mazin' lonesome."

"Cap'n Pennel, you 're gettin' to make an idol of that 'ere child," said Miss Ruey. "We have to watch our hearts. It minds me of the hymn,—

"'The fondness of a creature's love,
How strong it strikes the sense,—

39

Thither the warm affections move,
Nor can we call them hence.'"

Miss Ruey's mode of getting off poetry, in a sort of high-pitched canter, with a strong thump on every accented syllable, might have provoked a smile in more sophisticated society, but Zephaniah listened to her with deep gravity, and answered,—

"I 'm 'fraid there 's truth in what you say, Aunt Ruey. When her mother was called away, I thought that was a warning I never should forget; but now I seem to be like Jonah,—I 'm restin' in the shadow of my gourd, and my heart is glad because of it. I kind o' trembled at the prayer meetin' when we was a-singin',—

"'The dearest idol I have known,
Whate'er that idol be,
Help me to tear it from Thy throne,
And worship only Thee.'"

"Yes," said Miss Ruey, "Roxy says if the Lord should take us up short on our prayers, it would make sad work with us sometimes."

"Somehow," said Mrs. Pennel, "it seems to me just her mother over again. She don't look like her. I think her hair and complexion comes from the Badger blood; my mother had that sort o' hair and skin,—but then she has ways like Naomi,—and it seems as if the Lord had kind o' given Naomi back to us; so I hope she 's goin' to be spared to us."

Mrs. Pennel had one of those natures—gentle, trustful, and hopeful, because not very deep; she was one of the little children of the world whose faith rests on childlike ignorance, and who know not the deeper needs of deeper natures; such see only the sunshine and forget the storm.

This conversation had been going on to the accompaniment of a clatter of plates and spoons and dishes, and the fizzling of sausages, prefacing the evening meal, to which all now sat down after a lengthened grace from Zephaniah.

"There's a tremendous gale a-brewin'," he said, as they sat at table. "I noticed the clouds to-night as I was comin' home, and somehow I felt kind o' as if I wanted all our folks snug indoors."

"Why, law, husband, Cap'n Kittridge's house is as good as ours, if it does blow. You never can seem to remember that houses don't run aground or strike on rocks in storms."

"The Cap'n puts me in mind of old Cap'n Jeduth Scranton," said Miss Ruey, "that built that queer house down by Middle Bay. The Cap'n he would insist on havin' on't jist like a ship, and the closet-shelves had holes for the tumblers and dishes, and he had all his tables and chairs battened down, and so when it came a gale, they say the old Cap'n used to sit in his chair and hold on to hear the wind blow."

"Well, I tell you," said Captain, "those that has followed the seas hears the wind with different ears from lands-people. When you lie with only a plank between you and eternity, and hear the voice of the Lord on the waters, it don't sound as it does on shore."

sea life

And in truth, as they were speaking, a fitful gust swept by the house, wailing and screaming and rattling the windows, and after it came the heavy, hollow moan of the surf on the beach, like the wild, angry howl of some savage animal just beginning to be lashed into fury.

"Sure enough, the wind is rising," said Miss Ruey, getting up from the table, and flattening her snub nose against the window-pane. "Dear me, how dark it is! Mercy on us, how the waves come in!—all of a sheet of foam. I pity the ships that's comin' on coast such a night."

The storm seemed to have burst out with a sudden fury, as if myriads of howling demons had all at once been loosened in the air. Now they piped and whistled with eldritch screech round the corners of the house—now they thundered down the chimney—and now they shook the door and rattled the casement—and anon mustering their forces with wild ado, seemed to career over the house, and sail high up into the murky air. The dash of the rising tide came with successive crash upon crash like the discharge of heavy artillery, seeming to shake the very house, and the spray borne by the wind dashed whizzing against the window-panes.

Zephaniah, rising from supper, drew up the little stand that had the family Bible on it, and the three old time-worn people sat themselves as seriously down to evening worship as if they had been an extensive congregation. They raised the old psalm-tune which our fathers called "Complaint," and the cracked, wavering voices of the women, with the deep, rough bass of the old sea-captain, rose in the uproar of the storm with a ghostly, strange wildness, like the scream of the curlew or the wailing of the wind:—

> "Spare us, O Lord, aloud we pray,
> Nor let our sun go down at noon:
> Thy years are an eternal day,
> And must thy children die so soon!"

Miss Ruey valued herself on singing a certain weird and exalted part which in ancient days used to be called counter, and which wailed and gyrated in unimaginable heights of the scale, much as you may hear a shrill, fine-voiced wind over a chimney-top; but altogether, the deep and earnest gravity with which the three filled up the pauses in the storm with their quaint minor key, had something singularly impressive. When the singing was over, Zephaniah read to the accompaniment of wind and sea, the words of poetry made on old Hebrew shores, in the dim, gray dawn of the world:—

"The voice of the Lord is upon the waters; the God of glory thundereth; the Lord is upon many waters. The voice of the Lord shaketh the wilderness; the Lord shaketh the wilderness of Kadesh. The Lord sitteth upon the floods, yea, the Lord sitteth King forever. The Lord will give strength to his people; yea, the Lord will bless his people with peace."

How natural and home-born sounded this old piece of Oriental poetry in the ears of the three! The wilderness of Kadesh, with its great cedars, was doubtless Orr's Island, where even now the goodly fellowship of black-winged trees were groaning and swaying, and creaking as the breath of the Lord passed over them.

And the three old people kneeling by their smouldering fireside, amid the general uproar, Zephaniah began in the words of a prayer which Moses the man of God made long ago under the shadows of Egyptian pyramids: "Lord, thou hast been our dwelling-place in all generations. Before the mountains were brought forth, or ever thou hadst formed the earth and the world, even from everlasting to everlasting, thou art God."

We hear sometimes in these days that the Bible is no more inspired of God than many other books of historic and poetic merit. It is a fact, however, that the Bible answers a strange and wholly exceptional purpose by thousands of firesides on all shores of the earth; and, till some other book can be found to do the same thing, it will not be surprising if a belief of its Divine origin be one of the ineffaceable ideas of the popular mind. It will be a long while before a translation from Homer or a chapter in the Koran, or any of the beauties of Shakespeare, will be read in a stormy night on Orr's Island with the same sense of a Divine presence as the Psalms of David, or the prayer of Moses, the man of God.

Boom! boom! "What 's that?" said Zephaniah, starting, as they rose up from prayer. "Hark! again, that 's a gun,—there 's a ship in distress."

"Poor souls," said Miss Ruey; "it 's an awful night!"

The captain began to put on his sea-coat.

"You ain't a-goin' out?" said his wife.

"I must go out along the beach a spell, and see if I can hear any more of that ship."

"Mercy on us; the wind 'll blow you over!" said Aunt Ruey.

"I rayther think I 've stood wind before in my day," said Zephaniah, a grim smile stealing over his weather-beaten cheeks. In fact, the man felt a sort of secret relationship to the storm, as if it were in some manner a family connection—a wild, roystering cousin, who drew him out by a rough attraction of comradeship.

"Well, at any rate," said Mrs. Pennel, producing a large tin lantern perforated with many holes, in which she placed a tallow candle, "take this with you, and don't stay out long."

The kitchen door opened, and the first gust of wind took off the old man's hat and nearly blew him prostrate. He came back and shut the door. "I ought to have known better," he said, knotting his pocket-handkerchief over his head, after which he waited for a momentary lull, and went out into the storm.

Miss Ruey looked through the window-pane, and saw the light go twinkling far down into the gloom, and ever and anon came the mournful boom of distant guns.

"Certainly there is a ship in trouble somewhere," she said.

"He never can be easy when he hears these guns," said Mrs. Pennel; "but what can he do, or anybody, in such a storm, the wind blowing right on to shore?"

"I should n't wonder if Cap'n Kittridge should be out on the beach, too," said Miss Ruey; "but laws, he ain't much more than one of these 'ere old grasshoppers you see after frost comes. Well, any way, there *ain't* much help in man if a ship comes ashore in such a gale as this, such a dark night too."

"It 's kind o' lonesome to have poor little Mara away such a night as this is," said Mrs. Pennel; "but who would a-thought it this afternoon, when Aunt Roxy took her?"

"I 'member my grandmother had a silver cream-pitcher that come ashore in a storm on Mare P'int," said Miss Ruey, as she sat trotting her knitting-needles. "Grand'ther found it, half full of sand, under a knot of seaweed way up on the beach. It had a coat of arms on it,—might have belonged to some grand family, that pitcher; in the Toothacre family yet."

"I remember when I was a girl," said Mrs. Pennel, "seeing the hull of a ship that went on Eagle Island; it run way up in a sort of gully between two rocks, and lay there years. They split pieces off it sometimes to make fires, when they wanted to make a chowder down on the beach."

"My aunt, Lois Toothacre, that lives down by Middle Bay," said Miss Ruey, "used to tell about a dreadful blow they had once in time of the equinoctial storm; and what was remarkable, she insisted that she heard a baby cryin' out in the storm,—she heard it just as plain as could be."

"Laws a-mercy," said Mrs. Pennel, nervously, "it was nothing but the wind,—it always screeches like a child crying; or maybe it was the seals; seals will cry just like babes."

"So they told her; but no,—she insisted she knew the difference,—it *was* a baby. Well, what do you think, when the storm cleared off, they found a baby's cradle washed ashore sure enough!"

"But they did n't find any baby," said Mrs. Pennel, nervously.

"No; they searched the beach far and near, and that cradle was all they found. Aunt Lois took it in—it was a very good cradle, and she took it to use, but every time there came up a gale, that ar cradle would rock, rock, jist as if somebody was a-sittin' by it; and you could stand across the room and see there wa'n't nobody there."

"You make me all of a shiver," said Mrs. Pennel.

This, of course, was just what Miss Ruey intended, and she went on:—

"Wal', you see they kind o' got used to it; they found there wa'n't no harm come of its rockin', and so they did n't mind; but Aunt Lois had a sister Cerinthy that was a weakly girl, and had the janders. Cerinthy was one of the sort that 's born with veils over their faces, and can see sperits; and one time Cerinthy was a-visitin' Lois after her second baby was born, and there came up a blow, and Cerinthy comes out of the keepin'-room, where the cradle was a-standin', and says, 'Sister,' says she, 'who 's that woman sittin' rockin' the cradle?' and Aunt Lois says she, 'Why, there ain't nobody. That ar cradle always will rock in a gale, but I 've got used to it, and don't mind it.' 'Well,' says Cerinthy, 'jist as true as you live, I just saw a woman with a silk gown on, and long black hair a-hangin' down, and her face was pale as a sheet, sittin' rockin' that ar cradle, and she looked round at me with her great black eyes kind o' mournful and wishful, and then she stooped down over the cradle.' 'Well,' says Lois, 'I ain't goin' to have no such doin's in my house,' and she went right in and took up the baby, and the very next day she jist had the cradle split up for kindlin'; and that night, if you 'll believe, when they was a-burnin' of it, they heard, jist as plain as could be, a baby scream, scream, screamin' round the house; but after that they never heard it no more."

"I don't like such stories," said Dame Pennel, "'specially to-night, when Mara's away. I shall get to hearing all sorts of noises in the wind. I wonder when Cap'n Pennel will be back."

And the good woman put more wood on the fire, and as the tongues of flame streamed up high and clear, she approached her face to the window-pane and started back with half a scream, as a pale, anxious visage with sad dark eyes seemed to approach her. It took a moment or two for her to discover that she had seen only the reflection of her own anxious, excited face, the pitchy blackness without having converted the window into a sort of dark mirror.

Miss Ruey meanwhile began solacing herself by singing, in her chimney-corner, a very favorite sacred melody, which contrasted oddly enough with the driving storm and howling sea:—

> "Haste, my beloved, haste away,
> Cut short the hours of thy delay;
> Fly like the bounding hart or roe,
> Over the hills where spices grow."

The tune was called "Invitation,"—one of those profusely florid in runs, and trills, and quavers, which delighted the ears of a former generation; and Miss Ruey, innocently unconscious of the effect of old age on her voice, ran them up and down, and out and in, in a way that would have made a laugh, had there been anybody there to notice or to laugh.

"I remember singin' that ar to Mary Jane Wilson the very night she died," said Aunt Ruey, stopping. "She wanted me to sing to her, and it was jist between two and three in the mornin'; there was jist the least red streak of daylight, and I opened the window and sat there and sung, and when I come to 'over the hills where spices grow,' I looked round and there was a change in Mary Jane, and I went to the bed, and says she very bright, 'Aunt Ruey, the Beloved has come,' and she was gone afore I could raise her up on her pillow. I always think of Mary Jane at them words; if ever there was a broken-hearted crittur took home, it was her."

At this moment Mrs. Pennel caught sight through the window of the gleam of the returning lantern, and in a moment Captain Pennel entered, dripping with rain and spray.

"Why, Cap'n! you 're e'en a'most drowned," said Aunt Ruey.

"How long have you been gone? You must have been a great ways," said Mrs. Pennel.

"Yes, I have been down to Cap'n Kittridge's. I met Kittridge out on the beach. We heard the guns plain enough, but could n't see anything. I went on down to Kittridge's to get a look at little Mara."

"Well, she 's all well enough?" said Mrs. Pennel, anxiously.

"Oh, yes, well enough. Miss Roxy showed her to me in the trundle-bed, 'long with Sally. The little thing was lying smiling in her sleep, with her cheek right up against Sally's. I took comfort looking at her. I could n't help thinking: 'So he giveth his beloved sleep!'"

VII

FROM THE SEA

During the night and storm, the little Mara had lain sleeping as quietly as if the cruel sea, that had made her an orphan from her birth, were her kind-tempered old grandfather singing her to sleep, as he often did,—with a somewhat hoarse voice truly, but with ever an undertone of protecting love. But toward daybreak, there came very clear and bright into her childish mind a dream, having that vivid distinctness which often characterizes the dreams of early childhood.

She thought she saw before her the little cove where she and Sally had been playing the day before, with its broad sparkling white beach of sand curving round its blue sea-mirror, and studded thickly with gold and silver shells. She saw the boat of Captain Kittridge upon the stocks, and his tar-kettle with the smouldering fires flickering under it; but, as often happens in dreams, a certain rainbow vividness and clearness invested everything, and she and Sally were jumping for joy at the beautiful things they found on the beach.

Suddenly, there stood before them a woman, dressed in a long white garment. She was very pale, with sweet, serious dark eyes, and she led by the hand a black-eyed boy, who seemed to be crying and looking about as for something lost. She dreamed that she stood still, and the woman came toward her, looking at her with sweet, sad eyes, till the child seemed to feel them in every fibre of her frame. The woman laid her hand on her head as if in blessing, and then put the boy's hand in hers, and said, "Take him, Mara, he is a playmate for you;" and with that the little boy's face flashed out into a merry laugh. The woman faded away, and the three children remained playing together, gathering shells and pebbles of a wonderful brightness. So vivid was this vision, that the little one awoke laughing with pleasure, and searched under her pillows for the strange and beautiful things that she had been gathering in dreamland.

"What 's Mara looking after?" said Sally, sitting up in her trundle-bed, and speaking in the patronizing motherly tone she commonly used to her little playmate.

"All gone, pitty boy—all gone!" said the child, looking round regretfully, and shaking her golden head; "pitty lady all gone!"

"How queer she talks!" said Sally, who had awakened with the project of building a sheet-house with her fairy neighbor, and was beginning to loosen the upper sheet and dispose the pillows with a view to this species of architecture. "Come, Mara, let 's make a pretty house!" she said.

"Pitty boy out dere—out dere!" said the little one, pointing to the window, with a deeper expression than ever of wishfulness in her eyes.

"Come, Sally Kittridge, get up this minute!" said the voice of her mother, entering the door at this moment; "and here, put these clothes on to Mara, the child must n't run round in her best; it 's strange, now, Mary Pennel never thinks of such things."

Sally, who was of an efficient temperament, was preparing energetically to second these commands of her mother, and en-due her little neighbor with a coarse brown stuff dress, somewhat faded and patched, which she herself had outgrown when of Mara's age; with shoes, which had been coarsely made to begin with, and very much battered by time; but, quite to her surprise, the child, generally so passive and tractable, opposed a most unexpected and desperate resistance to this operation. She began to cry and to sob and shake her curly head, throwing her tiny hands out in a wild species of freakish opposition, which had, notwithstanding, a quaint and singular grace about it, while she stated her objections in all the little English at her command.

"Mara don't want—Mara want pitty boo des—and *pitty* shoes."

"Why, was ever anything like it?" said Mrs. Kittridge to Miss Roxy, as they both were drawn to the door by the outcry; "here 's this child won't have decent every-day clothes put on her,—she must be kept dressed up like a princess. Now, that ar 's French calico!" said Mrs. Kittridge, holding up the controverted blue dress, "and that ar never cost a cent under five-and-sixpence a yard; it takes a yard and a half to make it, and it must have been a good day's work to make it up; call that three-and-six-pence more, and with them pearl buttons and thread and all, that ar dress never cost less than a dollar and seventy-five, and here she 's goin' to run out every day in it!"

"Well, well!" said Miss Roxy, who had taken the sobbing fair one in her lap, "you know, Mis' Kittridge, this 'ere 's a kind o' pet lamb, an old-folks' darling, and things be with her as they be, and we can't make her over, and she 's such a nervous little thing we must n't cross her." Saying which, she proceeded to dress the child in her own clothes.

"If you had a good large checked apron, I would n't mind putting that on her!" added Miss Roxy, after she had arrayed the child.

"Here's one," said Mrs. Kittridge; "that may save her clothes some."

Miss Roxy began to put on the wholesome garment; but, rather to her mortification, the little fairy began to weep again in a most heart-broken manner.

"Don't want che't apon."

"Why don't Mara want nice checked apron?" said Miss Roxy, in that extra cheerful tone by which children are to be made to believe they have mistaken their own mind.

"Don't want it!" with a decided wave of the little hand; "I 's too pitty to wear che't apon."

"Well! well!" said Mrs. Kittridge, rolling up her eyes, "did I ever! no, I never did. If there ain't depraved natur' a-comin' out early. Well, if she says she 's pretty now, what 'll it be when she 's fifteen?"

"She 'll learn to tell a lie about it by that time," said Miss Roxy, "and say she thinks she 's horrid. The child *is* pretty, and the truth comes uppermost with her now."

"Haw! haw! haw!" burst with a great crash from Captain Kittridge, who had come in behind, and stood silently listening during this conversation; "that 's musical now; come here, my little maid, you *are* too pretty for checked aprons, and no mistake;" and seizing the child in his long arms, he tossed her up like a butterfly, while her sunny curls shone in the morning light.

"There 's one comfort about the child, Miss Kittridge," said Aunt Roxy: "she 's one of them that dirt won't stick to. I never knew her to stain or tear her clothes,—she always come in jist so nice."

"She ain't much like Sally, then!" said Mrs. Kittridge. "That girl 'll run through more clothes! Only last week she walked the crown out of my old black straw bonnet, and left it hanging on the top of a blackberry-bush."

"Wal', wal'," said Captain Kittridge, "as to dressin' this 'ere child,—why, ef Pennel's a mind to dress her in cloth of gold, it's none of our business! He's rich enough for all he wants to do, and so let's eat our breakfast and mind our own business."

After breakfast Captain Kittridge took the two children down to the cove, to investigate the state of his boat and tar-kettle, set high above the highest tide-mark. The sun had risen gloriously, the sky was of an intense, vivid blue, and only great snowy islands of clouds, lying in silver banks on the horizon, showed vestiges of last night's storm. The whole wide sea was one glorious scene of forming and dissolving mountains of blue and purple, breaking at the crest into brilliant silver. All round the island the waves were constantly leaping and springing into jets and columns of brilliant foam, throwing themselves high up, in silvery cataracts, into the very arms of the solemn ever-green forests which overhung the shore.

The sands of the little cove seemed harder and whiter than ever, and were thickly bestrewn with the shells and seaweed which the upturnings of the night had brought in. There lay what might have been fringes and fragments of sea-gods' vestures,—blue, crimson, purple, and orange seaweeds, wreathed in tangled ropes of kelp and sea-grass, or lying separately scattered on the sands. The children ran wildly, shouting as they began gathering sea-treasures; and Sally, with the air of an experienced hand in the business, untwisted the coils of rosy seaweed, from which every moment she disengaged some new treasure, in some rarer shell or smoother pebble.

Suddenly, the child shook out something from a knotted mass of sea-grass, which she held up with a perfect shriek of delight. It was a bracelet of hair, fastened by a brilliant clasp of green, sparkling stones, such as she had never seen before. She redoubled her cries of delight, as she saw it sparkle between her and the sun, calling upon her father.

"Father! father! do come here, and see what I 've found!"

He came quickly, and took the bracelet from the child's hand; but, at the same moment, looking over her head, he caught sight of an object partially concealed behind a projecting rock. He took a step forward, and uttered an exclamation,—

"Well, well! sure enough! poor things!"

There lay, bedded in sand and seaweed, a woman with a little boy clasped in her arms! Both had been carefully lashed to a spar, but the child was held to the bosom of the woman, with a pressure closer than any knot that mortal hands could tie. Both were deep sunk in the sand, into which had streamed the woman's long, dark hair, which sparkled with glittering morsels of sand and pebbles, and with those tiny, brilliant, yellow shells which are so numerous on that shore.

The woman was both young and beautiful. The forehead, damp with ocean-spray, was like sculptured marble,—the eyebrows dark and decided in their outline; but the long, heavy, black fringes had shut down, as a solemn curtain, over all the history of mortal joy or sorrow that those eyes had looked upon. A wedding-ring gleamed on the marble hand; but the sea had divorced all human ties, and taken her as a bride to itself. And, in truth, it seemed to have made to her a worthy bed, for she was all folded and inwreathed in sand and shells and seaweeds, and a great, weird-looking leaf of kelp, some yards in length, lay twined around her like a shroud. The child that lay in her bosom had hair, and face, and eyelashes like her own, and his little hands were holding tightly a portion of the black dress which she wore.

"Cold,—cold,—stone dead!" was the muttered exclamation of the old seaman, as he bent over the woman.

"She must have struck her head there," he mused, as he laid his finger on a dark, bruised spot on her temple. He laid his hand on the child's heart, and put one finger under the arm to see if there was any lingering vital heat, and then hastily cut the lashings that bound the pair to the spar, and with difficulty disengaged the child from the cold clasp in which dying love had bound him to a heart which should beat no more with mortal joy or sorrow.

Sally, after the first moment, had run screaming toward the house, with all a child's forward eagerness, to be the bearer of news; but the little Mara stood, looking anxiously, with a wishful earnestness of face.

"Pitty boy,—pitty boy,—come!" she said often; but the old man was so busy, he scarcely regarded her.

"Now, Cap'n Kittridge, do tell!" said Miss Roxy, meeting him in all haste, with a cap-border stiff in air, while Dame Kittridge exclaimed,—

"Now, you don't! Well, well! did n't I say that was a ship last night? And what a solemnizing thought it was that souls might be goin' into eternity!"

"We must have blankets and hot bottles, right away," said Miss Roxy, who always took the earthly view of matters, and who was, in her own person, a personified humane society. "Miss Kittridge, you jist dip out your dishwater into the smallest tub, and we 'll put him in. Stand away, Mara! Sally, you take her out of the way! We 'll fetch this child to, perhaps. I 've fetched 'em to, when they 's seemed to be dead as door-nails!"

"Cap'n Kittridge, you 're sure the woman's dead?"

"Laws, yes; she had a blow right on her temple here. There 's no bringing her to till the resurrection."

"Well, then, you jist go and get Cap'n Pennel to come down and help you, and get the body into the house, and we 'll attend to layin' it out by and by. Tell Ruey to come down."

Aunt Roxy issued her orders with all the military vigor and precision of a general in case of a sudden attack. It was her habit. Sickness and death were her opportunities; where they were, she felt herself at home, and she addressed herself to the task before her with undoubting faith.

Before many hours a pair of large, dark eyes slowly emerged from under the black-fringed lids of the little drowned boy,— they rolled dreamily round for a moment, and dropped again in heavy languor.

The little Mara had, with the quiet persistence which formed a trait in her baby character, dragged stools and chairs to the back of the bed, which she at last succeeded in scaling, and sat opposite to where the child lay, grave and still, watching with intense earnestness the process that was going on. At the moment when the eyes had opened, she stretched forth her little arms, and said, eagerly, "Pitty boy, come,"—and then, as they closed again, she dropped her hands with a sigh of disappointment. Yet, before night, the little stranger sat up in bed, and laughed with pleasure at the treasures of shells and pebbles which the children spread out on the bed before him.

He was a vigorous, well-made, handsome child, with brilliant eyes and teeth, but the few words that he spoke were in a language unknown to most present. Captain Kittridge declared it to be Spanish, and that a call which he most passionately and often repeated was for his mother. But he was of that happy age when sorrow can be easily effaced, and the efforts of the children called forth joyous smiles. When his playthings did not go to his liking, he showed sparkles of a fiery, irascible spirit.

The little Mara seemed to appropriate him in feminine fashion, as a chosen idol and graven image. She gave him at once all her slender stock of infantine treasures, and seemed to watch with an ecstatic devotion his every movement,—often repeating, as she looked delightedly around, "Pitty boy, come."

She had no words to explain the strange dream of the morning; it lay in her, struggling for expression, and giving her an interest in the new-comer as in something belonging to herself. Whence it came,—whence come multitudes like it, which spring up as strange, enchanted flowers, every now and then in the dull, material pathway of life,—who knows? It may be that our present faculties have among them a rudimentary one, like the germs of wings in the chrysalis, by which the spiritual world becomes sometimes an object of perception; there may be natures in which the walls of the material are so fine and translucent that the spiritual is seen through them as through a glass darkly. It may be, too, that the love which is stronger than death has a power sometimes to make itself heard and felt through the walls of our mortality, when it would plead for the defenseless ones it has left behind. All these things *may* be,—who knows?

"There," said Miss Roxy, coming out of the keeping-room at sunset; "I would n't ask to see a better-lookin' corpse. That ar woman was a sight to behold this morning. I guess I shook a double handful of stones and them little shells out of her hair,—now she reely looks beautiful. Captain Kittridge has made a coffin out o' some cedar-boards he happened to have, and I lined it with bleached cotton, and stuffed the pillow nice and full, and when we come to get her in, she reely will look lovely."

"I s'pose, Mis' Kittridge, you 'll have the funeral to-morrow,—it 's Sunday."

"Why, yes, Aunt Roxy,—I think everybody must want to improve such a dispensation. Have you took little Mara in to look at the corpse?"

"Well, no," said Miss Roxy; "Mis' Pennel 's gettin' ready to take her home."

"I think it 's an opportunity we ought to improve," said Mrs.

Kittridge, "to learn children what death is. I think we can't begin to solemnize their minds too young."

At this moment Sally and the little Mara entered the room.

"Come here, children," said Mrs. Kittridge, taking a hand of either one, and leading them to the closed door of the keeping-room; "I 've got somethin' to show you."

The room looked ghostly and dim,—the rays of light fell through the closed shutter on an object mysteriously muffled in a white sheet.

Sally's bright face expressed only the vague curiosity of a child to see something new; but the little Mara resisted and hung back with all her force, so that Mrs. Kittridge was obliged to take her up and hold her.

She folded back the sheet from the chill and wintry form which lay so icily, lonely, and cold. Sally walked around it, and gratified her curiosity by seeing it from every point of view, and laying her warm, busy hand on the lifeless and cold one; but Mara clung to Mrs. Kittridge, with eyes that expressed a distressed astonishment. The good woman stooped over and placed the child's little hand for a moment on the icy forehead. The little one gave a piercing scream, and struggled to get away; and as soon as she was put down, she ran and hid her face in Aunt Roxy's dress, sobbing bitterly.

"That child 'll grow up to follow vanity," said Mrs. Kittridge; "her little head is full of dress now, and she hates anything serious,—it 's easy to see that."

The little Mara had no words to tell what a strange, distressful chill had passed up her arm and through her brain, as she felt that icy cold of death,—that cold so different from all others. It was an impression of fear and pain that lasted weeks and months, so that she would start out of sleep and cry with a terror which she had not yet a sufficiency of language to describe.

"You seem to forget, Mis' Kittridge, that this 'ere child ain't rugged like our Sally," said Aunt Roxy, as she raised the little Mara in her arms. "She was a seven-months' baby, and hard to raise at all, and a shivery, scary little creature."

"Well, then, she ought to be hardened," said Dame Kittridge. "But Mary Pennel never had no sort of idea of bringin' up children; 't was jist so with Naomi,—the girl never had no sort o' resolution, and she just died for want o' resolution,—that 's what came of it. I tell ye, children 's got to learn to take the world as it is; and 't ain't no use bringin' on 'em up too tender. Teach 'em to begin as they 've got to go out,—that 's my maxim."

"Mis' Kittridge," said Aunt Roxy, "there 's reason in all things, and there 's difference in children. 'What 's one's meat 's another's pison.' You could n't fetch up Mis' Pennel's children, and she could n't fetch up your'n,—so let 's say no more 'bout it."

"I 'm always a-tellin' my wife that ar," said Captain Kittridge; "she 's always wantin' to make everybody over after her pattern."

"Cap'n Kittridge, I don't think *you* need to speak," resumed his wife. "When such a loud providence is a-knockin' at *your* door, I think you 'd better be a-searchin' your own heart,—here it is the eleventh hour, and you hain't come into the Lord's vineyard yet."

"Oh! come, come, Mis' Kittridge, don't twit a feller afore folks," said the Captain. "I 'm goin' over to Harpswell Neck this blessed minute after the minister to 'tend the funeral,—so we 'll let *him* preach."

VIII

The Seen
and the Unseen

Life on any shore is a dull affair,—ever degenerating into commonplace; and this may account for the eagerness with which even a great calamity is sometimes accepted in a neighborhood, as affording wherewithal to stir the deeper feelings of our nature. Thus, though Mrs. Kittridge was by no means a hardhearted woman, and would not for the world have had a ship wrecked on her particular account, yet since a ship had been wrecked and a body floated ashore at her very door, as it were, it afforded her no inconsiderable satisfaction to dwell on the details and to arrange for the funeral.

It was something to talk about and to think of, and likely to furnish subject-matter for talk for years to come when she should go out to tea with any of her acquaintances who lived at Middle Bay, or Maquoit, or Harpswell Neck. For although in those days,—the number of light-houses being much smaller than it is now,—it was no uncommon thing for ships to be driven on shore in storms, yet this incident had undeniably more that was stirring and romantic in it than any within the memory of any tea-table gossip in the vicinity. Mrs. Kittridge, therefore, looked forward to the funeral services on Sunday afternoon as to a species of solemn fête, which imparted a sort of consequence to her dwelling and herself. Notice of it was to be given out in "meeting" after service, and she might expect both keeping-room and kitchen to be full. Mrs. Pennel had offered to do her share of Christian and neighborly kindness, in taking home to her own dwelling the little boy. In fact, it became necessary to do so in order to appease the feelings of the little Mara, who clung to the new acquisition with most devoted fondness, and wept bitterly when he was separated from her even for a few moments. Therefore, in the afternoon of the day when the body was found, Mrs. Pennel, who had come down to assist, went back in company with Aunt Ruey and the two children.

The September evening set in brisk and chill, and the cheerful fire that snapped and roared up the ample chimney of Captain Kittridge's kitchen was a pleasing feature. The days of our story were before the advent of those sullen gnomes, the "airtights," or even those more sociable and cheery domestic genii, the cooking-stoves. They were the days of the genial open kitchen-fire, with the crane, the pot-hooks, and trammels,— where hissed and boiled the social tea-kettle, where steamed the huge dinner-pot, in whose ample depths beets, carrots, potatoes, and turnips boiled in jolly sociability with the pork or corned beef which they were destined to flank at the coming meal.

On the present evening, Miss Roxy sat bolt upright, as was her wont, in one corner of the fireplace, with her spectacles on her nose, and an unwonted show of candles on the little stand beside her, having resumed the task of the silk dress which had been for a season interrupted. Mrs. Kittridge, with her spectacles also mounted, was carefully and warily "running-up breadths," stopping every few minutes to examine her work, and to inquire submissively of Miss Roxy if "it will do?"

Captain Kittridge sat in the other corner busily whittling on a little boat which he was shaping to please Sally, who sat on a low stool by his side with her knitting, evidently more intent on what her father was producing than on the evening task of "ten bouts," which her mother exacted before she could freely give her mind to anything on her own account. As Sally was rigorously sent to bed exactly at eight o'clock, it became her to be diligent if she wished to do anything for her own amusement before that hour.

And in the next room, cold and still, was lying that faded image of youth and beauty which the sea had so strangely given up. Without a name, without a history, without a single accompaniment from which her past could even be surmised,—there she lay, sealed in eternal silence.

"It 's strange," said Captain Kittridge, as he whittled away,— "it 's very strange we don't find anything more of that ar ship. I 've been all up and down the beach a-lookin'. There was a spar and some broken bits of boards and timbers come ashore down on the beach, but nothin' to speak of."

"It won't be known till the sea gives up its dead," said Miss Roxy, shaking her head solemnly, "and there 'll be a great givin' up then, I 'm a-thinkin'."

"Yes, indeed," said Mrs. Kittridge, with an emphatic nod.

"Father," said Sally, "how many, many things there must be at the bottom of the sea,—so many ships are sunk with all their fine things on board. Why don't people contrive some way to go down and get them?"

"They do, child," said Captain Kittridge; "they have diving-bells, and men go down in 'em with caps over their faces, and long tubes to get the air through, and they walk about on the bottom of the ocean."

"Did you ever go down in one, father?"

"Why, yes, child, to be sure; and strange enough it was, to be sure. There you could see great big sea critters, with ever so many eyes and long arms, swimming right up to catch you, and all you could do would be to muddy the water on the bottom, so they could n't see you."

"I never heard of that, Cap'n Kittridge," said his wife, drawing herself up with a reproving coolness.

"Wal', Mis' Kittridge, you hain't heard of everything that ever happened," said the Captain, imperturbably, "though you *do* know a sight."

"And how does the bottom of the ocean look, father?" said Sally.

"Laws, child, why trees and bushes grow there, just as they do on land; and great plants,—blue and purple and green and yellow, and lots of great pearls lie round. I 've seen 'em big as chippin'-birds' eggs."

"Cap'n Kittridge!" said his wife.

"I have, and big as robins' eggs, too, but them was off the coast of Ceylon and Malabar, and way round the Equator," said the Captain, prudently resolved to throw his romance to a sufficient distance.

"It 's a pity you did n't get a few of them pearls," said his wife, with an indignant appearance of scorn.

"I did get lots on 'em, and traded 'em off to the Nabobs in the interior for Cashmere shawls and India silks and sich," said the Captain, composedly; "and brought 'em home and sold 'em at a good figure, too."

"Oh, father!" said Sally, earnestly, "I wish you had saved just one or two for us."

"Laws, child, I wish now I had," said the Captain, good-naturedly. "Why, when I was in India, I went up to Lucknow, and Benares, and round, and saw all the Nabobs and Biggums,—

why, they don't make no more of gold and silver and precious stones than we do of the shells we find on the beach. Why, I 've seen one of them fellers with a diamond in his turban as big as my fist."

"Cap'n Kittridge, what are you telling?" said his wife once more.

"Fact,—as big as my fist," said the Captain, obdurately; "and all the clothes he wore was jist a stiff crust of pearls and precious stones. I tell you, he looked like something in the Revelations,—a real New Jerusalem look he had."

"I call that ar talk wicked, Cap'n Kittridge, usin' Scriptur' that ar way," said his wife.

"Why, don't it tell about all sorts of gold and precious stones in the Revelations?" said the Captain; "that 's all I meant. Them ar countries off in Asia ain't like our'n,—stands to reason they should n't be; them 's Scripture countries, and everything is different there."

"Father, did n't you ever get any of those splendid things?" said Sally.

"Laws, yes, child. Why, I had a great green ring, an emerald, that one of the princes giv' me, and ever so many pearls and diamonds. I used to go with 'em rattlin' loose in my vest pocket. I was young and gay in them days, and thought of bringin' of 'em home for the gals, but somehow I always got opportunities for swappin' of 'em off for goods and sich. That ar shawl your mother keeps in her camfire chist was what I got for one on 'em."

"Well, well," said Mrs. Kittridge, "there 's never any catchin' you, 'cause you 've been where we have n't."

"You 've caught me once, and that ought'r do," said the Captain, with unruffled good-nature. "I tell you, Sally, your mother was the handsomest gal in Harpswell in them days."

"I should think you was too old for such nonsense, Cap'n," said Mrs. Kittridge, with a toss of her head, and a voice that sounded far less inexorable than her former admonition. In fact, though the old Captain was as unmanageable under his wife's fireside *régime* as any brisk old cricket that skipped and sang around the hearth, and though he hopped over all moral boundaries with a cheerful alertness of conscience that was quite discouraging, still there was no resisting the spell of his inexhaustible good-nature.

By this time he had finished the little boat, and to Sally's great delight, began sailing it for her in a pail of water.

"I wonder," said Mrs. Kittridge, "what's to be done with that ar child. I suppose the selectmen will take care on't; it'll be brought up by the town."

"I should n't wonder," said Miss Roxy, "if Cap'n Pennel should adopt it."

"You don't think so," said Mrs. Kittridge. "'T would be taking a great care and expense on their hands at their time of life."

"I would n't want no better fun than to bring up that little shaver," said Captain Kittridge; "he's a bright un, I promise you."

"You, Cap'n Kittridge! I wonder you can talk so," said his wife. "It's an awful responsibility, and I wonder you don't think whether or no you're fit for it."

"Why, down here on the shore, I'd as lives undertake a boy as a Newfoundland pup," said the Captain. "Plenty in the sea to eat, drink, and wear. That ar young un may be the staff of their old age yet."

"You see," said Miss Roxy, "I think they'll adopt it to be company for little Mara; they're bound up in her, and the little thing pines bein' alone."

"Well, they make a real graven image of that ar child," said

Mrs. Kittridge, "and fairly bow down to her and worship her."

"Well, it 's natural," said Miss Roxy. "Besides, the little thing is cunnin'; she 's about the cunnin'est little crittur that I ever saw, and has such enticin' ways."

The fact was, as the reader may perceive, that Miss Roxy had been thawed into an unusual attachment for the little Mara, and this affection was beginning to spread a warming element through her whole being. It was as if a rough granite rock had suddenly awakened to a passionate consciousness of the beauty of some fluttering white anemone that nestled in its cleft, and felt warm thrills running through all its veins at every tender motion and shadow. A word spoken against the little one seemed to rouse her combativeness. Nor did Dame Kittridge bear the child the slightest ill-will, but she was one of those naturally care-taking people whom Providence seems to design to perform the picket duties for the rest of society, and who, therefore, challenge everybody and everything to stand and give an account of themselves. Miss Roxy herself belonged to this class, but sometimes found herself so stoutly overhauled by the guns of Mrs. Kittridge's battery, that she could only stand modestly on the defensive.

One of Mrs. Kittridge's favorite hobbies was education, or, as she phrased it, the "fetchin' up" of children, which she held should be performed to the letter of the old stiff rule. In this manner she had already trained up six sons, who were all following their fortunes upon the seas, and, on this account, she had no small conceit of her abilities; and when she thought she discerned a lamb being left to frisk heedlessly out of bounds, her zeal was stirred to bring it under proper sheepfold regulations.

"Come, Sally, it 's eight o'clock," said the good woman.

Sally's dark brows lowered over her large, black eyes, and she gave an appealing look to her father.

"Law, mother, let the child sit up a quarter of an hour later, jist for once."

"Cap'n Kittridge, if I was to hear to you, there 'd never be no rule in this house. Sally, you go 'long this minute, and be sure you put your knittin' away in its place."

The Captain gave a humorous nod of submissive good-nature to his daughter as she went out. In fact, putting Sally to bed was taking away his plaything, and leaving him nothing to do but study faces in the coals, or watch the fleeting sparks which chased each other in flocks up the sooty back of the chimney.

It was Saturday night, and the morrow was Sunday,—never a very pleasant prospect to the poor Captain, who, having, unfortunately, no spiritual tastes, found it very difficult to get through the day in compliance with his wife's views of propriety, for he, alas! soared no higher in his aims.

"I b'lieve, on the hull, Polly, I 'll go to bed, too," said he, suddenly starting up.

"Well, father, your clean shirt is in the right-hand corner of the upper drawer, and your Sunday clothes on the back of the chair by the bed."

The fact was that the Captain promised himself the pleasure of a long conversation with Sally, who nestled in the trundle-bed under the paternal couch, to whom he could relate long, many-colored yarns, without the danger of interruption from her mother's sharp, truth-seeking voice.

A moralist might, perhaps, be puzzled exactly what account to make of the Captain's disposition to romancing and embroidery. In all real, matter-of-fact transactions, as between man and man, his word was as good as another's, and he was held to be honest and just in his dealings. It was only when he mounted the stilts of foreign travel that his paces became so enormous. Perhaps, after all, a rude poetic and artistic faculty possessed the man. He might have been a humbler phase of the "mute, in-glorious Milton." Perhaps his narrations required the privileges and allowances due to the inventive arts generally. Certain it was that, in common with other artists, he required an atmos-phere of sympathy and confidence in which to develop himself fully; and, when left alone with children, his mind ran such riot, that the bounds between the real and unreal became foggier than the banks of Newfoundland.

The two women sat up, and the night wore on apace, while they kept together that customary vigil which it was thought necessary to hold over the lifeless casket from which an immor-tal jewel had recently been withdrawn.

"I re'lly did hope," said Mrs. Kittridge, mournfully, "that this 'ere solemn Providence would have been sent home to the Cap'n's mind; but he seems jist as light and triflin' as ever."

"There don't nobody see these 'ere things unless they 's effec-tually called," said Miss Roxy, "and the Cap'n's time ain't come."

"It 's gettin' to be t'ward the eleventh hour," said Mrs. Kit-tridge, "as I was a-tellin' him this afternoon."

"Well," said Miss Roxy, "you know

> " 'While the lamp holds out to burn,
> The vilest sinner may return.' "

"Yes, I know that," said Mrs. Kittridge, rising and taking up the candle. "Don't you think, Aunt Roxy, we may as well give a look in there at the corpse?"

It was past midnight as they went together into the keeping-room. All was so still that the clash of the rising tide and the ticking of the clock assumed that solemn and mournful dis-tinctness which even tones less impressive take on in the night-watches. Miss Roxy went mechanically through with certain arrangements of the white drapery around the cold sleeper, and uncovering the face and bust for a moment, looked critically at the still, unconscious countenance.

"Not one thing to let us know who or what she is," she said; "that boy, if he lives, would give a good deal to know, some day."

"What is it one's duty to do about this bracelet?" said Mrs. Kittridge, taking from a drawer the article in question, which had been found on the beach in the morning.

"Well, I s'pose it belongs to the child, whatever it 's worth," said Miss Roxy.

"Then if the Pennels conclude to take him, I may as well give it to them," said Mrs. Kittridge, laying it back in the drawer.

Miss Roxy folded the cloth back over the face, and the two went out into the kitchen. The fire had sunk low—the crickets were chirruping gleefully. Mrs. Kittridge added more wood, and put on the tea-kettle that their watching might be refreshed by the aid of its talkative and inspiring beverage. The two solemn, hard-visaged women drew up to each other by the fire, and insensibly their very voices assumed a tone of drowsy and confidential mystery.

"If this 'ere poor woman was hopefully pious, and could see what was goin' on here," said Mrs. Kittridge, "it would seem to be a comfort to her that her child has fallen into such good hands. It seems a'most a pity she could n't know it."

"How do you know she don't?" said Miss Roxy, brusquely.

"Why, you know the hymn," said Mrs. Kittridge, quoting those somewhat saddusaical lines from the popular psalm-book:—

> " 'The living know that they must die,
> But all the dead forgotten lie—
> *Their memory and their senses gone,*
> *Alike unknowing and unknown.'* "

"Well, I don't know 'bout that," said Miss Roxy, flavoring her cup of tea; "hymn-book ain't Scriptur', and I 'm pretty sure that ar ain't true always;" and she nodded her head as if she could say more if she chose.

Now Miss Roxy's reputation of vast experience in all the facts relating to those last fateful hours, which are the only certain event in every human existence, caused her to be regarded as a sort of Delphic oracle in such matters, and therefore Mrs. Kittridge, not without a share of the latent superstition to which each human heart must confess at some hours, drew confidentially near to Miss Roxy, and asked if she had anything particular on her mind.

"Well, Mis' Kittridge," said Miss Roxy, "I ain't one of the sort as likes to make a talk of what I 've seen, but mebbe if I was, I 've seen some things *as* remarkable as anybody. I tell you, Mis' Kittridge, folks don't tend the sick and dyin' bed year in and out, at all hours, day and night, and not see some remarkable things; that 's my opinion."

"Well, Miss Roxy, did you ever see a sperit?"

"I won't say as I have, and I won't say as I have n't," said Miss Roxy; "only as I have seen some remarkable things."

There was a pause, in which Mrs. Kittridge stirred her tea, looking intensely curious, while the old kitchen-clock seemed to tick with one of those fits of loud insistence which seem to take clocks at times when all is still, as if they had something that they were getting ready to say pretty soon, if nobody else spoke.

But Miss Roxy evidently had something to say, and so she began:—

"Mis' Kittridge, this 'ere 's a very particular subject to be talkin' of. I 've had opportunities to observe that most have n't, and I don't care if I jist say to you, that I 'm pretty sure spirits that has left the body do come to their friends sometimes."

The clock ticked with still more *empressement,* and Mrs. Kittridge glared through the horn bows of her glasses with eyes of eager curiosity.

"Now, you remember Cap'n Titcomb's wife, that died fifteen years ago when her husband had gone to Archangel, and you remember that he took her son John out with him—and of all her boys, John was the one she was particular sot on."

"Yes, and John died at Archangel; I remember that."

"Jes' so," said Miss Roxy, laying her hand on Mrs. Kittridge's; "he died at Archangel the very day his mother died, and jist the hour, for the Cap'n had it down in his log-book."

"You don't say so!"

"Yes, I do. Well, now," said Miss Roxy, sinking her voice, "this 'ere was remarkable. Mis' Titcomb was one of the fearful sort, tho' one of the best women that ever lived. Our minister used to call her 'Mis' Muchafraid'—you know, in the 'Pilgrim's Progress'—but he was satisfied with her evidences, and told her so; she used to say she was 'afraid of the dark valley,' and she told our minister so when he went out, that ar last day he called; and his last words, as he stood with his hand on the knob of the door, was 'Mis' Titcomb, the Lord will find ways to bring you thro' the dark valley.' Well, she sunk away about three o'clock in the morning. I remember the time, 'cause the Cap'n's chronometer watch that he left with her lay on the stand for her to take her drops by. I heard her kind o' restless, and I went up, and I saw she was struck with death, and she looked sort o' anxious and distressed.

"'Oh, Aunt Roxy,' says she, 'it's so dark, who will go with me?' and in a minute her whole face brightened up, and says she, 'John is going with me,' and she jist gave the least little sigh and never breathed no more—she jist died as easy as a bird. I told our minister of it next morning, and he asked if I'd made a note of the hour, and I told him I had, and says he, 'You did right, Aunt Roxy.'"

"What did he seem to think of it?"

"Well, he did n't seem inclined to speak freely. 'Miss Roxy,' says he, 'all natur 's in the Lord's hands, and there 's no saying why he uses this or that; them that 's strong enough to go by faith, he lets 'em, but there 's no saying what he won't do for the weak ones.'"

"Wa'n't the Cap'n overcome when you told him?" said Mrs. Kittridge.

"Indeed he was; he was jist as white as a sheet."

Miss Roxy now proceeded to pour out another cup of tea, and having mixed and flavored it, she looked in a weird and sibylline manner across it, and inquired,—

"Mis' Kittridge, do you remember that ar Mr. Wadkins that come to Brunswick twenty years ago, in President Averill's days?"

"Yes, I remember the pale, thin, long-nosed gentleman that used to sit in President Averill's pew at church. Nobody knew who he was, or where he came from. The college students used to call him Thaddeus of Warsaw. Nobody knew who he was but the President, 'cause he could speak all the foreign tongues — one about as well as another; but the President he knew his story, and said he was a good man, and he used to stay to the sacrament regular, I remember."

"Yes," said Miss Roxy, "he used to live in a room all alone, and keep himself. Folks said he was quite a gentleman, too, and fond of reading."

"I heard Cap'n Atkins tell," said Mrs. Kittridge, "how they came to take him up on the shores of Holland. You see, when he was somewhere in a port in Denmark, some men come to him and offered him a pretty good sum of money if he 'd be at such a place on the coast of Holland on such a day, and take whoever should come. So the Cap'n he went, and sure enough on that day there come a troop of men on horseback down to the beach with this man, and they all bid him good-by, and seemed to make much of him, but he never told 'em nothin on board ship, only he seemed kind o' sad and pinin'."

"Well," said Miss Roxy; "Ruey and I we took care o' that man in his last sickness, and we watched with him the night he died, and there was something quite remarkable."

"Do tell now," said Mrs. Kittridge.

"Well, you see," said Miss Roxy, "he 'd been low and poorly all day, kind o' tossin' and restless, and a little light-headed, and the Doctor said he thought he would n't last till morning, and so Ruey and I we set up with him, and between twelve and one Ruey said she thought she 'd jist lop down a few minutes on the old sofa at the foot of the bed, and I made me a cup of tea like as I 'm a-doin' now, and set with my back to him."

"Well?" said Mrs. Kittridge, eagerly.

"Well, you see he kept a-tossin' and throwin' off the clothes, and I kept a-gettin' up to straighten 'em; and once he threw out his arms, and something bright fell out on to the pillow, and I went and looked, and it was a likeness that he wore by a ribbon round his neck. It was a woman—a real handsome one—and she had on a low-necked black dress, of the cut they used to call Marie Louise, and she had a string of pearls round her neck, and her hair curled with pearls in it, and very wide blue eyes. Well, you see, I did n't look but a minute before he seemed to wake up, and he caught at it and hid it in his clothes. Well, I went and sat down, and I grew kind o' sleepy over the fire; but pretty soon I heard him speak out very clear, and kind o' surprised, in a tongue I did n't understand, and I looked round."

Miss Roxy here made a pause, and put another lump of sugar into her tea.

"Well?" said Mrs. Kittridge, ready to burst with curiosity.

"Well, now, I don't like to tell about these 'ere things, and you must n't never speak about it; but as sure as you live, Polly Kittridge, I see that ar very woman standin' at the back of the bed, right in the partin' of the curtains, jist as she looked in the pictur'—blue eyes and curly hair and pearls on her neck, and black dress."

"What did you do?" said Mrs. Kittridge.

"Do? Why, I jist held my breath and looked, and in a minute it kind o' faded away, and I got up and went to the bed, but the man was gone. He lay there with the pleasantest smile on his face that ever you see; and I woke up Ruey, and told her about it."

Mrs. Kittridge drew a long breath. "What do you think it was?"

"Well," said Miss Roxy, "I know what I think, but I don't think best to tell. I told Doctor Meritts, and he said there were more things in heaven and earth than folks knew about—and so I think."

⁂

Meanwhile, on this same evening, the little Mara frisked like a household fairy round the hearth of Zephaniah Pennel.

The boy was a strong-limbed, merry-hearted little urchin, and did full justice to the abundant hospitalities of Mrs. Pennel's tea-table; and after supper little Mara employed herself in bringing apronful after apronful of her choicest treasures, and laying them down at his feet. His great black eyes flashed with pleasure, and he gamboled about the hearth with his new playmate in perfect forgetfulness, apparently, of all the past night of fear and anguish.

When the great family Bible was brought out for prayers, and little Mara composed herself on a low stool by her grandmother's side, he, however, did not conduct himself as a babe of grace. He resisted all Miss Ruey's efforts to make him sit down beside her, and stood staring with his great, black, irreverent eyes during the Bible-reading, and laughed out in the most inappropriate manner when the psalm-singing began, and seemed disposed to mingle incoherent remarks of his own even in the prayers.

"This is a pretty self-willed youngster," said Miss Ruey, as they rose from the exercises, "and I should n't think he 'd been used to religious privileges."

"Perhaps not," said Zephaniah Pennel; "but who can say but what this providence is a message of the Lord to us—such as Pharaoh's daughter sent about Moses, 'Take this child, and bring him up for me'?"

"I 'd like to take him, if I thought I was capable," said Mrs. Pennel, timidly. "It seems a real providence to give Mara some company; the poor child pines so for want of it."

"Well, then, Mary, if you say so, we will bring him up with our little Mara," said Zephaniah, drawing the child toward him. "May the Lord bless him!" he added, laying his great brown hands on the shining black curls of the child.

IX

MOSES

Sunday morning rose clear and bright on Harpswell Bay. The whole sea was a waveless, blue looking-glass, streaked with bands of white, and flecked with sailing cloud-shadows from the skies above. Orr's Island, with its blue-black spruces, its silver firs, its golden larches, its scarlet sumachs, lay on the bosom of the deep like a great many-colored gem on an enchanted mirror. A vague, dreamlike sense of rest and Sabbath stillness seemed to brood in the air. The very spruce-trees seemed to know that it was Sunday, and to point solemnly upward with their dusky fingers; and the small tide-waves that chased each other up on the shelly beach, or broke against projecting rocks, seemed to do it with a chastened decorum, as if each blue-haired wave whispered to his brother, "Be still—be still."

Yes, Sunday it was along all the beautiful shores of Maine—netted in green and azure by its thousand islands, all glorious with their majestic pines, all musical and silvery with the caresses of the sea-waves, that loved to wander and lose themselves in their numberless shelly coves and tiny beaches among their cedar shadows.

Not merely as a burdensome restraint, or a weary endurance, came the shadow of that Puritan Sabbath. It brought with it all the sweetness that belongs to rest, all the sacredness that hallows home, all the memories of patient thrift, of sober order, of chastened yet intense family feeling, of calmness, purity, and self-respecting dignity which distinguish the Puritan household. It seemed a solemn pause in all the sights and sounds of earth. And he whose moral nature was not yet enough developed to fill the blank with visions of heaven was yet wholesomely instructed by his weariness into the secret of his own spiritual poverty.

Zephaniah Pennel, in his best Sunday clothes, with his hard visage glowing with a sort of interior tenderness, ministered this morning at his family-altar—one of those thousand priests of God's ordaining that tend the sacred fire in as many families of New England. He had risen with the morning star and been forth to meditate, and came in with his mind softened and glowing. The trance-like calm of earth and sea found a solemn answer with him, as he read what a poet wrote by the sea-shores of the Mediterranean, ages ago: "Bless the Lord, O my soul. O Lord my God, thou art very great; thou art clothed with honor and majesty. Who coverest thyself with light as with a garment: who stretchest out the heavens like a curtain: who layeth the beams of his chambers in the waters: who maketh the clouds his chariot: who walketh upon the wings of the wind. The trees of the Lord are full of sap; the cedars of Lebanon, which he hath planted; where the birds make their nests; as for the stork, the fir-trees are her house. O Lord, how manifold are thy works! in wisdom hast thou made them all."

Ages ago the cedars that the poet saw have rotted into dust, and from their cones have risen generations of others, wide-winged and grand. But the words of that poet have been wafted like seed to our days, and sprung up in flowers of trust and faith in a thousand households.

"Well, now," said Miss Ruey, when the morning rite was over, "Mis' Pennel, I s'pose you and the Cap'n will be wantin' to go to the meetin', so don't you gin yourse'ves a mite of trouble about the children, for I 'll stay at home with 'em. The little feller was starty and fretful in his sleep last night, and did n't seem to be quite well."

"No wonder, poor dear," said Mrs. Pennel; "it 's a wonder children can forget as they do."

"Yes," said Miss Ruey; "you know them lines in the 'English Reader,'—

> 'Gay hope is theirs by fancy led,
> Least pleasing when possessed;
> The tear forgot as soon as shed,
> The sunshine of the breast.'

Them lines all'ys seemed to me affectin'."

Miss Ruey's sentiment was here interrupted by a loud cry from the bedroom, and something between a sneeze and a howl.

"Massy! what is that ar young un up to!" she exclaimed, rushing into the adjoining bedroom.

There stood the young Master Hopeful of our story, with streaming eyes and much-bedaubed face, having just, after much labor, succeeded in making Miss Ruey's snuff-box fly open, which he did with such force as to send the contents in a perfect cloud into eyes, nose, and mouth. The scene of struggling and confusion that ensued cannot be described. The washings, and wipings, and sobbings, and exhortings, and the sympathetic sobs of the little Mara, formed a small tempest for the time being that was rather appalling.

"Well, this 'ere 's a youngster that 's a-goin' to make work," said Miss Ruey, when all things were tolerably restored. "Seems to make himself at home first thing."

"Poor little dear," said Mrs. Pennel, in the excess of loving-kindness, "I hope he will; he's welcome, I'm sure."

"Not to my snuff-box," said Miss Ruey, who had felt herself attacked in a very tender point.

"He 's got the notion of lookin' into things pretty early," said Captain Pennel, with an indulgent smile.

"Well, Aunt Ruey," said Mrs. Pennel, when this disturbance was somewhat abated, "I feel kind o' sorry to deprive you of your privileges to-day."

"Oh! never mind me," said Miss Ruey, briskly. "I 've got the big Bible, and I can sing a hymn or two by myself. My voice ain't quite what it used to be, but then I get a good deal of pleasure out of it." Aunt Ruey, it must be known, had in her youth been one of the foremost leaders in the "singers' seats," and now was in the habit of speaking of herself much as a retired *prima donna* might, whose past successes were yet in the minds of her generation.

After giving a look out of the window, to see that the children were within sight, she opened the big Bible at the story of the ten plagues of Egypt, and adjusting her horn spectacles with a sort of sideway twist on her little pug nose, she seemed intent on her Sunday duties. A moment after she looked up and said, "I don't know but I must send a message by you over to Mis' Deacon Badger, about a worldly matter, if 't is Sunday; but I 've been thinkin', Mis' Pennel, that there 'll have to be clothes made up for this 'ere child next week, and so perhaps Roxy and I had better stop here a day or two longer, and you tell Mis' Badger that we 'll come to her a Wednesday, and so she 'll have time to have that new press-board done,—the old one used to pester me so."

"Well, I 'll remember," said Mrs. Pennel.

"It seems a'most impossible to prevent one's thoughts wanderin' Sundays," said Aunt Ruey; "but I could n't help a-thinkin' I could get such a nice pair o' trousers out of them old Sunday ones of the Cap'n's in the garret. I was a-lookin' at 'em last Thursday, and thinkin' what a pity 't was you had n't nobody to cut down for; but this 'ere young un 's going to be such a tearer, he 'll want somethin' real stout; but I 'll try and put it out of my mind till Monday. Mis' Pennel, you 'll be sure to ask Mis' Titcomb how Harriet's toothache is, and whether them drops cured her that I gin her last Sunday; and ef you 'll jist look in a minute at Major Broad's, and tell 'em to use bayberry wax for his blister, it 's so healin'; and do jist ask if Sally's baby's eye-tooth has come through yet."

"Well, Aunt Ruey, I 'll try to remember all," said Mrs. Pennel, as she stood at the glass in her bedroom, carefully adjusting the respectable black silk shawl over her shoulders, and tying her neat bonnet-strings.

"I s'pose," said Aunt Ruey, "that the notice of the funeral 'll be gin out after sermon."

"Yes, I think so," said Mrs. Pennel.

"It 's another loud call," said Miss Ruey, "and I hope it will turn the young people from their thoughts of dress and vanity,—there 's Mary Jane Sanborn was all took up with gettin' feathers and velvet for her fall bonnet. I don't think I shall get no bonnet this year till snow comes. My bonnet 's respectable enough,—don't you think so?"

"Certainly, Aunt Ruey, it looks very well."

"Well, I 'll have the pork and beans and brown-bread all hot on table agin you come back," said Miss Ruey, "and then after dinner we 'll all go down to the funeral together. Mis' Pennel, there 's one thing on my mind,—what you goin' to call this 'ere boy?"

"Father and I 've been thinkin' that over," said Mrs. Pennel.

"Would n't think of giv'n him the Cap'n's name?" said Aunt Ruey.

"He must have a name of his own," said Captain Pennel. "Come here, sonny," he called to the child, who was playing just beside the door.

The child lowered his head, shook down his long black curls, and looked through them as elfishly as a Skye terrier, but showed no inclination to come.

"One thing he has n't learned, evidently," said Captain Pennel, "and that is to mind."

"Here!" he said, turning to the boy with a little of the tone he had used of old on the quarter-deck, and taking his small hand firmly.

The child surrendered, and let the good man lift him on his knee and stroke aside the clustering curls; the boy then looked fixedly at him with his great gloomy black eyes, his little firm-set mouth and bridled chin,—a perfect little miniature of proud manliness.

"What 's your name, little boy?"

The great eyes continued looking in the same solemn quiet.

"Law, he don't understand a word," said Zephaniah, putting his hand kindly on the child's head; "our tongue is all strange to him. Kittridge says he 's a Spanish child; may be from the West Indies; but nobody knows,—we never shall know his name."

"Well, I dare say it was some Popish nonsense or other," said Aunt Ruey; "and now he 's come to a land of Christian privileges, we ought to give him a good Scripture name, and start him well in the world."

"Let 's call him Moses," said Zephaniah, "because we drew him out of the water."

"Now, did I ever!" said Miss Ruey; "there 's something in the Bible to fit everything, ain't there?"

"I like Moses, because I had a brother of that name," said Mrs. Pennel.

The child had slid down from his protector's knee, and stood looking from one to the other gravely while this discussion was going on. What change of destiny was then going on for him in this simple formula of adoption, none could tell; but, surely, never orphan stranded on a foreign shore found home with hearts more true and loving.

"Well, wife, I suppose we must be goin'," said Zephaniah.

About a stone's throw from the open door, the little fishing-craft lay courtesying daintily on the small tide-waves that came licking up the white pebbly shore. Mrs. Pennel seated herself in the end of the boat, and a pretty placid picture she was, with her smooth, parted hair, her modest, cool, drab bonnet, and her bright hazel eyes, in which was the Sabbath calm of a loving and tender heart. Zephaniah loosed the sail, and the two children stood on the beach and saw them go off. A pleasant little wind carried them away, and back on the breeze came the sound of Zephaniah's Sunday-morning psalm:—

> "Lord, in the morning thou shalt hear
> My voice ascending high;
> To thee will I direct my prayer,
> To thee lift up mine eye.
>
> "Unto thy house will I resort,
> To taste thy mercies there;
> I will frequent thy holy court,
> And worship in thy fear."

The surface of the glassy bay was dotted here and there with the white sails of other little craft bound for the same point and for the same purpose. It was as pleasant a sight as one might wish to see.

Left in charge of the house, Miss Ruey drew a long breath, took a consoling pinch of snuff, sang "Bridgewater" in an uncommonly high key, and then began reading in the prophecies. With her good head full of the "daughter of Zion" and the house of Israel and Judah, she was recalled to terrestrial things by loud screams from the barn, accompanied by a general flutter and cackling among the hens.

Away plodded the good soul, and opening the barn-door saw the little boy perched on the top of the hay-mow, screaming and shrieking,—his face the picture of dismay,—while poor little Mara's cries came in a more muffled manner from some unexplored lower region. In fact, she was found to have slipped through a hole in the hay-mow into the nest of a very domestic sitting-hen, whose clamors at the invasion of her family privacy added no little to the general confusion.

The little princess, whose nicety as to her dress and sensitiveness as to anything unpleasant about her pretty person we have seen, was lifted up streaming with tears and broken eggs, but otherwise not seriously injured, having fallen on the very substantial substratum of hay which Dame Poulet had selected as the foundation of her domestic hopes.

"Well, now, did I ever!" said Miss Ruey, when she had ascertained that no bones were broken; "if that ar young un is n't a limb! I declare for 't I pity Mis' Pennel,—she don't know what she 's undertook. How upon 'arth the critter managed to get Mara on to the hay, I 'm sure I can't tell,—that ar little thing never got into no such scrapes before."

Far from seeming impressed with any wholesome remorse of conscience, the little culprit frowned fierce defiance at Miss Ruey, when, after having repaired the damages of little Mara's toilet, she essayed the good old plan of shutting him into the closet. He fought and struggled so fiercely that Aunt Ruey's carroty frisette came off in the skirmish, and her head-gear, always rather original, assumed an aspect verging on the supernatural. Miss Ruey thought of Philistines and Moabites, and all the other terrible people she had been reading about that morning, and came as near getting into a passion with the little elf as so good-humored and Christian an old body could possibly do. Human virtue is frail, and every one has some vulnerable point. The old Roman senator could not control himself when his beard was invaded, and the like sensitiveness resides in an old woman's cap; and when young master irreverently clawed off her Sunday best, Aunt Ruey, in her confusion of mind, administered a sound cuff on either ear.

Little Mara, who had screamed loudly through the whole scene, now conceiving that her precious new-found treasure was endangered, flew at poor Miss Ruey with both little hands; and throwing her arms round her "boy," as she constantly called him, she drew him backward, and looked defiance at the common enemy. Miss Ruey was dumb-struck.

"I declare for 't, I b'lieve he 's bewitched her," she said, stupefied, having never seen anything like the martial expression which now gleamed from those soft brown eyes. "Why, Mara dear,—putty little Mara."

But Mara was busy wiping away the angry tears that stood on the hot, glowing cheeks of the boy, and offering her little rosebud of a mouth to kiss him, as she stood on tiptoe.

"Poor boy,—no kie,—Mara's boy," she said; "Mara love boy;" and then giving an angry glance at Aunt Ruey, who sat much disheartened and confused, she struck out her little pearly hand, and cried, "Go way,—go way, naughty!"

The child jabbered unintelligibly and earnestly to Mara, and she seemed to have the air of being perfectly satisfied with his view of the case, and both regarded Miss Ruey with frowning looks. Under these peculiar circumstances, the good soul began to bethink her of some mode of compromise, and going to the closet took out a couple of slices of cake, which she offered to the little rebels with pacificatory words.

Mara was appeased at once, and ran to Aunt Ruey; but the boy struck the cake out of her hand, and looked at her with steady defiance. The little one picked it up, and with much chippering and many little feminine manœuvres, at last succeeded in making him taste it, after which appetite got the better of his valorous resolutions,—he ate and was comforted; and after a little time, the three were on the best possible footing. And Miss Ruey having smoothed her hair, and arranged her frisette and cap, began to reflect upon herself as the cause of the whole disturbance. If she had not let them run while she indulged in reading and singing, this would not have happened. So the toilful good soul kept them at her knee for the next hour or two, while they looked through all the pictures in the old family Bible.

The evening of that day witnessed a crowded funeral in the small rooms of Captain Kittridge. Mrs. Kittridge was in her glory. Solemn and lugubrious to the last degree, she supplied in her own proper person the want of the whole corps of mourners, who generally attract sympathy on such occasions. But what drew artless pity from all was the unconscious orphan, who came in, led by Mrs. Pennel by the one hand, and with the little Mara by the other.

The simple rite of baptism administered to the wondering little creature so strongly recalled that other scene three years before, that Mrs. Pennel hid her face in her handkerchief, and Zephaniah's firm hand shook a little as he took the boy to offer him to the rite. The child received the ceremony with a look of grave surprise, put up his hand quickly and wiped the holy drops from his brow, as if they annoyed him; and shrinking back, seized hold of the gown of Mrs. Pennel. His great beauty, and, still more, the air of haughty, defiant firmness with which he regarded the company, drew all eyes, and many were the whispered comments.

"Pennel 'll have his hands full with that ar chap," said Captain Kittridge to Miss Roxy.

Mrs. Kittridge darted an admonitory glance at her husband, to remind him that she was looking at him, and immediately he collapsed into solemnity.

The evening sunbeams slanted over the blackberry bushes and mullein stalks of the graveyard, when the lonely voyager was lowered to the rest from which she should not rise till the heavens be no more. As the purple sea at that hour retained no trace of the ships that had furrowed its waves, so of this mortal traveler no trace remained, not even in that infant soul that was to her so passionately dear.

X

THE MINISTER

Mrs. Kittridge's advantages and immunities resulting from the shipwreck were not yet at an end. Not only had one of the most "solemn providences" known within the memory of the neighborhood fallen out at her door,—not only had the most interesting funeral that had occurred for three or four years taken place in her parlor, but she was still further to be distinguished in having the minister to tea after the performances were all over. To this end she had risen early, and taken down her best china tea-cups, which had been marked with her and her husband's joint initials in Canton, and which only came forth on high and solemn occasions. In view of this probable distinction, on Saturday, immediately after the discovery of the calamity, Mrs. Kittridge had found time to rush to her kitchen, and make up a loaf of pound-cake and some doughnuts, that the great occasion which she foresaw might not find her below her reputation as a forehanded housewife.

It was a fine golden hour when the minister and funeral train turned away from the grave. Unlike other funerals, there was no draught on the sympathies in favor of mourners—no wife, or husband, or parent, left a heart in that grave; and so when the rites were all over, they turned with the more cheerfulness back into life, from the contrast of its freshness with those shadows into which, for the hour, they had been gazing.

The Rev. Theophilus Sewell was one of the few ministers who preserved the costume of a former generation, with something of that imposing dignity with which, in earlier times, the habits of the clergy were invested. He was tall and majestic in stature, and carried to advantage the powdered wig and three-cornered hat, the broad-skirted coat, knee-breeches, high shoes, and plated buckles of the ancient costume. There was just a sufficient degree of the formality of olden times to give a certain quaintness to all he said and did. He was a man of a considerable degree of talent, force, and originality, and in fact had been held in his day to be one of the most promising graduates of Harvard University. But, being a good man, he had proposed to himself no higher ambition than to succeed to the pulpit of his father in Harpswell.

His parish included not only a somewhat scattered seafaring population on the mainland, but also the care of several islands. Like many other of the New England clergy of those times, he united in himself numerous different offices for the benefit of the people whom he served. As there was neither lawyer nor physician in the town, he had acquired by his reading, and still more by his experience, enough knowledge in both these departments to enable him to administer to the ordinary wants of a very healthy and peaceable people.

It was said that most of the deeds and legal conveyances in his parish were in his handwriting, and in the medical line his authority was only rivaled by that of Miss Roxy, who claimed a very obvious advantage over him in a certain class of cases, from the fact of her being a woman, which was still further increased by the circumstance that the good man had retained steadfastly his bachelor estate. "So, of course," Miss Roxy used to say, "poor man! what could he know about a woman, you know?"

This state of bachelorhood gave occasion to much surmising; but when spoken to about it, he was accustomed to remark with gallantry, that he should have too much regard for any lady whom he could think of as a wife, to ask her to share his straitened circumstances. His income, indeed, consisted of only about two hundred dollars a year; but upon this he and a very brisk, cheerful maiden sister contrived to keep up a thrifty and comfortable establishment, in which everything appeared to be pervaded by a spirit of quaint cheerfulness.

In fact, the man might be seen to be an original in his way, and all the springs of his life were kept oiled by a quiet humor, which sometimes broke out in playful sparkles, despite the gravity of the pulpit and the awfulness of the cocked hat. He had a placid way of amusing himself with the quaint and picturesque side of life, as it appeared in all his visitings among a very primitive, yet very shrewd-minded people.

There are those people who possess a peculiar faculty of mingling in the affairs of this life as spectators as well as actors. It does not, of course, suppose any coldness of nature or want of human interest or sympathy—nay, it often exists most completely with people of the tenderest human feeling. It rather seems to be a kind of distinct faculty working harmoniously with all the others; but he who possesses it needs never to be at a loss for interest or amusement; he is always a spectator at a tragedy or comedy, and sees in real life a humor and a pathos beyond anything he can find shadowed in books.

Mr. Sewell sometimes, in his pastoral visitations, took a quiet pleasure in playing upon these simple minds, and amusing himself with the odd harmonies and singular resolutions of chords which started out under his fingers. Surely he had a right to something in addition to his limited salary, and this innocent, unsuspected entertainment helped to make up the balance for his many labors.

His sister was one of the best-hearted and most unsuspicious of the class of female idolaters, and worshiped her brother with the most undoubting faith and devotion—wholly ignorant of the constant amusement she gave him by a thousand little feminine peculiarities, which struck him with a continual sense of oddity. It was infinitely diverting to him to see the solemnity of her interest in his shirts and stockings, and Sunday clothes, and to listen to the subtle distinctions which she would draw between best and second-best, and every-day; to receive her somewhat prolix admonition how he was to demean himself in respect of the wearing of each one; for Miss Emily Sewell was a gentlewoman, and held rigidly to various traditions of gentility which had been handed down in the Sewell family, and which afforded her brother too much quiet amusement to be disturbed. He would not have overthrown one of her quiddities for the world; it would be taking away a part of his capital in existence.

Miss Emily was a trim, genteel little person, with dancing black eyes, and cheeks which had the roses of youth well dried into them. It was easy to see that she had been quite pretty in her days; and her neat figure, her brisk little vivacious ways, her unceasing good-nature and kindness of heart, still made her an object both of admiration and interest in the parish. She was great in drying herbs and preparing recipes; in knitting and sewing, and cutting and contriving; in saving every possible snip and chip either of food or clothing; and no less liberal was she in bestowing advice and aid in the parish, where she moved about with all the sense of consequence which her brother's position warranted.

The fact of his bachelorhood caused his relations to the female part of his flock to be even more shrouded in sacredness and mystery than is commonly the case with the great man of the parish; but Miss Emily delighted to act as interpreter. She was charmed to serve out to the willing ears of his parish from time to time such scraps of information as regarded his life, habits, and opinions as might gratify their ever new curiosity. Instructed by her, all the good wives knew the difference between his very best long silk stocking and his second best, and how carefully the first had to be kept under lock and key, where he could not get at them; for he was understood, good as he was, to have concealed in him all the thriftless and pernicious inconsiderateness of the male nature, ready at any moment to break out into unheard-of improprieties. But the good man submitted himself to Miss Emily's rule, and suffered himself to be led about by her with an air of half whimsical consciousness.

Mrs. Kittridge that day had felt the full delicacy of the compliment when she ascertained by a hasty glance, before the first prayer, that the good man had been brought out to her funeral in all his very best things, not excepting the long silk stockings, for she knew the second-best pair by means of a certain skillful darn which Miss Emily had once shown her, which commemorated the spot where a hole had been. The absence of this darn struck to Mrs. Kittridge's heart at once as a delicate attention.

"Mis' Simpkins," said Mrs. Kittridge to her pastor, as they were seated at the tea-table, "told me that she wished when you were going home that you would call in to see Mary Jane; she could n't come out to the funeral on account of a dreffle sore throat. I was tellin' on her to gargle it with blackberry-root tea—don't you think that is a good gargle, Mr. Sewell?"

"Yes, I think it a very good gargle," replied the minister, gravely.

"Ma'sh rosemary is the gargle that I always use," said Miss Roxy; "it cleans out your throat so."

"Marsh rosemary is a very excellent gargle," said Mr. Sewell.

"Why, brother, don't you think that rose leaves and vitriol is a good gargle?" said little Miss Emily; "I always thought that you liked rose leaves and vitriol for a gargle."

"So I do," said the imperturbable Mr. Sewell, drinking his tea with the air of a sphinx.

"Well, now, you 'll have to tell which on 'em will be most likely to cure Mary Jane," said Captain Kittridge, "or there 'll be a pullin' of caps, I 'm thinkin'; or else the poor girl will have to drink them all, which is generally the way."

"There won't any of them cure Mary Jane's throat," said the minister, quietly.

"Why, brother!" "Why, Mr. Sewell!" "Why, you don't!" burst in different tones from each of the women.

"I thought you said that blackberry-root tea was good," said Mrs. Kittridge.

"I understood that you 'proved of ma'sh rosemary," said Miss Roxy, touched in her professional pride.

"And I am sure, brother, that I have heard you say, often and often, that there was n't a better gargle than rose leaves and vitriol," said Miss Emily.

"You are quite right, ladies, all of you. I think these are all good gargles—excellent ones."

"But I thought you said that they did n't do any good?" said all the ladies in a breath.

"No, they don't—not the least in the world," said Mr. Sewell; "but they are all excellent gargles, and as long as people must have gargles, I think one is about as good as another."

"Now you have got it," said Captain Kittridge.

"Brother, you do say the strangest things," said Miss Emily.

"Well, I must say," said Miss Roxy, "it is a new idea to me, long as I 've been nussin', and I nussed through one season of scarlet fever when sometimes there was five died in one house; and if ma'sh rosemary did n't do good then, I should like to know what did."

"So would a good many others," said the minister.

"Law, now, Miss Roxy, you mus'n't mind him. Do you know that I believe he says these sort of things just to hear us talk? Of course he would n't think of puttin' his experience against yours."

"But, Mis' Kittridge," said Miss Emily, with a view of summoning a less controverted subject, "what a beautiful little boy that was, and what a striking providence that brought him into such a good family!"

"Yes," said Mrs. Kittridge; "but I 'm sure I don't see what Mary Pennel is goin' to do with that boy, for she ain't got no more government than a twisted tow-string."

"Oh, the Cap'n, he 'll lend a hand," said Miss Roxy, "it won't be easy gettin' roun' him; Cap'n bears a pretty steady hand when he sets out to drive."

"Well," said Miss Emily, "I do think that bringin' up children is the most awful responsibility, and I always wonder when I hear that any one dares to undertake it."

"It requires a great deal of resolution, certainly," said Mrs. Kittridge; "I 'm sure I used to get a'most discouraged when my boys was young: they was a reg'lar set of wild ass's colts," she added, not perceiving the reflection on their paternity.

But the countenance of Mr. Sewell was all aglow with merriment, which did not break into a smile.

"Wal', Mis' Kittridge," said the Captain, "strikes me that "you 're gettin' pussonal."

"No, I ain't neither," said the literal Mrs. Kittridge, ignorant of the cause of the amusement which she saw around her; "but you wa' n't no help to me, you know; you was always off to sea, and the whole wear and tear on't came on me."

"Well, well, Polly, all 's well that ends well; don't you think so, Mr. Sewell?"

"I have n't much experience in these matters," said Mr. Sewell, politely.

"No, indeed, that 's what he hasn't, for he never will have a child round the house that he don't turn everything topsy-turvy for them," said Miss Emily.

"But I was going to remark," said Mr. Sewell, "that a friend of mine said once, that the woman that had brought up six boys deserved a seat among the martyrs; and that is rather my opinion."

"Wal', Polly, if you git up there, I hope you 'll keep a seat for me."

"Cap'n Kittridge, what levity!" said his wife.

"I did n't begin it, anyhow," said the Captain.

Miss Emily interposed, and led the conversation back to the subject. "What a pity it is," she said, "that this poor child's family can never know anything about him. There may be those who would give all the world to know what has become of him; and when he comes to grow up, how sad he will feel to have no father and mother!"

"Sister," said Mr. Sewell, "you cannot think that a child brought up by Captain Pennel and his wife would ever feel as without father and mother."

"Why, no, brother, to be sure not. There 's no doubt he will have everything done for him that a child could. But then it 's a loss to lose one's real home."

"It may be a gracious deliverance," said Mr. Sewell—"who knows? We may as well take a cheerful view, and think that some kind wave has drifted the child away from an unfortunate destiny to a family where we are quite sure he will be brought up industriously and soberly, and in the fear of God."

"Well, I never thought of that," said Miss Roxy.

Miss Emily, looking at her brother, saw that he was speaking with a suppressed vehemence, as if some inner fountain of recollection at the moment were disturbed. But Miss Emily knew no more of the deeper parts of her brother's nature than a little bird that dips its beak into the sunny waters of some spring knows of its depths of coldness and shadow.

"Mis' Pennel was a-sayin' to me," said Mrs. Kittridge, "that I should ask you what was to be done about the bracelet they found. We don't know whether 't is real gold and precious stones, or only glass and pinchbeck. Cap'n Kittridge he thinks it 's real; and if 't is, why then the question is, whether or no to try to sell it, or keep it for the boy agin he grows up. It may help find out who and what he is."

"And why should he want to find out?" said Mr. Sewell. "Why should he not grow up and think himself the son of Captain and Mrs. Pennel? What better lot could a boy be born to?"

"That may be, brother, but it can't be kept from him. Everybody knows how he was found, and you may be sure every bird of the air will tell him, and he 'll grow up restless and wanting to know. Mis' Kittridge, have you got the bracelet handy?"

The fact was, little Miss Emily was just dying with curiosity to set her dancing black eyes upon it.

"Here it is," said Mrs. Kittridge, taking it from a drawer.

It was a bracelet of hair, of some curious foreign workmanship. A green enameled serpent, studded thickly with emeralds and with eyes of ruby, was curled around the clasp. A crystal plate covered a wide flat braid of hair, on which the letters "D. M." were curiously embroidered in a cipher of seed pearls.

The whole was in style and workmanship quite different from any jewelry which ordinarily meets one's eye.

But what was remarkable was the expression in Mr. Sewell's face when this bracelet was put into his hand. Miss Emily had risen from table and brought it to him, leaning over him as she did so, and he turned his head a little to hold it in the light from the window, so that only she remarked the sudden expression of blank surprise and startled recognition which fell upon it. He seemed like a man who chokes down an exclamation; and rising hastily, he took the bracelet to the window, and standing with his back to the company, seemed to examine it with the minutest interest. After a few moments he turned and said, in a very composed tone, as if the subject were of no particular interest,—

"It is a singular article, so far as workmanship is concerned. The value of the gems in themselves is not great enough to make it worth while to sell it. It will be worth more as a curiosity than anything else. It will doubtless be an interesting relic to keep for the boy when he grows up."

"Well, Mr. Sewell, you keep it," said Mrs. Kittridge; "the Pennels told me to give it into your care."

"I shall commit it to Emily here; women have a native sympathy with anything in the jewelry line. She 'll be sure to lay it up so securely that she won't even know where it is herself."

"Brother!"

"Come, Emily," said Mr. Sewell, "your hens will all go to roost on the wrong perch if you are not at home to see to them; so, if the Captain will set us across to Harpswell, I think we may as well be going."

"Why, what 's your hurry?" said Mrs. Kittridge.

"Well," said Mr. Sewell, "firstly, there 's the hens; secondly, the pigs; and lastly, the cow. Besides I should n't wonder if some of Emily's admirers should call on her this evening,—never any saying when Captain Broad may come in."

"Now, brother, you are too bad," said Miss Emily, as she bustled about her bonnet and shawl. "Now, that's all made up out of whole cloth. Captain Broad called last week a Monday, to talk to you about the pews, and hardly spoke a word to me. You ought n't to say such things, 'cause it raises reports."

"Ah, well, then, I won't again," said her brother. "I believe, after all, it was Captain Badger that called twice."

"Brother!"

"And left you a basket of apples the second time."

"Brother, you know he only called to get some of my hoarhound for Mehitable's cough."

"Oh, yes, I remember."

"If you don't take care," said Miss Emily, "I 'll tell where you call."

"Come, Miss Emily, you must not mind him," said Miss Roxy; "we all know his ways."

And now took place the grand leave-taking, which consisted first of the three women's standing in a knot and all talking at once, as if their very lives depended upon saying everything they could possibly think of before they separated, while Mr. Sewell and Captain Kittridge stood patiently waiting with the resigned air which the male sex commonly assume on such occasions; and when, after two or three "Come, Emily's," the group broke up only to form again on the door-step, where they were at it harder than ever, and a third occasion of the same sort took place at the bottom of the steps, Mr. Sewell was at last obliged by main force to drag his sister away in the middle of a sentence.

Miss Emily watched her brother shrewdly all the way home, but all traces of any uncommon feeling had passed away; and yet, with the restlessness of female curiosity, she felt quite sure that she had laid hold of the end of some skein of mystery, could she only find skill enough to unwind it.

She took up the bracelet, and held it in the fading evening light, and broke into various observations with regard to the singularity of the workmanship. Her brother seemed entirely absorbed in talking with Captain Kittridge about the brig Anna Maria, which was going to be launched from Pennel's wharf next Wednesday. But she, therefore, internally resolved to lie in wait for the secret in that confidential hour which usually preceded going to bed. Therefore, as soon as she had arrived at their quiet dwelling, she put in operation the most seducing little fire that ever crackled and snapped in a chimney, well knowing that nothing was more calculated to throw light into any hidden or concealed chamber of the soul than that enlivening blaze, which danced so merrily on her well-polished andirons, and made the old chintz sofa and the time-worn furniture so rich in remembrances of family comfort.

She then proceeded to divest her brother of his wig and his dress-coat, and to induct him into the flowing ease of a study-gown, crowning his well-shaven head with a black cap, and placing his slippers before the corner of a sofa nearest the fire. She observed him with satisfaction sliding into his seat, and then she trotted to a closet with a glass door in the corner of the room, and took down an old, quaintly-shaped silver cup, which had been an heirloom in their family, and was the only piece of plate which their modern domestic establishment could boast; and with this, down cellar she tripped, her little heels tapping lightly on each stair, and the hum of a song coming back after her as she sought the cider-barrel. Up again she came, and set the silver cup, with its clear amber contents, down by the fire, and then busied herself in making just the crispest, nicest square of toast to be eaten with it; for Miss Emily had conceived the idea that some little ceremony of this sort was absolutely necessary to do away all possible ill effects from a day's labor, and secure an uninterrupted night's repose. Having done all this, she took her knitting-work, and stationed herself just opposite to her brother.

It was fortunate for Miss Emily that the era of daily journals had not yet arisen upon the earth, because if it had, after all her care and pains, her brother would probably have taken up the evening paper, and holding it between his face and her, have read an hour or so in silence; but Mr. Sewell had not this resort. He knew perfectly well that he had excited his sister's curiosity on a subject where he could not gratify it, and therefore he took refuge in a kind of mild, abstracted air of quietude which bid defiance to all her little suggestions.

After in vain trying every indirect form, Miss Emily approached the subject more pointedly. "I thought that you looked very much interested in that poor woman to-day."

"She had an interesting face," said her brother, dryly.

"Was it like anybody that you ever saw?" said Miss Emily.

Her brother did not seem to hear her, but, taking the tongs, picked up the two ends of a stick that had just fallen apart, and arranged them so as to make a new blaze.

Miss Emily was obliged to repeat her question, whereat he started as one awakened out of a dream, and said, —

"Why, yes, he did n't know but she did; there were a good many women with black eyes and black hair, — Mrs. Kittridge, for instance."

"Why, I don't think that she looked like Mrs. Kittridge in the least," said Miss Emily, warmly.

"Oh, well! I did n't say she did," said her brother, looking drowsily at his watch; "why, Emily, it 's getting rather late."

"What made you look so when I showed you that bracelet?" said Miss Emily, determined now to push the war to the heart of the enemy's country.

"Look how?" said her brother, leisurely moistening a bit of toast in his cider.

"Why, I never saw anybody look more wild and astonished than you did for a minute or two."

"I did, did I?" said her brother, in the same indifferent tone. "My dear child, what an active imagination you have. Did you ever look through a prism, Emily?"

"Why, no, Theophilus; what do you mean?"

"Well, if you should, you would see everybody and everything with a nice little bordering of rainbow around them; now the rainbow is n't on the things, but in the prism."

"Well, what 's that to the purpose?" said Miss Emily, rather bewildered.

"Why, just this: you women are so nervous and excitable, that you are very apt to see your friends and the world in general with some coloring just as unreal. I am sorry for you, childie, but really I can't help you to get up a romance out of this bracelet. Well, good-night, Emily; take good care of yourself and go to bed;" and Mr. Sewell went to his room, leaving poor Miss Emily almost persuaded out of the sight of her own eyes.

XI

LITTLE ADVENTURERS

The little boy who had been added to the family of Zephaniah Pennel and his wife soon became a source of grave solicitude to that mild and long-suffering woman. For, as the reader may have seen, he was a resolute, self-willed little elf, and whatever his former life may have been, it was quite evident that these traits had been developed without any restraint.

Mrs. Pennel, whose whole domestic experience had consisted in rearing one very sensitive and timid daughter, who needed for her development only an extreme of tenderness, and whose conscientiousness was a law unto herself, stood utterly confounded before the turbulent little spirit to which her loving-kindness had opened so ready an asylum, and she soon discovered that it is one thing to take a human being to bring up, and another to know what to do with it after it is taken.

The child had the instinctive awe of Zephaniah which his manly nature and habits of command were fitted to inspire, so that morning and evening, when he was at home, he was demure enough; but while the good man was away all day, and sometimes on fishing excursions which often lasted a week, there was a chronic state of domestic warfare—a succession of skirmishes, pitched battles, long treaties, with divers articles of capitulation, ending, as treaties are apt to do, in open rupture on the first convenient opportunity.

Mrs. Pennel sometimes reflected with herself mournfully, and with many self-disparaging sighs, what was the reason that young master somehow contrived to keep her far more in awe of him than he was of her. Was she not evidently, as yet at least, bigger and stronger than he, able to hold his rebellious little hands, to lift and carry him, and to shut him up, if so she willed, in a dark closet, and even to administer to him that discipline of the birch which Mrs. Kittridge often and forcibly recommended as the great secret of her family prosperity? Was it not her duty, as everybody told her, to break his will while he was young?—a duty which hung like a millstone round the peaceable creature's neck, and weighed her down with a distressing sense of responsibility.

Now, Mrs. Pennel was one of the people to whom self-sacrifice is constitutionally so much a nature, that self-denial for her must have consisted in standing up for her own rights, or having her own way when it crossed the will and pleasure of any one around her. All she wanted of a child, or in fact of any human creature, was something to love and serve. We leave it entirely to theologians to reconcile such facts with the theory of total depravity; but it *is* a fact that there are a considerable number of women of this class. Their life would flow on very naturally if it might consist only in giving, never in withholding—only in praise, never in blame—only in acquiescence, never in conflict; and the chief comfort of such women in religion is that it gives them at last an object for love without criticism, and for whom the utmost degree of self-abandonment is not idolatry, but worship.

Mrs. Pennel would gladly have placed herself and all she possessed at the disposition of the children; they might have broken her china, dug in the garden with her silver spoons, made turf alleys in her best room, drummed on her mahogany tea-table, filled her muslin drawer with their choicest shells and seaweed; only Mrs. Pennel knew that such kindness was no kindness, and that in the dreadful word responsibility, familiar to every New England mother's ear, there lay an awful summons to deny and to conflict where she could so much easier have conceded.

She saw that the tyrant little will would reign without mercy, if it reigned at all; and ever present with her was the uneasy sense that it was her duty to bring this erratic little comet within the laws of a well-ordered solar system,—a task to which she felt about as competent as to make a new ring for Saturn. Then, too, there was a secret feeling, if the truth must be told, of what Mrs. Kittridge would think about it; for duty is never more formidable than when she gets on the cap and gown of a neighbor; and Mrs. Kittridge, with her resolute voice and declamatory family government, had always been a secret source of uneasiness to poor Mrs. Pennel, who was one of those sensitive souls who can feel for a mile or more the sphere of a stronger neighbor. During all the years that they had lived side by side, there had been this shadowy, unconfessed feeling on the part of poor Mrs. Pennel, that Mrs. Kittridge thought her deficient in her favorite virtue of "resolution," as, in fact, in her inmost soul she knew she was;—but who wants to have one's weak places looked into by the sharp eyes of a neighbor who is strong precisely where we are weak? The trouble that one neighbor may give to another, simply by living within a mile of one, is incredible; but until this new accession to her family, Mrs. Pennel had always been able to comfort herself with the idea that the child under her particular training was as well-behaved as any of those of her more demonstrative friend. But now, all this consolation had been put to flight; she could not meet Mrs. Kittridge without most humiliating recollections.

On Sundays, when those sharp black eyes gleamed upon her through the rails of the neighboring pew, her very soul shrank within her, as she recollected all the compromises and defeats of the week before. It seemed to her that Mrs. Kittridge saw it all,—how she had ingloriously bought peace with gingerbread, instead of maintaining it by rightful authority,—how young master had sat up till nine o'clock on divers occasions, and even kept little Mara up for his lordly pleasure.

How she trembled at every movement of the child in the pew, dreading some patent and open impropriety which should bring scandal on her government! This was the more to be feared, as the first effort to initiate the youthful neophyte in the decorums of the sanctuary had proved anything but a success,—insomuch that Zephaniah Pennel had been obliged to carry him out from the church; therefore, poor Mrs. Pennel was thankful every Sunday when she got her little charge home without any distinct scandal and breach of the peace.

But, after all, he was such a handsome and engaging little wretch, attracting all eyes wherever he went, and so full of saucy drolleries, that it seemed to Mrs. Pennel that everything and everybody conspired to help her spoil him. There are two classes of human beings in this world: one class seem made to give love, and the other to take it. Now Mrs. Pennel and Mara belonged to the first class, and little Master Moses to the latter.

It was, perhaps, of service to the little girl to give to her delicate, shrinking, highly nervous organization the constant support of a companion so courageous, so richly blooded, and highly vitalized as the boy seemed to be. There was a fervid, tropical richness in his air that gave one a sense of warmth in looking at him, and made his Oriental name seem in good-keeping. He seemed an exotic that might have waked up under fervid Egyptian suns, and been found cradled among the lotus blossoms of old Nile; and the fair golden-haired girl seemed to be gladdened by his companionship, as if he supplied an element of vital warmth to her being. She seemed to incline toward him as naturally as a needle to a magnet.

The child's quickness of ear and the facility with which he picked up English were marvelous to observe. Evidently, he had been somewhat accustomed to the sound of it before, for there dropped out of his vocabulary, after he began to speak, phrases which would seem to betoken a longer familiarity with its idioms than could be equally accounted for by his present experience. Though the English evidently was not his native language, there had yet apparently been some effort to teach it to him, although the terror and confusion of the shipwreck seemed at first to have washed every former impression from his mind.

But whenever any attempt was made to draw him to speak of the past, of his mother, or of where he came from, his brow lowered gloomily, and he assumed that kind of moody, impenetrable gravity, which children at times will so strangely put on, and which baffle all attempts to look within them. Zephaniah Pennel used to call it putting up his dead-lights. Perhaps it was the dreadful association of agony and terror connected with the shipwreck, that thus confused and darkened the mirror of his mind the moment it was turned backward; but it was thought wisest by his new friends to avoid that class of subjects altogether—indeed, it was their wish that he might forget the past entirely, and remember them as his only parents.

Miss Roxy and Miss Ruey came duly, as appointed, to initiate the young pilgrim into the habiliments of a Yankee boy, endeav-oring, at the same time, to drop into his mind such seeds of moral wisdom as might make the internal economy in time cor-respond to the exterior. But Miss Roxy declared that "of all the children that ever she see, he beat all for finding out new mis-chief, — the moment you 'd make him understand he must n't do one thing, he was right at another."

One of his exploits, however, had very nearly been the means of cutting short the materials of our story in the outset.

It was a warm, sunny afternoon, and the three women, being busy together with their stitching, had tied a sun-bonnet on lit-tle Mara, and turned the two loose upon the beach to pick up shells. All was serene, and quiet, and retired, and no possible danger could be apprehended. So up and down they trotted, till the spirit of adventure which ever burned in the breast of little Moses caught sight of a small canoe which had been moored just under the shadow of a cedar-covered rock. Forthwith he persuaded his little neighbor to go into it, and for a while they made themselves very gay, rocking it from side to side.

The tide was going out, and each retreating wave washed the boat up and down, till it came into the boy's curly head how beautiful it would be to sail out as he had seen men do, — and so, with much puffing and earnest tugging of his little brown hands, the boat at last was loosed from her moorings and pushed out on the tide, when both children laughed gayly to find themselves swinging and balancing on the amber surface, and watching the rings and sparkles of sunshine and the white pebbles below. Little Moses was glorious, — his adventures had begun, — and with a fairy-princess in his boat, he was going to stretch away to some of the islands of dreamland. He per-suaded Mara to give him her pink sun-bonnet, which he placed for a pennon on a stick at the end of the boat, while he made a vehement dashing with another, first on one side of the boat and then on the other,—spattering the water in diamond showers, to the infinite amusement of the little maiden.

Meanwhile the tide waves danced them out and still outward, and as they went farther and farther from shore, the more glorious felt the boy. He had got Mara all to himself, and was going away with her from all grown people, who would n't let children do as they pleased,—who made them sit still in prayer-time, and took them to meeting, and kept so many things which they must not touch, or open, or play with. Two white sea-gulls came flying toward the children, and they stretched their little arms in welcome, nothing doubting but these fair creatures were coming at once to take passage with them for fairy-land. But the birds only dived and shifted and veered, turning their silvery sides toward the sun, and careering in circles round the children. A brisk little breeze, that came hurrying down from the land, seemed disposed to favor their unsubstantial enterprise,—for your winds, being a fanciful, uncertain tribe of people, are always for falling in with anything that is contrary to common sense. So the wind trolled them merrily along, nothing doubting that there might be time, if they hurried, to land their boat on the shore of some of the low-banked red clouds that lay in the sunset, where they could pick up shells,—blue and pink and purple,—enough to make them rich for life. The children were all excitement at the rapidity with which their little bark danced and rocked, as it floated outward to the broad, open ocean; at the blue, freshening waves, at the silver-glancing gulls, at the floating, white-winged ships, and at vague expectations of going rapidly somewhere, to something more beautiful still. And what is the happiness of the brightest hours of grown people more than this?

"Roxy," said Aunt Ruey innocently, "seems to me I have n't

heard nothin' o' them children lately. They 're so still, I 'm 'fraid there 's some mischief."

"Well, Ruey, you jist go and give a look at 'em," said Miss Roxy. "I declare, that boy! I never know what he will do next; but there did n't seem to be nothin' to get into out there but the sea, and the beach is so shelving, a body can't well fall into that."

Alas! good Miss Roxy, the children are at this moment tilting up and down on the waves, half a mile out to sea, as airily happy as the sea-gulls; and little Moses now thinks, with glorious scorn, of you and your press-board, as of grim shadows of restraint and bondage that shall never darken his free life more.

Both Miss Roxy and Mrs. Pennel were, however, startled into a paroxysm of alarm when poor Miss Ruey came screaming, as she entered the door,—

"As sure as you 're alive, them chil'en are off in the boat,— they 're out to sea, sure as I 'm alive! What shall we do? The boat 'll upset, and the sharks 'll get 'em."

Miss Roxy ran to the window, and saw dancing and courtesying on the blue waves the little pinnace, with its fanciful pink pennon fluttered gayly by the indiscreet and flattering wind.

Poor Mrs. Pennel ran to the shore, and stretched her arms wildly, as if she would have followed them across the treacherous blue floor that heaved and sparkled between them.

"Oh, Mara, Mara! Oh, my poor little girl! Oh, poor children!"

"Well, if ever I see such a young un as that," soliloquized Miss Roxy from the chamber-window; "there they be, dancin' and giggitin' about; they 'll have the boat upset in a minit, and the sharks are waitin' for 'em, no doubt. *I* b'lieve that ar young un 's helped by the Evil One,— not a boat round, else I 'd push off after 'em. Well, I don't see but we must trust in the Lord,— there don't seem to be much else to trust to," said the spinster, as she drew her head in grimly.

To say the truth, there was some reason for the terror of these most fearful suggestions; for not far from the place where the children embarked was Zephaniah's fish-drying ground, and multitudes of sharks came up with every rising tide, allured by the offal that was here constantly thrown into the sea. Two of these prowlers, outward-bound from their quest, were even now assiduously attending the little boat, and the children derived no small amusement from watching their motions in the pellucid water,—the boy occasionally almost upsetting the boat by valorous plunges at them with his stick. It was the most exhilarating and piquant entertainment he had found for many a day; and little Mara laughed in chorus at every lunge that he made.

What would have been the end of it all, it is difficult to say, had not some mortal power interfered before they had sailed finally away into the sunset. But it so happened, on this very afternoon, Rev. Mr. Sewell was out in a boat, busy in the very apostolic employment of catching fish, and looking up from one of the contemplative pauses which his occupation induced, he rubbed his eyes at the apparition which presented itself. A tiny little shell of a boat came drifting toward him, in which was a black-eyed boy, with cheeks like a pomegranate and lustrous tendrils of silky dark hair, and a little golden-haired girl, white as a water-lily, and looking ethereal enough to have risen out of the sea-foam. Both were in the very sparkle and effervescence of that fanciful glee which bubbles up from the golden, untried fountains of early childhood. Mr. Sewell, at a glance, comprehended the whole, and at once overhauling the tiny craft, he broke the spell of fairy-land, and constrained the little people to return to the confines, dull and dreary, of real and actual life.

Neither of them had known a doubt or a fear in that joyous trance of forbidden pleasure which shadowed with so many fears the wiser and more far-seeing heads and hearts of the grown people; nor was there enough language yet in common between the two classes to make the little ones comprehend the risk they had run. Perhaps so do our elder brothers, in our Father's house, look anxiously out when we are sailing gayly over life's sea,—over unknown depths,—amid threatening monsters,—but want words to tell us why what seems so bright is so dangerous.

Duty herself could not have worn a more rigid aspect than Miss Roxy, as she stood on the beach, press-board in hand; for she had forgotten to lay it down in the eagerness of her anxiety. She essayed to lay hold of the little hand of Moses to pull him from the boat, but he drew back, and, looking at her with a world of defiance in his great eyes, jumped magnanimously upon the beach. The spirit of Sir Francis Drake and of Christopher Columbus was swelling in his little body, and was he to be brought under by a dry-visaged woman with a press-board? In fact, nothing is more ludicrous about the escapades of children than the utter insensibility they feel to the dangers they have run, and the light esteem in which they hold the deep tragedy they create.

That night, when Zephaniah, in his evening exercise, poured forth most fervent thanksgivings for the deliverance, while Mrs. Pennel was sobbing in her handkerchief, Miss Roxy was much scandalized by seeing the young cause of all the disturbance sitting upon his heels, regarding the emotion of the kneeling party with his wide bright eyes, without a wink of compunction.

"Well, for her part," she said, "she hoped Cap'n Pennel would be blessed in takin' that ar boy; but she was sure she did n't see much that looked like it now."

The Rev. Mr. Sewell fished no more that day, for the draught from fairy-land with which he had filled his boat brought up many thoughts into his mind, which he pondered anxiously.

"Strange ways of God," he thought, "that should send to my door this child, and should wash upon the beach the only sign by which he could be identified. To what end or purpose? Hath the Lord a will in this matter, and what is it?"

So he thought as he slowly rowed homeward, and so did his thoughts work upon him that half way across the bay to Harpswell he slackened his oar without knowing it, and the boat lay drifting on the purple and gold-tinted mirror, like a speck between two eternities. Under such circumstances, even heads that have worn the clerical wig for years at times get a little dizzy and dreamy. Perhaps it was because of the impression made upon him by the sudden apparition of those great dark eyes and sable curls, that he now thought of the boy that he had found floating that afternoon, looking as if some tropical flower had been washed landward by a monsoon; and as the boat rocked and tilted, and the minister gazed dreamily downward into the wavering rings of purple, orange, and gold which spread out and out from it, gradually it seemed to him that a face much like the child's formed itself in the waters; but it was the face of a girl, young and radiantly beautiful, yet with those same eyes and curls,—he saw her distinctly, with her thousand rings of silky hair, bound with strings of pearls and clasped with strange gems, and she raised one arm imploringly to him, and on the wrist he saw the bracelet embroidered with seed pearls, and the letters D. M. "Ah, Dolores," he said, "well wert thou called so. Poor Dolores! I cannot help thee."

"What am I dreaming of?" said the Rev. Mr. Sewell. "It is my Thursday evening lecture on Justification, and Emily has got tea ready, and here I am catching cold out on the bay."

XII

SEA TALES

Mr. Sewell, as the reader may perhaps have inferred, was of a nature profoundly secretive. It was in most things quite as pleasant for him to keep matters to himself, as it was to Miss Emily to tell them to somebody else. She resembled more than anything one of those trotting, chattering little brooks that enliven the "back lot" of many a New England home, while he was like one of those wells you shall sometimes see by a deserted homestead, so long unused that ferns and lichens feather every stone down to the dark, cool water.

Dear to him was the stillness and coolness of inner thoughts with which no stranger intermeddles; dear to him every pendent fern-leaf of memory, every dripping moss of old recollection; and though the waters of his soul came up healthy and refreshing enough when one really must have them, yet one had to go armed with bucket and line and draw them up,—they never flowed. One of his favorite maxims was, that the only way to keep a secret was never to let any one suspect that you have one. And as he had one now, he had, as you have seen, done his best to baffle and put to sleep the feminine curiosity of his sister.

He rather wanted to tell her, too, for he was a good-natured brother, and would have liked to have given her the amount of pleasure the confidence would have produced; but then he reflected with dismay on the number of women in his parish with whom Miss Emily was on tea-drinking terms,—he thought of the wondrous solvent powers of that beverage in whose amber depths so many resolutions yea, and solemn vows, of utter silence have been dissolved like Cleopatra's pearls. He knew that an infusion of his secret would steam up from every cup of tea Emily should drink for six months to come, till gradually every particle would be dissolved and float in the air of common fame. No; it would not do.

You would have thought, however, that something was the matter with Mr. Sewell, had you seen him after he retired for the night, after he had so very indifferently dismissed the subject of Miss Emily's inquiries. For instead of retiring quietly to bed, as had been his habit for years at that hour, he locked his door, and then unlocked a desk of private papers, and emptied certain pigeon-holes of their contents, and for an hour or two sat unfolding and looking over old letters and papers; and when all this was done, he pushed them from him, and sat for a long time buried in thoughts which went down very, very deep into that dark and mossy well of which we have spoken.

Then he took a pen and wrote a letter, and addressed it to a direction for which he had searched through many piles of paper, and having done so, seemed to ponder, uncertainly, whether to send it or not. The Harpswell post-office was kept in Mr. Silas Perrit's store, and the letters were every one of them carefully and curiously investigated by all the gossips of the village, and as this was addressed to St. Augustine in Florida, he foresaw that before Sunday the news would be in every mouth in the parish that the minister had written to so and so in Florida, "and what do you s'pose it's about?"

"No, no," he said to himself, "that will never do; but at all events there is no hurry," and he put back the papers in order, put the letter with them, and locking his desk, looked at his watch and found it to be two o'clock, and so he went to bed to think the matter over.

Now, there may be some reader so simple as to feel a portion of Miss Emily's curiosity. But, my friend, restrain it, for Mr. Sewell will certainly, as we foresee, become less rather than more communicative on this subject, as he thinks upon it. Nevertheless, whatever it be that he knows or suspects, it is something which leads him to contemplate with more than usual interest this little mortal waif that has so strangely come ashore in his parish. He mentally resolves to study the child as minutely as possible, without betraying that he has any particular reason for being interested in him.

Therefore, in the latter part of this mild November afternoon, which he has devoted to pastoral visiting, about two months after the funeral, he steps into his little sail-boat, and stretches away for the shores of Orr's Island. He knows the sun will be down before he reaches there; but he sees, in the opposite horizon, the spectral, shadowy moon, only waiting for daylight to be gone to come out, calm and radiant, like a saintly friend neglected in the flush of prosperity, who waits patiently to enliven our hours of darkness.

As his boat-keel grazed the sands on the other side, a shout of laughter came upon his ear from behind a cedar-covered rock, and soon emerged Captain Kittridge, as long and lean and brown as the Ancient Mariner, carrying little Mara on one shoulder, while Sally and little Moses Pennel trotted on before.

It was difficult to say who in this whole group was in the highest spirits. The fact was that Mrs. Kittridge had gone to a tea-drinking over at Maquoit, and left the Captain as housekeeper and general overseer; and little Mara and Moses and Sally had been gloriously keeping holiday with him down by the boat-cove, where, to say the truth, few shavings were made, except those necessary to adorn the children's heads with flowing suits of curls of a most extraordinary effect. The aprons of all of them were full of these most unsubstantial specimens of woody treasure, which hung out in long festoons, looking of a yellow transparency in the evening light. But the delight of the children in their acquisitions was only equaled by that of grown-up people in possessions equally fanciful in value.

The mirth of the little party, however, came to a sudden pause as they met the minister. Mara clung tight to the Captain's neck, and looked out slyly under her curls. But the little Moses made a step forward, and fixed his bold, dark, inquisitive eyes upon him. The fact was, that the minister had been impressed upon the boy, in his few visits to the "meeting," as such a grand and mysterious reason for good behavior, that he seemed resolved to embrace the first opportunity to study him close at hand.

"Well, my little man," said Mr. Sewell, with an affability which he could readily assume with children, "you seem to like to look at me."

"I do like to look at you," said the boy gravely, continuing to fix his great black eyes upon him.

"I see you do, my little fellow."

"Are you the Lord?" said the child, solemnly.

"Am I what?"

"The Lord," said the boy.

"No, indeed, my lad," said Mr. Sewell, smiling. "Why, what put that into your little head?"

"I thought you were," said the boy, still continuing to study the pastor with attention. "Miss Roxy said so."

"It 's curious what notions chil'en will get in their heads," said Captain Kittridge. "They put this and that together and think it over, and come out with such queer things."

"But," said the minister, "I have brought something for you all;" saying which he drew from his pocket three little bright-cheeked apples, and gave one to each child; and then taking the hand of the little Moses in his own, he walked with him toward the house-door.

Mrs. Pennel was sitting in her clean kitchen, busily spinning at the little wheel, and rose flushed with pleasure at the honor that was done her.

"Pray, walk in, Mr. Sewell," she said, rising, and leading the way toward the penetralia of the best room.

"Now, Mrs. Pennel, I am come here for a good sit-down by your kitchen-fire, this evening," said Mr. Sewell. "Emily has gone out to sit with old Mrs. Broad, who is laid up with the rheumatism, and so I am turned loose to pick up my living on the parish, and you must give me a seat for a while in your kitchen corner. Best rooms are always cold."

"The minister 's right," said Captain Kittridge. "When rooms ain't much set in, folks never feel so kind o' natural in 'em. So you jist let me put on a good back-log and forestick, and build up a fire to tell stories by this evening. My wife 's gone out to tea, too," he said, with an elastic skip.

And in a few moments the Captain had produced in the great cavernous chimney a foundation for a fire that promised breadth, solidity, and continuance. A great back-log, embroidered here and there with tufts of green or grayish moss, was first flung into the capacious arms of the fireplace, and a smaller log placed above it. "Now, all you young uns go out and bring in chips," said the Captain. "There 's capital ones out to the wood-pile."

Mr. Sewell was pleased to see the flash that came from the

eyes of little Moses at this order, how energetically he ran before the others, and came with glowing cheeks and distended arms, throwing down great white chips with their green mossy bark, scattering tufts on the floor. "Good," said he softly to himself, as he leaned on the top of his gold-headed cane; "there's energy, ambition, muscle;" and he nodded his head once or twice to some internal decision.

"There!" said the Captain, rising out of a perfect whirlwind of chips and pine kindlings with which in his zeal he had bestrown the wide, black stone hearth, and pointing to the tongues of flame that were leaping and blazing up through the crevices of the dry pine wood which he had intermingled plentifully with the more substantial fuel,—"there, Mis' Pennel, ain't I a master-hand at a fire? But I'm really sorry I've dirtied your floor," he said, as he brushed down his pantaloons, which were covered with bits of grizzly moss, and looked on the surrounding desolations; "give me a broom, I can sweep up now as well as any woman."

"Oh, never mind," said Mrs. Pennel, laughing, "I'll sweep up."

"Well, now, Mis' Pennel, you're one of the women that don't get put out easy; ain't ye?" said the Captain, still contemplating his fire with a proud and watchful eye.

"Law me!" he exclaimed, glancing through the window, "there's the Cap'n a-comin'. I'm jist goin' to give a look at what he's brought in. Come, chil'en," and the Captain disappeared with all three of the children at his heels, to go down to examine the treasures of the fishing-smack.

Mr. Sewell seated himself cozily in the chimney corner and sank into a state of half-dreamy reverie; his eyes fixed on the fairest sight one can see of a frosty autumn twilight—a crackling wood-fire.

Mrs. Pennel moved soft-footed to and fro, arraying her tea-table in her own finest and pure damask, and bringing from hidden stores her best china and newest silver, her choicest sweetmeats and cake—whatever was fairest and nicest in her house—to honor her unexpected guest.

Mr. Sewell's eyes followed her occasionally about the room, with an expression of pleased and curious satisfaction. He was taking it all in as an artistic picture—that simple, kindly hearth, with its mossy logs, yet steaming with the moisture of the wild woods; the table so neat, so cheery with its many little delicacies, and refinements of appointment, and its ample varieties to tempt the appetite; and then the Captain coming in, yet fresh and hungry from his afternoon's toil, with the children trotting before him.

"And this is the inheritance he comes into," he murmured; "healthy—wholesome—cheerful—secure: how much better than hot, stifling luxury!"

Here the minister's meditations were interrupted by the entrance of all the children, joyful and loquacious. Little Moses held up a string of mackerel, with their graceful bodies and elegantly cut fins.

"Just a specimen of the best, Mary," said Captain Pennel. "I thought I'd bring 'em for Miss Emily."

"Miss Emily will be a thousand times obliged to you," said Mr. Sewell, rising up.

As to Mara and Sally, they were reveling in apronfuls of shells and seaweed, which they bustled into the other room to bestow in their spacious baby-house.

And now, after due time for Zephaniah to assume a land toilet, all sat down to the evening meal.

After supper was over, the Captain was besieged by the children. Little Mara mounted first into his lap, and nestled herself quietly under his coat—Moses and Sally stood at each knee.

"Come, now," said Moses, "you said you would tell us about the mermen to-night."

"Yes, and the mermaids," said Sally. "Tell them all you told me the other night in the trundle-bed."

Sally valued herself no little on the score of the Captain's talent as a romancer.

"You see, Moses," she said, volubly, "father saw mermen and mermaids a plenty of them in the West Indies."

"Oh, never mind about 'em now," said Captain Kittridge, looking at Mr. Sewell's corner.

"Why not, father? mother is n't here," said Sally, innocently.

A smile passed round the faces of the company, and Mr. Sewell said, "Come, Captain, no modesty; we all know you have as good a faculty for telling a story as for making a fire."

"Do tell me what mermen are," said Moses.

"Wal'," said the Captain, sinking his voice confidentially, and hitching his chair a little around, "mermen and maids is a kind o' people that have their world jist like our'n, only it's down in the bottom of the sea, 'cause the bottom of the sea has its mountains and its valleys, and its trees and its bushes, and it stands to reason there should be people there too."

Moses opened his broad black eyes wider than usual, and looked absorbed attention.

"Tell 'em about how you saw 'em," said Sally.

"Wal', yes," said Captain Kittridge; "once when I was to the Bahamas,—it was one Sunday morning in June, the first Sunday in the month,—we cast anchor pretty nigh a reef of coral, and I was jist a-sittin' down to read my Bible, when up comes a merman over the side of the ship, all dressed as fine as any old beau that ever ye see, with cocked hat and silk stockings, and shoe-buckles, and his clothes were sea-green, and his shoe-buckles shone like diamonds."

"Do you suppose they were diamonds, really?" said Sally.

"Wal', child, I did n't ask him, but I should n't be surprised, from all I know of their ways, if they was," said the Captain, who had now got so wholly into the spirit of his fiction that he no longer felt embarrassed by the minister's presence, nor saw the look of amusement with which he was listening to him in his chimney-corner. "But, as I was sayin', he came up to me, and made the politest bow that ever ye see, and says he, 'Cap'n Kittridge, I presume,' and says I, 'Yes, sir.' 'I 'm sorry to interrupt your reading,' says he; and says I, 'Oh, no matter, sir.' 'But,' says he, 'if you would only be so good as to move your anchor. You 've cast anchor right before my front-door, and my wife and family can't get out to go to meetin'.'"

"Why, do they go to meeting in the bottom of the sea?" said Moses.

"Law, bless you sonny, yes. Why, Sunday morning, when the sea was all still, I used to hear the bass-viol a-soundin' down under the waters, jist as plain as could be,—and psalms and preachin'. I 've reason to think there 's as many hopefully pious mermaids as there be folks," said the Captain.

"But," said Moses, "you said the anchor was before the front-door, so the family could n't get out,—how did the merman get out?"

"Oh! he got out of the scuttle on the roof," said the Captain, promptly.

"And did you move your anchor?" said Moses.

"Why, child, yes, to be sure I did; he was such a gentleman I wanted to oblige him,—it shows you how important it is always to be polite," said the Captain, by way of giving a moral turn to his narrative.

Mr. Sewell, during the progress of this story, examined the Captain with eyes of amused curiosity. His countenance was as fixed and steady, and his whole manner of reciting as matter-of-fact and collected, as if he were relating some of the every-day affairs of his boat-building.

"Wal', Sally," said the Captain, rising, after his yarn had proceeded for an indefinite length in this manner, "you and I must be goin'. I promised your ma you should n't be up late, and we have a long walk home,—besides it 's time these little folks was in bed."

The children all clung round the Captain, and could hardly be persuaded to let him go.

When he was gone, Mrs. Pennel took the little ones to their nest in an adjoining room.

Mr. Sewell approached his chair to that of Captain Pennel, and began talking to him in a tone of voice so low, that we have never been able to make out exactly what he was saying. Whatever it might be, however, it seemed to give rise to an anxious consultation. "I did not think it advisable to tell *any* one this but yourself, Captain Pennel. It is for you to decide, in view of the probabilities I have told you, what you will do."

"Well," said Zephaniah, "since you leave it to me, I say, let us keep him. It certainly seems a marked providence that he has been thrown upon us as he has, and the Lord seemed to prepare a way for him in our hearts. I am well able to afford it, and Mis' Pennel, she agrees to it, and on the whole I don't think we 'd best go back on our steps; besides, our little Mara has thrived since he came under our roof. He is, to be sure, kind o' masterful, and I shall have to take him off Mis' Pennel's hands before long, and put him into the sloop. But, after all, there seems to be the makin' of a man in him, and when we are called away, why he 'll be as a brother to poor little Mara. Yes, I think it 's best as 't is."

The minister, as he flitted across the bay by moonlight, felt relieved of a burden. His secret was locked up as safe in the breast of Zephaniah Pennel as it could be in his own.

XIII

🌲🌲🌲🌲

BOY AND GIRL

Zephaniah Pennel was what might be called a Hebrew of the Hebrews.

New England, in her earlier days, founding her institutions on the Hebrew Scriptures, bred better Jews than Moses could, because she read Moses with the amendments of Christ.

The state of society in some of the districts of Maine, in these days, much resembled in its spirit that which Moses labored to produce in ruder ages. It was entirely democratic, simple, grave, hearty, and sincere,—solemn and religious in its daily tone, and yet, as to all material good, full of wholesome thrift and prosperity. Perhaps, taking the average mass of the people, a more healthful and desirable state of society never existed. Its better specimens had a simple Doric grandeur unsurpassed in any age. The bringing up a child in this state of society was a far more simple enterprise than in our modern times, when the factious wants and aspirations are so much more developed.

Zephaniah Pennel was as high as anybody in the land. He owned not only the neat little schooner, "Brilliant," with divers small fishing-boats, but also a snug farm, adjoining the brown house, together with some fresh, juicy pasture-lots on neighboring islands, where he raised mutton, unsurpassed even by the English South-down, and wool, which furnished homespun to clothe his family on all every-day occasions.

Mrs. Pennel, to be sure, had silks and satins, and flowered India chintz, and even a Cashmere shawl, the fruits of some of her husband's earlier voyages, which were, however, carefully stowed away for occasions so high and mighty, that they seldom saw the light. *Not to wear best things every day* was a maxim of New England thrift as little disputed as any verse of the catechism; and so Mrs. Pennel found the stuff gown of her own dyeing and spinning so respectable for most purposes, that it figured even in the meeting-house itself, except on the very finest of Sundays, when heaven and earth seemed alike propitious. A person can well afford to wear homespun stuff to meeting, who is buoyed up by a secret consciousness of an abundance of fine things that could be worn, if one were so disposed, and everybody respected Mrs. Pennel's homespun the more, because they thought of the things she did n't wear.

As to advantages of education, the island, like all other New England districts, had its common school, where one got the key of knowledge,—for having learned to read, write, and cipher, the young fellow of those regions commonly regarded himself as in possession of all that a man needs, to help himself to any further acquisitions he might desire. The boys then made fishing voyages to the Banks, and those who were so disposed took their books with them. If a boy did not wish to be bored with study, there was nobody to force him; but if a bright one saw visions of future success in life lying through the avenues of knowledge, he found many a leisure hour to pore over his books, and work out the problems of navigation directly over the element they were meant to control.

Four years having glided by since the commencement of our story, we find in the brown house of Zephaniah Pennel a tall, well-knit, handsome boy of ten years, who knows no fear of wind or sea; who can set you over from Orr's Island to Harpswell, either in sail or row-boat, he thinks, as well as any man living; who knows every rope of the schooner Brilliant, and fancies he could command it as well as "father" himself; and is supporting himself this spring, during the tamer drudgeries of driving plough, and dropping potatoes, with the glorious vision of being taken this year on the annual trip to "the Banks," which comes on after planting. He reads fluently,—witness the "Robinson Crusoe," which never departs from under his pillow, and Goldsmith's "History of Greece and Rome," which good Mr. Sewell has lent him,—and he often brings shrewd criticisms on the character and course of Romulus or Alexander into the common current of everyday life, in a way that brings a smile over the grave face of Zephaniah, and makes Mrs. Pennel think the boy certainly ought to be sent to college.

As for Mara, she is now a child of seven, still adorned with long golden curls, still looking dreamily out of soft hazel eyes into some unknown future not her own. She has no dreams for herself—they are all for Moses. For his sake she has learned all the womanly little accomplishments which Mrs. Kittridge has dragooned into Sally. She knits his mittens and his stockings, and hems his pocket-handkerchiefs, and aspires to make his shirts all herself. Whatever book Moses reads, forthwith she aspires to read too, and though three years younger, reads with a far more precocious insight.

Her little form is slight and frail, and her cheek has a clear transparent brilliancy quite different from the rounded one of the boy; she looks not exactly in ill health, but has that sort of transparent appearance which one fancies might be an attribute of fairies and sylphs. All her outward senses are finer and more acute than his, and finer and more delicate all the attributes of her mind. Those who contend against giving woman the same education as man do it on the ground that it would make the woman unfeminine, as if Nature had done her work so slightly that it could be so easily raveled and knit over. In fact, there is a masculine and a feminine element in all knowledge, and a man and a woman put to the same study extract only what their nature fits them to see, so that knowledge can be fully orbed only when the two unite in the search and share the spoils.

When Moses was full of Romulus and Numa, Mara pondered the story of the nymph Egeria—sweet parable, in which lies all we have been saying. Her trust in him was boundless. He was a constant hero in her eyes, and in her he found a steadfast believer as to all possible feats and exploits to which he felt himself competent, for the boy often had privately assured her that he could command the Brilliant as well as father himself.

Spring had already come, loosing the chains of ice in all the bays and coves round Harpswell, Orr's Island, Maquoit, and Middle Bay. The magnificent spruces stood forth in their gala-dresses, tipped on every point with vivid emerald; the silver firs exuded from their tender shoots the fragrance of ripe pineapple; the white pines shot forth long weird fingers at the end of their fringy boughs; and even every little mimic evergreen in the shadows at their feet was made beautiful by the addition of a vivid border of green on the sombre coloring of its last year's leaves. Arbutus, fragrant with its clean, wholesome odors, gave forth its thousand dewy pink blossoms, and the trailing Linnea borealis hung its pendent twin bells round every mossy stump and old rock damp with green forest mould. The green and vermilion matting of the partridge-berry was impearled with white velvet blossoms, the checkerberry hung forth a translucent bell under its varnished green leaf, and a thousand more fairy bells, white or red, hung on blueberry and huckleberry bushes. The little Pearl of Orr's Island had wandered many an hour gathering bouquets of all these, to fill the brown house with sweetness when her grandfather and Moses should come in from work.

The love of flowers seemed to be one of her earliest characteristics, and the young spring flowers of New England, in their airy delicacy and fragility, were much like herself; and so strong seemed the affinity between them, that not only Mrs. Pennel's best India china vases on the keeping-room mantel were filled, but here stood a tumbler of scarlet rock columbine, and there a bowl of blue and white violets, and in another place a saucer of shell-tinted crow-foot, blue liverwort, and white anemone, so that Zephaniah Pennel was wont to say there was n't a drink of water to be got, for Mara's flowers; but he always said it with a smile that made his weather-beaten, hard features look like a rock lit up by a sunbeam. Little Mara was the pearl of the old seaman's life, every finer particle of his nature came out in her concentrated and polished, and he often wondered at a creature so ethereal belonging to him—as if down on some shaggy sea-green rock an old pearl oyster should muse and marvel on the strange silvery mystery of beauty that was growing in the silence of his heart.

But May has passed; the arbutus and the Linnea are gone from the woods, and the pine tips have grown into young shoots, which wilt at noon under a direct reflection from sun and sea, and the blue sky has that metallic clearness and brilliancy which distinguishes those regions, and the planting is at last over, and this very morning Moses is to set off in the Brilliant for his first voyage to the Banks. Glorious knight he! the world all before him, and the blood of ten years racing and throbbing in his veins as he talks knowingly of hooks, and sinkers, and bait, and lines, and wears proudly the red flannel shirt which Mara had just finished for him.

"How I do wish I were going with you!" she says. "I could do something, could n't I—take care of your hooks, or something?"

"Pooh!" said Moses, sublimely regarding her while he settled the collar of his shirt, "you 're a girl; and what can girls do at sea? you never like to catch fish—it always makes you cry to see 'em flop."

"Oh, yes, poor fish!" said Mara, perplexed between her sympathy for the fish and her desire for the glory of her hero, which must be founded on their pain; "I can't help feeling sorry when they gasp so."

"Well, and what do you suppose you would do when the men are pulling up twenty and forty pounder?" said Moses, striding sublimely. "Why, they flop so, they 'd knock you over in a minute."

"Do they? Oh, Moses, do be careful. What if they should hurt you?"

"Hurt me!" said Moses, laughing; "that 's a good one. I 'd like to see a fish that could hurt me."

"Do hear that boy talk!" said Mrs. Pennel to her husband, as they stood within their chamber-door.

"Yes, yes," said Captain Pennel, smiling; "he 's full of the matter. I believe he 'd take the command of the schooner this morning, if I 'd let him."

The Brilliant lay all this while courtesying on the waves, which kissed and whispered to the little coquettish craft. A fairer June morning had not risen on the shores that week; the blue mirror of the ocean was all dotted over with the tiny white sails of fishing-craft bound on the same errand, and the breeze that was just crisping the waters had the very spirit of energy and adventure in it.

Everything and everybody was now on board, and she began

to spread her fair wings, and slowly and gracefully to retreat from the shore. Little Moses stood on the deck, his black curls blowing in the wind, and his large eyes dancing with excitement,—his clear olive complexion and glowing cheeks well set off by his red shirt.

Mrs. Pennel stood with Mara on the shore to see them go. The fair little golden-haired Ariadne shaded her eyes with one arm, and stretched the other after her Theseus, till the vessel grew smaller, and finally seemed to melt away into the eternal blue. Many be the wives and lovers that have watched those little fishing-craft as they went gayly out like this, but have waited long—too long—and seen them again no more. In night and fog they have gone down under the keel of some ocean packet or Indiaman, and sunk with brave hearts and hands, like a bubble in the mighty waters. Yet Mrs. Pennel did not turn back to her house in apprehension of this. Her husband had made so many voyages, and always returned safely, that she confidently expected before long to see them home again.

The next Sunday the seat of Zephaniah Pennel was vacant in church. According to custom, a note was put up asking prayers for his safe return, and then everybody knew that he was gone to the Banks; and as the roguish, handsome face of Moses was also missing, Miss Roxy whispered to Miss Ruey, "There! Captain Pennel's took Moses on his first voyage. We must contrive to call round on Mis' Pennel afore long. She 'll be lonesome."

Sunday evening Mrs. Pennel was sitting pensively with little Mara by the kitchen hearth, where they had been boiling the tea-kettle for their solitary meal. They heard a brisk step without, and soon Captain and Mrs. Kittridge made their appearance.

"Good evening, Mis' Pennel," said the Captain; "I 's a-tellin' my good woman we must come down and see how you 's a-getting along. It 's raly a work of necessity and mercy proper for the Lord's day. Rather lonesome, now the Captain 's gone, ain't ye? Took little Moses, too, I see. Was n't at meetin' to-day, so I says, Mis' Kittridge, we 'll just step down and chirk 'em up a little."

"I did n't really know how to come," said Mrs. Kittridge, as she allowed Mrs. Pennel to take her bonnet; "but Aunt Roxy 's to our house now, and she said she 'd see to Sally. So you 've let the boy go to the Banks? He 's young, ain't he, for that?"

"Not a bit of it," said Captain Kittridge. "Why, I was off to the Banks long afore I was his age, and a capital time we had of it, too. Golly! how them fish did bite! We stood up to our knees in fish before we 'd fished half an hour."

Mara, who had always a shy affinity for the Captain, now drew towards him and climbed on his knee. "Did the wind blow very hard?" she said.

"What, my little maid?"

"Does the wind blow at the Banks?"

"Why, yes, my little girl, that it does, sometimes; but then there ain't the least danger. Our craft ride out storms like live creatures. I 've stood it out in gales that was tight enough, I 'm sure. 'Member once I turned in 'tween twelve and one, and had n't more 'n got asleep, afore I came *clump* out of my berth, and found everything upside down. And 'stead of goin' upstairs to get on deck, I had to go right down. Fact was, that 'ere vessel jist turned clean over in the water, and come right side up like a duck."

"Well, now, Cap'n, I would n't be tellin' such a story as that," said his help-meet.

"Why, Polly, what do you know about it? you never was to sea. We did turn clear over, for I 'member I saw a bunch of sea-weed big as a peck measure stickin' top of the mast next day. Jist shows how safe them ar little fishing craft is,—for all they look like an egg-shell on the mighty deep, as Parson Sewell calls it."

"I was very much pleased with Mr. Sewell's exercise in prayer this morning," said Mrs. Kittridge; "it must have been a comfort to you, Mis' Pennel."

"It was, to be sure," said Mrs. Pennel.

"Puts me in mind of poor Mary Jane Simpson. Her husband went out, you know, last June, and hain't been heard of since. Mary Jane don't really know whether to put on mourning or not."

"Law! I don't think Mary Jane need give up yet," said the Captain. "'Member one year I was out, we got blowed clear up to Baffin's Bay, and got shut up in the ice, and had to go ashore and live jist as we could among them Esquimaux. Did n't get home for a year. Old folks had clean giv' us up. Don't need never despair of folks gone to sea, for they 's sure to turn up, first or last."

"But I hope," said Mara, apprehensively, "that grandpapa won't get blown up to Baffin's Bay. I 've seen that on his chart,—it 's a good ways."

"And then there 's them 'ere icebergs," said Mrs. Kittridge; "I 'm always 'fraid of running into them in the fog."

"Law!" said Captain Kittridge, "I 've met 'em bigger than all the colleges up to Brunswick,—great white bears on 'em,—hungry as Time in the Primer. Once we came kersmash on to one of 'em, and if the Flying Betsey had n't been made of whalebone and injer-rubber, she 'd a-been stove all to pieces. Them white bears, they was so hungry, that they stood there with the water jist runnin' out of their chops in a perfect stream."

"Oh, dear, dear," said Mara, with wide round eyes, "what will Moses do if they get on the icebergs?"

"Yes," said Mrs. Kittridge, looking solemnly at the child through the black bows of her spectacles, "we can truly say:—

" 'Dangers stand thick through all the ground,
    To push us to the tomb,'

as the hymn-book says."

The kind-hearted Captain, feeling the fluttering heart of little Mara, and seeing the tears start in her eyes, addressed himself forthwith to consolation. "Oh, never you mind, Mara," he said, "there won't nothing hurt 'em. Look at me. Why, I 've been everywhere on the face of the earth. I 've been on icebergs, and among white bears and Indians, and seen storms that would blow the very hair off your head, and here I am, dry and tight as ever. You 'll see 'em back before long."

The cheerful laugh with which the Captain was wont to chorus his sentences sounded like the crackling of dry pine wood on the social hearth. One would hardly hear it without being lightened in heart; and little Mara gazed at his long, dry, ropy figure, and wrinkled thin face, as a sort of monument of hope; and his uproarious laugh, which Mrs. Kittridge sometimes ungraciously compared to "the crackling of thorns under a pot," seemed to her the most delightful thing in the world.

"Mary Jane was a-tellin' me," resumed Mrs. Kittridge, "that when her husband had been out a month, she dreamed she see him, and three other men, a-floatin' on an iceberg."

"Laws," said Captain Kittridge, "that 's jist what my old mother dreamed about me, and 't was true enough, too, till we got off the ice on to the shore up in the Esquimaux territory, as I was a-tellin'. So you tell Mary Jane she need n't look out for a second husband *yet,* for that ar dream 's a sartin sign he 'll be back."

"Cap'n Kittridge!" said his help-meet, drawing herself up, and giving him an austere glance over her spectacles; "how often must I tell you that there *is* subjects which should n't be treated with levity?"

"Who's been a-treatin' of 'em with levity?" said the Captain. "I'm sure I ain't. Mary Jane's good-lookin', and there's plenty of young fellows as sees it as well as me. I declare, she looked as pretty as any young gal when she ris up in the singers' seats to-day. Put me in mind of you, Polly, when I first come home from the Injies."

"Oh, come now, Cap'n Kittridge! we're gettin' too old for that sort o' talk."

"We ain't too old, be we, Mara?" said the Captain, trotting the little girl gayly on his knee; "and we ain't afraid of icebergs and no sich, be we? I tell you they's a fine sight of a bright day; they has millions of steeples, all white and glistering, like the New Jerusalem, and the white bears have capital times trampin' round on 'em. Would n't little Mara like a great, nice white bear to ride on, with his white fur, so soft and warm, and a saddle made of pearls, and a gold bridle?"

"You have n't seen any little girls ride so," said Mara, doubtfully.

"I should n't wonder if I had; but you see, Mis' Kittridge there, she won't let me tell all I know," said the Captain, sinking his voice to a confidential tone; "you jist wait till we get alone."

"But, you are sure," said Mara, confidingly, in return, "that white bears will be kind to Moses?"

"Lord bless you, yes, child, the kindest critturs in the world they be, if you only get the right side of 'em," said the Captain.

"Oh, yes! because," said Mara, "I know how good a wolf was to Romulus and Remus once, and nursed them when they were cast out to die. I read that in the Roman history."

"Jist so," said the Captain, enchanted at this historic confirmation of his apocrypha.

"And so," said Mara, "if Moses should happen to get on an iceberg, a bear might take care of him, you know."

"Jist so, jist so," said the Captain; "so don't you worry your little curly head one bit. Some time when you come down to see Sally, we 'll go down to the cove, and I 'll tell you lots of stories about chil'en that have been fetched up by white bears, jist like Romulus and what 's his name there."

"Come, Mis' Kittridge," added the cheery Captain; "you and I must n't be keepin' the folks up till nine o'clock."

"Well now," said Mrs. Kittridge, in a doleful tone, as she began to put on her bonnet, "Mis' Pennel, you must keep up your spirits—it 's one's duty to take cheerful views of things. I 'm sure many 's the night, when the Captain 's been gone to sea, I 've laid and shook in my bed, hearin' the wind blow, and thinking what if I should be left a lone widow."

"There 'd a-been a dozen fellows a-wanting to get you in six months, Polly," interposed the Captain. "Well, good-night, Mis' Pennel; there 'll be a splendid haul of fish at the Banks this year, or there 's no truth in signs. Come, my little Mara, got a kiss for the dry old daddy? That 's my good girl. Well, good night, and the Lord bless you."

And so the cheery Captain took up his line of march homeward, leaving little Mara's head full of dazzling visions of the land of romance to which Moses had gone. She was yet on that shadowy boundary between the dreamland of childhood and the real land of life; so all things looked to her quite possible; and gentle white bears, with warm, soft fur and pearl and gold saddles, walked through her dreams, and the victorious curls of Moses appeared, with his bright eyes and cheeks, over glittering pinnacles of frost in the ice-land.

XIV

THE ENCHANTED ISLAND

June and July passed, and the lonely two lived a quiet life in the brown house. Everything was so still and fair—no sound but the coming and going tide, and the swaying wind among the pine-trees, and the tick of the clock, and the whirr of the little wheel as Mrs. Pennel sat spinning in her door in the mild weather. Mara read the Roman history through again, and began it a third time, and read over and over again the stories and prophecies that pleased her in the Bible, and pondered the wood-cuts and texts in a very old edition of Æsop's Fables; and as she wandered in the woods, picking fragrant bay-berries and gathering hemlock, checkerberry, and sassafras to put in the beer which her grandmother brewed, she mused on the things that she read till her little mind became a tabernacle of solemn, quaint, dreamy forms, where old Judean kings and prophets, and Roman senators and warriors, marched in and out in shadowy rounds. She invented long dramas and conversations in which they performed imaginary parts, and it would not have appeared to the child in the least degree surprising either to have met an angel in the woods, or to have formed an intimacy with some talking wolf or bear, such as she read of in Æsop's Fables.

One day, as she was exploring the garret, she found in an old barrel of cast-off rubbish a bit of reading which she begged of her grandmother for her own. It was the play of the "Tempest," torn from an old edition of Shakespeare, and was in that delightfully fragmentary condition which most particularly pleases children, because they conceive a mutilated treasure thus found to be more especially their own property—something like a rare wild-flower or sea-shell. The pleasure which thoughtful and imaginative children sometimes take in reading that which they do not and cannot fully comprehend is one of the most common and curious phenomena of childhood.

And so little Mara would lie for hours stretched out on the pebbly beach, with the broad open ocean before her and the whispering pines and hemlocks behind her, and pore over this poem, from which she collected dim, delightful images of a lonely island, an old enchanter, a beautiful girl, and a spirit not quite like those in the Bible, but a very probable one to her mode of thinking. As for old Caliban, she fancied him with a face much like that of a huge skate-fish she had once seen drawn ashore in one of her grandfather's nets; and then there was the beautiful young Prince Ferdinand, much like what Moses would be when he was grown up—and how glad she would be to pile up his wood for him, if any old enchanter should set him to work!

One attribute of the child was a peculiar shamefacedness and shyness about her inner thoughts, and therefore the wonder that this new treasure excited, the host of surmises and dreams to which it gave rise, were never mentioned to anybody. That it was all of it as much authentic fact as the Roman history, she did not doubt, but whether it had happened on Orr's Island or some of the neighboring ones, she had not exactly made up her mind. She resolved at her earliest leisure to consult Captain Kittridge on the subject, wisely considering that it much resembled some of his fishy and aquatic experiences.

Some of the little songs fixed themselves in her memory, and she would hum them as she wandered up and down the beach.

> "Come unto these yellow sands,
>   And then take hands;
> Courtsied when you have and kissed
>   The wild waves whist,
> Foot it featly here and there;
> And, sweet sprites, the burthen bear."

And another which pleased her still more:—

> "Full fathom five thy father lies;
>   Of his bones are coral made,
> Those are pearls that were his eyes:
>   Nothing of him that can fade
> But doth suffer a sea-change
> Into something rich and strange;
> Sea-nymphs hourly ring his knell:
> Hark, now I hear them—ding-dong, bell."

These words she pondered very long, gravely revolving in her little head whether they described the usual course of things in the mysterious under-world that lay beneath that blue spangled floor of the sea; whether everybody's eyes changed to pearl, and their bones to coral, if they sunk down there; and whether the sea-nymphs spoken of were the same as the mermaids that Captain Kittridge had told of. Had he not said that the bell rung for church of a Sunday morning down under the waters?

Mara vividly remembered the scene on the sea-beach, the

finding of little Moses and his mother, the dream of the pale lady that seemed to bring him to her; and not one of the conversations that had transpired before her among different gossips had been lost on her quiet, listening little ears. These pale, still children that play without making any noise are deep wells into which drop many things which lie long and quietly on the bottom, and come up in after years whole and new, when everybody else has forgotten them.

So she had heard surmises as to the remaining crew of that unfortunate ship, where, perhaps, Moses had a father. And sometimes she wondered if *he* were lying fathoms deep with sea-nymphs ringing his knell, and whether Moses ever thought about him; and yet she could no more have asked him a question about it than if she had been born dumb. She decided that she should never show him this poetry—it might make him feel unhappy.

One bright afternoon, when the sea lay all dead asleep, and the long, steady respiration of its tides scarcely disturbed the glassy tranquillity of its bosom, Mrs. Pennel sat at her kitchen-door spinning, when Captain Kittridge appeared.

"Good afternoon, Mis' Pennel; how ye gettin' along?"

"Oh, pretty well, Captain; won't you walk in and have a glass of beer?"

"Well, thank you," said the Captain, raising his hat and wiping his forehead, "I be pretty dry, it 's a fact."

Mrs. Pennel hastened to a cask which was kept standing in a corner of the kitchen, and drew from thence a mug of her own home-brewed, fragrant with the smell of juniper, hemlock, and wintergreen, which she presented to the Captain, who sat down in the door-way and discussed it in leisurely sips.

"Wal', s'pose it 's most time to be lookin' for 'em home, ain't it?" he said.

"I *am* lookin' every day," said Mrs. Pennel, involuntarily glancing upward at the sea.

At the word appeared the vision of little Mara, who rose up like a spirit from a dusky corner, where she had been stooping over her reading.

"Why, little Mara," said the Captain, "you ris up like a ghost all of a sudden. I thought you 's out to play. I come down a-purpose arter you. Mis' Kittridge has gone shoppin' up to Brunswick, and left Sally a 'stent' to do; and I promised her if she 'd clap to and do it quick, I 'd go up and fetch you down, and we 'd have a play in the cove."

Mara's eyes brightened, as they always did at this prospect, and Mrs. Pennel said, "Well, I 'm glad to have the child go; she seems so kind o' still and lonesome since Moses went away; really one feels as if that boy took all the noise there was with him. I get tired myself sometimes hearing the clock tick. Mara, when she 's alone, takes to her book more than 's good for a child."

"She does, does she? Well, we 'll see about that. Come, little Mara, get on your sun-bonnet. Sally 's sewin' fast as ever she can, and we 're goin' to dig some clams, and make a fire, and have a chowder; that 'll be nice, won't it? Don't you want to come, too, Mis' Pennel?"

"Oh, thank you, Captain, but I 've got so many things on hand to do afore they come home, I don't really think I can. I 'll trust Mara to you any day."

Mara had run into her own little room and secured her precious fragment of treasure, which she wrapped up carefully in her handkerchief, resolving to enlighten Sally with the story, and to consult the Captain on any nice points of criticism. Arrived at the cove, they found Sally already there in advance of them, clapping her hands and dancing in a manner which made her black elf-locks fly like those of a distracted creature.

"Now, Sally," said the Captain, imitating, in a humble way, his wife's manner, "are you sure you 've finished your work well?"

"Yes, father, every stitch on't."

"And stuck in your needle, and folded it up, and put it in the drawer, and put away your thimble, and shet the drawer, and all the rest on 't?" said the Captain.

"Yes, father," said Sally, gleefully, "I 've done everything I could think of."

" 'Cause you know your ma 'll be arter ye, if you don't leave everything straight."

"Oh, never you fear, father, I 've done it all half an hour ago, and I 've found the most capital bed of clams just round the point here; and you take care of Mara there, and make up a fire while I dig 'em. If she comes, she 'll be sure to wet her shoes, or spoil her frock, or something."

"Wal', she likes no better fun now," said the Captain, watching Sally, as she disappeared round the rock with a bright tin pan.

He then proceeded to construct an extemporary fireplace of loose stones, and to put together chips and shavings for the fire,—in which work little Mara eagerly assisted; but the fire was crackling and burning cheerily long before Sally appeared with her clams, and so the Captain, with a pile of hemlock boughs by his side, sat on a stone feeding the fire leisurely from time to time with crackling boughs. Now was the time for Mara to make her inquiries; her heart beat, she knew not why, for she was full of those little timidities and shames that so often embarrass children in their attempts to get at the meanings of things in this great world, where they are such ignorant spectators.

"Captain Kittridge," she said at last, "do the mermaids toll any bells for people when they are drowned?"

Now the Captain had never been known to indicate the least

ignorance on any subject in heaven or earth, which any one wished his opinion on; he therefore leisurely poked another great crackling bough of green hemlock into the fire, and, Yankee-like, answered one question by asking another.

"What put that into your curly pate?" he said.

"A book I 've been reading says they do,—that is, sea-nymphs do. Ain't sea-nymphs and mermaids the same thing?"

"Wal', I guess they be, pretty much," said the Captain, rubbing down his pantaloons; "yes, they be," he added, after reflection.

"And when people are drowned, how long does it take for their bones to turn into coral, and their eyes into pearl?" said little Mara.

"Well, that depends upon circumstances," said the Captain, who was n't going to be posed; "but let me jist see your book you 've been reading these things out of."

"I found it in a barrel up garret, and grandma gave it to me," said Mara, unrolling her handkerchief; "it 's a beautiful book,—it tells about an island, and there was an old enchanter lived on it, and he had one daughter, and there was a spirit they called Ariel, whom a wicked old witch fastened in a split of a pine-tree, till the enchanter got him out. He was a beautiful spirit, and rode in the curled clouds and hung in flowers,—because he could make himself big or little, you see."

"Ah, yes, I see, to be sure," said the Captain, nodding his head.

"Well, that about sea-nymphs ringing his knell is here," Mara added, beginning to read the passage with wide, dilated eyes and great emphasis. "You see," she went on speaking very fast, "this enchanter had been a prince, and a wicked brother had contrived to send him to sea with his poor little daughter, in a ship so leaky that the very rats had left it."

"Bad business that!" said the Captain, attentively.

"Well," said Mara, "they got cast ashore on this desolate island, where they lived together. But once, when a ship was going by on the sea that had his wicked brother and his son—a real good, handsome young prince—in it, why then he made a storm by magic arts."

"Jist so," said the Captain; "that 's been often done, to my sartin knowledge."

"And he made the ship be wrecked, and all the people thrown ashore, but there was n't any of 'em drowned, and this handsome prince heard Ariel singing this song about his father, and it made him think he was dead."

"Well, what became of 'em?" interposed Sally, who had come up with her pan of clams in time to hear this story, to which she had listened with breathless interest.

"Oh, the beautiful young prince married the beautiful young lady," said Mara.

"Wal'," said the Captain, who by this time had found his soundings; "that you 've been a-tellin' is what they call a play, and I 've seen 'em act it at a theatre, when I was to Liverpool once. I know all about it. Shakespeare wrote it, and he 's a great English poet."

"But did it ever happen?" said Mara, trembling between hope and fear. "Is it like the Bible and Roman history?"

"Why, no," said Captain Kittridge, "not exactly; but things jist like it, you know. Mermaids and sich is common in foreign parts, and they has funerals for drowned sailors. 'Member once when we was sailing near the Bermudas by a reef where the Lively Fanny went down, and I heard a kind o' ding-dongin',— and the waters there is clear as the sky,—and I looked down and see the coral all a-growin', and the sea-plants a-wavin' as handsome as a pictur', and the mermaids they was a-singin'. It was beautiful; they sung kind o' mournful; and Jack Hubbard, he would have it they was a-singin' for the poor fellows that was a-lyin' there round under the seaweed."

"But," said Mara, "did you ever see an enchanter that could make storms?"

"Wal', there be witches and conjurers that make storms. 'Member once when we was crossin' the line, about twelve o'clock at night, there was an old man with a long white beard that shone like silver, came and stood at the masthead, and he had a pitchfork in one hand, and a lantern in the other, and there was great balls of fire as big as my fist came out all round in the rigging. And I'll tell you if we did n't get a blow that ar night! I thought to my soul we should all go to the bottom."

"Why," said Mara, her eyes staring with excitement, "that was just like this shipwreck; and 't was Ariel made those balls of fire; he says so; he said he 'flamed amazement' all over the ship."

"I 've heard Miss Roxy tell about witches that made storms," said Sally.

The Captain leisurely proceeded to open the clams, separating from the shells the contents, which he threw into a pan, meanwhile placing a black pot over the fire in which he had previously arranged certain slices of salt pork, which soon began frizzling in the heat.

"Now, Sally, you peel them potatoes, and mind you slice 'em thin," he said, and Sally soon was busy with her work.

"Yes," said the Captain, going on with his part of the arrangement, "there was old Polly Twitchell, that lived in that ar old tumble-down house on Mure P'int; people used to say she brewed storms, and went to sea in a sieve."

"Went in a sieve!" said both children; "why a sieve would n't swim!"

"No more it would n't, in any Christian way," said the Captain; "but that was to show what a great witch she was."

"But this was a good enchanter," said Mara, "and he did it all by a book and a rod."

"Yes, yes," said the Captain; "that ar 's the gen'l way magicians do, ever since Moses's time in Egypt. 'Member once I was to Alexandria, in Egypt, and I saw a magician there that could jist see everything you ever did in your life in a drop of ink that he held in his hand."

"He could, father!"

"To be sure he could! told me all about the old folks at home; and described our house as natural as if he 'd a-been there. He used to carry snakes round with him,—a kind so p'ison that it was certain death to have 'em bite you; but he played with 'em as if they was kittens."

"Well," said Mara, "my enchanter was a king; and when he got through all he wanted, and got his daughter married to the beautiful young prince, he said he would break his staff, and deeper than plummet sounded he would bury his book."

"It was pretty much the best thing he could do," said the Captain, "because the Bible is agin such things."

"Is it?" said Mara; "why, he was a real good man."

"Oh, well, you know, we all on us does what ain't quite right sometimes, when we gets pushed up," said the Captain, who now began arranging the clams and sliced potatoes in alternate layers with sea-biscuit, strewing in salt and pepper as he went on; and, in a few moments, a smell, fragrant to hungry senses, began to steam upward, and Sally began washing and preparing some mammoth clam-shells, to serve as ladles and plates for the future chowder.

Mara, who sat with her morsel of a book in her lap, seemed deeply pondering the past conversation. At last she said,

"What did you mean by saying you 'd seen 'em act that at a theatre?"

"Why, they make it all seem real; and they have a shipwreck, and you see it all jist right afore your eyes."

"And the Enchanter, and Ariel, and Caliban, and all?" said Mara.

"Yes, all on't,—plain as printing."

"Why, that is by magic, ain't it?" said Mara.

"No; they hes ways to jist make it up; but,"—added the Captain, "Sally, you need n't say nothin' to your ma 'bout the theatre, 'cause she would n't think I 's fit to go to meetin' for six months arter, if she heard on 't."

"Why, ain't theatres good?" said Sally.

"Wal', there 's a middlin' sight o' bad things in 'em," said the Captain, "that I must say; but as long as folks *is* folks, why, they will be *folksy;*—but there 's never any makin' women folk understand about them ar things."

"I am sorry they are bad," said Mara; "I want to see them."

"Wal', wal'," said the Captain, "on the hull I 've seen real things a good deal more wonderful than all their shows, and they hain't no make-b'lieve to 'em; but theatres is takin' arter all. But, Sally, mind you don't say nothin' to Mis' Kittridge."

A few moments more and all discussion was lost in preparations for the meal, and each one, receiving a portion of the savory stew in a large shell, made a spoon of a small cockle, and with some slices of bread and butter, the evening meal went off merrily. The sun was sloping toward the ocean; the wide blue floor was bedropped here and there with rosy shadows of sailing clouds. Suddenly the Captain sprang up, calling out,—

"Sure as I 'm alive, there they be!"

"Who?" exclaimed the children.

"Why, Captain Pennel and Moses; don't you see?"

And, in fact, on the outer circle of the horizon came drifting a line of small white-breasted vessels, looking like so many doves.

"Them 's 'em," said the Captain, while Mara danced for joy.

"How soon will they be here?"

"Afore long," said the Captain; "so, Mara, I guess you 'll want to be getting hum."

XV

✦✦✦✦

THE HOME COMING

Mrs. Pennel, too, had seen the white, dove-like cloud on the horizon, and had hurried to make biscuits, and conduct other culinary preparations which should welcome the wanderers home.

The sun was just dipping into the great blue sea—a round ball of fire—and sending long, slanting tracks of light across the top of each wave, when a boat was moored at the beach, and the minister sprang out,—not in his suit of ceremony, but attired in fisherman's garb.

"Good afternoon, Mrs. Pennel," he said. "I was out fishing, and I thought I saw your husband's schooner in the distance. I thought I 'd come and tell you."

"Thank you, Mr. Sewell. I thought I saw it, but I was not certain. Do come in; the Captain would be delighted to see you here."

"We miss your husband in our meetings," said Mr. Sewell; "it will be good news for us all when he comes home; he is one of those I depend on to help me preach."

"I 'm sure you don't preach to anybody who enjoys it more,"

said Mrs. Pennel. "He often tells me that the greatest trouble about his voyages to the Banks is that he loses so many sanctuary privileges; though he always keeps Sunday on his ship, and reads and sings his psalms; but, he says, after all, there's nothing like going to Mount Zion."

"And little Moses has gone on his first voyage?" said the minister.

"Yes, indeed; the child has been teasing to go for more than a year. Finally the Cap'n told him if he 'd be faithful in the ploughing and planting, he should go. You see, he 's rather unsteady, and apt to be off after other things,—very different from Mara. Whatever you give her to do, she always keeps at it till it 's done."

"And pray, where is the little lady?" said the minister; "is she gone?"

"Well, Cap'n Kittridge came in this afternoon to take her down to see Sally. The Cap'n 's always so fond of Mara, and she has always taken to him ever since she was a baby."

"The Captain is a curious creature," said the minister, smiling.

Mrs. Pennel smiled also; and it is to be remarked that nobody ever mentioned the poor Captain's name without the same curious smile.

"The Cap'n is a good-hearted, obliging creature," said Mrs. Pennel, "and a master-hand for telling stories to the children."

"Yes, a perfect 'Arabian Nights' Entertainment,'" said Mr. Sewell.

"Well, I really believe the Cap'n believes his own stories," said Mrs. Pennel; "he always seems to, and certainly a more obliging man and a kinder neighbor could n't be. He has been in and out almost every day since I 've been alone, to see if I wanted anything. He would insist on chopping wood and splitting kindlings for me, though I told him the Cap'n and Moses had left a plenty to last till they came home."

At this moment the subject of their conversation appeared striding along the beach, with a large, red lobster in one hand, while with the other he held little Mara upon his shoulder, she the while clapping her hands and singing merrily, as she saw the Brilliant out on the open blue sea, its white sails looking of a rosy purple in the evening light, careering gayly homeward.

"There is Captain Kittridge this very minute," said Mrs. Pennel, setting down a teacup she had been wiping, and going to the door.

"Good evening, Mis' Pennel," said the Captain. "I s'pose you see your folks are comin'. I brought down one of these 'ere ready b'iled, 'cause I thought it might make out your supper."

"Thank you, Captain; you must stay and take some with us."

"Wal', me and the children have pooty much done our supper," said the Captain. "We made a real fust-rate chowder down there to the cove; but I 'll jist stay and see what the Cap'n's luck is. Massy!" he added, as he looked in at the door, "if you hain't got the minister there! Wal', now, I come jist as I be," he added, with a glance down at his clothes.

"Never mind, Captain," said Mr. Sewell; "I 'm in my fishing-clothes, so we 're even."

As to little Mara, she had run down to the beach, and stood so near the sea, that every dash of the tide-wave forced her little feet to tread an inch backward, stretching out her hands eagerly toward the schooner, which was standing straight toward the small wharf, not far from their door. Already she could see on deck figures moving about, and her sharp little eyes made out a small personage in a red shirt that was among the most active. Soon all the figures grew distinct, and she could see her grandfather's gray head, and alert, active form, and could see, by the signs he made, that he had perceived the little blowy figure that stood, with hair streaming in the wind, like some flower bent seaward.

And now they are come nearer, and Moses shouts and dances on the deck, and the Captain and Mrs. Pennel come running from the house down to the shore, and a few minutes more, and all are landed safe and sound, and little Mara is carried up to the house in her grandfather's arms, while Captain Kittridge stops to have a few moments' gossip with Ben Halliday and Tom Scranton before they go to their own resting-places.

Meanwhile Moses loses not a moment in boasting of his heroic exploits to Mara.

"Oh, Mara! you 've no idea what times we 've had! I can fish equal to any of 'em, and I can take in sail and tend the helm like anything, and I know all the names of everything; and you ought to have seen us catch fish! Why, they bit just as fast as we could throw; and it was just throw and bite, — throw and bite, — throw and bite; and my hands got blistered pulling in, but I did n't mind it, — I was determined no one should beat me."

"Oh! did you blister your hands?" said Mara, pitifully.

"Oh, to be sure! Now, you girls think that 's a dreadful thing, but we men don't mind it. My hands are getting so hard, you 've no idea. And, Mara, we caught a great shark."

"A shark! — oh, how dreadful! Is n't he dangerous?"

"Dangerous! I guess not. We served him out, I tell you. He 'll never eat any more people, I tell you, the old wretch!"

"But, poor shark, it is n't his fault that he eats people. He was made so," said Mara, unconsciously touching a deep theological mystery.

"Well, I don't know but he was," said Moses; "but sharks that we catch never eat any more, I'll bet you."

"Oh, Moses, did you see any icebergs?"

"Icebergs! yes; we passed right by one,—a real grand one."

"Were there any bears on it?"

"Bears! No; we did n't see any."

"Captain Kittridge says there are white bears live on 'em."

"Oh, Captain Kittridge," said Moses, with a toss of superb contempt; "if you 're going to believe all *he* says, you 've got your hands full."

"Why, Moses, you don't think he tells lies?" said Mara, the tears actually starting in her eyes. "I think he is *real* good, and tells nothing but the truth."

"Well, well, you are young yet," said Moses, turning away with an air of easy grandeur, "and only a girl besides," he added.

Mara was nettled at this speech. First, it pained her to have her child's faith shaken in anything, and particularly in her good old friend, the Captain; and next, she felt, with more force than ever she did before, the continual disparaging tone in which Moses spoke of her girlhood.

"I 'm sure," she said to herself, "he ought n't to feel so about girls and women. There was Deborah was a prophetess, and judged Israel; and there was Egeria,—she taught Numa Pompilius all his wisdom."

But it was not the little maiden's way to speak when anything thwarted or hurt her, but rather to fold all her feelings and thoughts inward, as some insects, with fine gauzy wings, draw them under a coat of horny concealment. Somehow, there was a shivering sense of disappointment in all this meeting with Moses. She had dwelt upon it, and fancied so much, and had so many things to say to him; and he had come home so self-absorbed and glorious, and seemed to have had so little need of or thought for her, that she felt a cold, sad sinking at her heart; and walking away very still and white, sat down demurely by her grandfather's knee.

"Well, so my little girl is glad grandfather's come," he said, lifting her fondly in his arms, and putting her golden head under his coat, as he had been wont to do from infancy; "grandpa thought a great deal about his little Mara."

The small heart swelled against his. Kind, faithful old grandpa! how much more he thought about her than Moses; and yet she had thought so much of Moses. And there he sat, this same ungrateful Moses, bright-eyed and rosy-cheeked, full of talk and gayety, full of energy and vigor, as ignorant as possible of the wound he had given to the little loving heart that was silently brooding under her grandfather's butternut-colored sea-coat. Not only was he ignorant, but he had not even those conditions within himself which made knowledge possible. All that there was developed of him, at present, was a fund of energy, self-esteem, hope, courage, and daring, the love of action, life, and adventure; his life was in the outward and present, not in the inward and reflective; he was a true ten-year old boy, in its healthiest and most animal perfection. What she was, the small pearl with the golden hair, with her frail and high-strung organization, her sensitive nerves, her half-spiritual fibres, her ponderings, and marvels, and dreams, her power of love, and yearning for self-devotion, our readers may, perhaps, have seen. But if ever two children, or two grown people, thus organized, are thrown into intimate relations, it follows, from the very laws of their being, that one must hurt the other, simply by being itself; one must always hunger for what the other has not to give.

It was a merry meal, however, when they all sat down to the tea-table once more, and Mara by her grandfather's side, who often stopped what he was saying to stroke her head fondly. Moses bore a more prominent part in the conversation than he had been wont to do before this voyage, and all seemed to listen to him with a kind of indulgence elders often accord to a handsome, manly boy, in the first flush of some successful enterprise. That ignorant confidence in one's self and one's future, which comes in life's first dawn, has a sort of mournful charm in experienced eyes, who know how much it all amounts to.

Gradually, little Mara quieted herself with listening to and admiring him. It is not comfortable to have any heart-quarrel with one's cherished idol, and everything of the feminine nature, therefore, can speedily find fifty good reasons for seeing one's self in the wrong and one's graven image in the right; and little Mara soon had said to herself, without words, that, of course, Moses could n't be expected to think as much of her as she of him. He was handsomer, cleverer, and had a thousand other things to do and to think of—he was a boy, in short, and going to be a glorious man and sail all over the world, while she could only hem handkerchiefs and knit stockings, and sit at home and wait for him to come back. This was about the *résumé* of life as it appeared to the little one, who went on from the moment worshiping her image with more undivided idolatry than ever, hoping that by and by he would think more of her.

Mr. Sewell appeared to study Moses carefully and thoughtfully, and encouraged the wild, gleeful frankness which he had brought home from his first voyage, as a knowing jockey tries the paces of a high-mettled colt.

"Did you get any time to read?" he interposed once, when the boy stopped in his account of their adventures.

"No, sir," said Moses; "at least," he added, blushing very deeply, "I did n't feel like reading. I had so much to do, and there was so much to see."

"It 's all new to him now," said Captain Pennel; "but when he comes to being, as I 've been, day after day, with nothing but sea and sky, he 'll be glad of a book, just to break the sameness."

"Laws, yes," said Captain Kittridge; "sailor's life ain't all apple-pie, as it seems when a boy first goes on a summer trip with his daddy—not by no manner o' means."

"But," said Mara, blushing and looking very eagerly at Mr. Sewell, "Moses has read a great deal. He read the Roman and the Grecian history through before he went away, and knows all about them."

"Indeed!" said Mr. Sewell, turning with an amused look towards the tiny little champion; "do you read them, too, my little maid?"

"Yes, indeed," said Mara, her eyes kindling; "I have read them a great deal since Moses went away—them and the Bible."

Mara did not dare to name her new-found treasure—there was something so mysterious about that, that she could not venture to produce it, except on the score of extreme intimacy.

"Come, sit by me, little Mara," said the minister, putting out his hand; "you and I must be friends, I see."

Mr. Sewell had a certain something of mesmeric power in his eyes which children seldom resisted; and with a shrinking movement, as if both attracted and repelled, the little girl got upon his knee.

"So you like the Bible and Roman history?" he said to her, making a little aside for her, while a brisk conversation was going on between Captain Kittridge and Captain Pennel on the fishing bounty for the year.

"Yes, sir," said Mara, blushing in a very guilty way.

"And which do you like the best?"

"I don't know, sir; I sometimes think it is the one, and sometimes the other."

"Well, what pleases you in the Roman history?"

"Oh, I like that about Quintus Curtius."

"Quintus Curtius?" said Mr. Sewell, pretending not to remember.

"Oh, don't you remember him? why, there was a great gulf

opened in the Forum, and the Augurs said that the country would not be saved unless some one would offer himself up for it, and so he jumped right in, all on horseback. I think that was grand. I should like to have done that," said little Mara, her eyes blazing out with a kind of starry light which they had when she was excited.

"And how would you have liked it, if you had been a Roman girl, and Moses were Quintus Curtius? would you like to have him give himself up for the good of the country?"

"Oh, no, no!" said Mara, instinctively shuddering.

"Don't you think it would be very grand of him?"

"Oh, yes, sir."

"And should n't we wish our friends to do what is brave and grand?"

"Yes, sir; but then," she added, "it would be so dreadful *never* to see him any more," and a large tear rolled from the great soft eyes and fell on the minister's hand.

"Come, come," thought Mr. Sewell, "this sort of experimenting is too bad—too much nerve here, too much solitude, too much pine-whispering and sea-dashing are going to the making up of this little piece of workmanship."

"Tell me," he said, motioning Moses to sit by him, "how *you* like the Roman history."

"I like it first-rate," said Moses. "The Romans were such smashers, and beat everybody; nobody could stand against them; and I like Alexander, too—I think he was splendid."

"True boy," said Mr. Sewell to himself, "unreflecting brother of the wind and the sea, and all that is vigorous and active—no precocious development of the moral here."

"Now you have come," said Mr. Sewell, "I will lend you another book."

"Thank you, sir; I love to read them when I 'm at home—it 's so still here. I should be dull if I did n't."

Mara's eyes looked eagerly attentive. Mr. Sewell noticed their hungry look when a book was spoken of.

"And you must read it, too, my little girl," he said.

"Thank you, sir," said Mara; "I always want to read everything Moses does."

"What book is it?" said Moses.

"It is called Plutarch's 'Lives,'" said the minister; "it has more particular accounts of the men you read about in history."

"Are there any lives of women?" said Mara.

"No, my dear," said Mr. Sewell; "in the old times, women did not get their lives written, though I don't doubt many of them were much better worth writing than the men's."

"I should like to be a great general," said Moses, with a toss of his head.

"The way to be great lies through books, now, and not through battles," said the minister; "there is more done with pens than swords; so, if you want to do anything, you must read and study."

"Do you think of giving this boy a liberal education?" said Mr. Sewell some time later in the evening, after Moses and Mara were gone to bed.

"Depends on the boy," said Zephaniah. "I 've been up to Brunswick, and seen the fellows there in the college. With a good many of 'em, going to college seems to be just nothing but a sort of ceremony; they go because they 're sent, and don't learn anything more 'n they can help. That 's what I call waste of time and money."

"But don't you think Moses shows some taste for reading and study?"

"Pretty well, pretty well!" said Zephaniah; "jist keep him a little hungry; not let him get all he wants, you see, and he 'll bite the sharper. If I want to catch cod, I don't begin with flingin' over a barrel o' bait. So with the boys, jist bait 'em with a book here and a book there, and kind o' let 'em feel their own way, and then, if nothin' will do but a fellow must go to college, give in to him—that 'd be *my* way."

"And a very good one, too!" said Mr. Sewell. "I 'll see if I can't bait my hook, so as to make Moses take after Latin this winter. I shall have plenty of time to teach him."

"Now, there 's Mara!" said the Captain, his face becoming phosphorescent with a sort of mild radiance of pleasure as it usually was when he spoke of her; "she 's real sharp set after books; she 's ready to fly out of her little skin at the sight of one."

"That child thinks too much, and feels too much, and knows too much for her years!" said Mr. Sewell. "If she were a boy, and you would take her away cod-fishing, as you have Moses, the sea-winds would blow away some of the thinking, and her little body would grow stout, and her mind less delicate and sensitive. But she 's a woman," he said, with a sigh, "and they are all alike. We can't do much for them, but let them come up as they will and make the best of it."

XVI

THE NATURAL
AND THE SPIRITUAL

"Emily," said Mr. Sewell, "did you ever take much notice of that little Mara Lincoln?"

"No, brother; why?"

"Because I think her a very uncommon child."

"She is a pretty little creature," said Miss Emily, "but that is all I know; modest—blushing to her eyes when a stranger speaks to her."

"She has wonderful eyes," said Mr. Sewell; "when she gets excited, they grow so large and so bright, it seems almost unnatural."

"Dear me! has she?" said Miss Emily, in a tone of one who had been called upon to do something about it. "Well?" she added, inquiringly.

"That little thing is only seven years old," said Mr. Sewell; "and she is thinking and feeling herself all into mere spirit—brain and nerves all active, and her little body so frail. She reads incessantly, and thinks over and over what she reads."

"Well?" said Miss Emily, winding very swiftly on a skein of black silk, and giving a little twitch, every now and then, to a knot to make it subservient.

It was commonly the way when Mr. Sewell began to talk with Miss Emily, that she constantly answered him with the manner of one who expects some immediate, practical proposition to flow from every train of thought. Now Mr. Sewell was one of the reflecting kind of men, whose thoughts have a thousand meandering paths, that lead nowhere in particular. His sister's brisk little "Well's?" and "Ah's!" and "Indeed's!" were sometimes the least bit in the world annoying.

"What is to be done?" said Miss Emily; "shall we speak to Mrs. Pennel?"

"Mrs. Pennel would know nothing about her."

"How strangely you talk!—who should, if she does n't?"

"I mean, she would n't understand the dangers of her case."

"Dangers! Do you think she has any disease? She seems to be a healthy child enough, I 'm sure. She has a lovely color in her cheeks."

Mr. Sewell seemed suddenly to become immersed in a book he was reading.

"There now," said Miss Emily, with a little tone of pique, "that 's the way you always do. You begin to talk with me, and just as I get interested in the conversation, you take up a book. It 's too bad."

"Emily," said Mr. Sewell, laying down his book, "I think I shall begin to give Moses Pennel Latin lessons this winter."

"Why, what do you undertake that for?" said Miss Emily. "You have enough to do without that, I 'm sure."

"He is an uncommonly bright boy, and he interests me."

"Now, brother, you need n't tell me; there is some mystery about the interest you take in that child, *you know* there is."

"I am fond of children," said Mr. Sewell, dryly.

"Well, but you don't take as much interest in other boys. I never heard of your teaching any of them Latin before."

"Well, Emily, he is an uncommonly interesting child, and the providential circumstances under which he came into our neighborhood"—

"Providential fiddlesticks!" said Miss Emily, with heightened color. "*I* believe you knew that boy's mother."

This sudden thrust brought a vivid color into Mr. Sewell's cheeks. To be interrupted so unceremoniously, in the midst of so very proper and ministerial a remark, was rather provoking, and he answered, with some asperity,—

"And suppose I had, Emily, and supposing there were any painful subject connected with this past event, you might have sufficient forbearance not to try to make me speak on what I do not wish to talk of."

Mr. Sewell was one of your gentle, dignified men, from whom Heaven deliver an inquisitive female friend! If such people would only get angry, and blow some unbecoming blast, one might make something of them; but speaking, as they always do, from the serene heights of immaculate propriety, one gets in the wrong before one knows it, and has nothing for it but to beg pardon. Miss Emily had, however, a feminine resource: she began to cry—wisely confining herself to the simple eloquence of tears and sobs. Mr. Sewell sat as awkwardly as if he had trodden on a kitten's toe, or brushed down a china cup, feeling as if he were a great, horrid, clumsy boor, and his poor little sister a martyr.

"Come, Emily," he said, in a softer tone, when the sobs subsided a little.

But Emily did n't "come," but went at it with a fresh burst. Mr. Sewell had a vision like that which drowning men are said to have, in which all Miss Emily's sisterly devotions, stocking-darnings, account-keepings, nursings and tendings, and infinite self-sacrifices, rose up before him: and there she was—crying!

"I 'm sorry I spoke harshly, Emily. Come, come; that 's a good girl."

"I 'm a silly fool," said Miss Emily, lifting her head, and wiping the tears from her merry little eyes, as she went on winding her silk.

"Perhaps he will tell me now," she thought, as she wound.

But he did n't.

"What I was going to say, Emily," said her brother, "was, that I thought it would be a good plan for little Mara to come sometimes with Moses; and then, by observing her more particularly, you might be of use to her; her little, active mind needs good practical guidance like yours."

Mr. Sewell spoke in a gentle, flattering tone, and Miss Emily was flattered; but she soon saw that she had gained nothing by the whole breeze, except a little kind of dread, which made her inwardly resolve never to touch the knocker of his fortress again. But she entered into her brother's scheme with the facile alacrity with which she usually seconded any schemes of his proposing.

"I might teach her painting and embroidery," said Miss Emily, glancing, with a satisfied air, at a framed piece of her own work which hung over the mantelpiece, revealing the state of the fine arts in this country, as exhibited in the performances of well-instructed young ladies of that period. Miss Emily had performed it under the tuition of a celebrated teacher of female accomplishments. It represented a white marble obelisk, which an inscription, in legible India ink letters, stated to be "Sacred to the memory of Theophilus Sewell," etc. This obelisk stood in the midst of a ground made very green by an embroidery of different shades of chenille and silk, and was overshadowed by an embroidered weeping-willow. Leaning on it, with her face concealed in a plentiful flow of white handkerchief, was a female figure in deep mourning, designed to represent the desolate widow. A young girl, in a very black dress, knelt in front of it, and a very lugubrious-looking young man, standing bolt upright on the other side, seemed to hold in his hand one end of a wreath of roses, which the girl was presenting, as an appropriate decoration for the tomb. The girl and gentleman were, of course, the young Theophilus and Miss Emily, and the appalling grief conveyed by the expression of their faces was a triumph of the pictorial art.

Miss Emily had in her bedroom a similar funeral trophy, sacred to the memory of her deceased mother,—besides which there were, framed and glazed, in the little sitting-room, two embroidered shepherdesses standing with rueful faces, in charge of certain animals of an uncertain breed between sheep and pigs. The poor little soul had mentally resolved to make Mara the heiress of all the skill and knowledge of the arts by which she had been enabled to consummate these marvels.

"She is naturally a lady-like little thing," she said to herself, "and if I know anything of accomplishments, she shall have them."

Just about the time that Miss Emily came to this resolution, had she been clairvoyant, she might have seen Mara sitting very quietly, busy in the solitude of her own room with a little sprig of partridge-berry before her, whose round green leaves and brilliant scarlet berries she had been for hours trying to imitate, as appeared from the scattered sketches and fragments around her. In fact, before Zephaniah started on his spring fishing, he had caught her one day very busy at work of the same kind, with bits of charcoal, and some colors compounded out of wild berries; and so out of his capacious pocket, after his return, he drew a little box of water-colors and a lead-pencil and square of India-rubber, which he had bought for her in Portland on his way home.

Hour after hour the child works, so still, so fervent, so

earnest,—going over and over, time after time, her simple, ignorant methods to make it "look like," and stopping, at times,
to give the true artist's sigh, as the little green and scarlet fragment lies there hopelessly, unapproachably perfect. Ignorantly
to herself, the hands of the little pilgrim are knocking at the
very door where Giotto and Cimabue knocked in the innocent
child-life of Italian art.

"Why won't it look round?" she said to Moses, who had come
in behind her.

"Why, Mara, did you do these?" said Moses, astonished;
"why, how well they are done! I should know in a minute what
they were meant for."

Mara flushed up at being praised by Moses, but heaved a
deep sigh as she looked back.

"It 's so pretty, that sprig," she said; "if I only could make it
just like"—

"Why, nobody expects *that*," said Moses, "it 's like enough, if
people only know what you mean it for. But come, now, get
your bonnet, and come with me in the boat. Captain Kittridge
has just brought down our new one, and I 'm going to take you
over to Eagle Island, and we 'll take our dinner and stay all day;
mother says so."

"Oh, how nice!" said the little girl, running cheerfully for her
sun-bonnet.

At the house-door they met Mrs. Pennel, with a little closely
covered tin pail.

"Here 's your dinner, children; and, Moses, mind and take
good care of her."

"Never fear *me*, mother, I 've been to the Banks; there was n't
a man there could manage a boat better than I could."

"Yes, grandmother," said Mara, "you ought to see how strong
his arms are; I believe he will be like Samson one of these days if
he keeps on."

So away they went. It was a glorious August forenoon, and the sombre spruces and shaggy hemlocks that dipped and rippled in the waters were penetrated to their deepest recesses with the clear brilliancy of the sky,—a true northern sky, without a cloud, without even a softening haze, defining every outline, revealing every minute point, cutting with sharp decision the form of every promontory and rock, and distant island.

The blue of the sea and the blue of the sky were so much the same, that when the children had rowed far out, the little boat seemed to float midway, poised in the centre of an azure sphere, with a firmament above and a firmament below. Mara leaned dreamily over the side of the boat, and drew her little hands through the waters as they rippled along to the swift oars' strokes, and she saw as the waves broke, and divided and shivered around the boat, a hundred little faces, with brown eyes and golden hair, gleaming up through the water, and dancing away over rippling waves, and thought that so the sea-nymphs might look who came up from the coral caves when they ring the knell of drowned people. Moses sat opposite to her, with his coat off, and his heavy black curls more wavy and glossy than ever, as the exercise made them damp with perspiration.

Eagle Island lay on the blue sea, a tangled thicket of evergreens,—white pine, spruce, arbor vitæ, and fragrant silver firs. A little strip of white beach bound it, like a silver setting to a gem. And there Moses at length moored his boat, and the children landed. The island was wholly solitary, and there is something to children quite delightful in feeling that they have a little lonely world all to themselves. Childhood is itself such an enchanted island, separated by mysterious depths from the mainland of nature, life, and reality.

Moses had subsided a little from the glorious heights on which he seemed to be in the first flush of his return, and he and Mara, in consequence, were the friends of old time. It is true he thought himself quite a man, but the manhood of a boy is only a tiny masquerade,—a fantastic, dreamy prevision of real manhood. It was curious that Mara, who was by all odds the most precociously developed of the two, never thought of asserting herself a woman; in fact, she seldom thought of herself at all, but dreamed and pondered of almost everything else.

"I declare," said Moses, looking up into a thick-branched, rugged old hemlock, which stood all shaggy, with heavy beards of gray moss drooping from its branches, "there 's an eagle's nest up there; I mean to go and see." And up he went into the gloomy embrace of the old tree, crackling the dead branches, wrenching off handfuls of gray moss, rising higher and higher, every once in a while turning and showing to Mara his glowing face and curly hair through a dusky green frame of boughs, and then mounting again. "I'm coming to it," he kept exclaiming.

Meanwhile his proceedings seemed to create a sensation among the feathered house-keepers, one of whom rose and sailed screaming away into the air. In a moment after there was a swoop of wings, and two eagles returned and began flapping and screaming about the head of the boy.

Mara, who stood at the foot of the tree, could not see clearly what was going on, for the thickness of the boughs; she only heard a great commotion and rattling of the branches, the scream of the birds, and the swooping of their wings, and Moses's valorous exclamations, as he seemed to be laying about him with a branch which he had broken off.

At last he descended victorious, with the eggs in his pocket. Mara stood at the foot of the tree, with her sun-bonnet blown back, her hair streaming, and her little arms upstretched, as if to catch him if he fell.

"Oh, I was so afraid!" she said, as he set foot on the ground.

"Afraid? Pooh! Who 's afraid? Why, you might know the old eagles could n't beat me."

"Ah, well, I know how strong you are; but, you know, I could n't help it. But the poor birds,—do hear 'em scream. Moses, don't you suppose they feel bad?"

"No, they 're only mad, to think they could n't beat me. I beat them just as the Romans used to beat folks,—I played their nest was a city, and I spoiled it."

"I should n't want to spoil cities!" said Mara.

"That 's 'cause you are a girl,—I 'm a man, and men always like war; I 've taken one city this afternoon, and mean to take a great many more."

"But, Moses, do you think war is right?"

"Right? why, yes, to be sure; if it ain't, it 's a pity; for it 's all that has ever been done in this world. In the Bible, or out, certainly it 's right. I wish I had a gun now, I 'd stop those old eagles' screeching."

"But, Moses, we should n't want any one to come and steal all our things, and then shoot us."

"How long you do think about things!" said Moses, impatient at her pertinacity. "I am older than you, and when I tell you a thing 's right, you ought to believe it. Besides, don't you take hens' eggs every day, in the barn? How do you suppose the hens like that?"

This was a home-thrust, and for the moment threw the little casuist off the track. She carefully folded up the idea, and laid it away on the inner shelves of her mind till she could think more about it. Pliable as she was to all outward appearances, the child had her own still, interior world, where all her little notions and opinions stood up crisp and fresh, like flowers that grow in cool, shady places. If anybody too rudely assailed a thought or suggestion she put forth, she drew it back again into this quiet inner chamber, and went on. Reader, there are some women of this habit; and there is no independence and pertinacity of opinion like that of these seemingly soft, quiet creatures, whom it is so easy to silence, and so difficult to convince. Mara, little and unformed as she yet was, belonged to the race of those spirits to whom is deputed the office of the angel in the Apocalypse, to whom was given the golden rod which measured the New Jerusalem. Infant though she was, she had ever in her hands that invisible measuring-rod, which she was laying to the foundations of all actions and thoughts. There may, perhaps, come a time when the saucy boy, who now steps so superbly, and predominates so proudly in virtue of his physical strength and daring, will learn to tremble at the golden measuring-rod, held in the hand of a woman.

"Howbeit, that is not first which is spiritual, but that which is natural." Moses is the type of the first unreflecting stage of development, in which are only the out-reachings of active faculties, the aspirations that tend toward manly accomplishments. Seldom do we meet sensitiveness of conscience or discriminating reflection as the indigenous growth of a very vigorous physical development. Your true healthy boy has the breezy, hearty virtues of a Newfoundland dog, the wild fullness of life of the young race-colt. Sentiment, sensibility, delicate perceptions, spiritual aspirations, are plants of later growth.

But there are, both of men and women, beings born into this world in whom from childhood the spiritual and the reflective predominate over the physical. In relation to other human beings, they seem to be organized much as birds are in relation to other animals. They are the artists, the poets, the unconscious seers, to whom the purer truths of spiritual instruction are open. Surveying man merely as an animal, these sensitively organized beings, with their feebler physical powers, are imperfect specimens of life. Looking from the spiritual side, they seem to have a noble strength, a divine force. The types of this latter class are more commonly among women than among men. Multitudes of them pass away in earlier years, and leave behind in many hearts the anxious wonder, why they came so fair only to mock the love they kindled. They who live to maturity are the priests and priestesses of the spiritual life, ordained of God to keep the balance between the rude but absolute necessities of physical life and the higher sphere to which that must at length give place.

XVII

LESSONS

Moses felt elevated some inches in the world by the gift of a new Latin grammar, which had been bought for him in Brunswick. It was a step upward in life; no graduate from a college ever felt more ennobled.

"Wal', now, I tell ye, Moses Pennel," said Miss Roxy, who, with her press-board and big flat-iron, was making her autumn sojourn in the brown house, "I tell ye Latin ain't just what you think 't is, steppin' round so crank; you must remember what the king of Israel said to Benhadad, king of Syria."

"I don't remember; what did he say?"

"I remember," said the soft voice of Mara; "he said, 'Let not him that putteth on the harness boast as him that putteth it off.'"

"Good for you, Mara," said Miss Roxy; "if some other folks read their Bibles as much as you do, they 'd know more."

Between Moses and Miss Roxy there had always been a state of sub-acute warfare since the days of his first arrival, she regarding him as an unhopeful interloper, and he regarding her as a grim-visaged, interfering gnome, whom he dis-

liked with all the intense, unreasoning antipathy of childhood.

"I hate that old woman," he said to Mara, as he flung out of
the door.

"Why, Moses, what for?" said Mara, who never could comprehend hating anybody.

"I do hate her, and Aunt Ruey, too. They are two old scratch-
ing cats; they hate me, and I hate them; they 're always trying to
bring me down, and I won't be brought down."

Mara had sufficient instinctive insight into the feminine rôle
in the domestic concert not to adventure a direct argument just
now in favor of her friends, and therefore she proposed that
they should sit down together under a cedar hard by, and look
over the first lesson.

"Miss Emily invited me to go over with you," she said, "and I
should like so much to hear you recite."

Moses thought this very proper, as would any other male person, young or old, who has been habitually admired by any
other female one. He did not doubt that, as in fishing and row-
ing, and all other things he had undertaken as yet, he should
win himself distinguished honors.

"See here," he said; "Mr. Sewell told me I might go as far as I
liked, and I mean to take all the declensions to begin with;
there 's five of 'em, and I shall learn them for the first lesson;
then I shall take the adjectives next, and next the verbs, and so
in a fortnight get into reading."

Mara heaved a sort of sigh. She wished she had been invited
to share this glorious race; but she looked on admiring when
Moses read, in a loud voice, "Penna, pennæ, pennæ, pennam,".
etc.

"There now, I believe I 've got it," he said, handing Mara the
book; and he was perfectly astonished to find that, with the

book withdrawn, he boggled, and blundered, and stumbled ingloriously. In vain Mara softly prompted, and looked at him
with pitiful eyes as he grew red in the face with his efforts to remember.

"Confound it all!" he said, with an angry flush, snatching
back the book; "it's more trouble than it's worth."

Again he began the repetition, saying it very loud and plain;
he said it over and over till his mind wandered far out to sea,
and while his tongue repeated "penna, pennæ," he was counting
the white sails of the fishing-smacks, and thinking of pulling up
codfish at the Banks.

"There now, Mara, try me," he said, and handed her the book
again; "I'm sure I *must* know it now."

But, alas! with the book the sounds glided away; and "penna"
and "pennam" and "pennis" and "pennæ" were confusedly and
indiscriminately mingled. He thought it must be Mara's fault;
she did n't read right, or she told him just as he was going to say
it, or she did n't tell him right; or was he a fool? or had he lost
his senses?

That first declension has been a valley of humiliation to many
a sturdy boy—to many a bright one, too; and often it is, that the
more full of thought and vigor the mind is, the more difficult it
is to narrow it down to the single dry issue of learning those
sounds. Heinrich Heine said the Romans would never have
found time to conquer the world, if they had had to learn their
own language; but that, luckily for them, they were born into
the knowledge of what nouns form their accusatives in "um."

Long before Moses had learned the first declension, Mara
knew it by heart; for her intense anxiety for him, and the eagerness and zeal with which she listened for each termination,
fixed them in her mind. Besides, she was naturally of a more
quiet and scholar-like turn than he,—more intellectually devel-

oped. Moses began to think, before that memorable day was through, that there was some sense in Aunt Roxy's quotation of the saying of the King of Israel, and materially to retrench his expectations as to the time it might take to master the grammar; but still, his pride and will were both committed, and he worked away in this new sort of labor with energy.

It was a fine, frosty November morning, when he rowed Mara across the bay in a little boat to recite his first lesson to Mr. Sewell.

Miss Emily had provided a plate of seed-cake, otherwise called cookies, for the children, as was a kindly custom of old times, when the little people were expected. Miss Emily had a dim idea that she was to do something for Mara in her own department, while Moses was reciting his lesson; and therefore producing a large sampler, displaying every form and variety of marking-stitch, she began questioning the little girl, in a low tone, as to her proficiency in that useful accomplishment.

Presently, however, she discovered that the child was restless and uneasy, and that she answered without knowing what she was saying. The fact was that she was listening, with her whole soul in her eyes, and feeling through all her nerves, every word Moses was saying. She knew all the critical places, where he was likely to go wrong; and when at last, in one place, he gave the wrong termination, she involuntarily called out the right one, starting up and turning towards them. In a moment she blushed deeply, seeing Mr. Sewell and Miss Emily both looking at her with surprise.

"Come here, pussy," said Mr. Sewell, stretching out his hand to her. "Can you say this?"

"I believe I could, sir."

"Well, try it."

She went through without missing a word. Mr. Sewell then,

for curiosity, heard her repeat all the other forms of the lesson. She had them perfectly.

"Very well, my little girl," he said, "have you been studying, too?"

"I heard Moses say them so often," said Mara, in an apologetic manner, "I could n't help learning them."

"Would you like to recite with Moses every day?"

"Oh, yes, sir, so much."

"Well, you shall. It is better for him to have company."

Mara's face brightened, and Miss Emily looked with a puzzled air at her brother.

"So," she said, when the children had gone home, "I thought you wanted me to take Mara under my care. I was going to begin and teach her some marking stitches, and you put her up to studying Latin. I don't understand you."

"Well, Emily, the fact is, the child has a natural turn for study, that no child of her age ought to have; and I have done just as people always will with such children; there 's no sense in it, but I wanted to do it. You can teach her marking and embroidery all the same; it would break her little heart, now, if I were to turn her back."

"I do not see of what use Latin can be to a woman."

"Of what use is embroidery?"

"Why, that is an accomplishment."

"Ah, indeed!" said Mr. Sewell, contemplating the weeping willow and tombstone trophy with a singular expression, which it was lucky for Miss Emily's peace she did not understand. The fact was, that Mr. Sewell had, at one period of his life, had an opportunity of studying and observing minutely some really fine works of art, and the remembrance of them sometimes rose up to his mind, in the presence of the *chefs-d'oeuvre* on which his sister rested with so much complacency. It was a part of his quiet interior store of amusement to look at these bits of Byzantine embroidery round the room, which affected him always with a subtle sense of drollery.

"You see, brother," said Miss Emily, "it is far better for women to be accomplished than learned."

"You are quite right in the main," said Mr. Sewell, "only you must let me have my own way just for once. One can't be consistent always."

So another Latin grammar was bought, and Moses began to feel a secret respect for his little companion, that he had never done before, when he saw how easily she walked through the labyrinths which at first so confused him. Before this, the comparison had been wholly in points where superiority arose from physical daring and vigor; now he became aware of the existence of another kind of strength with which he had not measured himself. Mara's opinion in their mutual studies began to assume a value in his eyes that her opinions on other subjects had never done, and she saw and felt, with a secret gratification, that she was becoming more to him through their mutual pursuit. To say the truth, it required this fellowship to inspire Moses with the patience and perseverance necessary for this species of acquisition. His active, daring temperament little inclined him to patient, quiet study. For anything that could be done by two hands, he was always ready; but to hold hands still and work silently in the inner forces was to him a species of undertaking that seemed against his very nature; but then he would do it—he would not disgrace himself before Mr. Sewell, and let a girl younger than himself outdo him.

But the thing, after all, that absorbed more of Moses's thoughts than all his lessons was the building and rigging of a small schooner, at which he worked assiduously in all his leisure moments. He had dozens of blocks of wood, into which he had cut anchor moulds; and the melting of lead, the running and shaping of anchors, the whittling of masts and spars took up many an hour. Mara entered into all these things readily, and was too happy to make herself useful in hemming the sails.

When the schooner was finished, they built some ways down by the sea, and invited Sally Kittridge over to see it launched.

"There!" he said, when the little thing skimmed down prosperously into the sea and floated gayly on the waters, "when I 'm a man, I 'll have a big ship; I 'll build her, and launch her, and command her, all myself; and I 'll give you and Sally both a passage in it, and we 'll go off to the East Indies—we 'll sail round the world!"

None of the three doubted the feasibility of this scheme; the little vessel they had just launched seemed the visible prophecy of such a future; and how pleasant it would be to sail off, with the world all before them, and winds ready to blow them to any port they might wish!

The three children arranged some bread and cheese and doughnuts on a rock on the shore, to represent the collation that was usually spread in those parts at a ship launch, and felt quite like grown people—acting life beforehand in that sort of shadowy pantomime which so delights little people. Happy, happy days—when ships can be made with a jack-knife and anchors run in pine blocks, and three children together can launch a schooner, and the voyage of the world can all be made in one sunny Saturday afternoon!

"Mother says you are going to college," said Sally to Moses.

"Not I, indeed," said Moses; "as soon as I get old enough, I 'm going up to Umbagog among the lumberers, and I 'm going to cut real, splendid timber for my ship, and I 'm going to get it on the stocks, and have it built to suit myself."

"What will you call her?" said Sally.

"I have n't thought of that," said Moses.

"Call her the Ariel," said Mara.

"What! after the spirit you were telling us about?" said Sally.

"Ariel is a pretty name," said Moses. "But what is that about a spirit?"

"Why," said Sally, "Mara read us a story about a ship that was wrecked, and a spirit called Ariel, that sang a song about the drowned mariners."

Mara gave a shy, apprehensive glance at Moses, to see if this allusion called up any painful recollections.

No; instead of this, he was following the motions of his little schooner on the waters with the briskest and most unconcerned air in the world.

"Why did n't you ever show me that story, Mara?" said Moses.

Mara colored and hesitated; the real reason she dared not say.

"Why, she read it to father and me down by the cove," said Sally, "the afternoon that you came home from the Banks; I remember how we saw you coming in; don't you, Mara?"

"What have you done with it?" said Moses.

"I 've got it at home," said Mara, in a faint voice; "I 'll show it to you, if you want to see it; there are such beautiful things in it."

That evening, as Moses sat busy, making some alterations in his darling schooner, Mara produced her treasure, and read and explained to him the story. He listened with interest, though without any of the extreme feeling which Mara had thought possible, and even interrupted her once in the middle of the celebrated—

"Full fathom five thy father lies,"

by asking her to hold up the mast a minute, while he drove in a peg to make it rake a little more. He was, evidently, thinking of no drowned father, and dreaming of no possible sea-caves, but acutely busy in fashioning a present reality; and yet he liked to hear Mara read, and, when she had done, told her that he thought it was a pretty—quite a pretty story, with such a total absence of recognition that the story had any affinities with his own history, that Mara was quite astonished.

She lay and thought about him hours, that night, after she had gone to bed; and he lay and thought about a new way of disposing a pulley for raising a sail, which he determined to try the effect of early in the morning.

What was the absolute truth in regard to the boy? Had he forgotten the scenes of his early life, the strange catastrophe that cast him into his present circumstances? To this we answer that all the efforts of Nature, during the early years of a healthy childhood, are bent on effacing and obliterating painful impressions, wiping out from each day the sorrows of the last, as the daily tide effaces the furrows on the seashore. The child that broods, day after day, over some fixed idea, is so far forth not a healthy one. It is Nature's way to make first a healthy animal, and then develop in it gradually higher faculties. We have seen our two children unequally matched hitherto, because unequally developed. There will come a time, by and by in the history of the boy, when the haze of dreamy curiosity will steam up likewise from his mind, and vague yearnings, and questionings, and longings possess and trouble him, but it must be some years hence.

⁂

Here for a season we leave both our child friends, and when ten years have passed over their heads,—when Moses shall be twenty, and Mara seventeen,—we will return again to tell their story, for then there will be one to tell. Let us suppose in the interval, how Moses and Mara read Virgil with the minister, and

how Mara works a shepherdess with Miss Emily, which aston-
ishes the neighborhood,—but how by herself she learns, after
divers trials, to paint partridge, and checkerberry, and trailing
arbutus,—how Moses makes better and better ships, and Sally
grows up a handsome girl, and goes up to Brunswick to the high
school,—how Captain Kittridge tells stories, and Miss Roxy
and Miss Ruey nurse and cut and make and mend for the still
rising generation,—how there are quiltings and tea-drinkings
and prayer meetings and Sunday sermons,—how Zephaniah
and Mary Pennel grow old gradually and graciously, as the sun
rises and sets, and the eternal silver tide rises and falls around
our little gem, Orr's Island.

XVIII

SALLY

"Now, where 's Sally Kittridge! There 's the clock striking five, and nobody to set the table. Sally, I say! Sally!"

"Why, Mis' Kittridge," said the Captain, "Sally 's gone out more 'n an hour ago, and I expect she 's gone down to Pennel's to see Mara; 'cause, you know, she come home from Portland to-day."

"Well, if she 's come home, I s'pose I may as well give up havin' any good of Sally, for that girl fairly bows down to Mara Lincoln and worships her."

"Well, good reason," said the Captain. "There ain't a puttier creature breathin'. I 'm a'most a mind to worship her myself."

"Captain Kittridge, you ought to be ashamed of yourself, at your age, talking as you do."

"Why, laws, mother, I don't feel my age," said the frisky Captain, giving a sort of skip. "It don't seem more 'n yesterday since you and I was a-courtin', Polly. What a life you did lead me in them days! I think you kep' me on the anxious seat a pretty middlin' spell."

"I do wish you would n't talk so. You ought to be ashamed to be triflin' round as you do. Come, now, can't you jest tramp over to Pennel's and tell Sally I want her?"

"Not I, mother. There ain't but two gals in two miles square here, and I ain't a-goin' to be the feller to shoo 'em apart. What 's the use of bein' gals, and young, and putty, if they can't get together and talk about their new gownds and the fellers? That ar 's what gals is for."

"I do wish you would n't talk in that way before Sally, father, for her head is full of all sorts of vanity now; and as to Mara, I never did see a more slack-twisted, flimsy thing than she 's grown up to be. Now Sally 's learnt to do something, thanks to me. She can brew, and she can make bread and cake and pickles, and spin, and cut, and make. But as to Mara, what does she do? Why, she paints pictur's. Mis' Pennel was a-showin' on me a blue-jay she painted, and I was a-thinkin' whether she could brile a bird fit to be eat if she tried; and she don't know the price of nothin'," continued Mrs. Kittridge, with wasteful profusion of negatives.

"Well," said the Captain, "the Lord makes some things jist to be looked at. Their work is to be putty, and that ar 's Mara's sphere. It never seemed to me she was cut out for hard work; but she 's got sweet ways and kind words for everybody, and it 's as good as a psalm to look at her."

"And what sort of a wife 'll she make, Captain Kittridge?"

"A real sweet, putty one," said the Captain, persistently.

"Well, as to beauty, I 'd rather have our Sally any day," said Mrs. Kittridge; "and she looks strong and hearty, and seems to be good for use."

"So she is, so she is," said the Captain, with fatherly pride. "Sally 's the very image of her ma at her age—black eyes, black hair, tall and trim as a spruce-tree, and steps off as if she had springs in her heels. I tell you, the feller 'll have to be spry that catches her. There 's two or three of 'em at it, I see; but Sally won't have nothin' to say to 'em. I hope she won't, yet awhile."

"Sally is a girl that has as good an eddication as money can give," said Mrs. Kittridge. "If I 'd a-had her advantages at her age, I should a-been a great deal more 'n I am. But we ha'n't spared nothin' for Sally; and when nothin' would do but Mara must be sent to Miss Plucher's school over in Portland, why, I sent Sally too—for all she 's our seventh child, and Pennel has n't but the one."

"You forget Moses," said the Captain.

"Well, he 's settin' up on his own account, I guess. They did talk o' giving him college eddication; but he was so unstiddy, there were n't no use in trying. A real wild ass's colt he was."

"Wal', wal', Moses was in the right on 't. He took the cross-lot track into life," said the Captain. "Colleges is well enough for your smooth, straight-grained lumber, for gen'ral buildin'; but come to fellers that 's got knots, and streaks, and cross-grains, like Moses Pennel, and the best way is to let 'em eddicate 'emselves, as he 's a-doin'. He 's cut out for the sea, plain enough, and he 'd better be up to Umbagog, cuttin' timber for his ship, than havin' rows with tutors, and blowin' the roof off the colleges, as one o' them 'ere kind o' fellers is apt to when he don't have work to use up his steam. Why, mother, there 's more gas got up in them Brunswick buildin's, from young men that are spilin' for hard work, than you could shake a stick at! But Mis' Pennel told me yesterday she was 'spectin' Moses home to-day."

"Oho! that 's at the bottom of Sally 's bein' up there," said Mrs. Kittridge.

"Mis' Kittridge," said the Captain, "I take it you ain't the woman as would expect a daughter of your bringin' up to be a-runnin' after any young chap, be he who he may," said the Captain.

Mrs. Kittridge for once was fairly silenced by this home-
thrust; nevertheless, she did not the less think it quite possible,
from all that she knew of Sally; for although that young lady
professed great hardness of heart and contempt for all the
young male generation of her acquaintance, yet she had evidently a turn for observing their ways—probably purely in the
way of philosophical inquiry.

XIX

EIGHTEEN

In fact, at this very moment our scene-shifter changes the picture. Away rolls the image of Mrs. Kittridge's kitchen, with its sanded floor, its scoured rows of bright pewter platters, its great, deep fireplace, with wide stone hearth, its little looking-glass with a bit of asparagus bush, like a green mist, over it. *Exeunt* the image of Mrs. Kittridge, with her hands floury from the bread she has been moulding, and the dry, ropy, lean Captain, who has been sitting tilting back in a splint-bottomed chair,— and the next scene comes rolling in. It is a chamber in the house of Zephaniah Pennel, whose windows present a blue panorama of sea and sky. Through two windows you look forth into the blue belt of Harpswell Bay, bordered on the farther edge by Harpswell Neck, dotted here and there with houses, among which rises the little white meeting-house, like a mother-bird among a flock of chickens. The third window, on the other side of the room, looks far out to sea, where only a group of low, rocky islands interrupts the clear sweep of the horizon line, with its blue infinitude of distance.

The furniture of this room, though of the barest and most frigid simplicity, is yet relieved by many of those touches of taste and fancy which the indwelling of a person of sensibility and imagination will shed off upon the physical surroundings. The bed was draped with a white spread, embroidered with a kind of knotted tracery, the working of which was considered among the female accomplishments of those days, and over the head of it was a painting of a bunch of crimson and white trillium, executed with a fidelity to Nature that showed the most delicate gifts of observation. Over the mantel-piece hung a painting of the Bay of Genoa, which had accidentally found a voyage home in Zephaniah Pennel's sea-chest, and which skillful fingers had surrounded with a frame curiously wrought of moss and sea-shells. Two vases of India china stood on the mantel, filled with spring flowers, crowfoot, anemones, and liverwort, with drooping bells of the twin-flower. The looking-glass that hung over the table in one corner of the room was fancifully webbed with long, drooping festoons of that gray moss which hangs in such graceful wreaths from the boughs of the pines in the deep forest shadows of Orr's Island. On the table below was a collection of books: a whole set of Shakespeare which Zephaniah Pennel had bought of a Portland bookseller; a selection, in prose and verse, from the best classic writers, presented to Mara Lincoln, the fly-leaf said, by her sincere friend, Theophilus Sewell; a Virgil, much thumbed, with an old, worn cover, which, however, some adroit fingers had concealed under a coating of delicately marbled paper;—there was a Latin dictionary, a set of Plutarch's Lives, the Mysteries of Udolpho, and Sir Charles Grandison, together with Edwards on the Affections, and Boston's Fourfold State;—there was an inkstand, curiously contrived from a sea-shell, with pens and paper in that phase of arrangement which betokened frequency of use; and, lastly, a little work-basket, containing a long strip of curious and delicate embroidery, in which the needle yet hanging showed that the work was in progress.

By a table at the sea-looking window sits our little Mara, now grown to the maturity of eighteen summers, but retaining still unmistakable signs of identity with the little golden-haired, dreamy, excitable, fanciful "Pearl" of Orr's Island.

She is not quite of a middle height, with something beautiful and childlike about the moulding of her delicate form. We still see those sad, wistful, hazel eyes, over which the lids droop with a dreamy languor, and whose dark lustre contrasts singularly with the golden hue of the abundant hair which waves in a thousand rippling undulations around her face. The impression she produces is not that of paleness, though there is no color in her cheek, but her complexion has everywhere that delicate pink tinting which one sees in healthy infants, and with the least emotion brightens into a fluttering bloom. Such a bloom is on her cheek at this moment, as she is working away, copying a bunch of scarlet rock-columbine which is in a wine-glass of water before her; every few moments stopping and holding her work at a distance, to contemplate its effect. At this moment there steps behind her chair a tall, lithe figure, a face with a rich Spanish complexion, large black eyes, glowing cheeks, marked eyebrows, and lustrous black hair arranged in shining braids around her head. It is our old friend, Sally Kittridge, whom common fame calls the handsomest girl of all the region round Harpswell, Macquoit, and Orr's Island. In truth, a wholesome, ruddy, blooming creature she was, the sight of whom cheered and warmed one like a good fire in December; and she seemed to have enough and to spare of the warmest gifts of vitality and joyous animal life. She had a well-formed mouth, but rather large, and a frank laugh which showed all her teeth sound—and a fortunate sight it was, considering that they were white and even as pearls; and the hand that she laid upon Mara's at this moment, though twice as large as that of the little artist, was yet in harmony with her vigorous, finely developed figure.

"Mara Lincoln," she said, "you are a witch, a perfect little witch, at painting. How you can make things look so like, I don't see. Now, I could paint the things we painted at Miss Plucher's; but then, dear me! they did n't look at all like flowers. One needed to write under them what they were made for."

"Does this look like to you, Sally?" said Mara. "I wish it would to me. Just see what a beautiful clear color that flower is. All I can do, I can't make one like it. My scarlet and yellows sink dead into the paper."

"Why, I think your flowers are wonderful! You are a real genius, that 's what you are! I am only a common girl; I can't do things as you can."

"You can do things a thousand times more useful, Sally. I don't pretend to compare with you in the useful arts, and I am only a bungler in ornamental ones. Sally, I feel like a useless little creature. If I could go round as you can, and do business, and make bargains, and push ahead in the world, I should feel that I was good for something; but somehow I can't."

"To be sure you can't," said Sally, laughing. "I should like to see you try it."

"Now," pursued Mara, in a tone of lamentation, "I could no more get into a carriage and drive to Brunswick as you can, than I could fly. I can't drive, Sally—something is the matter with me; and the horses always know it the minute I take the reins; they always twitch their ears and stare round into the chaise at me, as much as to say, 'What! you there?' and I feel sure they never will mind me. And then how you can make those wonderful bargains you do, I can't see!—you talk up to the clerks and the men, and somehow you talk everybody round; but as for me, if I only open my mouth in the humblest way to dispute the price, everybody puts me down. I always tremble when I go into a store, and people talk to me just as if I was a little girl, and once or twice they have made me buy things that I knew I did n't want, just because they will talk me down."

"Oh, Mara, Mara," said Sally, laughing till the tears rolled down her cheeks, "what do *you* ever go a-shopping for?—of course you ought always to send me. Why, look at this dress— real India chintz; do you know I made old Pennywhistle's clerk up in Brunswick give it to me just for the price of common cotton? You see there was a yard of it had got faded by lying in the shop-window, and there were one or two holes and imperfections in it, and you ought to have heard the talk I made! I abused it to right and left, and actually at last I brought the poor wretch to believe that he ought to be grateful to me for taking it off his hands. Well, you see the dress I 've made of it. The imperfections did n't hurt it the least in the world as I managed it,—and the faded breadth makes a good apron, so you see. And just so I got that red spotted flannel dress I wore last winter. It was moth-eaten in one or two places, and I made them let me have it at half-price;—made exactly as good a dress. But after all, Mara, I can't trim a bonnet as you can, and I can't come up to your embroidery, nor your lace-work, nor I can't draw and paint as you can, and I can't sing like you; and then as to all those things you talk with Mr. Sewell about, why they're beyond my depth,—that 's all I 've got to say. Now, you are made to have poetry written to you, and all that kind of thing one reads of in novels. Nobody would ever think of writing poetry to me, now, or sending me flowers and rings, and such things. If a fellow likes me, he gives me a quince, or a big apple; but, then, Mara, there ain't any fellows round here that are fit to speak to."

"I 'm sure, Sally, there always is a train following you everywhere, at singing-school and Thursday lecture."

"Yes—but what do I care for 'em?" said Sally, with a toss of her head. "Why they follow me, I don't see. I don't do anything to make 'em, and I tell 'em all that they tire me to death; and still they will hang round. What is the reason, do you suppose?"

"What can it be?" said Mara, with a quiet kind of arch drollery which suffused her face, as she bent over her painting.

"Well, you know I can't bear fellows — I think they are hateful."

"What! even Tom Hiers?" said Mara, continuing her painting.

"Tom Hiers! Do you suppose I care for him? He would insist on waiting on me round all last winter, taking me over in his boat to Portland, and up in his sleigh to Brunswick; but I did n't care for him."

"Well, there 's Jimmy Wilson, up at Brunswick."

"What! that little snip of a clerk! You don't suppose I care for him, do you? — only he almost runs his head off following me round when I go up there shopping; he 's nothing but a little dressed-up yard-stick! I never saw a fellow yet that I 'd cross the street to have another look at. By the by, Mara, Miss Roxy told me Sunday that Moses was coming down from Umbagog this week."

"Yes, he is," said Mara; "we are looking for him every day."

"You must want to see him. How long is it since you saw him?"

"It is three years," said Mara. "I scarcely know what he is like now. I was visiting in Boston when he came home from his three-years' voyage, and he was gone into the lumbering country when I came back. He seems almost a stranger to me."

"He 's pretty good-looking," said Sally. "I saw him on Sunday when he was here, but he was off on Monday, and never called on old friends. Does he write to you often?"

"Not very," said Mara; "in fact, almost never; and when he does, there is so little in his letters."

"Well, I tell you, Mara, you must not expect fellows to write as girls can. They don't do it. Now, our boys, when they write home, they tell the latitude and longitude, and soil and productions, and such things. But if you or I were only there, don't you think we should find something more to say? Of course we should,—fifty thousand little things that they never think of."

Mara made no reply to this, but went on very intently with her painting. A close observer might have noticed a suppressed sigh that seemed to retreat far down into her heart. Sally did not notice it.

What was in that sigh? It was the sigh of a long, deep, inner history, unwritten and untold—such as are transpiring daily by thousands, and of which we take no heed.

XX

R EBELLION

We have introduced Mara to our readers as she appears in her seventeenth year, at the time when she is expecting the return of Moses as a young man of twenty; but we cannot do justice to the feelings which are roused in her heart by this expectation, without giving a chapter or two to tracing the history of Moses since we left him as a boy commencing the study of the Latin grammar with Mr. Sewell. The reader must see the forces that acted upon his early development, and what they have made of him.

It is common for people who write treatises on education to give forth their rules and theories with a self-satisfied air, as if a human being were a thing to be made up, like a batch of bread, out of a given number of materials combined by an infallible recipe. Take your child, and do thus and so for a given number of years, and he comes out a thoroughly educated individual.

But in fact, education is in many cases nothing more than a blind struggle of parents and guardians with the evolutions of some strong, predetermined character, individual, obstinate, unreceptive, and seeking by an inevitable law of its being to develop itself and gain free expression in its own way. Captain

Kittridge's confidence that he would as soon undertake a boy as a Newfoundland pup, is good for those whose idea of what is to be done for a human being are only what would be done for a dog, namely, give food, shelter, and world-room, and leave each to act out his own nature without let or hindrance.

But everybody takes an embryo human being with some plan of one's own what it shall do or be. The child's future shall shape out some darling purpose or plan, and fulfill some long unfulfilled expectation of the parent. And thus, though the wind of every generation sweeps its hopes and plans like forest-leaves, none are whirled and tossed with more piteous moans than those which come out green and fresh to shade the happy spring-time of the cradle. For the temperaments of children are often as oddly unsuited to parents as if capricious fairies had been filling cradles with changelings.

A meek member of the Peace Society, a tender, devout, poetical clergyman, receives an heir from heaven, and straightway devotes him to the Christian ministry. But lo! the boy proves a young war-horse, neighing for battle, burning for gunpowder and guns, for bowie-knives and revolvers, and for every form and expression of physical force;—he might make a splendid trapper, an energetic sea-captain, a bold, daring military man, but his whole boyhood is full of rebukes and disciplines for sins which are only the blind effort of the creature to express a nature which his parent does not and cannot understand. So again, the son that was to have upheld the old, proud merchant's time-honored firm, that should have been mighty in ledgers and great upon 'Change, breaks his father's heart by an unintelligible fancy for weaving poems and romances. A father of literary aspirations, balked of privileges of early education, bends over the cradle of his son with but one idea. This child shall have the full advantages of regular college-training; and so for years he battles with a boy abhorring study, and fitted only for a life of out-door energy and bold adventure,—on whom Latin forms and Greek quantities fall and melt aimless and useless, as snow-flakes on the hide of a buffalo. Then the secret agonies,—the long years of sorrowful watchings of those gentler nurses of humanity who receive the infant into their bosom out of the void unknown, and strive to read its horoscope through the mists of their prayers and tears!—what perplexities,—what confusion! Especially is this so in a community where the moral and religious sense is so cultivated as in New England, and frail, trembling, self-distrustful mothers are told that the shaping and ordering not only of this present life, but of an immortal destiny, is in their hands.

On the whole, those who succeed best in the rearing of children are the tolerant and easy persons who instinctively follow nature and accept without much inquiry whatever she sends; or that far smaller class, wise to discern spirits and apt to adopt means to their culture and development, who can prudently and carefully train every nature according to its true and characteristic ideal.

Zephaniah Pennel was a shrewd old Yankee, whose instincts taught him from the first, that the waif that had been so mysteriously washed out of the gloom of the sea into his family, was of some different class and lineage from that which might have filled a cradle of his own, and of a nature which he could not perfectly understand. So he prudently watched and waited, only using restraint enough to keep the boy anchored in society, and letting him otherwise grow up in the solitary freedom of his lonely seafaring life.

The boy was from childhood, although singularly attractive, of a moody, fitful, unrestful nature,—eager, earnest, but unsteady,—with varying phases of imprudent frankness and of the most stubborn and unfathomable secretiveness. He was a creature of unreasoning antipathies and attractions. As Zephaniah Pennel said of him, he was as full of hitches as an old bureau drawer. His peculiar beauty, and a certain electrical power of attraction, seemed to form a constant circle of protection and forgiveness around him in the home of his foster-parents; and great as was the anxiety and pain which he often gave them, they somehow never felt the charge of him as a weariness.

We left him a boy beginning Latin with Mr. Sewell in company with the little Mara. This arrangement progressed prosperously for a time, and the good clergyman, all whose ideas of education ran through the halls of a college, began to have hopes of turning out a choice scholar. But when the boy's ship of life came into the breakers of that narrow and intricate channel which divides boyhood from manhood, the difficulties that had always attended his guidance and management wore an intensified form. How much family happiness is wrecked just then and there! How many mothers' and sisters' hearts are broken in the wild and confused tossings and tearings of that stormy transition! A whole new nature is blindly upheaving itself, with cravings and clamorings, which neither the boy himself nor often surrounding friends understand.

A shrewd observer has significantly characterized the period as the time when the boy wishes he were dead, and everybody else wishes so too. The wretched, half-fledged, half-conscious, anomalous creature has all the desires of the man, and none of the rights; has a double and triple share of nervous edge and intensity in every part of his nature, and no definitely perceived objects on which to bestow it,—and, of course, all sorts of unreasonable moods and phases are the result.

One of the most common signs of this period, in some natures, is the love of contradiction and opposition,—a blind desire to go contrary to everything that is commonly received among the older people. The boy disparages the minister, quizzes the deacon, thinks the school-master an ass, and does n't believe in the Bible, and seems to be rather pleased than otherwise with the shock and flutter that all these announcements create among peaceably disposed grown people. No respectable hen that ever hatched out a brood of ducks was more puzzled what to do with them than was poor Mrs. Pennel when her adopted nursling came into this state. Was he a boy? an immortal soul? a reasonable human being? or only a handsome goblin sent to torment her?

"What shall we do with him, father?" said she, one Sunday, to Zephaniah, as he stood shaving before the little looking-glass in their bedroom. "He can't be governed like a child, and he won't govern himself like a man."

Zephaniah stopped and strapped his razor reflectively.

"We must cast out anchor and wait for day," he answered. "Prayer is a long rope with a strong hold."

It was just at this critical period of life that Moses Pennel was drawn into associations which awoke the alarm of all his friends, and from which the characteristic willfulness of his nature made it difficult to attempt to extricate him.

In order that our readers may fully understand this part of our history, we must give some few particulars as to the peculiar scenery of Orr's Island and the state of the country at this time.

The coast of Maine, as we have elsewhere said, is remarkable for a singular interpenetration of the sea with the land, forming amid its dense primeval forests secluded bays, narrow and deep, into which vessels might float with the tide, and where they might nestle unseen and unsuspected amid the dense shadows of the overhanging forest.

At this time there was a very brisk business done all along the coast of Maine in the way of smuggling. Small vessels, lightly built and swift of sail, would run up into these sylvan fastnesses, and there make their deposits and transact their business so as entirely to elude the vigilance of government officers.

It may seem strange that practices of this kind should ever have obtained a strong foothold in a community peculiar for its rigid morality and its orderly submission to law; but in this case, as in many others, contempt of law grew out of weak and unworthy legislation. The celebrated embargo of Jefferson stopped at once the whole trade of New England, and condemned her thousand ships to rot at the wharves, and caused the ruin of thousands of families.

The merchants of the country regarded this as a flagrant, high-handed piece of injustice, expressly designed to cripple New England commerce, and evasions of this unjust law found everywhere a degree of sympathy, even in the breasts of well-disposed and conscientious people. In resistance to the law, vessels were constantly fitted out which ran upon trading voyages to the West Indies and other places; and although the practice was punishable as smuggling, yet it found extensive connivance. From this beginning smuggling of all kinds gradually grew up in the community, and gained such a foothold that even after the repeal of the embargo it still continued to be extensively practiced. Secret depositories of contraband goods still existed in many of the lonely haunts of islands off the coast of Maine. Hid in deep forest shadows, visited only in the darkness of the night, were these illegal stores of merchandise. And from these secluded resorts they found their way, no one knew or cared to say how, into houses for miles around.

There was no doubt that the practice, like all other illegal ones, was demoralizing to the community, and particularly fatal to the character of that class of bold, enterprising young men who would be most likely to be drawn into it.

Zephaniah Pennel, who was made of a kind of straight-grained, uncompromising oaken timber such as built the Mayflower of old, had always borne his testimony at home and abroad against any violations of the laws of the land, however veiled under the pretext of righting a wrong or resisting an injustice, and had done what he could in his neighborhood to enable government officers to detect and break up these unlawful depositories. This exposed him particularly to the hatred and ill-will of the operators concerned in such affairs, and a plot was laid by a few of the most daring and determined of them to establish one of their depositories on Orr's Island, and to implicate the family of Pennel himself in the trade. This would accomplish two purposes, as they hoped,—it would be a mortification and defeat to him,—a revenge which they coveted; and it would, they thought, insure his silence and complicity for the strongest reasons.

The situation and characteristics of Orr's Island peculiarly fitted it for the carrying out of a scheme of this kind, and for this purpose we must try to give our readers a more definite idea of it.

The traveler who wants a ride through scenery of more varied and singular beauty than can ordinarily be found on the shores of any land whatever, should start some fine clear day along the clean sandy road, ribboned with strips of green grass, that leads through the flat pitch-pine forests of Brunswick toward the sea. As he approaches the salt water, a succession of the most beautiful and picturesque lakes seems to be lying softly cradled in the arms of wild, rocky forest shores, whose outlines are ever changing with the windings of the road.

At a distance of about six or eight miles from Brunswick he crosses an arm of the sea, and comes upon the first of the interlacing group of islands which beautifies the shore. A ride across this island is a constant succession of pictures, whose wild and solitary beauty entirely distances all power of description. The magnificence of the evergreen forests,—their peculiar air of sombre stillness,—the rich intermingling ever and anon of groves of birch, beech, and oak, in picturesque knots and tufts, as if set for effect by some skillful landscape-gardner,—produce a sort of strange dreamy wonder; while the sea, breaking forth both on the right hand and the left of the road into the most romantic glimpses, seems to flash and glitter like some strange gem which every moment shows itself through the framework of a new setting. Here and there little secluded coves push in from the sea, around which lie soft tracts of green meadowland, hemmed in and guarded by rocky pine-crowned ridges. In such sheltered spots may be seen neat white houses, nestling like sheltered doves in the beautiful solitude.

When one has ridden nearly to the end of Great Island, which is about four miles across, he sees rising before him, from the sea, a bold romantic point of land, uplifting a crown of rich evergreen and forest trees over shores of perpendicular rock. This is Orr's Island.

It was not an easy matter in the days of our past experience to guide a horse and carriage down the steep, wild shores of Great Island to the long bridge that connects it with Orr's. The sense of wild seclusion reaches here the highest degree; and one crosses the bridge with a feeling as if genii might have built it, and one might be going over it to fairy-land. From the bridge the path rises on to a high granite ridge, which runs from one end of the island to the other, and has been called the Devil's Back, with that superstitious generosity which seems to have abandoned all romantic places to so undeserving an owner.

By the side of this ridge of granite is a deep, narrow chasm, running a mile and a half or two miles parallel with the road, and veiled by the darkest and most solemn shadows of the primeval forest. Here scream the jays and the eagles, and fish-hawks make their nests undisturbed; and the tide rises and falls under black branches of evergreen, from which depend long, light festoons of delicate gray moss. The darkness of the forest is relieved by the delicate foliage and the silvery trunks of the great white birches, which the solitude of centuries has allowed to grow in this spot to a height and size seldom attained else-where.

It was this narrow, rocky cove that had been chosen by the smuggler Atkinson and his accomplices as a safe and secluded resort for their operations. He was a seafaring man of Bath, one of that class who always prefer uncertain and doubtful courses to those which are safe and reputable. He was possessed of many of those traits calculated to make him a hero in the eyes of young men; was dashing, free, and frank in his manners, with a fund of humor and an abundance of ready anecdote which made his society fascinating; but he concealed beneath all these attractions a character of hard, grasping, unscrupulous selfish-ness, and an utter destitution of moral principle.

Moses, now in his sixteenth year, and supposed to be in a general way doing well, under the care of the minister, was left free to come and go at his own pleasure, unwatched by Zepha-niah, whose fishing operations often took him for weeks from home. Atkinson hung about the boy's path, engaging him first in fishing or hunting enterprises; plied him with choice prepa-rations of liquor, with which he would enhance the hilarity of their expeditions; and finally worked on his love of adventure and that impatient restlessness incident to his period of life to draw him fully into his schemes. Moses lost all interest in his lessons, often neglecting them for days at a time—accounting for his negligence by excuses which were far from satisfactory. When Mara would expostulate with him about this, he would break out upon her with a fierce irritation. Was he always going to be tied to a girl's apron-string? He was tired of study, and tired of old Sewell, whom he declared an old granny in a white wig, who knew nothing of the world. He was n't going to college—it was altogether too slow for him—he was going to see life and push ahead for himself.

Mara's life during this time was intensely wearing. A frail, slender, delicate girl of thirteen, she carried a heart prematurely old with the most distressing responsibility of mature life. Her love for Moses had always had in it a large admixture of that maternal and care-taking element which, in some shape or other, qualifies the affection of woman to man. Ever since that dream of babyhood, when the vision of a pale mother had led the beautiful boy to her arms, Mara had accepted him as something exclusively her own, with an intensity of ownership that seemed almost to merge her personal identity with his. She felt, and saw, and enjoyed, and suffered in him, and yet was conscious of a higher nature in herself, by which unwillingly he was often judged and condemned. His faults affected her with a kind of guilty pain, as if they were her own; his sins were borne bleeding in her heart in silence, and with a jealous watchfulness to hide them from every eye but hers. She busied herself day and night interceding and making excuses for him, first to her own sensitive moral nature, and then with everybody around, for with one or another he was coming into constant collision. She felt at this time a fearful load of suspicion, which she dared not express to a human being.

Up to this period she had always been the only confidant of Moses, who poured into her ear without reserve all the good and the evil of his nature, and who loved her with all the intensity with which he was capable of loving anything. Nothing so much shows what a human being is in moral advancement as the quality of his love. Moses Pennel's love was egotistic, exacting, tyrannical, and capricious—sometimes venting itself in expressions of a passionate fondness, which had a savor of protecting generosity in them, and then receding to the icy pole of surly petulance. For all that, there was no resisting the magnetic attraction with which in his amiable moods he drew those whom he liked to himself.

Such people are not very wholesome companions for those who are sensitively organized and predisposed to self-sacrificing love. They keep the heart in a perpetual freeze and thaw, which, like the American northern climate, is so particularly fatal to plants of a delicate habit. They could live through the hot summer and the cold winter, but they cannot endure the three or four months when it freezes one day and melts the next,—when all the buds are started out by a week of genial sunshine, and then frozen for a fortnight. These fitful persons are of all others most engrossing, because you are always sure in their good moods that they are just going to be angels,—an expectation which no number of disappointments seems finally to do away. Mara believed in Moses's future as she did in her own existence. He was going to do something great and good,—that she was certain of. He would be a splendid man! Nobody, she thought, knew him as she did; nobody could know how good and generous he was *sometimes,* and how frankly he would confess his faults, and what noble aspirations he had!

But there was no concealing from her watchful sense that Moses was beginning to have secrets from her. He was cloudy and murky; and at some of the most harmless inquiries in the world, would flash out with a sudden temper, as if she had touched some sore spot. Her bedroom was opposite to his; and she became quite sure that night after night, while she lay thinking of him, she heard him steal down out of the house between two and three o'clock, and not return till a little before day-dawn. Where he went, and with whom, and what he was doing, was to her an awful mystery,—and it was one she dared not share with a human being. If she told her kind old grandfather, she feared that any inquiry from him would only light as a spark on that inflammable spirit of pride and insubordination that was rising within him, and bring on an instantaneous explosion. Mr. Sewell's influence she could hope little more from; and as to poor Mrs. Pennel, such communications would only weary and distress her, without doing any manner of good. There was, therefore, only that one unfailing Confidant—the Invisible Friend to whom the solitary child could pour out her heart, and whose inspirations of comfort and guidance never fail to come again in return to true souls.

One moonlight night, as she lay thus praying, her senses, sharpened by watching, discerned a sound of steps treading under her window, and then a low whistle. Her heart beat violently, and she soon heard the door of Moses's room open, and then the old chamber-stairs gave forth those inconsiderate creaks and snaps that garrulous old stairs always will when anybody is desirous of making them accomplices in a night-secret. Mara rose, and undrawing her curtain, saw three men standing before the house, and saw Moses come out and join them. Quick as thought she threw on her clothes and wrapping her little form in a dark cloak, with a hood, followed them out. She kept at a safe distance behind them,—so far back as just to keep them in sight. They never looked back, and seemed to say but little till they approached the edge of that deep belt of forest which shrouds so large a portion of the island. She hurried along, now nearer to them lest they should be lost to view in the deep shadows, while they went on crackling and plunging through the dense underbrush.

XXI

THE TEMPTER

It was well for Mara that so much of her life had been passed in wild forest rambles. She looked frail as the rays of moonbeam which slid down the old white-bearded hemlocks, but her limbs were agile and supple as steel; and while the party went crashing on before, she followed with such lightness that the slight sound of her movements was entirely lost in the heavy crackling plunges of the party. Her little heart was beating fast and hard; but could any one have seen her face, as it now and then came into a spot of moonshine, they might have seen it fixed in a deadly expression of resolve and determination. She was going after *him*—no matter where; she was resolved to know who and what it was that was leading him away, as her heart told her, to no good. Deeper and deeper into the shadows of the forest they went, and the child easily kept up with them.

Mara had often rambled for whole solitary days in this lonely wood, and knew all its rocks and dells the whole three miles to the long bridge at the other end of the island. But she had never before seen it under the solemn stillness of midnight moonlight, which gives to the most familiar objects such a strange, ghostly charm. After they had gone a mile into the forest, she could see through the black spruces silver gleams of the sea, and hear, amid the whirr and sway of the pine-tops, the dash of the ever restless tide which pushed up the long cove. It was at the full, as she could discern with a rapid glance of her practiced eye, expertly versed in the knowledge of every change of the solitary nature around.

And now the party began to plunge straight down the rocky ledge of the Devil's Back, on which they had been walking hitherto, into the deep ravine where lay the cove. It was a scrambling, precipitous way, over perpendicular walls of rock, whose crevices furnished anchoring-places for grand old hemlocks or silver-birches, and whose rough sides, leathery with black flaps of lichen, were all tangled and interlaced with thick netted bushes. The men plunged down laughing, shouting, and swearing at their occasional missteps, and silently as moonbeam or thistledown the light-footed shadow went down after them.

She suddenly paused behind a pile of rock, as, through an opening between two great spruces, the sea gleamed out like a sheet of looking-glass set in a black frame. And here the child saw a small vessel swinging at anchor, with the moonlight full on its slack sails, and she could hear the gentle gurgle and lick of the green-tongued waves as they dashed under it toward the rocky shore.

Mara stopped with a beating heart as she saw the company making for the schooner. The tide is high; will they go on board and sail away with him where she cannot follow? What could she do? In an ecstasy of fear she kneeled down and asked God not to let him go,—to give her at least one more chance to save him.

For the pure and pious child had heard enough of the words of these men, as she walked behind them, to fill her with horror. She had never before heard an oath, but there came back from these men coarse, brutal tones and words of blasphemy that froze her blood with horror. And Moses was going with them! She felt somehow as if they must be a company of fiends bearing him to his ruin.

For some time she kneeled there watching behind the rock, while Moses and his companions went on board the little schooner. She had no feeling of horror at the loneliness of her own situation, for her solitary life had made every woodland thing dear and familiar to her. She was cowering down on a loose, spongy bed of moss, which was all threaded through and through with the green vines and pale pink blossoms of the mayflower, and she felt its fragrant breath streaming up in the moist moonlight. As she leaned forward to look through a rocky crevice, her arms rested on a bed of that brittle white moss she had often gathered with so much admiration, and a scarlet rock-columbine, such as she loved to paint, brushed her cheek,—and all these mute fair things seemed to strive to keep her company in her chill suspense of watchfulness. Two whip-poorwills, from a clump of silvery birches, kept calling to each other in melancholy iteration, while she stayed there still listening, and knowing by an occasional sound of laughing, or the explosion of some oath, that the men were not yet gone. At last they all appeared again, and came to a cleared place among the dry leaves, quite near to the rock where she was concealed, and kindled a fire which they kept snapping and crackling by a constant supply of green resinous hemlock branches.

The red flame danced and leaped through the green fuel, and leaping upward in tongues of flame, cast ruddy bronze reflections on the old pine-trees with their long branches waving with beards of white moss,—and by the firelight Mara could see two men in sailor's dress with pistols in their belts, and the man Atkinson, whom she had recollected as having seen once or twice at her grandfather's. She remembered how she had always shrunk from him with a strange instinctive dislike, half fear, half disgust, when he had addressed her with that kind of free admiration which men of his class often feel themselves at liberty to express to a pretty girl of her early age. He was a man that might have been handsome, had it not been for a certain strange expression of covert wickedness. It was as if some vile evil spirit, walking, as the Scriptures say, through dry places, had lighted on a comely man's body, in which he had set up housekeeping, making it look like a fair house abused by an unclean owner.

As Mara watched his demeanor with Moses, she could think only of a loathsome black snake that she had once seen in those solitary rocks;—she felt as if his handsome but evil eye were charming him with an evil charm to his destruction.

"Well, Mo, my boy," she heard him say,—slapping Moses on the shoulder,—"this is something like. We 'll have a 'tempus,' as the college fellows say,—put down the clams to roast, and I 'll mix the punch," he said, setting over the fire a tea-kettle which they brought from the ship.

After their preparations were finished, all sat down to eat and drink. Mara listened with anxiety and horror to a conversation such as she never heard or conceived before. It is not often that women hear men talk in the undisguised manner which they use among themselves; but the conversation of men of unprincipled lives, and low, brutal habits, unchecked by the presence of respectable female society, might well convey to the horror-struck child a feeling as if she were listening at the mouth of hell. Almost every word was preceded or emphasized by an oath; and what struck with a death chill to her heart was, that Moses swore too, and seemed to show that desperate anxiety to seem *au fait* in the language of wickedness, which boys often do at that age, when they fancy that to be ignorant of vice is a mark of disgraceful greenness. Moses evidently was bent on showing that he was not green,—ignorant of the pure ear to which every such word came like the blast of death.

He drank a great deal, too, and the mirth among them grew furious and terrific. Mara, horrified and shocked as she was, did not, however, lose that intense and alert presence of mind, natural to persons in whom there is moral strength, however delicate be their physical frame. She felt at once that these men were playing upon Moses; that they had an object in view; that they were flattering and cajoling him, and leading him to drink, that they might work out some fiendish purpose of their own. The man called Atkinson related story after story of wild adventure, in which sudden fortunes had been made by men who, he said, were not afraid to take "the short cut across lots." He told of piratical adventures in the West Indies,—of the fun of chasing and overhauling ships,—and gave dazzling accounts of the treasures found on board. It was observable that all these stories were told on the line between joke and earnest,—as frolics, as specimens of good fun, and seeing life, etc.

At last came a suggestion,—What if they should start off together some fine day, "just for a spree," and try a cruise in the West Indies, to see what they could pick up? They had arms, and a gang of fine, whole-souled fellows. Moses had been tied to Ma'am Pennel's apron-string long enough. And "hark ye," said one of them, "Moses, they say old Pennel has lots of dollars in that old sea-chest of his'n. It would be a kindness to him to invest them for him in an adventure."

Moses answered with a streak of the boy innocence which often remains under the tramping of evil men, like ribbons of green turf in the middle of roads:—

"You don't know Father Pennel,—why, he 'd no more come into it than"—

A perfect roar of laughter cut short this declaration, and Atkinson, slapping Moses on the back, said,—

"By——, Mo! you are the jolliest green dog! I shall die a-laughing of your innocence some day. Why, my boy, can't you see? Pennel's money can be invested without asking him."

"Why, he keeps it locked," said Moses.

"And supposing you pick the lock?"

"Not I, indeed," said Moses, making a sudden movement to rise.

Mara almost screamed in her ecstasy, but she had sense enough to hold her breath.

"Ho! see him now," said Atkinson, lying back, and holding his sides while he laughed, and rolled over; "you can get off anything on that muff,—any hoax in the world,—he's so soft! Come, come, my dear boy, sit down. I was only seeing how wide I could make you open those great black eyes of your'n,—that's all."

"You'd better take care how you joke with me," said Moses, with that look of gloomy determination which Mara was quite familiar with of old. It was the rallying effort of a boy who had abandoned the first outworks of virtue to make a stand for the citadel. And Atkinson, like a prudent besieger after a repulse, returned to lie on his arms.

He began talking volubly on other subjects, telling stories, and singing songs, and pressing Moses to drink.

Mara was comforted to see that he declined drinking,—that he looked gloomy and thoughtful, in spite of the jokes of his companions; but she trembled to see, by the following conversation, how Atkinson was skillfully and prudently making apparent to Moses the extent to which he had him in his power. He seemed to Mara like an ugly spider skillfully weaving his web around a fly. She felt cold and faint; but within her there was a heroic strength.

She was not going to faint; she would make herself bear up. She was going to do something to get Moses out of this snare,—but what? At last they rose.

"It is past three o'clock," she heard one of them say.

"I say, Mo," said Atkinson, "you must make tracks for home, or you won't be in bed when Mother Pennel calls you."

The men all laughed at this joke, as they turned to go on board the schooner.

When they were gone, Moses threw himself down and hid his face in his hands. He knew not what pitying little face was looking down upon him from the hemlock shadows, what brave little heart was determined to save him. He was in one of those great crises of agony that boys pass through when they first awake from the fun and frolic of unlawful enterprises to find themselves sold under sin, and feel the terrible logic of evil which constrains them to pass from the less to greater crime. He felt that he was in the power of bad, unprincipled, heartless men, who, if he refused to do their bidding, had the power to expose him. All he had been doing would come out. His kind old foster-parents would know it. Mara would know it. Mr. Sewell and Miss Emily would know the secrets of his life that past month. He felt as if they were all looking at him now. He had disgraced himself,—had sunk below his education,—had been false to all his better knowledge and the past expectations of his friends, living a mean, miserable, dishonorable life,—and now the ground was fast sliding from under him, and the next plunge might be down a precipice from which there would be no return. What he had done up to this hour had been done in the roystering, inconsiderate gamesomeness of boyhood. It had been represented to himself only as "sowing wild oats," "having steep times," "seeing a little of life," and so on; but this night he had had propositions of piracy and robbery made to him, and he had not dared to knock down the man that made them,— had not dared at once to break away from his company. He must meet him again,—must go on with him, or—he groaned in agony at the thought.

It was a strong indication of that repressed, considerate habit of mind which love had wrought in the child, that when Mara heard the boy's sobs rising in the stillness, she did not, as she wished to, rush out and throw her arms around his neck and try to comfort him.

But she felt instinctively that she must not do this. She must not let him know that she had discovered his secret by stealing after him thus in the night shadows. She knew how nervously he had resented even the compassionate glances she had cast upon him in his restless, turbid intervals during the past few weeks, and the fierceness with which he had replied to a few timid inquiries. No,—though her heart was breaking for him, it was a shrewd, wise little heart, and resolved not to spoil all by yielding to its first untaught impulses. She repressed herself as the mother does who refrains from crying out when she sees her unconscious little one on the verge of a precipice.

When Moses rose and moodily began walking homeward, she followed at a distance. She could now keep farther off, for she knew the way through every part of the forest, and she only wanted to keep within sound of his footsteps to make sure that he was going home. When he emerged from the forest into the open moonlight, she sat down in its shadows and watched him as he walked over the open distance between her and the house. He went in; and then she waited a little longer for him to be quite retired. She thought he would throw himself on the bed, and then she could steal in after him. So she sat there quite in the shadows.

The grand full moon was riding high and calm in the purple sky, and Harpswell Bay on the one hand, and the wide, open ocean on the other, lay all in a silver shimmer of light. There was not a sound save the plash of the tide, now beginning to go out, and rolling and rattling the pebbles up and down as it came and went, and once in a while the distant, mournful intoning of the whippoorwill. There were silent lonely ships, sailing slowly to and fro far out to sea, turning their fair wings now into bright light and now into shadow, as they moved over the glassy still-ness. Mara could see all the houses on Harpswell Neck and the white church as clear as in the daylight. It seemed to her some strange, unearthly dream.

As she sat there, she thought over her whole little life, all full of one thought, one purpose, one love, one prayer, for this be-ing so strangely given to her out of that silent sea, which lay so like a still eternity around her,—and she revolved again what meant the vision of her childhood. Did it not mean that she was to watch over him and save him from some dreadful dan-ger? That poor mother was lying now silent and peaceful under the turf in the little graveyard not far off, and *she* must care for her boy.

A strong motherly feeling swelled out the girl's heart,—she felt that she *must,* she would, somehow save that treasure which had so mysteriously been committed to her. So, when she thought she had given time enough for Moses to be quietly asleep in his room, she arose and ran with quick footsteps across the moonlit plain to the house.

The front-door was standing wide open, as was always the in-nocent fashion in these regions, with a half-angle of moonlight and shadow lying within its dusky depths. Mara listened a mo-ment,—no sound: he had gone to bed then. "Poor boy," she said, "I hope he is asleep; how he must feel, poor fellow! It's all the fault of those dreadful men!" said the little dark shadow to herself, as she stole up the stairs past his room as guiltily as if she were the sinner. Once the stairs creaked, and her heart was in her mouth, but she gained her room and shut and bolted the door. She kneeled down by her little white bed, and thanked

God that she had come in safe, and then prayed him to teach her what to do next. She felt chilly and shivering, and crept into bed, and lay with her great soft brown eyes wide open, intently thinking what she should do.

Should she tell her grandfather? Something instinctively said No; that the first word from him which showed Moses he was detected would at once send him off with those wicked men. "He would never, never bear to have this known," she said. Mr. Sewell?—ah, that was worse. She herself shrank from letting him know what Moses had been doing; she could not bear to lower him so much in his eyes. He could not make allowances, she thought. He is good, to be sure, but he is so old and grave, and does n't know how much Moses has been tempted by these dreadful men; and then perhaps he would tell Miss Emily, and they never would want Moses to come there any more.

"What shall I do?" she said to herself. "I must get somebody to help me or tell me what to do. I can't tell grandmamma; it would only make her ill, and she would n't know what to do any more than I. Ah, I know what I will do,—I 'll tell Captain Kittridge; he was always so kind to me; and he has been to sea and seen all sorts of men, and Moses won't care so much perhaps to have him know, because the Captain is such a funny man, and don't take everything so seriously. Yes, that 's it. I 'll go right down to the cove in the morning. God will bring me through, I know He will;" and the little weary head fell back on the pillow asleep. And as she slept, a smile settled over her face, perhaps a reflection from the face of her good angel, who always beholdeth the face of our Father in Heaven.

XXII

A FRIEND IN NEED

Mara was so wearied with her night walk and the agitation she had been through, that once asleep she slept long after the early breakfast hour of the family. She was surprised on awaking to hear the slow old clock downstairs striking eight. She hastily jumped up and looked around with a confused wonder, and then slowly the events of the past night came back upon her like a remembered dream. She dressed herself quickly, and went down to find the breakfast things all washed and put away, and Mrs. Pennel spinning.

"Why, dear heart," said the old lady, "how came you to sleep so?—I spoke to you twice, but I could not make you hear."

"Has Moses been down, grandma?" said Mara, intent on the sole thought in her heart.

"Why, yes, dear, long ago,—and cross enough he was; that boy does get to be a trial,—but come, dear, I've saved some hot cakes for you,—sit down now and eat your breakfast."

Mara made a feint of eating what her grandmother with fond officiousness would put before her, and then rising up she put on her sun-bonnet and started down toward the cove to find her old friend.

The queer, dry, lean old Captain had been to her all her life like a faithful kobold or brownie, an unquestioning servant of all her gentle biddings. She dared tell him anything without diffidence or shamefacedness; and she felt that in this trial of her life he might have in his sea-receptacle some odd old amulet or spell that should be of power to help her. Instinctively she avoided the house, lest Sally should see and fly out and seize her. She took a narrow path through the cedars down to the little boat cove where the old Captain worked so merrily ten years ago, in the beginning of our story, and where she found him now, with his coat off, busily planing a board.

"Wal', now,—if this 'ere don't beat all!" he said, looking up and seeing her; "why, you 're looking after Sally, I s'pose? She 's up to the house."

"No, Captain Kittridge, I 'm come to see *you*."

"You *be?*" said the Captain, "I swow! if I ain't a lucky feller. But what 's the matter?" he said, suddenly observing her pale face and the tears in her eyes. "Hain't nothin' bad happened,— hes there?"

"Oh! Captain Kittridge, something dreadful; and nobody but you can help me."

"Want to know, now!" said the Captain, with a grave face. "Well, come here, now, and sit down, and tell me all about it. Don't you cry, there 's a good girl! Don't, now."

Mara began her story, and went through with it in a rapid and agitated manner; and the good Captain listened in a fidgety state of interest, occasionally relieving his mind by interjecting "Do tell, now!" "I swan,—if that ar ain't too bad."

"That ar 's rediculous conduct in Atkinson. He ought to be talked to," said the Captain, when she had finished, and then he whistled and put a shaving in his mouth, which he chewed reflectively.

"Don't you be a mite worried, Mara," he said. "You did a great deal better to come to me than to go to Mr. Sewell or your grand'ther either; 'cause you see these 'ere wild chaps they 'll take things from me they would n't from a church-member or a minister. Folks must n't pull 'em up with *too* short a rein,—they must kind o' flatter 'em off. But that ar Atkinson 's too rediculous for anything; and if he don't mind, I 'll serve him out. I know a thing or two about him that I shall shake over his head if he don't behave. Now I don't think so much of smugglin' as some folks," said the Captain, lowering his voice to a confidential tone. "I reely don't, now; but come to goin' off piratin',— and tryin' to put a young boy up to robbin' his best friends,— why, there ain't no kind o' sense in that. It 's p'ison mean of Atkinson. I shall tell him so, and I shall talk to Moses."

"Oh! I 'm afraid to have you," said Mara, apprehensively.

"Why, chickabiddy," said the old Captain, "you don't understand me. I ain't goin' at him with no sermons,—I shall jest talk to him this way: Look here now, Moses, I shall say, there 's Badger's ship goin' to sail in a fortnight for China, and they want likely fellers aboard, and I 've got a hundred dollars that I 'd like to send on a venture; if you 'll take it and go, why, we 'll share the profits. I shall talk like that, you know. Mebbe I sha' n't let him know what I know, and mebbe I shall; jest tip him a wink, you know; it depends on circumstances. But bless you, child, these 'ere fellers ain't none of 'em 'fraid o' me, you see, 'cause they know I know the ropes."

"And can you make that horrid man let him alone?" said Mara, fearfully.

"Calculate I can. 'Spect if I 's to tell Atkinson a few things I know, he 'd be for bein' scase in our parts. Now, you see, I hain't minded doin' a small bit o' trade now and then with them ar fellers myself; but this 'ere," said the Captain, stopping and looking extremely disgusted, "why, it 's contemptible, it 's rediculous!"

"Do you think I 'd better tell grandpapa?" said Mara.

"Don't worry your little head. I 'll step up and have a talk with Pennel, this evening. He knows as well as I that there is times when chaps must be seen to, and no remarks made. Pennel knows that ar. Why, now, Mis' Kittridge thinks our boys turned out so well all along of her bringin' up, and I let her think so; keeps her sort o' in spirits, you see. But Lord bless ye, child, there 's been times with Job, and Sam, and Pass, and Dass, and Dile, and all on 'em finally, when, if I had n't jest pulled a rope here and turned a screw there, and said nothin' to nobody, they 'd a-been all gone to smash. I never told Mis' Kittridge none o' their didos; bless you, 't would n't been o' no use. I never told *them,* neither; but I jest kind o' worked 'em off, you know; and they 's all putty 'spectable men now, as men go, you know; not like Parson Sewell, but good, honest mates and shipmasters,—kind o' middlin' people, you know. It takes a good many o' sich to make up a world, d 'ye see."

"But oh, Captain Kittridge, did any of them use to swear?" said Mara, in a faltering voice.

"Wal', they did, consid'able," said the Captain;—then seeing the trembling of Mara's lip, he added,—

"Ef you could a-found this 'ere out any other way, it 's most a pity you 'd a-heard him; 'cause he would n't never have let out afore you. It don't do for gals to hear the fellers talk when they 's alone, 'cause fellers,—wal', you see, fellers will be fellers, partic'larly when they 're young. Some on 'em, they never gits over it all their lives finally."

"But oh! Captain Kittridge, that talk last night was so dreadfully wicked! and Moses!—oh, it was dreadful to hear him!"

"Wal', yes, it was," said the Captain, consolingly; "but don't you cry, and don't you break your little heart. I expect he 'll come all right, and jine the church one of these days; 'cause there 's old Pennel, he prays,—fact now, I think there 's consid'able in some people's prayers, and he 's one of the sort. And you pray, too; and I 'm quite sure the good Lord *must* hear you. I declare sometimes I wish you 'd jest say a good word to Him for me; I should like to get the hang o' things a little better than I do, somehow, I reely should. I 've gi'n up swearing years ago. Mis' Kittridge, she broke me o' that, and now I don't never go further than 'I vum' or 'I swow,' or somethin' o' that sort; but you see I 'm old;—Moses is young; but then he 's got eddication and friends, and he 'll come all right. Now you jest see ef he don't!"

This miscellaneous budget of personal experiences and friendly consolation which the good Captain conveyed to Mara may possibly make you laugh, my reader, but the good, ropy brown man was doing his best to console his little friend; and as Mara looked at him he was almost glorified in her eyes—he had power to save Moses, and he would do it. She went home to dinner that day with her heart considerably lightened. She refrained, in a guilty way, from even looking at Moses, who was gloomy and moody.

Mara had from nature a good endowment of that kind of innocent hypocrisy which is needed as a staple in the lives of women who bridge a thousand awful chasms with smiling, unconscious looks, and walk, singing and scattering flowers, over abysses of fear, while their hearts are dying within them.

She talked more volubly than was her wont with Mrs. Pennel, and with her old grandfather; she laughed and seemed in more than usual spirits, and only once did she look up and catch the gloomy eye of Moses. It had that murky, troubled look that one may see in the eye of a boy when those evil waters which cast up mire and dirt have once been stirred in his soul. They fell under her clear glance, and he made a rapid, impatient movement, as if it hurt him to be looked at. The evil spirit in boy or man cannot bear the "touch of celestial temper;" and the sensitiveness to eyebeams is one of the earliest signs of conscious, inward guilt.

Mara was relieved, as he flung out of the house after dinner, to see the long, dry figure of Captain Kittridge coming up and seizing Moses by the button. From the window she saw the Captain assuming a confidential air with him; and when they had talked together a few moments, she saw Moses going with great readiness after him down the road to his house.

In less than a fortnight, it was settled Moses was to sail for China, and Mara was deep in the preparations for his outfit. Once she would have felt this departure as the most dreadful trial of her life. Now it seemed to her a deliverance for him, and she worked with a cheerful alacrity, which seemed to Moses more than was proper, considering *he* was going away.

For Moses, like many others of his sex, boy or man, had quietly settled in his own mind that the whole love of Mara's heart was to be his, to have and to hold, to use and to draw on, when and as he liked. He reckoned on it as a sort of inexhaustible, uncounted treasure that was his own peculiar right and property, and therefore he felt abused at what he supposed was a disclosure of some deficiency on her part.

"You seem to be very glad to be rid of me," he said to her in a bitter tone one day, as she was earnestly busy in her preparations.

Now the fact was, that Moses had been assiduously making himself disagreeable to Mara for the fortnight past, by all sorts of unkind sayings and doings; and he knew it too; yet he felt a right to feel very much abused at the thought that she could

possibly want him to be going. If she had been utterly desolate
about it, and torn her hair and sobbed and wailed, he would
have asked what she could be crying about, and begged not to
be bored with scenes; but as it was, this cheerful composure
was quite unfeeling.

Now pray don't suppose Moses to be a monster of an uncommon species. We take him to be an average specimen of a boy of
a certain kind of temperament in the transition period of life.
Everything is chaos within; the flesh lusteth against the spirit,
and the spirit against the flesh, and "light and darkness, and
mind and dust, and passion and pure thoughts, mingle and contend," without end or order. He wondered at himself sometimes that he could say such cruel things as he did to his faithful
little friend—to one whom, after all, he did love and trust before all other human beings.

There is no saying why it is that a man or a boy, not radically
destitute of generous comprehensions, will often cruelly torture and tyrannize over a woman whom he both loves and
reveres, who stands in his soul in his best hours as the very im-
personation of all that is good and beautiful. It is as if some evil
spirit at times possessed him, and compelled him to utter
words which were felt at the moment to be mean and hateful.
Moses often wondered at himself, as he lay awake nights, how
he could have said and done the things he had, and felt miser-
ably resolved to make it up somehow before he went away; but
he did not.

He could not say, "Mara, I have done wrong," though he every day meant to do it, and sometimes sat an hour in her presence, feeling murky and stony, as if possessed by a dumb spirit;
then he would get up and fling stormily out of the house.

Poor Mara wondered if he really would go without one kind
word. She thought of all the years they had been together, and

how he had been her only thought and love. What had become of her brother?—the Moses that once she used to know—frank, careless, not ill-tempered, and who sometimes seemed to love her and think she was the best little girl in the world? Where was he gone to—this friend and brother of her childhood, and would he never come back?

At last came the evening before his parting; the sea-chest was all made up and packed; and Mara's fingers had been busy with everything, from more substantial garments down to all those little comforts and nameless conveniences that only a woman knows how to improvise. Mara thought certainly she should get a few kind words, as Moses looked it over. But he only said, "All right;" and then added that "there was a button off one of the shirts." Mara's busy fingers quickly replaced it, and Moses was annoyed at the tear that fell on the button. What was she crying for now? He knew very well, but he felt stubborn and cruel. Afterwards he lay awake many a night in his berth, and acted this last scene over differently. He took Mara in his arms and kissed her; he told her she was his best friend, his good angel, and that he was not worthy to kiss the hem of her garment; but the next day, when he thought of writing a letter to her, he did n't, and the good mood passed away. Boys do not acquire an ease of expression in letter-writing as early as girls, and a voyage to China furnished opportunities few and far between of sending letters.

Now and then, through some sailing ship, came missives which seemed to Mara altogether colder and more unsatisfactory than they would have done could she have appreciated the difference between a boy and a girl in power of epistolary expression; for the power of really representing one's heart on paper, which is one of the first spring flowers of early womanhood, is the latest blossom on the slow-growing tree of manhood. To do Moses justice, these seeming cold letters were often written with a choking lump in his throat, caused by thinking over his many sins against his little good angel; but then that past account was so long, and had so much that it pained him to think of, that he dashed it all off in the shortest fashion, and said to himself, "One of these days when I see her I 'll make it all up."

No man—especially one that is living a rough, busy, out-of-doors life—can form the slightest conception of that veiled and secluded life which exists in the heart of a sensitive woman, whose sphere is narrow, whose external diversions are few, and whose mind, therefore, acts by a continual introversion upon itself. They know nothing how their careless words and actions are pondered and turned again in weary, quiet hours of fruitless questioning. What did he mean by this? and what did he intend by that?—while he, the careless buffalo, meant nothing, or has forgotten what it was, if he did. Man's utter ignorance of woman's nature is a cause of a great deal of unsuspected cruelty which he practices toward her.

Mara found one or two opportunities of writing to Moses; but her letters were timid and constrained by a sort of frosty, discouraged sense of loneliness; and Moses, though he knew he had no earthly right to expect this to be otherwise, took upon him to feel as an abused individual, whom nobody loved—whose way in the world was destined to be lonely and desolate. So when, at the end of three years, he arrived suddenly at Brunswick in the beginning of winter, and came, all burning with impatience, to the home at Orr's Island, and found that Mara had gone to Boston on a visit, he resented it as a personal slight.

He might have inquired why she should expect him, and whether her whole life was to be spent in looking out of the window to watch for him. He might have remembered that he had warned her of his approach by no letter. But no. "Mara did n't care for him—she had forgotten all about him—she was having a good time in Boston, just as likely as not with some train of admirers, and he had been tossing on the stormy ocean, and she had thought nothing of it." How many things he had meant to say! He had never felt so good and so affectionate. He would have confessed all the sins of his life to her, and asked her pardon—and she was n't there!

Mrs. Pennel suggested that he might go to Boston after her.

No, he was not going to do that. He would not intrude on her pleasures with the memory of a rough, hard-working sailor. He was alone in the world, and had his own way to make, and so best go at once up among lumbermen, and cut the timber for the ship that was to carry Cæsar and his fortunes.

When Mara was informed by a letter from Mrs. Pennel, ex-pressed in the few brief words in which that good woman gen-erally embodied her epistolary communications, that Moses had been at home, and gone to Umbagog without seeing her, she felt at her heart only a little closer stricture of cold, quiet pain, which had become a habit of her inner life.

"He did not love her—he was cold and selfish," said the inner voice. And faintly she pleaded, in answer, "He is a man—he has seen the world—and has so much to do and think of, no won-der."

In fact, during the last three years that had parted them, the great change of life had been consummated in both. They had parted boy and girl; they would meet man and woman. The time of this meeting had been announced.

And all this is the history of that sigh, so very quiet that Sally Kittridge never checked the rattling flow of her conversation to observe it.

XXIII

🌲🌲🌲

The Beginning
of the Story

We have in the last three chapters brought up the history of our characters to the time when our story opens, when Mara and Sally Kittridge were discussing the expected return of Moses. Sally was persuaded by Mara to stay and spend the night with her, and did so without much fear of what her mother would say when she returned; for though Mrs. Kittridge still made bustling demonstrations of authority, it was quite evident to every one that the handsome grown-up girl had got the sceptre into her own hands, and was reigning in the full confidence of being, in one way or another, able to bring her mother into all her views.

So Sally stayed—to have one of those long night-talks in which girls delight, in the course of which all sorts of intimacies and confidences, that shun the daylight, open like the night-blooming cereus in strange successions. One often wonders by daylight at the things one says very naturally in the dark.

So the two girls talked about Moses, and Sally dilated upon his handsome, manly air the one Sunday that he had appeared in Harpswell meeting-house.

"He did n't know me at all, if you 'll believe it," said Sally. "I was standing with father when he came out, and he shook hands with him, and looked at me as if I 'd been an entire stranger."

"I 'm not in the least surprised," said Mara; "you 're grown so and altered."

"Well, now, you 'd hardly know him, Mara," said Sally. "He is a man—a real man; everything about him is different; he holds up his head in such a proud way. Well, he always did that when he was a boy; but when he speaks, he has such a deep voice! How boys do alter in a year or two!"

"Do you think I have altered much, Sally?" said Mara; "at least, do you think *he* would think so?"

"Why, Mara, you and I have been together so much, I can't tell. We don't notice what goes on before us every day. I really should like to see what Moses Pennel will think when he sees you. At any rate, he can't order you about with such a grand air as he used to when you were younger."

"I think sometimes he has quite forgotten about me," said Mara.

"Well, if I were you, I should put him in mind of myself by one or two little ways," said Sally. "I 'd plague him and tease him. I 'd lead him such a life that he could n't forget me,—that 's what I would."

"I don't doubt you would, Sally; and he might like you all the better for it. But you know that sort of thing is n't my way. People must act in character."

"Do you know, Mara," said Sally, "I always thought Moses was hateful in his treatment of you? Now I 'd no more marry that fellow than I 'd walk into the fire; but it would be a just punishment for his sins to have to marry me! Would n't I serve him out, though!"

With which threat of vengeance on her mind Sally Kittridge fell asleep, while Mara lay awake pondering,—wondering if Moses would come to-morrow, and what he would be like if he did come.

The next morning as the two girls were wiping breakfast dishes in a room adjoining the kitchen, a step was heard on the kitchen-floor, and the first that Mara knew she found herself lifted from the floor in the arms of a tall dark-eyed young man, who was kissing her just as if he had a right to. She knew it must be Moses, but it seemed strange as a dream, for all she had tried to imagine it beforehand.

He kissed her over and over, and then holding her off at arm's length, said, "Why, Mara, you have grown to be a beauty!"

"And what was she, I'd like to know, when you went away, Mr. Moses?" said Sally, who could not long keep out of a conversation. "She was handsome when you were only a great ugly boy."

"Thank you, Miss Sally!" said Moses, making a profound bow.

"Thank me for what?" said Sally, with a toss.

"For your intimation that I am a handsome young man now," said Moses, sitting with his arm around Mara, and her hand in his.

And in truth he was as handsome now for a man as he was in the promise of his early childhood. All the oafishness and surly awkwardness of the half-boy period was gone. His great black eyes were clear and confident: his dark hair clustering in short curls round his well-shaped head; his black lashes, and fine form, and a certain confident ease of manner, set him off to the greatest advantage.

Mara felt a peculiar dreamy sense of strangeness at this brother who was not a brother,—this Moses so different from the one she had known. The very tone of his voice, which when he left had the uncertain cracked notes which indicate the unformed man, were now mellowed and settled. Mara regarded him shyly as he talked, blushed uneasily, and drew away from his arm around her, as if this handsome, self-confident young man were being too familiar. In fact, she made apology to go out into the other room to call Mrs. Pennel.

Moses looked after her as she went with admiration. "What a little woman she has grown!" he said, naïvely.

"And what did you expect she would grow?" said Sally. "You did n't expect to find her a girl in short clothes, did you?"

"Not exactly, Miss Sally," said Moses, turning his attention to her; "and some other people are changed too."

"Like enough," said Sally, carelessly. "I should think so, since somebody never spoke a word to one the Sunday he was at meeting."

"Oh, you remember that, do you? On my word, Sally"—

"Miss Kittridge, if you please, sir," said Sally, turning round with the air of an empress.

"Well, then, Miss Kittridge," said Moses, making a bow; "now let me finish my sentence. I never dreamed who you were."

"Complimentary," said Sally, pouting.

"Well, hear me through," said Moses; "you had grown so handsome, Miss Kittridge."

"Oh! that indeed! I suppose you mean to say I was a fright when you left?"

"Not at all—not at all," said Moses; "but handsome things may grow handsomer, you know."

"I don't like flattery," said Sally.

"I never flatter, Miss Kittridge," said Moses.

Our young gentleman and young lady of Orr's Island went through with this customary little lie of civilized society with as much gravity as if they were practicing in the court of Versailles,—she looking out from the corner of her eye to watch the effect of her words, and he laying his hand on his heart in the most edifying gravity. They perfectly understood one another.

But, says the reader, seems to me Sally Kittridge does all the talking! So she does,—so she always will,—for it is her nature to be bright, noisy, and restless; and one of these girls always overcrows a timid and thoughtful one, and makes her, for the time, seem dim and faded, as does rose color when put beside scarlet.

Sally was a born coquette. It was as natural for her to want to flirt with every man she saw, as for a kitten to scamper after a pin-ball. Does the kitten care a fig for the pin-ball, or the dry leaves, which she whisks, and frisks, and boxes, and pats, and races round and round after? No; it's nothing but kittenhood; every hair of her fur is alive with it. Her sleepy green eyes, when she pretends to be dozing, are full of it; and though she looks wise a moment, and seems resolved to be a discreet young cat, let but a leaf sway—off she goes again, with a frisk and a rap. So, though Sally had scolded and flounced about Moses's inattention to Mara in advance, she contrived even in this first interview to keep him talking with nobody but herself;—not because she wanted to draw him from Mara, or meant to; not because she cared a pin for him; but because it was her nature, as a frisky young cat. And Moses let himself be drawn, between bantering and contradicting, and jest and earnest, at some moments almost to forget that Mara was in the room.

She took her sewing and sat with a pleased smile, sometimes breaking into the lively flow of conversation, or eagerly appealed to by both parties to settle some rising quarrel.

Once, as they were talking, Moses looked up and saw Mara's head, as a stray sunbeam falling upon the golden hair seemed to make a halo around her face. Her large eyes were fixed upon him with an expression so intense and penetrative, that he felt a sort of wincing uneasiness. "What makes you look at me so, Mara?" he said, suddenly.

A bright flush came in her cheek as she answered, "I did n't know I was looking. It all seems so strange to me. I am trying to make out who and what you are."

"It 's not best to look too deep," Moses said, laughing, but with a slight shade of uneasiness.

When Sally, late in the afternoon, declared that she must go home, she could n't stay another minute, Moses rose to go with her.

"What are you getting up for?" she said to Moses, as he took his hat.

"To go home with you, to be sure."

"Nobody asked you to," said Sally.

"I 'm accustomed to asking myself," said Moses.

"Well, I suppose I must have you along," said Sally. "Father will be glad to see you, of course."

"You 'll be back to tea, Moses," said Mara, "will you not? Grandfather will be home, and want to see you."

"Oh, I shall be right back," said Moses, "I have a little business to settle with Captain Kittridge."

But Moses, however, did stay at tea with Mrs. Kittridge, who looked graciously at him through the bows of her black horn spectacles, having heard her liege lord observe that Moses was a smart chap, and had done pretty well in a money way.

How came he to stay? Sally told him every other minute to go; and then when he had got fairly out of the door, called him back to tell him that there was something she had heard about him. And Moses of course came back; wanted to know what it was; and could n't be told, it was a secret; and then he would be ordered off, and reminded that he promised to go straight home; and then when he got a little farther off she called after him a second time, to tell him that he would be very much surprised if he knew how she found it out, etc., etc.,—till at last tea being ready, there was no reason why he should n't have a cup. And so it was sober moonrise before Moses found himself going home.

"Hang that girl!" he said to himself; "don't she know what she 's about, though?"

There our hero was mistaken. Sally never did know what she was about,—had no plan or purpose more than a blackbird; and when Moses was gone laughed to think how many times she had made him come back.

"Now, confound it all," said Moses, "I care more for our little Mara than a dozen of her; and what have I been fooling all this time for?—now Mara will think I don't love her."

And, in fact, our young gentleman rather set his heart on the sensation he was going to make when he got home. It is flattering, after all, to feel one 's power over a susceptible nature; and Moses, remembering how entirely and devotedly Mara had loved him all through childhood, never doubted but he was the sole possessor of uncounted treasure in her heart, which he could develop at his leisure and use as he pleased. He did not calculate for one force which had grown up in the meanwhile between them,—and that was the power of womanhood. He did not know the intensity of that kind of pride, which is the very life of the female nature, and which is most vivid and vigorous in the most timid and retiring.

Our little Mara was tender, self-devoting, humble, and religious, but she was woman after all to the tips of her fingers,— quick to feel slights, and determined with the intensest determination, that no man should wrest from her one of those few humble rights and privileges, which Nature allows to woman.

Something swelled and trembled in her when she felt the confident pressure of that bold arm around her waist,—like the instinct of a wild bird to fly. Something in the deep, manly voice, the determined, self-confident air, aroused a vague feeling of defiance and resistance in her which she could scarcely explain to herself. Was he to assume a right to her in this way without even asking? When he did not come to tea nor long after, and Mrs. Pennel and her grandfather wondered, she laughed, and said gayly,—

"Oh, he knows he 'll have time enough to see me. Sally seems more like a stranger."

But when Moses came home after moonrise, determined to go and console Mara for his absence, he was surprised to hear the sound of a rapid and pleasant conversation, in which a masculine and feminine voice were intermingled in a lively duet. Coming a little nearer, he saw Mara sitting knitting in the doorway, and a very good-looking young man seated on a stone at her feet, with his straw hat flung on the ground, while he was looking up into her face, as young men often do into pretty faces seen by moonlight. Mara rose and introduced Mr. Adams of Boston to Mr. Moses Pennel.

Moses measured the young man with his eye as if he could have shot him with a good will. And his temper was not at all bettered as he observed that he had the easy air of a man of fashion and culture, and learned by a few moments of the succeeding conversation, that the acquaintance had commenced during Mara's winter visit to Boston.

"I was staying a day or two at Mr. Sewell's," he said, carelessly, "and the night was so fine I could n't resist the temptation to row over."

It was now Moses's turn to listen to a conversation in which he could bear little part, it being about persons and places and things unfamiliar to him; and though he could give no earthly reason why the conversation was not the most proper in the world,—yet he found that it made him angry.

In the pauses, Mara inquired, prettily, how he found the Kittridges, and reproved him playfully for staying, in despite of his promise to come home. Moses answered with an effort to appear easy and playful, that there was no reason, it appeared, to hurry on her account, since she had been so pleasantly engaged.

"That is true," said Mara, quietly; "but then grandpapa and grandmamma expected you, and they have gone to bed, as you know they always do after tea."

"They 'll keep till morning, I suppose," said Moses, rather gruffly.

"Oh yes; but then as you had been gone two or three months, naturally they wanted to see a little of you at first."

The stranger now joined in the conversation, and began talking with Moses about his experiences in foreign parts, in a manner which showed a man of sense and breeding. Moses had a jealous fear of people of breeding,—an apprehension lest they should look down on one whose life had been laid out of the course of their conventional ideas; and therefore, though he had sufficient ability and vigor of mind to acquit himself to advantage in this conversation, it gave him all the while a secret uneasiness. After a few moments, he rose up moodily, and saying that he was very much fatigued, he went into the house to retire.

Mr. Adams rose to go also, and Moses might have felt in a more Christian frame of mind, had he listened to the last words of the conversation between him and Mara.

"Do you remain long in Harpswell?" she asked.

"That depends on circumstances," he replied. "If I do, may I be permitted to visit you?"

"As a friend—yes," said Mara; "I shall always be happy to see you."

"No more?"

"No more," replied Mara.

"I had hoped," he said, "that you would reconsider."

"It is impossible," said she; and soft voices can pronounce that word, *impossible,* in a very fateful and decisive manner.

"Well, God bless you, then, Miss Lincoln," he said, and was gone.

Mara stood in the doorway and saw him loosen his boat from its moorings and float off in the moonlight, with a long train of silver sparkles behind.

A moment after Moses was looking gloomily over her shoulder.

"Who is that puppy?" he said.

"He is not a puppy, but a very fine young man," said Mara.

"Well, that very fine young man, then?"

"I thought I told you. He is a Mr. Adams of Boston, and a distant connection of the Sewells. I met him when I was visiting at Judge Sewell's in Boston."

"You seemed to be having a very pleasant time together?"

"We were," said Mara, quietly.

"It 's a pity I came home as I did. I 'm sorry I interrupted you," said Moses, with a sarcastic laugh.

"You did n't interrupt us; he had been here almost two hours."

Now Mara saw plainly enough that Moses was displeased and hurt, and had it been in the days of her fourteenth summer, she would have thrown her arms around his neck, and said, "Moses, I don't care a fig for that man, and I love you better than all the world." But this the young lady of eighteen would not do; so she wished him goodnight very prettily, and pretended not to see anything about it.

Mara was as near being a saint as human dust ever is; but—she was a woman saint; and therefore may be excused for a little gentle vindictiveness. She was, in a merciful way, rather glad that Moses had gone to bed dissatisfied, and rather glad that he did not know what she might have told him—quite resolved that he should not know at present. Was he to know that she liked nobody so much as him? Not he, unless he loved her more than all the world, and said so first. Mara was resolved upon that. He might go where he liked—flirt with whom he liked—come back as late as he pleased; never would she, by word or look, give him reason to think she cared.

XXIV

DESIRES
AND DREAMS

Moses passed rather a restless and uneasy night on his return to the home-roof which had sheltered his childhood. All his life past, and all his life expected, seemed to boil and seethe and ferment in his thoughts, and to go round and round in never-ceasing circles before him.

Moses was *par excellence* proud, ambitious, and willful. These words, generally supposed to describe positive vices of the mind, in fact are only the overaction of certain very valuable portions of our nature, since one can conceive all three to raise a man immensely in the scale of moral being, simply by being applied to right objects. He who is too proud even to admit a mean thought—who is ambitious only of ideal excellence—who has an inflexible will only in the pursuit of truth and righteousness—may be a saint and a hero.

But Moses was neither a saint nor a hero, but an undeveloped chaotic young man, whose pride made him sensitive and restless; whose ambition was fixed on wealth and worldly success; whose willfulness was for the most part a blind determination to compass his own points, with the leave of Providence or without. There was no God in his estimate of life—and a sort of secret unsuspected determination at the bottom of his heart that there should be none. He feared religion, from a suspicion which he entertained that it might hamper some of his future schemes. He did not wish to put himself under its rules, lest he might find them in some future time inconveniently strict.

With such determinations and feelings, the Bible—necessarily an excessively uninteresting book to him—he never read, and satisfied himself with determining in a general way that it was not worth reading, and, as was the custom with many young men in America at that period, announced himself as a skeptic, and seemed to value himself not a little on the distinction. Pride in skepticism is a peculiar distinction of young men. It takes years and maturity to make the discovery that the power of faith is nobler than the power of doubt; and that there is a celestial wisdom in the ingenuous propensity to trust, which belongs to honest and noble natures. Elderly skeptics generally regard their unbelief as a misfortune.

Not that Moses was, after all, without "the angel in him." He had a good deal of the susceptibility to poetic feeling, the power of vague and dreamy aspiration, the longing after the good and beautiful, which is God's witness in the soul. A noble sentiment in poetry, a fine scene in nature, had power to bring tears in his great dark eyes, and he had, under the influence of such things, brief inspired moments in which he vaguely longed to do, or be, something grand or noble. But this, however, was something apart from the real purpose of his life,—a sort of voice crying in the wilderness,—to which he gave little heed. Practically, he was determined with all his might, to have a good time in this life, whatever another might be,—if there were one; and that he would do it by the strength of his right arm. Wealth he saw to be the lamp of Aladdin, which commanded all other things. And the pursuit of wealth was therefore the first step in his programme.

As for plans of the heart and domestic life, Moses was one of that very common class who had more desire to be loved than power of loving. His cravings and dreams were not for somebody to be devoted to, but for somebody who should be devoted to him. And, like most people who possess this characteristic, he mistook it for an affectionate disposition.

Now the chief treasure of his heart had always been his little sister Mara, chiefly from his conviction that he was the one absorbing thought and love of her heart. He had never figured life to himself otherwise than with Mara at his side, his unquestioning, devoted friend. Of course he and his plans, his ways and wants, would always be in the future, as they always had been, her sole thought. These sleeping partnerships in the interchange of affection, which support one's heart with a basis of uncounted wealth, and leave one free to come and go, and buy and sell, without exaction or interference, are a convenience certainly, and the loss of them in any way is like the sudden breaking of a bank in which all one's deposits are laid.

It had never occurred to Moses how or in what capacity he should always stand banker to the whole wealth of love that there was in Mara's heart, and what provision he should make on his part for returning this incalculable debt. But the interview of this evening had raised a new thought in his mind. Mara, as he saw that day, was no longer a little girl in a pink sunbonnet. She was a woman,—a little one, it is true, but every inch a woman,—and a woman invested with a singular poetic charm of appearance, which, more than beauty, has the power of awakening feeling in the other sex.

He felt in himself, in the experience of that one day, that there was something subtle and veiled about her, which set the imagination at work; that the wistful, plaintive expression of her dark eyes, and a thousand little shy and tremulous movements of her face, affected him more than the most brilliant of Sally Kittridge's sprightly sallies. Yes, there would be people falling in love with her fast enough, he thought even here, where she is as secluded as a pearl in an oyster-shell,—it seems means were found to come after her,—and then all the love of her heart, that priceless love, would go to another.

Mara would be absorbed in some one else, would love some one else, as he knew she could, with heart and soul and mind and strength. When he thought of this, it affected him much as it would if one were turned out of a warm, smiling apartment into a bleak December storm. What should he do, if that treasure which he had taken most for granted in all his valuations of life should suddenly be found to belong to another? Who was this fellow that seemed so free to visit her, and what had passed between them? Was Mara in love with him, or going to be? There is no saying how the consideration of this question enhanced in our hero's opinion both her beauty and all her other good qualities.

Such a brave little heart! such a good, clear little head! and such a pretty hand and foot! She was always so cheerful, so unselfish, so devoted! When had he ever seen her angry, except when she had taken up some childish quarrel of his, and fought for him like a little Spartan? Then she was pious, too. She was born religious, thought our hero, who, in common with many men professing skepticism for their own particular part, set a great value on religion in that unknown future person whom they are fond of designating in advance as "my wife." Yes, Moses meant his wife should be pious, and pray for him, while he did as he pleased.

"Now there's that witch of a Sally Kittridge," he said to himself; "I would n't have such a girl for a wife. Nothing to her but foam and frisk,—no heart more than a bobolink! But is n't she amusing? By George! is n't she, though?"

"But," thought Moses, "it 's time I settled this matter who is to be my wife. I won't marry till I 'm rich,—that 's flat. My wife is n't to rub and grub. So at it I must go to raise the wind. I wonder if old Sewell really does know anything about my parents. Miss Emily would have it that there was some mystery that he had the key of; but I never could get anything from him. He always put me off in such a smooth way that I could n't tell whether he did or he did n't. But, now, supposing I have relatives, family connections, then who knows but what there may be property coming to me? That 's an idea worth looking after, surely."

There 's no saying with what vividness ideas and images go through one's wakeful brain when the midnight moon is making an exact shadow of your window-sash, with panes of light, on your chamber-floor. How vividly we all have loved and hated and planned and hoped and feared and desired and dreamed, as we tossed and turned to and fro upon such watchful, still nights. In the stillness, the tide upon one side of the Island replied to the dash on the other side in unbroken symphony, and Moses began to remember all the stories gossips had told him of how he had floated ashore there, like a fragment of tropical seaweed borne landward by a great gale. He positively wondered at himself that he had never thought of it more, and the more he meditated, the more mysterious and inexplicable he felt. Then he had heard Miss Roxy once speaking something about a bracelet, he was sure he had; but afterwards it was hushed up, and no one seemed to know anything about it when he inquired. But in those days he was a boy,—he was nobody,— now he was a young man. He could go to Mr. Sewell, and demand as his right a fair answer to any questions he might ask. If he found, as was quite likely, that there was nothing to be known, his mind would be thus far settled,—he should trust only to his own resources.

So far as the state of the young man's finances were concerned, it would be considered in those simple times and regions an auspicious beginning of life. The sum intrusted to him by Captain Kittridge had been more than doubled by the liberality of Zephaniah Pennel, and Moses had traded upon it in foreign parts with a skill and energy that brought a very fair return, and gave him, in the eyes of the shrewd, thrifty neighbors, the prestige of a young man who was marked for success in the world.

He had already formed an advantageous arrangement with his grandfather and Captain Kittridge, by which a ship was to be built, which he should command, and thus the old Saturday afternoon dream of their childhood be fulfilled. As he thought of it, there arose in his mind a picture of Mara, with her golden hair and plaintive eyes and little white hands, reigning as a fairy queen in the captain's cabin, with a sort of wish to carry her off and make sure that no one else ever should get her from him.

But these midnight dreams were all sobered down by the plain matter-of-fact beams of the morning sun, and nothing remained of immediate definite purpose except the resolve, which came strongly upon Moses as he looked across the blue band of Harpswell Bay, that he would go that morning and have a talk with Mr. Sewell.

XXV

MISS EMILY

Miss Roxy Toothacre was seated by the window of the little keeping-room where Miss Emily Sewell sat on every-day occasions. Around her were the insignia of her power and sway. Her big tailor's goose was heating between Miss Emily's bright brass fire-irons; her great pin-cushion was by her side, bristling with pins of all sizes, and with broken needles thriftily made into pins by heads of red sealing-wax, and with needles threaded with all varieties of cotton, silk, and linen; her scissors hung martially by her side; her black bombazette work-apron was on; and the expression of her iron features was that of deep responsibility, for she was making the minister a new Sunday vest!

The good soul looks not a day older than when we left her, ten years ago. Like the gray, weather-beaten rocks of her native shore, her strong features had an unchangeable identity beyond that of anything fair and blooming. There was of course no chance for a gray streak in her stiff, uncompromising mohair frisette, which still pushed up her cap-border bristlingly as of old, and the clear, high winds and bracing atmosphere of that rough coast kept her in an admirable state of preservation.

Miss Emily had now and then a white hair among her soft, pretty brown ones, and looked a little thinner; but the round, bright spot of bloom on each cheek was there just as of yore,— and just as of yore she was thinking of her brother, and filling her little head with endless calculations to keep him looking fresh and respectable, and his housekeeping comfortable and easy, on very limited means. She was now officiously and anxiously attending on Miss Roxy, who was in the midst of the responsible operation which should conduce greatly to this end.

"Does that twist work well?" she said, nervously; "because I believe I 've got some other upstairs in my India box."

Miss Roxy surveyed the article; bit a fragment off, as if she meant to taste it; threaded a needle and made a few cabalistical stitches; and then pronounced, *ex cathedrâ,* that it would do. Miss Emily gave a sigh of relief. After buttons and tapes and linings, and various other items had been also discussed, the conversation began to flow into general channels.

"Did you know Moses Pennel had got home from Umbagog?" said Miss Roxy.

"Yes. Captain Kittridge told brother so this morning. I wonder he does n't call over to see us."

"Your brother took a sight of interest in that boy," said Miss Roxy. "I was saying to Ruey, this morning, that if Moses Pennel ever did turn out well, he ought to have a large share of the credit."

"Brother always did feel a peculiar interest in him; it was such a strange providence that seemed to cast in his lot among us," said Miss Emily.

"As sure as you live, there he is a-coming to the front door," said Miss Roxy.

"Dear me," said Miss Emily, "and here I have on this old

faded chintz. Just so sure as one puts on any old rag, and thinks nobody will come, company is sure to call."

"Law, I 'm sure I should n't think of calling him company," said Miss Roxy.

A rap at the door put an end to this conversation, and very soon Miss Emily introduced our hero into the little sitting-room, in the midst of a perfect stream of apologies relating to her old dress and the littered condition of the sitting-room, for Miss Emily held to the doctrine of those who consider any sign of human occupation and existence in a room as being disorder—however reputable and respectable be the cause of it.

"Well, really," she said, after she had seated Moses by the fire, "how time does pass, to be sure; it don't seem more than yesterday since you used to come with your Latin books, and now here you are a grown man! I must run and tell Mr. Sewell. He will be so glad to see you."

Mr. Sewell soon appeared from his study in morning-gown and slippers, and seemed heartily responsive to the proposition which Moses soon made to him to have some private conversation with him in his study.

"I declare," said Miss Emily, as soon as the study-door had closed upon her brother and Moses, "what a handsome young man he is! and what a beautiful way he has with him!—so deferential! A great many young men nowadays seem to think nothing of their minister; but he comes to seek advice. Very proper. It is n't every young man that appreciates the privilege of having elderly friends. I declare, what a beautiful couple he and Mara Lincoln would make! Don't Providence seem in a peculiar way to have designed them for each other?"

"I hope not," said Miss Roxy, with her grimmest expression.

"You don't! Why not?"

"I never liked him," said Miss Roxy, who had possessed herself of her great heavy goose, and was now thumping and squeaking it emphatically on the press-board. "She 's a thousand times too good for Moses Pennel,"—thump. "I ne'er had no faith in him,"—thump. "He 's dreffle unstiddy,"—thump. "He 's handsome, but he knows it,"—thump. "He won't never love nobody so much as he does himself,"—thump, *fortissimo con spirito.*

"Well, really now, Miss Roxy, you must n't always remember the sins of his youth. Boys must sow their wild oats. He was unsteady for a while, but now everybody says he 's doing well; and as to his knowing he 's handsome, and all that, I don't see as he does. See how polite and deferential he was to us all, this morning; and he spoke so handsomely to you."

"I don't want none of his politeness," said Miss Roxy, inexorably; "and as to Mara Lincoln, she might have better than him any day. Miss Badger was a-tellin' Captain Brown, Sunday noon, that she was very much admired in Boston."

"So she was," said Miss Emily, bridling. "I never reveal secrets, or I might tell something,—but there has been a young man,—but I promised not to speak of it, and I sha'n't."

"If you mean Mr. Adams," said Miss Roxy, "you need n't worry about keepin' that secret, 'cause that ar was all talked over atween meetin's a-Sunday noon; for Mis' Kittridge she used to know his aunt Jerushy, her that married Solomon Peters, and Mis' Captain Badger she says that he has a very good property, and is a professor in the Old South church in Boston."

"Dear me," said Miss Emily, "how things do get about!"

"People will talk, there ain't no use trying to help it," said Miss Roxy; "but it 's strongly borne in on my mind that it ain't Adams, nor 't ain't Moses Pennel that 's to marry her. I 've had peculiar exercises of mind about that ar child,—well I have;" and Miss Roxy pulled a large spotted bandanna handkerchief out of her pocket, and blew her nose like a trumpet, and then wiped the withered corners of her eyes, which were humid as some old Orr's Island rock wet with sea-spray.

Miss Emily had a secret love of romancing. It was one of the recreations of her quiet, monotonous life to build air-castles, which she furnished regardless of expense, and in which she set up at housekeeping her various friends and acquaintances, and she had always been bent on weaving a romance on the history of Mara and Moses Pennel. The good little body had done her best to second Mr. Sewell's attempts toward the education of the children. It was little busy Miss Emily who persuaded honest Zephaniah and Mary Pennel that talents such as Mara's ought to be cultivated, and that ended in sending her to Miss Plucher's school in Portland. There her artistic faculties were trained into creating funereal monuments out of chenille embroidery, fully equal to Miss Emily's own; also to painting landscapes, in which the ground and all the trees were one unvarying tint of blue-green; and also to creating flowers of a new and particular construction, which, as Sally Kittridge remarked, were pretty, but did not look like anything in heaven or earth. Mara had obediently and patiently done all these things; and solaced herself with copying flowers and birds and landscapes as near as possible like nature, as a recreation from these more dignified toils.

Miss Emily also had been the means of getting Mara invited to Boston, where she saw some really polished society, and gained as much knowledge of the forms of artificial life as a nature so wholly and strongly individual could obtain. So little Miss Emily regarded Mara as her godchild, and was intent on finishing her up into a romance in real life, of which a handsome young man, who had been washed ashore in a shipwreck, should be the hero.

What would she have said could she have heard the conversation that was passing in her brother's study? Little could she dream that the mystery, about which she had timidly nibbled for years, was now about to be unrolled;—but it was even so. But, upon what she does not see, good reader, you and I, following invisibly on tiptoe, will make our observations.

When Moses was first ushered into Mr. Sewell's study, and found himself quite alone, with the door shut, his heart beat so that he fancied the good man must hear it. He knew well what he wanted and meant to say, but he found in himself all that shrinking and nervous repugnance which always attends the proposing of any decisive question.

"I thought it proper," he began, "that I should call and express my sense of obligation to you, sir, for all the kindness you showed me when a boy. I 'm afraid in those thoughtless days I did not seem to appreciate it so much as I do now."

As Moses said this, the color rose in his cheeks, and his fine eyes grew moist with a sort of subdued feeling that made his face for the moment more than usually beautiful.

Mr. Sewell looked at him with an expression of peculiar interest, which seemed to have something almost of pain in it, and answered with a degree of feeling more than he commonly showed,—

"It has been a pleasure to me to do anything I could for you, my young friend. I only wish it could have been more. I congratulate you on your present prospects in life. You have perfect health; you have energy and enterprise; you are courageous and self-reliant, and, I trust, your habits are pure and virtuous. It only remains that you add to all this that fear of the Lord which is the beginning of wisdom."

Moses bowed his head respectfully, and then sat silent a moment, as if he were looking through some cloud where he vainly tried to discover objects.

Mr. Sewell continued, gravely,—

"You have the greatest reason to bless the kind Providence which has cast your lot in such a family, in such a community. I have had some means in my youth of comparing other parts of the country with our New England, and it is my opinion that a young man could not ask a better introduction into life than the wholesome nurture of a Christian family in our favored land."

"Mr. Sewell," said Moses, raising his head, and suddenly looking him straight in the eyes, "do you know anything of my family?"

The question was so point-blank and sudden, that for a moment Mr. Sewell made a sort of motion as if he dodged a pistol-shot, and then his face assumed an expression of grave thoughtfulness, while Moses drew a long breath. It was out,—the question had been asked.

"My son," replied Mr. Sewell, "it has always been my intention, when you had arrived at years of discretion, to make you acquainted with all that I know or suspect in regard to your life. I trust that when I tell you all I do know, you will see that I have acted for the best in the matter. It has been my study and my prayer to do so."

Mr. Sewell then rose, and unlocking the cabinet, of which we have before made mention, in his apartment, drew forth a very yellow and time-worn package of papers, which he untied. From these he selected one which enveloped an old-fashioned miniature case.

"I am going to show you," he said, "what only you and my God know that I possess. I have not looked at it now for ten years, but I have no doubt that it is the likeness of your mother."

Moses took it in his hand, and for a few moments there came a mist over his eyes,—he could not see clearly. He walked to the window as if needing a clearer light.

What he saw was a painting of a beautiful young girl, with large melancholy eyes, and a clustering abundance of black, curly hair. The face was of a beautiful, clear oval, with that warm brunette tint in which the Italian painters delight. The black eyebrows were strongly and clearly defined, and there was in the face an indescribable expression of childish innocence and shyness, mingled with a kind of confiding frankness, that gave the picture the charm which sometimes fixes itself in faces for which we involuntarily make a history. She was represented as simply attired in a white muslin, made low in the neck, and the hands and arms were singularly beautiful. The picture, as Moses looked at it, seemed to stand smiling at him with a childish grace,—a tender, ignorant innocence which affected him deeply.

"My young friend," said Mr. Sewell, "I have written all that I know of the original of this picture, and the reasons I have for thinking her your mother.

"You will find it all in this paper, which, if I had been providentially removed, was to have been given you in your twenty-first year. You will see in the delicate nature of the narrative that it could not properly have been imparted to you till you had arrived at years of understanding. I trust when you know all that you will be satisfied with the course I have pursued. You will read it at your leisure, and after reading I shall be happy to see you again."

Moses took the package, and after exchanging salutations with Mr. Sewell, hastily left the house and sought his boat.

When one has suddenly come into possession of a letter or paper in which is known to be hidden the solution of some long-pondered secret, of the decision of fate with regard to some long-cherished desire, who has not been conscious of a sort of pain,—an unwillingness at once to know what is therein? We turn the letter again and again, we lay it by and return to it, and defer from moment to moment the opening of it. So Moses did not sit down in the first retired spot to ponder the paper. He put it in the breast pocket of his coat, and then, taking up his oars, rowed across the bay. He did not land at the house, but passed around the south point of the Island, and rowed up the other side to seek a solitary retreat in the rocks, which had always been a favorite with him in his early days.

The shores of the Island, as we have said, are a precipitous wall of rock, whose long, ribbed ledges extend far out into the sea. At high tide these ledges are covered with the smooth blue sea quite up to the precipitous shore. There was a place, however, where the rocky shore shelved over, forming between two ledges a sort of grotto, whose smooth floor of shells and many-colored pebbles was never wet by the rising tide. It had been the delight of Moses when a boy, to come here and watch the gradual rise of the tide till the grotto was entirely cut off from all approach, and then to look out in a sort of hermit-like security over the open ocean that stretched before him. Many an hour he had sat there and dreamed of all the possible fortunes that might be found for him when he should launch away into that blue smiling futurity.

It was now about half-tide, and Moses left his boat and made his way over the ledge of rocks toward his retreat. They were all shaggy and slippery with yellow seaweeds, with here and there among them wide crystal pools, where purple and lilac and green mosses unfolded their delicate threads, and thousands of curious little shell-fish were tranquilly pursuing their quiet life. The rocks where the pellucid water lay were in some places crusted with barnacles, which were opening and shutting the little white scaly doors of their tiny houses, and drawing in and out those delicate pink plumes which seem to be their nerves of enjoyment. Moses and Mara had rambled and played here many hours of their childhood, amusing themselves with catching crabs and young lobsters and various little fish for these rocky aquariums, and then studying at their leisure their various ways. Now he had come hither a man, to learn the secret of his life.

Moses stretched himself down on the clean pebbly shore of the grotto, and drew forth Mr. Sewell's letter.

XXVI

🌲🌲🌲🌲🌲

DOLORES

Mr. Sewell's letter ran as follows:—

My Dear Young Friend,—It has always been my intention when you arrived at years of maturity to acquaint you with some circumstances which have given me reason to conjecture your true parentage, and to let you know what steps I have taken to satisfy my own mind in relation to these conjectures. In order to do this, it will be necessary for me to go back to the earlier years of my life, and give you the history of some incidents which are known to none of my most intimate friends. I trust I may rely on your honor that they will ever remain as secrets with you.

I graduated from Harvard University in——. At the time I was suffering somewhat from an affection of the lungs, which occasioned great alarm to my mother, many of whose family had died of consumption. In order to allay her uneasiness, and also for the purpose of raising funds for the pursuit of my professional studies, I accepted a position as tutor in the family of a wealthy gentleman at St. Augustine, in Florida.

I cannot do justice to myself,—to the motives which actuated me in the events which took place in this family, without speaking with the most undisguised freedom of the character of all the parties with whom I was connected.

Don José Mendoza was a Spanish gentleman of large property, who had emigrated from the Spanish West Indies to Florida, bringing with him an only daughter, who had been left an orphan by the death of her mother at a very early age. He brought to this country a large number of slaves;—and shortly after his arrival, married an American lady: a widow with three children. By her he had four other children. And thus it will appear that the family was made up of such a variety of elements as only the most judicious care could harmonize. But the character of the father and mother was such that judicious care was a thing not to be expected of either.

Don José was extremely ignorant and proud, and had lived a life of the grossest dissipation. Habits of absolute authority in the midst of a community of a very low moral standard had produced in him all the worst vices of despots. He was cruel, overbearing, and dreadfully passionate. His wife was a woman who had pretensions to beauty, and at times could make herself agreeable, and even fascinating, but she was possessed of a temper quite as violent and ungoverned as his own.

Imagine now two classes of slaves, the one belonging to the mistress, and the other brought into the country by the master, and each animated by a party spirit and jealousy;—imagine children of different marriages, inheriting from their parents violent tempers and stubborn wills, flattered and fawned on by slaves, and alternately petted or stormed at, now by this parent and now by that, and you will have some idea of the task which I undertook in being tutor in this family.

I was young and fearless in those days, as you are now, and

the difficulties of the position, instead of exciting apprehension, only awakened the spirit of enterprise and adventure.

The whole arrangements of the household, to me fresh from the simplicity and order of New England, had a singular and wild sort of novelty which was attractive rather than otherwise. I was well recommended in the family by an influential and wealthy gentleman of Boston, who represented my family, as indeed it was, as among the oldest and most respectable of Boston, and spoke in such terms of me, personally, as I should not have ventured to use in relation to myself. When I arrived, I found that two or three tutors, who had endeavored to bear rule in this tempestuous family, had thrown up the command after a short trial, and that the parents felt some little apprehension of not being able to secure the services of another,—a circumstance which I did not fail to improve in making my preliminary arrangements. I assumed an air of grave hauteur, was very exacting in all my requisitions and stipulations, and would give no promise of doing more than to give the situation a temporary trial. I put on an air of supreme indifference as to my continuance, and acted in fact rather on the assumption that I should confer a favor by remaining.

In this way I succeeded in obtaining at the outset a position of more respect and deference than had been enjoyed by any of my predecessors. I had a fine apartment, a servant exclusively devoted to me, a horse for riding, and saw myself treated among the servants as a person of consideration and distinction.

Don José and his wife both had in fact a very strong desire to retain my services, when after the trial of a week or two, it was found that I really could make their discordant and turbulent children to some extent obedient and studious during certain portions of the day; and in fact I soon acquired in the whole family that ascendency which a well-bred person who respects himself, and can keep his temper, must have over passionate and undisciplined natures.

I became the receptacle of the complaints of all, and a sort of confidential adviser. Don José imparted to me with more frankness than good taste his chagrins with regard to his wife's indolence, ill-temper, and bad management, and his wife in turn omitted no opportunity to vent complaints against her husband for similar reasons. I endeavored, to the best of my ability, to act a friendly part by both. It never was in my nature to see anything that needed to be done without trying to do it, and it was impossible to work at all without becoming so interested in my work as to do far more than I had agreed to do. I assisted Don José about many of his affairs; brought his neglected accounts into order; and suggested from time to time arrangements which relieved the difficulties which had been brought on by disorder and neglect. In fact, I became, as he said, quite a necessary of life to him.

In regard to the children, I had a more difficult task. The children of Don José by his present wife had been systematically stimulated by the negroes into a chronic habit of dislike and jealousy toward her children by a former husband. On the slightest pretext, they were constantly running to their father with complaints; and as the mother warmly espoused the cause of her first children, criminations and recriminations often convulsed the whole family.

In ill-regulated families in that region, the care of the children is from the first in the hands of half-barbarized negroes, whose power of moulding and assimilating childish minds is peculiar, so that the teacher has to contend constantly with a savage element in the children which seems to have been drawn in with the mother's milk. It is, in a modified way, something the same result as if the child had formed its manners in Dahomey or on the coast of Guinea. In the fierce quarrels which were carried on between the children of this family, I had frequent occasion to observe this strange, savage element, which sometimes led to expressions and actions which would seem incredible in civilized society.

The three children by Madame Mendoza's former husband were two girls of sixteen and eighteen and a boy of fourteen. The four children of the second marriage consisted of three boys and a daughter,—the eldest being not more than thirteen.

The natural capacity of all the children was good, although, from self-will and indolence, they had grown up in a degree of ignorance which could not have been tolerated except in a family living an isolated plantation life in the midst of barbarized dependents. Savage and untaught and passionate as they were, the work of teaching them was not without its interest to me. A power of control was with me a natural gift; and then that command of temper which is the common attribute of well-trained persons in the Northern states, was something so singular in this family as to invest its possessor with a certain awe; and my calm, energetic voice, and determined manner, often acted as a charm on their stormy natures.

But there was one member of the family of whom I have not yet spoken,—and yet all this letter is about her,—the daughter of Don José by his first marriage. Poor Dolores! poor child! God grant she may have entered into his rest!

I need not describe her. You have seen her picture. And in the wild, rude, discordant family, she always reminded me of the words, "a lily among thorns." She was in her nature unlike all the rest, and, I may say, unlike any one I ever saw. She seemed to live a lonely kind of life in this disorderly household, often marked out as the object of the spites and petty tyrannies of both parties. She was regarded with bitter hatred and jeal-

ousy by Madame Mendoza, who was sure to visit her with un-
sparing bitterness and cruelty after the occasional demonstrations of fondness she received from her father. Her exquisite
beauty and the gentle softness of her manners made her such a
contrast to her sisters as constantly excited their ill-will. Unlike
them all, she was fastidiously neat in her personal habits, and
orderly in all the little arrangements of life.

She seemed to me in this family to be like some shy, beautiful
pet creature in the hands of rude, unappreciative owners,
hunted from quarter to quarter, and finding rest only by stealth.
Yet she seemed to have no perception of the harshness and cruelty with which she was treated. She had grown up with it; it
was the habit of her life to study peaceable methods of averting
or avoiding the various inconveniences and annoyances of her
lot, and secure to herself a little quiet.

It not unfrequently happened, amid the cabals and storms
which shook the family, that one party or the other took up and
patronized Dolores for a while, more, as it would appear, out of
hatred for the other than any real love to her. At such times it
was really affecting to see with what warmth the poor child
would receive these equivocal demonstrations of good-will—
the nearest approaches to affection which she had ever
known—and the bitterness with which she would mourn when
they were capriciously withdrawn again. With a heart full of affection, she reminded me of some delicate, climbing plant trying vainly to ascend the slippery side of an inhospitable wall,
and throwing its neglected tendrils around every weed for support.

Her only fast, unfailing friend was her old negro nurse, or
Mammy, as the children called her. This old creature, with the
cunning and subtlety which had grown up from years of servi-
tude, watched and waited upon the interests of her little mistress, and contrived to carry many points for her in the con-

fused household. Her young mistress was her one thought and purpose in living. She would have gone through fire and water to serve her; and this faithful, devoted heart, blind and ignorant though it were, was the only unfailing refuge and solace of the poor hunted child.

Dolores, of course, became my pupil among the rest. Like the others, she had suffered by the neglect and interruptions in the education of the family, but she was intelligent and docile, and learned with a surprising rapidity. It was not astonishing that she should soon have formed an enthusiastic attachment to me, as I was the only intelligent, cultivated person she had ever seen, and treated her with unvarying consideration and delicacy. The poor thing had been so accustomed to barbarous words and manners that simple politeness and the usages of good society seemed to her cause for the most boundless gratitude.

It is due to myself, in view of what follows, to say that I was from the first aware of the very obvious danger which lay in my path in finding myself brought into close and daily relations with a young creature so confiding, so attractive, and so singularly circumstanced. I knew that it would be in the highest degree dishonorable to make the slightest advances toward gaining from her that kind of affection which might interfere with her happiness in such future relations as her father might arrange for her. According to the European fashion, I knew that Dolores was in her father's hands, to be disposed of for life according to his pleasure, as absolutely as if she had been one of his slaves. I had every reason to think that his plans on this subject were matured, and only waited for a little more teaching and training on my part, and her fuller development in womanhood, to be announced to her.

In looking back over the past, therefore, I have not to reproach myself with any dishonest and dishonorable breach of trust; for I was from the first upon my guard, and so much so that even the jealousy of my other scholars never accused me of partiality. I was not in the habit of giving very warm praise, and was in my general management anxious rather to be just than conciliatory, knowing that with the kind of spirits I had to deal with, firmness and justice went farther than anything else. If I approved Dolores oftener than the rest, it was seen to be because she never failed in a duty; if I spent more time with her lessons, it was because her enthusiasm for study led her to learn longer ones and study more things; but I am sure there was never a look or a word toward her that went beyond the proprieties of my position.

But yet I could not so well guard my heart. I was young and full of feeling. She was beautiful; and more than that, there was something in her Spanish nature at once so warm and simple, so artless and yet so unconsciously poetic, that her presence was a continual charm. How well I remember her now,—all her little ways,—the movements of her pretty little hands,—the expression of her changeful face as she recited to me,—the grave, rapt earnestness with which she listened to all my instructions!

I had not been with her many weeks before I felt conscious that it was her presence that charmed the whole house, and made the otherwise perplexing and distasteful details of my situation agreeable. I had a dim perception that this growing passion was a dangerous thing for myself; but was it a reason, I asked, why I should relinquish a position in which I felt that I was useful, and when I could do for this lovely child what no one else could do? I call her a child,—she always impressed me as such,—though she was in her sixteenth year and had the early womanly development of Southern climates. She seemed to me like something frail and precious, needing to be guarded and cared for; and when reason told me that I risked my own happiness in holding my position, love argued on the other hand that I was her only friend, and that I should be willing to risk something myself for the sake of protecting and shielding her. For there was no doubt that my presence in the family was a restraint upon the passions which formerly vented themselves so recklessly on her, and established a sort of order in which she found more peace than she had ever known before.

For a long time in our intercourse I was in the habit of looking on myself as the only party in danger. It did not occur to me that this heart, so beautiful and so lonely, might, in the want of all natural and appropriate objects of attachment, fasten itself on me unsolicited, from the mere necessity of loving. She seemed to me so much too beautiful, too perfect, to belong to a lot in life like mine, that I could not suppose it possible this could occur without the most blameworthy solicitation on my part; and it is the saddest and most affecting proof to me how this poor child had been starved for sympathy and love, that she should have repaid such cold services as mine with such an entire devotion. At first her feelings were expressed openly toward me, with the dutiful air of a good child. She placed flowers on my desk in the morning, and made quaint little nosegays in the Spanish fashion, which she gave me, and busied her leisure with various ingenious little knick-knacks of fancy work, which she brought me. I treated them all as the offerings of a child while with her, but I kept them sacredly in my own room. To tell the truth, I have some of the poor little things now.

But after a while I could not help seeing how she loved me; and then I felt as if I ought to go; but how could I? The pain to myself I could have borne; but how could I leave her to all the misery of her bleak, ungenial position? She, poor thing, was so unconscious of what I knew,—for I was made clear-sighted by love. I tried the more strictly to keep to the path I had marked out for myself, but I fear I did not always do it; in fact, many things seemed to conspire to throw us together. The sisters, who were sometimes invited out to visit on neighboring estates, were glad enough to dispense with the presence and attractions of Dolores, and so she was frequently left at home to study with me in their absence. As to Don José, although he always treated me with civility, yet he had such an ingrained and deep-rooted idea of his own superiority of position, that I suppose he would as soon have imagined the possibility of his daughter's falling in love with one of his horses. I was a great convenience to him. I had a knack of governing and carrying points in his family that it had always troubled and fatigued him to endeavor to arrange,—and that was all. So that my intercourse with Dolores was as free and unwatched, and gave me as many opportunities of enjoying her undisturbed society, as heart could desire.

At last came the crisis, however. After breakfast one morning, Don José called Dolores into his library and announced to her that he had concluded for her a treaty of marriage, and expected her husband to arrive in a few days. He expected that this news would be received by her with the glee with which a young girl hears of a new dress or of a ball-ticket, and was quite confounded at the grave and mournful silence in which she received it. She said no word, made no opposition, but went out from the room and shut herself up in her own apartment, and spent the day in tears and sobs.

Don José, who had rather a greater regard for Dolores than for any creature living, and who had confidently expected to give great delight by the news he had imparted, was quite confounded by this turn of things. If there had been one word of either expostulation or argument, he would have blazed and stormed in a fury of passion; but as it was, this broken-hearted submission, though vexatious, was perplexing. He sent for me, and opened his mind, and begged me to talk with Dolores and show her the advantages of the alliance, which the poor foolish child, he said, did not seem to comprehend. The man was immensely rich, and had a splendid estate in Cuba. It was a most desirable thing.

I ventured to inquire whether his person and manners were such as would be pleasing to a young girl, and could gather only that he was a man of about fifty, who had been most of his life in the military service, and was now desirous of making an establishment for the repose of his latter days, at the head of which he would place a handsome and tractable woman, and do well by her.

I represented that it would perhaps be safer to say no more on the subject until Dolores had seen him, and to this he agreed. Madame Mendoza was very zealous in the affair, for the sake of getting clear of the presence of Dolores in the family, and her sisters laughed at her for her dejected appearance. They only wished, they said, that so much luck might happen to them. For myself, I endeavored to take as little notice as possible of the affair, though what I felt may be conjectured. I knew,—I was perfectly certain,—that Dolores loved me as I loved her. I knew that she had one of those simple and unworldly natures which wealth and splendor could not satisfy, and whose life would lie entirely in her affections. Sometimes I violently debated with myself whether honor required me to sacrifice her happiness as well as my own, and I felt the strongest temptation to ask her to be my wife and fly with me to the Northern states, where I did not doubt my ability to make for her a humble and happy home.

But the sense of honor is often stronger than all reasoning, and I felt that such a course would be the betrayal of a trust; and I determined at least to command myself till I should see the character of the man who was destined to be her husband.

Meanwhile the whole manner of Dolores was changed. She maintained a stony, gloomy silence, performed all her duties in a listless way, and occasionally, when I commented on anything in her lessons or exercises, would break into little flashes of petulance, most strange and unnatural in her. Sometimes I could feel that she was looking at me earnestly, but if I turned my eyes toward her, hers were instantly averted; but there was in her eyes a peculiar expression at times, such as I have seen in the eye of a hunted animal when it turned at bay,—a sort of desperate resistance,—which, taken in connection with her fragile form and lovely face, produced a mournful impression.

One morning I found Dolores sitting alone in the schoolroom, leaning her head on her arms. She had on her wrist a bracelet of peculiar workmanship, which she always wore,— the bracelet which was afterwards the means of confirming her identity. She sat thus some moments in silence, and then she raised her head and began turning this bracelet round and round upon her arm, while she looked fixedly before her. At last she spoke abruptly, and said,—

"Did I ever tell you that this was *my mother's* hair? It is my mother's hair,—and she was the only one that ever loved me; except poor old Mammy, nobody else loves me,—nobody ever will."

"My dear Miss Dolores," I began.

"Don't call me dear," she said; "you don't care for me,—nobody does,—papa does n't, and I always loved him; everybody in the house wants to get rid of me, whether I like to go or not. I have always tried to be good and do all you wanted, and I should think *you* might care for me a little, but you don't."

"Dolores," I said, "I do care for you more than I do for any one in the world; I love you more than my own soul."

These were the very words I never meant to say, but somehow they seemed to utter themselves against my will. She looked at me for a moment as if she could not believe her hearing, and then the blood flushed her face, and she laid her head down on her arms.

At this moment Madame Mendoza and the other girls came into the room in a clamor of admiration about a diamond bracelet which had just arrived as a present from her future husband. It was a splendid thing, and had for its clasp his miniature, surrounded by the largest brilliants.

The enthusiasm of the party even at this moment could not say anything in favor of the beauty of this miniature, which, though painted on ivory, gave the impression of a coarse-featured man, with a scar across one eye.

"No matter for the beauty," said one of the girls, "so long as it is set with such diamonds."

"Come, Dolores," said another, giving her the present, "pull off that old hair bracelet, and try this on."

Dolores threw the diamond bracelet from her with a vehemence so unlike her gentle self as to startle every one.

"I shall not take off my mother's bracelet for a gift from a man I never knew," she said. "I hate diamonds. I wish those who like such things might have them."

"Was ever anything so odd?" said Madame Mendoza.

"Dolores always was odd," said another of the girls; "nobody ever could tell what she would like."

XXVII

HIDDEN THINGS

The next day Señor Don Guzman de Cardona arrived, and the whole house was in a commotion of excitement. There was to be no school, and everything was bustle and confusion. I passed my time in my own room in reflecting severely upon myself for the imprudent words by which I had thrown one more difficulty in the way of this poor harassed child.

Dolores this day seemed perfectly passive in the hands of her mother and sisters, who appeared disposed to show her great attention. She allowed them to array her in her most becoming dress, and made no objection to anything except removing the bracelet from her arm. "Nobody's gifts should take the place of her mother's," she said, and they were obliged to be content with her wearing of the diamond bracelet on the other arm.

Don Guzman was a large, plethoric man, with coarse features and heavy gait. Besides the scar I have spoken of, his face was adorned here and there with pimples, which were not set down in the miniature. In the course of the first hour's study, I saw him to be a man of much the same stamp as Dolores's father—sensual, tyrannical, passionate. He seemed in his own way to be much struck with the beauty of his intended wife, and was not wanting in efforts to please her. All that I could see in her was the settled, passive paleness of despair. She played, sang, exhibited her embroidery and painting, at the command of Madame Mendoza, with the air of an automaton; and Don Guzman remarked to her father on the passive obedience as a proper and hopeful trait. Once only when he, in presenting her a flower, took the liberty of kissing her cheek, did I observe the flashing of her eye and a movement of disgust and impatience, that she seemed scarcely able to restrain.

The marriage was announced to take place the next week, and a holiday was declared through the house. Nothing was talked of or discussed but the *corbeille de mariage* which the bridegroom had brought—the dresses, laces, sets of jewels, and cashmere shawls. Dolores never had been treated with such attention by the family in her life. She rose immeasurably in the eyes of all as the future possessor of such wealth and such an establishment as awaited her. Madame Mendoza had visions of future visits in Cuba rising before her mind, and overwhelmed her daughter-in-law with flatteries and caresses, which she received in the same passive silence as she did everything else.

For my own part, I tried to keep entirely by myself. I remained in my room reading, and took my daily rides, accompanied by my servant—seeing Dolores only at mealtimes, when I scarcely ventured to look at her. One night, however, as I was walking through a lonely part of the garden, Dolores suddenly stepped out from the shrubbery and stood before me. It was bright moonlight, by which her face and person were distinctly shown. How well I remember her as she looked then! She was dressed in white muslin, as she was fond of being, but it had been torn and disordered by the haste with which she had come through the shrubbery. Her face was fearfully pale, and her great, dark eyes had an unnatural brightness. She laid hold on my arm.

"Look here," she said, "I saw you and came down to speak with you."

She panted and trembled, so that for some moments she could not speak another word. "I want to ask you," she gasped, after a pause, "whether I heard you right? Did you say"—

"Yes, Dolores, you did. I did say what I had no right to say, like a dishonorable man."

"But is it true? Are you sure it is true?" she said, scarcely seeming to hear my words.

"God knows it is," said I despairingly.

"Then why don't you save me? Why do you let them sell me to this dreadful man? He don't love me—he never will. Can't you take me away?"

"Dolores, I am a poor man. I cannot give you any of these splendors your father desires for you."

"Do you think I care for them? I love you more than all the world together. And if you do really love me, why should we not be happy with each other?"

"Dolores," I said, with a last effort to keep calm, "I am much older than you, and know the world, and ought not to take advantage of your simplicity. You have been so accustomed to abundant wealth and all it can give, that you cannot form an idea of what the hardships and discomforts of marrying a poor man would be. You are unused to having the least care, or making the least exertion for yourself. All the world would say that I acted a very dishonorable part to take you from a position which offers you wealth, splendor, and ease, to one of comparative hardship. Perhaps some day you would think so yourself."

While I was speaking, Dolores turned me toward the moonlight, and fixed her great dark eyes piercingly upon me, as if she wanted to read my soul. "Is that all?" she said; "is that the only reason?"

"I do not understand you," said I.

She gave me such a desolate look, and answered in a tone of utter dejection, "Oh, I did n't know, but perhaps *you* might not want me. All the rest are so glad to sell me to anybody that will take me. But you really do love me, don't you?" she added, laying her hand on mine.

What answer I made I cannot say. I only know that every vestige of what is called reason and common sense left me at that moment, and that there followed an hour of delirium in which I—we both were *very* happy—we forgot everything but each other, and we arranged all our plans for flight. There was fortunately a ship lying in the harbor of St. Augustine, the captain of which was known to me. In course of a day or two passage was taken, and my effects transported on board. Nobody seemed to suspect us. Everything went on quietly up to the day before that appointed for sailing. I took my usual rides, and did everything as much as possible in my ordinary way, to disarm suspicion, and none seemed to exist. The needed preparations went gayly forward. On the day I mentioned, when I had ridden some distance from the house, a messenger came posthaste after me. It was a boy who belonged specially to Dolores. He gave me a little hurried note. I copy it:—

"Papa has found all out, and it is dreadful. No one else knows, and he means to kill you when you come back. Do, if you love me, hurry and get on board the ship. I shall never get over it, if evil comes on you for my sake. I shall let them do what they please with me, if God will only save *you*. I will try to be good. Perhaps if I bear my trials well, he will let me die soon. That is all I ask. I love you, and always shall, to death and after.

Dolores."

There was the end of it all. I escaped on the ship. I read the marriage in the paper. Incidentally I afterwards heard of her as

living in Cuba, but I never saw her again till I saw her in her cof-
fin. Sorrow and death had changed her so much that at first the
sight of her awakened only a vague, painful remembrance. The
sight of the hair bracelet which I had seen on her arm brought
all back, and I felt sure that my poor Dolores had strangely
come to sleep her last sleep near me.

Immediately after I became satisfied who you were, I felt a
painful degree of responsibility for the knowledge. I wrote at
once to a friend of mine in the neighborhood of St. Augustine,
to find out any particulars of the Mendoza family. I learned that
its history had been like that of many others in that region.
Don José had died in a bilious fever, brought on by excessive
dissipation, and at his death the estate was found to be so in-
cumbered that the whole was sold at auction. The slaves were
scattered hither and thither to different owners, and Madame
Mendoza, with her children and remains of fortune, had gone
to live in New Orleans.

Of Dolores he had heard but once since her marriage. A
friend had visited Don Guzman's estates in Cuba. He was living
in great splendor, but bore the character of a hard, cruel, tyrannical master, and an overbearing man. His wife was spoken of as
being in very delicate health,—avoiding society and devoting
herself to religion.

I would here take occasion to say that it was understood
when I went into the family of Don José, that I should not in
any way interfere with the religious faith of the children, the
family being understood to belong to the Roman Catholic
Church. There was so little like religion of any kind in the family, that the idea of their belonging to any faith savored something of the ludicrous. In the case of poor Dolores, however, it
was different. The earnestness of her nature would always have
made any religious form a reality to her. In her case I was glad
to remember that the Romish Church, amid many corruptions,

preserves all the essential beliefs necessary for our salvation, and that many holy souls have gone to heaven through its doors. I therefore was only careful to direct her principal attention to the more spiritual parts of her own faith, and to dwell on the great themes which all Christian people hold in common.

Many of my persuasion would not have felt free to do this, but my liberty of conscience in this respect was perfect. I have seen that if you break the cup out of which a soul has been used to take the wine of the gospel, you often spill the very wine itself. And after all, these forms are but shadows of which the substance is Christ.

I am free to say, therefore, that the thought that your poor mother was devoting herself earnestly to religion, although after the forms of a church with which I differ, was to me a source of great consolation, because I knew that in that way alone could a soul like hers find peace.

I have never rested from my efforts to obtain more information. A short time before the incident which cast you upon our shore, I conversed with a sea-captain who had returned from Cuba. He stated that there had been an attempt at insurrection among the slaves of Don Guzman, in which a large part of the buildings and out-houses of the estate had been consumed by fire. On subsequent inquiry I learned that Don Guzman had sold his estates and embarked for Boston with his wife and family, and that nothing had subsequently been heard of him.

Thus, my young friend, I have told you all that I know of those singular circumstances which have cast your lot on our shores. I do not expect at your time of life you will take the same view of this event that I do. You may possibly—very probably will—consider it a loss not to have been brought up as you might have been in the splendid establishment of Don

Guzman, and found yourself heir to wealth and pleasure without labor or exertion. Yet I am quite sure in that case that your value as a human being would have been immeasurably less. I think I have seen in you the elements of passions, which luxury and idleness and the too early possession of irresponsible power, might have developed with fatal results. You have simply to reflect whether you would rather be an energetic, intelligent, self-controlled man, capable of guiding the affairs of life and of acquiring its prizes,—or to be the reverse of all this, with its prizes bought for you by the wealth of parents. I hope mature reflection will teach you to regard with gratitude that disposition of the All-Wise, which cast your lot as it has been cast.

Let me ask one thing in closing. I have written for you here many things most painful for me to remember, because I wanted you to love and honor the memory of your mother. I wanted that her memory should have something such a charm for you as it has for me. With me, her image has always stood between me and all other women; but I have never even intimated to a living being that such a passage in my history ever occurred,—no, not even to my sister, who is nearer to me than any other earthly creature.

In some respects I am a singular person in my habits, and having once written this, you will pardon me if I observe that it will never be agreeable to me to have the subject named between us. Look upon me always as a friend, who would regard nothing as a hardship by which he might serve the son of one so dear.

I have hesitated whether I ought to add one circumstance more. I think I will do so, trusting to your good sense not to give it any undue weight.

I have never ceased making inquiries in Cuba, as I found opportunity, in regard to your father's property, and late investigations have led me to the conclusion that he left a considerable sum of money in the hands of a notary, whose address I have, which, if your identity could be proved, would come in course of law to you. I have written an account of all the circumstances which, in my view, identify you as the son of Don Guzman de Cardona, and had them properly attested in legal form.

This, together with your mother's picture and the bracelet, I recommend you to take on your next voyage, and to see what may result from the attempt. How considerable the sum may be which will result from this, I cannot say, but as Don Guzman's fortune was very large, I am in hopes it may prove something worth attention.

At any time you may wish to call, I will have all these things ready for you.

I am, with warm regard,
    Your sincere friend,
        Theophilus Sewell.

When Moses had finished reading this letter, he laid it down on the pebbles beside him, and, leaning back against a rock, looked moodily out to sea. The tide had washed quite up to within a short distance of his feet, completely isolating the little grotto where he sat from all the surrounding scenery, and before him, passing and repassing on the blue bright solitude of the sea, were silent ships, going on their wondrous pathless ways to unknown lands. The letter had stirred all within him that was dreamy and poetic: he felt somehow like a leaf torn from a romance, and blown strangely into the hollow of those rocks. Something too of ambition and pride stirred within him. He had been born an heir of wealth and power, little as they had done for the happiness of his poor mother; and when he thought he might have had these two wild horses which have run away with so many young men, he felt, as young men all do, an impetuous desire for their possession, and he thought as so many do, "Give them to me, and I 'll risk my character,—I 'll risk my happiness."

The letter opened a future before him which was something to speculate upon, even though his reason told him it was uncertain, and he lay there dreamily piling one air-castle on another, —unsubstantial as the great islands of white cloud that sailed through the sky and dropped their shadows in the blue sea.

It was late in the afternoon when he bethought him he must return home, and so climbing from rock to rock he swung himself upward on to the island, and sought the brown cottage. As he passed by the open window he caught a glimpse of Mara sewing. He walked softly up to look in without her seeing him. She was sitting with the various articles of his wardrobe around her, quietly and deftly mending his linen, singing soft snatches of an old psalm-tune.

She seemed to have resumed quite naturally that quiet care of him and his, which she had in all the earlier years of their life. He noticed again her little hands,—they seemed a sort of wonder to him. Why had he never seen, when a boy, how pretty they were? And she had such dainty little ways of taking up and putting down things as she measured and clipped; it seemed so pleasant to have her handling his things; it was as if a good fairy were touching them, whose touch brought back peace. But then, he thought, by and by she will do all this for some one else. The thought made him angry. He really felt abused in anticipation. She was doing all this for him just in sisterly kindness, and likely as not thinking of somebody else whom she loved better all the time. It is astonishing how cool and dignified this consideration made our hero as he faced up to the window. He was, after all, in hopes she might blush, and look agitated at seeing him suddenly; but she did not. The foolish boy did not know the quick wits of a girl, and that all the while that he had supposed himself so sly, and been holding his breath to observe, Mara had been perfectly cognizant of his presence, and had been schooling herself to look as unconscious and natural as possible. So she did, — only saying, —

"Oh, Moses, is that you? Where have you been all day?"

"Oh, I went over to see Parson Sewell, and get my pastoral lecture, you know."

"And did you stay to dinner?"

"No; I came home and went rambling round the rocks, and got into our old cave, and never knew how the time passed."

"Why, then you 've had no dinner, poor boy," said Mara, rising suddenly. "Come in quick, you must be fed, or you 'll get dangerous and eat somebody."

"No, no, don't get anything," said Moses, "it 's almost supper-time, and I 'm not hungry."

And Moses threw himself into a chair, and began abstractedly snipping a piece of tape with Mara's very best scissors.

"If you please, sir, don't demolish that; I was going to stay one of your collars with it," said Mara.

"Oh, hang it, I 'm always in mischief among girls' things," said Moses, putting down the scissors and picking up a bit of white wax, which with equal unconsciousness, he began kneading in his hands, while he was dreaming over the strange contents of the morning's letter.

"I hope Mr. Sewell did n't say anything to make you look so very gloomy," said Mara.

"Mr. Sewell?" said Moses, starting; "no, he did n't; in fact, I had a pleasant call there; and there was that confounded old sphinx of a Miss Roxy there. Why don't she die? She must be somewhere near a hundred years old by this time."

"Never thought to ask her why she did n't die," said Mara; "but I presume she has the best of reasons for living."

"Yes, that 's so," said Moses; "every old toadstool, and burdock, and mullein lives and thrives and lasts; no danger of their dying."

"You seem to be in a charitable frame of mind," said Mara.

"Confound it all! I hate this world. If I could have my own way now,—if I could have just what I wanted, and do just as I please exactly, I might make a pretty good thing of it."

"And pray what would you have?" said Mara.

"Well, in the first place, riches."

"In the first place?"

"Yes, in the first place, I say; for money buys everything else."

"Well, supposing so," said Mara, "for argument's sake, what would you buy with it?"

"Position in society, respect, consideration,—and I 'd have a splendid place, with everything elegant. I have ideas enough, only give me the means. And then I 'd have a wife, of course."

"And how much would you pay for her?" said Mara, looking quite cool.

"I 'd buy her with all the rest,—a girl that would n't look at *me* as I am,—would take me for all the rest, you know,—that 's the way of the world."

"It is, is it?" said Mara. "I don't understand such matters much."

"Yes; it 's the way with all you girls," said Moses; "it 's the way you 'll marry when you do."

"Don't be so fierce about it. I have n't done it yet," said Mara; "but now, really, I must go and set the supper-table when I have put these things away,"—and Mara gathered an armful of things together, and tripped singing upstairs, and arranged them in the drawer of Moses's room. "Will his wife like to do all these little things for him as I do?" she thought. "It 's natural I should. I grew up with him, and love him, just as if he were my own brother,—he is all the brother I ever had. I love him more than anything else in the world, and this wife he talks about could do no more."

"She don't care a pin about me," thought Moses; "it 's only a habit she has got, and her strict notions of duty, that 's all. She is housewifely in her instincts, and seizes all neglected linen and garments as her lawful prey,—she would do it just the same for her grandfather;" and Moses drummed moodily on the window-pane.

XXVIII

A COQUETTE

The timbers of the ship which was to carry the fortunes of our hero were laid by the side of Middle Bay, and all these romantic shores could hardly present a lovelier scene. This beautiful sheet of water separates Harpswell from a portion of Brunswick. Its shores are rocky and pine-crowned, and display the most picturesque variety of outline. Eagle Island, Shelter Island, and one or two smaller ones, lie on the glassy surface like soft clouds of green foliage pierced through by the steel-blue tops of arrowy pinetrees.

There were a goodly number of shareholders in the projected vessel; some among the most substantial men in the vicinity. Zephaniah Pennel had invested there quite a solid sum, as had also our friend Captain Kittridge. Moses had placed therein the proceeds of his recent voyage, which enabled him to buy a certain number of shares, and he secretly revolved in his mind whether the sum of money left by his father might not enable him to buy the whole ship. Then a few prosperous voyages, and his fortune was made!

He went into the business of building the new vessel with all the enthusiasm with which he used, when a boy, to plan ships and mould anchors. Every day he was off at early dawn in his working-clothes, and labored steadily among the men till evening. No matter how early he rose, however, he always found that a good fairy had been before him and prepared his dinner, daintily sometimes adding thereto a fragrant little bunch of flowers. But when his boat returned home at evening, he no longer saw her as in the days of girlhood waiting far out on the farthest point of rock for his return. Not that she did not watch for it and run out many times toward sunset; but the moment she had made out that it was surely he, she would run back into the house, and very likely find an errand in her own room, where she would be so deeply engaged that it would be necessary for him to call her down before she could make her appearance. Then she came smiling, chatty, always gracious, and ready to go or to come as he requested,—the very cheer-fulest of household fairies,—but yet for all that there was a cob-web invisible barrier around her that for some reason or other he could not break over. It vexed and perplexed him, and day after day he determined to whistle it down,—ride over it rough-shod,—and be as free as he chose with this apparently soft, un-resistant, airy being, who seemed so accessible. Why should n't he kiss her when he chose, and sit with his arm around her waist, and draw her familiarly upon his knee,—this little child-woman, who was as a sister to him? Why, to be sure? Had she ever frowned or scolded as Sally Kittridge did when he at-tempted to pass the air-line that divides man from woman-hood? Not at all. She had neither blushed nor laughed, nor ran away. If he kissed her, she took it with the most matter-of-fact composure; if he passed his arm around her, she let it remain with unmoved calmness; and so somehow he did these things less and less, and wondered why.

The fact is, our hero had begun an experiment with his little friend that we would never advise a young man to try on one of these intense, quiet, soft-seeming women, whose whole life is inward. He had determined to find out whether she loved him before he committed himself to her; and the strength of a whole book of martyrs is in women to endure and to bear without flinching before they will surrender the gate of this citadel of silence. Moreover, our hero had begun his siege with precisely the worst weapons.

For on the night that he returned and found Mara conversing with a stranger, the suspicion arose in his mind that somehow Mara might be particularly interested in him, and instead of asking her, which anybody might consider the most feasible step in the case, he asked Sally Kittridge.

Sally's inborn, inherent love of teasing was up in a moment. Did she know anything of that Mr. Adams? Of course she did,—a young lawyer of one of the best Boston families,—a splendid fellow; she wished any such luck might happen to her! Was Mara engaged to him? What would he give to know? Why did n't he ask Mara? Did he expect her to reveal her friend's secrets? Well, she should n't,—report said Mr. Adams was well-to-do in the world, and had expectations from an uncle,—and did n't Moses think he was interesting in conversation? Everybody said what a conquest it was for an Orr's Island girl, etc., etc. And Sally said the rest with many a malicious toss and wink and sly twinkle of the dimples of her cheek, which might mean more or less, as a young man of imaginative temperament was disposed to view it. Now this was all done in pure simple love of teasing. We incline to think phrenologists have as yet been very incomplete in their classification of faculties, or they would have appointed a separate organ for this propensity of human nature. Certain persons, often the most kind-hearted in the world, and who would not give pain in any serious matter, seem to have an insatiable appetite for those small annoyances we commonly denominate teasing,—and Sally was one of this number.

She diverted herself infinitely in playing upon the excitability of Moses,—in awaking his curiosity, and baffling it, and tormenting him with a whole phantasmagoria of suggestions and assertions, which played along so near the line of probability, that one could never tell which might be fancy and which might be fact.

Moses therefore pursued the line of tactics for such cases made and provided, and strove to awaken jealousy in Mara by paying marked and violent attentions to Sally. He went there evening after evening, leaving Mara to sit alone at home. He made secrets with her, and alluded to them before Mara. He proposed calling his new vessel the Sally Kittridge; but whether all these things made Mara jealous or not, he could never determine. Mara had no peculiar gift for acting, except in this one point; but here all the vitality of nature rallied to her support, and enabled her to preserve an air of the most unperceiving serenity. If she shed any tears when she spent a long, lonesome evening, she was quite particular to be looking in a very placid frame when Moses returned, and to give such an account of the books, or the work, or paintings which had interested her, that Moses was sure to be vexed. Never were her inquiries for Sally more cordial,—never did she seem inspired by a more ardent affection for her.

Whatever may have been the result of this state of things in regard to Mara, it is certain that Moses succeeded in convincing the common fame of that district that he and Sally were destined for each other, and the thing was regularly discussed at quilting frolics and tea-drinkings around, much to Miss Emily's

disgust and Aunt Roxy's grave satisfaction, who declared that
"Mara was altogether too good for Moses Pennel, but Sally Kittridge would make him stand round,"—by which expression
she was understood to intimate that Sally had in her the rudi-
ments of the same kind of domestic discipline which had oper-
ated so favorably in the case of Captain Kittridge.

These things, of course, had come to Mara's ears. She had
overheard the discussions on Sunday noons as the people between meetings sat over their doughnuts and cheese, and ana-
lyzed their neighbors' affairs, and she seemed to smile at them
all. Sally only laughed, and declared that it was no such thing;
that she would no more marry Moses Pennel, or any other fellow, than she would put her head into the fire. What did she
want of any of them? She knew too much to get married,—that
she did. She was going to have her liberty for one while yet to
come, etc., etc.; but all these assertions were of course supposed to mean nothing but the usual declarations in such cases.
Mara among the rest thought it quite likely that this thing was
yet to be.

So she struggled and tried to reason down a pain which constantly ached in her heart when she thought of this. She ought
to have foreseen that it must some time end in this way. Of
course she must have known that Moses would some time
choose a wife; and how fortunate that, instead of a stranger, he
had chosen her most intimate friend. Sally was careless and
thoughtless, to be sure, but she had a good generous heart at
the bottom, and she hoped she would love Moses at least as
well as *she* did, and then she would always live with them, and
think of any little things that Sally might forget.

After all, Sally was so much more capable and efficient a person than herself,—so much more bustling and energetic, she
would make altogether a better housekeeper, and doubtless a

better wife for Moses. But then it was so hard that he did not tell her about it. Was she not his sister?—his confidant for all his childhood?—and why should he shut up his heart from her now? But then she must guard herself from being jealous,—that would be mean and wicked. So Mara, in her zeal of self-discipline, pushed on matters; invited Sally to tea to meet Moses; and when she came, left them alone together while she busied herself in hospitable cares. She sent Moses with errands and commissions to Sally, which he was sure to improve into protracted visits; and in short, no young match-maker ever showed more good-will to forward the union of two chosen friends than Mara showed to unite Moses and Sally.

So the flirtation went on all summer, like a ship under full sail, with prosperous breezes; and Mara, in the many hours that her two best friends were together, tried heroically to persuade herself that she was not unhappy. She said to herself constantly that she never had loved Moses other than as a brother, and repeated and dwelt upon the fact to her own mind with a pertinacity which might have led her to suspect the reality of the fact, had she had experience enough to look closer. True, it was rather lonely, she said, but that she was used to,—she always had been and always should be. Nobody would ever love her in return as she loved; which sentence she did not analyze very closely, or she might have remembered Mr. Adams and one or two others, who had professed more for her than she had found herself able to return. That general proposition about nobody is commonly found, if sifted to the bottom, to have specific relation to somebody whose name never appears in the record.

Nobody could have conjectured from Mara's calm, gentle cheerfulness of demeanor, that any sorrow lay at the bottom of her heart; she would not have owned it to herself.

There are griefs which grow with years, which have no

marked beginnings,—no especial dates; they are not events, but slow perceptions of disappointment, which bear down on the heart with a constant and equable pressure like the weight of the atmosphere, and these things are never named or counted in words among life's sorrows; yet through them, as through an unsuspected inward wound, life, energy, and vigor slowly bleed away, and the persons, never owning even to themselves the weight of the pressure,—standing, to all appearance, fair and cheerful, are still undermined with a secret wear of this inner current, and ready to fall with the first external pressure.

There are persons often brought into near contact by the relations of life, and bound to each other by a love so close, that they are perfectly indispensable to each other, who yet act upon each other as a file upon a diamond, by a slow and gradual friction, the pain of which is so equable, so constantly diffused through life, as scarcely ever at any time to force itself upon the mind as a reality.

Such had been the history of the affection of Mara for Moses. It had been a deep, inward, concentrated passion that had almost absorbed self-consciousness, and made her keenly alive to all the moody, restless, passionate changes of his nature; it had brought with it that craving for sympathy and return which such love ever will, and yet it was fixed upon a nature so different and so uncomprehending that the action had for years been one of pain more than pleasure. Even now, when she had him at home with her and busied herself with constant cares for him, there was a sort of disturbing, unquiet element in the history of every day. The longing for him to come home at night,—the wish that he would stay with her,—the uncertainty whether he would or would not go and spend the evening with Sally,—the musing during the day over all that he had done and said the day before, were a constant interior excitement. For

Moses, besides being in his moods quite variable and change-able, had also a good deal of the dramatic element in him, and put on sundry appearances in the way of experiment.

He would feign to have quarreled with Sally, that he might detect whether Mara would betray some gladness; but she only evinced concern and a desire to make up the difficulty. He would discuss her character and her fitness to make a man happy in matrimony in the style that young gentlemen use who think their happiness a point of great consequence in the cre-ation; and Mara, always cool, and firm, and sensible, would talk with him in the most maternal style possible, and caution him against trifling with her affections. Then again he would be lav-ish in his praise of Sally's beauty, vivacity, and energy, and Mara would join with the most apparently unaffected delight. Some-times he ventured, on the other side, to rally her on some fu-ture husband, and predict the days when all the attentions which she was daily bestowing on him would be for another; and here, as everywhere else, he found his little Sphinx per-fectly inscrutable. Instinct teaches the grassbird, who hides her eggs under long meadow grass, to creep timidly yards from the nest, and then fly up boldly in the wrong place; and a like in-stinct teaches shy girls all kinds of unconscious stratagems when the one secret of their life is approached. They may be as truthful in all other things as the strictest Puritan, but here they deceive by an infallible necessity. And meanwhile, where was Sally Kittridge in all this matter? Was her heart in the least touched by the black eyes and long lashes? Who can say? Had she a heart? Well, Sally was a good girl. When one got suffi-ciently far down through the foam and froth of the surface to find what was in the depths of her nature, there was abundance there of good womanly feeling, generous and strong, if one could but get at it.

She was the best and brightest of daughters to the old Captain, whose accounts she kept, whose clothes she mended, whose dinner she often dressed and carried to him, from loving choice; and Mrs. Kittridge regarded her house-wifely accomplishments with pride, though she never spoke to her otherwise than in words of criticism and rebuke, as in her view an honest mother should who means to keep a flourishing sprig of a daughter within limits of a proper humility.

But as for any sentiment or love toward any person of the other sex, Sally, as yet, had it not. Her numerous admirers were only so many subjects for the exercise of her dear delight of teasing, and Moses Pennel, the last and most considerable, differed from the rest only in the fact that he was a match for her in this redoubtable art and science, and this made the game she was playing with him altogether more stimulating than that she had carried on with any other of her admirers. For Moses could sulk and storm for effect, and clear off as bright as Harpswell Bay after a thunder-storm—for effect also. Moses could play jealous, and make believe all those thousand-and-one shadowy nothings that coquettes, male and female, get up to carry their points with; and so their quarrels and their makings-up were as manifold as the sea-breezes that ruffled the ocean before the Captain's door.

There is but one danger in play of this kind, and that is, that deep down in the breast of every slippery, frothy, elfish Undine sleeps the germ of an unawakened soul, which suddenly, in the course of some such trafficking with the outward shows and seemings of affection, may wake up and make of the teasing, tricksy elf a sad and earnest woman—a creature of loves and self-denials and faithfulness unto death—in short, something altogether too good, too sacred to be trifled with; and when a man enters the game protected by a previous attachment which absorbs all his nature, and the woman awakes in all her depth and strength to feel the real meaning of love and life, she finds that she has played with one stronger than she, at a terrible disadvantage.

Is this mine lying dark and evil under the saucy little feet of our Sally? Well, we should not of course be surprised some day to find it so.

XXIX

♠♠♠♠♠

NIGHT TALKS

October is come, and among the black glooms of the pine forests flare out the scarlet branches of the rock-maple, and the beech-groves are all arrayed in gold, through which the sunlight streams in subdued richness. October is come with long, bright, hazy days, swathing in purple mists the rainbow brightness of the forests, and blending the otherwise gaudy and flaunting colors into wondrous harmonies of splendor. And Moses Pennel's ship is all built and ready, waiting only a favorable day for her launching.

And just at this moment Moses is sauntering home from Captain Kittridge's in company with Sally, for Mara has sent him to bring her to tea with them. Moses is in high spirits; everything has succeeded to his wishes; and as the two walk along the high, bold, rocky shore, his eye glances out to the open ocean, where the sun is setting, and the fresh wind blowing, and the white sails flying, and already fancies himself a sea-king, commanding his own place, and going from land to land.

"There has n't been a more beautiful ship built here these twenty years," he says, in triumph.

"Oho, Mr. Conceit," said Sally, "that's only because it's yours now—your geese are all swans. I wish you could have seen the Typhoon, that Ben Drummond sailed in—a real handsome fellow he was. What a pity there are n't more like him!"

"I don't enter on the merits of Ben Drummond's beauty," said Moses; "but I don't believe the Typhoon was one whit superior to our ship. Besides, Miss Sally, I thought you were going to take it under your especial patronage, and let me honor it with your name."

"How absurd you always will be talking about that—why don't you call it after Mara?"

"After Mara?" said Moses. "I don't want to—it would n't be appropriate—one wants a different kind of girl to name a ship after—something bold and bright and dashing!"

"Thank you, sir, but I prefer not to have my bold and dashing qualities immortalized in this way," said Sally; "besides, sir, how do I know that you would n't run me on a rock the very first thing? When I give my name to a ship, it must have an experienced commander," she added, maliciously, for she knew that Moses was specially vulnerable on this point.

"As you please," said Moses, with heightened color. "Allow me to remark that he who shall ever undertake to command the 'Sally Kittridge' will have need of all his experience—and then, perhaps, not be able to know the ways of the craft."

"See him now," said Sally, with a malicious laugh; "we are getting wrathy, are we?"

"Not I," said Moses; "it would cost altogether too much exertion to get angry at every teasing thing you choose to say, Miss Sally. By and by I shall be gone, and then won't your conscience trouble you?"

"My conscience is all easy, so far as you are concerned, sir; your self-esteem is too deep-rooted to suffer much from my poor little nips—they produce no more impression than a cat-bird pecking at the cones of that spruce-tree yonder. Now don't you put your hand where your heart is supposed to be—there's nobody at home there, you know. There's Mara coming to meet us;" and Sally bounded forward to meet Mara with all those demonstrations of extreme delight which young girls are fond of showering on each other.

"It's such a beautiful evening," said Mara, "and we are all in such good spirits about Moses's ship, and I told him you must come down and hold counsel with us as to what was to be done about the launching; and the name, you know, that is to be decided on—are you going to let it be called after you?"

"Not I, indeed. I should always be reading in the papers of horrible accidents that had happened to the 'Sally Kittridge.'"

"Sally has so set her heart on my being unlucky," said Moses, "that I believe if I make a prosperous voyage, the disappointment would injure her health."

"She does n't mean what she says," said Mara; "but I think there are some objections in a young lady's name being given to a ship."

"Then I suppose, Mara," said Moses, "that you would not have yours either?"

"I would be glad to accommodate you in anything *but* that," said Mara, quietly; but she added, "Why need the ship be named for anybody? A ship is such a beautiful, graceful thing, it should have a fancy name."

"Well, suggest one," said Moses.

"Don't you remember," said Mara, "one Saturday afternoon, when you and Sally and I launched your little ship down in the cove after you had come from your first voyage at the Banks?"

"I do," said Sally. "We called that the Ariel, Mara, after that old torn play you were so fond of. That's a pretty name for a ship."

"Why not take that?" said Mara.

"I bow to the decree," said Moses. "The Ariel it shall be."

"Yes; and you remember," said Sally, "Mr. Moses here promised at that time that he would build a ship, and take us two round the world with him."

Moses's eyes fell upon Mara as Sally said these words with a sort of sudden earnestness of expression which struck her. He was really feeling very much about something, under all the bantering disguise of his demeanor, she said to herself. Could it be that he felt unhappy about his prospects with Sally? That careless liveliness of hers might wound him perhaps now, when he felt that he was soon to leave her.

Mara was conscious herself of a deep undercurrent of sadness as the time approached for the ship to sail that should carry Moses from her, and she could not but think some such feeling must possess her mind. In vain she looked into Sally's great Spanish eyes for any signs of a lurking softness or tenderness concealed under her sparkling vivacity. Sally's eyes were admirable windows of exactly the right size and color for an earnest, tender spirit to look out of, but just now there was nobody at the casement but a slippery elf peering out in tricksy defiance.

When the three arrived at the house, tea was waiting on the table for them. Mara fancied that Moses looked sad and preoccupied as they sat down to the tea-table, which Mrs. Pennel had set forth festively, with the best china and the finest tablecloth and the choicest sweetmeats. In fact, Moses did feel that sort of tumult and upheaving of the soul which a young man experiences when the great crisis comes which is to plunge him into the struggles of manhood. It is a time when he wants sympathy and is grated upon by uncomprehending merriment, and therefore his answers to Sally grew brief and even harsh at times, and Mara sometimes perceived him looking at herself with a singular fixedness of expression, though he withdrew his eyes whenever she turned hers to look on him. Like many another little woman, she had fixed a theory about her friends, into which she was steadily interweaving all the facts she saw. Sally *must* love Moses, because she had known her from childhood as a good and affectionate girl, and it was impossible that she could have been going on with Moses as she had for the last six months without loving him. She must evidently have seen that he cared for her; and in how many ways had she shown that she liked his society and him! But then evidently she did not understand him, and Mara felt a little womanly self-pluming on the thought that *she* knew him so much better. She was resolved that she would talk with Sally about it, and show her that she was disappointing Moses and hurting his feelings. Yes, she said to herself, Sally has a kind heart, and her coquettish desire to conceal from him the extent of her affection ought now to give way to the outspoken tenderness of real love.

So Mara pressed Sally with the old-times request to stay and sleep with her; for these two, the only young girls in so lonely a neighborhood, had no means of excitement or dissipation beyond this occasional sleeping together—by which is meant, of course, lying awake all night talking.

When they were alone together in their chamber, Sally let down her long black hair, and stood with her back to Mara brushing it. Mara sat looking out of the window, where the moon was making a wide sheet of silver-sparkling water. Everything was so quiet that the restless dash of the tide could be plainly heard. Sally was rattling away with her usual gayety.

"And so the launching is to come off next Thursday. What shall you wear?"

"I 'm sure I have n't thought," said Mara.

"Well, I shall try and finish my blue merino for the occasion. What fun it will be! I never was on a ship when it was launched, and I think it will be something perfectly splendid!"

"But does n't it sometimes seem sad to think that after all this Moses will leave us to be gone so long?"

"What do I care?" said Sally, tossing back her long hair as she brushed it, and then stopping to examine one of her eyelashes.

"Sally dear, you often speak in that way," said Mara, "but really and seriously, you do yourself great injustice. You could not certainly have been going on as you have these six months past with a man you did not care for."

"Well, I do care for him, 'sort o',' " said Sally; "but is that any reason I should break my heart for his going? — that 's too much for any man."

"But, Sally, you *must* know that Moses loves you."

"I 'm not so sure," said Sally, freakishly tossing her head and laughing.

"If he did not," said Mara, "why has he sought you so much, and taken every opportunity to be with you? I 'm sure I 've been left here alone hour after hour, when my only comfort was that it was because my two best friends loved each other, as I know they must some time love some one better than they do me."

The most practiced self-control must fail some time, and Mara's voice faltered on these last words, and she put her hands over her eyes. Sally turned quickly and looked at her, then giving her hair a sudden fold round her shoulders, and running to her friend, she kneeled down on the floor by her, and put her arms round her waist, and looked up into her face with an air of more gravity than she commonly used.

"Now, Mara, what a wicked, inconsistent fool I have been! Did you feel lonesome? — did you care? I ought to have seen that; but I 'm selfish, I love admiration, and I love to have some one to flatter me, and run after me; and so I 've been going on and on in this silly way. But I did n't know you cared—indeed, I did n't—you are such a deep little thing. Nobody can ever tell what you feel. I never shall forgive myself, if you have been lonesome, for you are worth five hundred times as much as I am. You really do love Moses. I don't."

"I do love him as a dear brother," said Mara.

"Dear fiddlestick," said Sally. "Love is love; and when a person loves all she can, it is n't much use to talk so. I 've been a wicked sinner, that I have. Love? Do you suppose I would bear with Moses Pennel all his ins and outs and ups and downs, and be always putting him before myself in everything, as you do? No, I could n't; I have n't it in me; but you have. He 's a sinner, too, and deserves to get me for a wife. But, Mara, I have tormented him well—there 's some comfort in that."

"It 's no comfort to me," said Mara. "I see his heart is set on you—the happiness of his life depends on you—and that he is pained and hurt when you give him only cold, trifling words when he needs real true love. It is a serious thing, dear, to have a strong man set his whole heart on you. It will do him a great good or a great evil, and you ought not to make light of it."

"Oh, pshaw, Mara, you don't know these fellows; they are only playing games with us. If they once catch us, they have no mercy; and for one here 's a child that is n't going to be caught. I can see plain enough that Moses Pennel has been trying to get me in love with him, but he does n't love me. No, he does n't," said Sally, reflectively. "He only wants to make a conquest of me, and I 'm just the same. I want to make a conquest of him,— at least I have been wanting to,—but now I see it 's a false, wicked kind of way to do as we 've been doing."

"And is it really possible, Sally, that you don't love him?" said Mara, her large, serious eyes looking into Sally's. "What! be with him so much,—seem to like him so much,—look at him as I have seen you do,—and not love him!"

"I can't help my eyes; they will look so," said Sally, hiding her face in Mara's lap with a sort of coquettish consciousness. "I tell you I 've been silly and wicked; but he 's just the same exactly."

"And you have worn his ring all summer?"

"Yes, and he has worn mine; and I have a lock of his hair, and he has a lock of mine; yet I don't believe he cares for them a bit. Oh, his heart is safe enough. If he has any, it is n't with me: that I know."

"But if you found it were, Sally? Suppose you found that, after all, you were the one love and hope of his life; that all he was doing and thinking was for you; that he was laboring, and toiling, and leaving home, so that he might some day offer you a heart and home, and be your best friend for life? Perhaps he dares not tell you how he really does feel."

"It 's no such thing! it 's no such thing!" said Sally, lifting up her head, with her eyes full of tears, which she dashed angrily away. "What am I crying for? I hate him. I 'm glad he 's going away. Lately it has been such a trouble to me to have things go on so. I 'm really getting to dislike him. You are the one he ought to love. Perhaps all this time you are the one he does love," said Sally, with a sudden energy, as if a new thought had dawned in her mind.

"Oh, no; he does not even love me as he once did, when we were children," said Mara. "He is so shut up in himself, so reserved, I know nothing about what passes in his heart."

"No more does anybody," said Sally. "Moses Pennel is n't one that says and does things straightforward because he feels so; but he says and does them to see what *you* will do. That 's his way. Nobody knows why he has been going on with me as he has. He has had his own reasons, doubtless, as I have had mine."

"He has admired you very much, Sally," said Mara, "and praised you to me very warmly. He thinks you are so handsome. I could tell you ever so many things he has said about you. He knows as I do that you are a more enterprising, practical sort of body than I am, too. Everybody thinks you are engaged. I have heard it spoken of everywhere."

"Everybody is mistaken, then, as usual," said Sally. "Perhaps Aunt Roxy was in the right of it when she said that Moses would never be in love with anybody but himself."

"Aunt Roxy has always been prejudiced and unjust to Moses," said Mara, her cheeks flushing. "She never liked him from a child, and she never can be made to see anything good in him. I know that he has a deep heart,—a nature that craves affection and sympathy; and it is only because he is so sensitive that he is so reserved and conceals his feelings so much. He has a noble, kind heart, and I believe he truly loves you, Sally; it must be so."

Sally rose from the floor and went on arranging her hair without speaking. Something seemed to disturb her mind. She bit her lip, and threw down the brush and comb violently. In the clear depths of the little square of looking-glass a face looked into hers, whose eyes were perturbed as if with the shadows of some coming inward storm; the black brows were knit, and the lips quivered. She drew a long breath and burst out into a loud laugh.

"What *are* you laughing at now?" said Mara, who stood in her white night-dress by the window, with her hair falling in golden waves about her face.

"Oh, because these fellows are so funny," said Sally; "it 's such fun to see their actions. Come now," she added, turning to Mara, "don't look so grave and sanctified. It 's better to laugh than cry about things, any time. It 's a great deal better to be made hard-hearted like me, and not care for anybody, than to be like you, for instance. The idea of any one's being in love is the drollest thing to me. I have n't the least idea how it feels. I wonder if I ever shall be in love!"

"It will come to you in its time, Sally."

"Oh, yes,—I suppose like the chicken-pox or the whooping cough," said Sally; "one of the things to be gone through with, and rather disagreeable while it lasts,—so I hope to put it off as long as possible."

"Well, come," said Mara, "we must not sit up all night."

After the two girls were nestled into bed and the light out, instead of the brisk chatter there fell a great silence between them. The full round moon cast the reflection of the window on the white bed, and the ever restless moan of the sea became more audible in the fixed stillness. The two faces, both young and fair, yet so different in their expression, lay each still on its pillow,—their wide-open eyes gleaming out in the shadow like mystical gems. Each was breathing softly, as if afraid of disturbing the other. At last Sally gave an impatient movement.

"How lonesome the sea sounds in the night," she said. "I wish it would ever be still."

"I like to hear it," said Mara. "When I was in Boston, for a while I thought I could not sleep, I used to miss it so much."

There was another silence, which lasted so long that each girl thought the other asleep, and moved softly, but at a restless movement from Sally, Mara spoke again.

"Sally,—you asleep?"

"No,—I thought you were."

"I wanted to ask you," said Mara, "did Moses ever say anything to you about me?—you know I told you how much he said about you."

"Yes; he asked me once if you were engaged to Mr. Adams."

"And what did you tell him?" said Mara, with increasing interest.

"Well, I only plagued him. I sometimes made him think you were, and sometimes that you were not; and then again, that there was a deep mystery in hand. But I praised and glorified Mr. Adams, and told him what a splendid match it would be, and put on any little bits of embroidery here and there that I could lay hands on. I used to make him sulky and gloomy for a whole evening sometimes. In that way it was one of the best weapons I had."

"Sally, what does make you love to tease people so?" said Mara.

"Why, you know the hymn says,—

> 'Let dogs delight to bark and bite,
>   For God hath made them so;
> Let bears and lions growl and fight,
>   For 't is their nature too.'

That 's all the account I can give of it."

"But," said Mara, "I never can rest easy a moment when I see I am making a person uncomfortable."

"Well, I don't tease anybody but the men. I don't tease father or mother or you,—but men are fair game; they are such thumby, blundering creatures, and we can confuse them so."

"Take care, Sally, it 's playing with edge tools; you may lose your heart some day in this kind of game."

"Never you fear," said Sally; "but are n't you sleepy?—let 's go to sleep."

Both girls turned their faces resolutely in opposite directions, and remained for an hour with their large eyes looking out into the moonlit chamber, like the fixed stars over Harpswell Bay. At last sleep drew softly down the fringy curtains.

XXX

THE LAUNCH OF
THE ARIEL

In the plain, simple regions we are describing,—where the sea is the great avenue of active life, and the pine forests are the great source of wealth,—ship-building is an engrossing interest, and there is no fête that calls forth the community like the launching of a vessel. And no wonder; for what is there belonging to this workaday world of ours that has such a never-failing fund of poetry and grace as a ship? A ship is a beauty and a mystery wherever we see it: its white wings touch the regions of the unknown and the imaginative; they seem to us full of the odors of quaint, strange, foreign shores, where life, we fondly dream, moves in brighter currents than the muddy, tranquil tides of every day.

Who that sees one bound outward, with her white breasts swelling and heaving, as if with a reaching expectancy, does not feel his own heart swell with a longing impulse to go with her to the far-off shores? Even at dingy, crowded wharves, amid the stir and tumult of great cities, the coming in of a ship is an event that never can lose its interest. But on these romantic shores of Maine, where all is so wild and still, and the blue sea lies embraced in the arms of dark, solitary forests, the sudden incoming of a ship from a distant voyage is a sort of romance. Who that has stood by the blue waters of Middle Bay, engirdled as it is by soft slopes of green farming land, interchanged here and there with heavy billows of forest-trees, or rocky, pine-crowned promontories, has not felt that sense of seclusion and solitude which is so delightful? And then what a wonder! There comes a ship from China, drifting in like a white cloud,—the gallant creature! how the waters hiss and foam before her! with what a great free, generous plash she throws out her anchors, as if she said a cheerful "Well done!" to some glorious work accomplished! The very life and spirit of strange romantic lands come with her; suggestions of sandal-wood and spice breathe through the pine-woods; she is an oriental queen, with hands full of mystical gifts; "all her garments smell of myrrh and cassia, out of the ivory palaces, whereby they have made her glad." No wonder men have loved ships like birds, and that there have been found brave, rough hearts that in fatal wrecks chose rather to go down with their ocean love than to leave her in the last throes of her death-agony.

A ship-building, a ship-sailing community has an unconscious poetry ever underlying its existence. Exotic ideas from foreign lands relieve the trite monotony of life; the ship-owner lives in communion with the whole world, and is less likely to fall into the petty commonplaces that infest the routine of inland life.

Never arose a clearer or lovelier October morning than that which was to start the Ariel on her watery pilgrimage. Moses had risen while the stars were yet twinkling over their own images in Middle Bay, to go down and see that everything was right; and in all the houses that we know in the vicinity, everybody woke with the one thought of being ready to go to the launching.

Mrs. Pennel and Mara were also up by starlight, busy over the provisions for the ample cold collation that was to be spread in a barn adjoining the scene,—the materials for which they were packing into baskets covered with nice clean linen cloths, ready for the little sail-boat which lay within a stone's throw of the door in the brightening dawn, her white sails looking rosy in the advancing light.

It had been agreed that the Pennels and the Kittridges should cross together in this boat with their contributions of good cheer.

The Kittridges, too, had been astir with the dawn, intent on their quota of the festive preparations, in which Dame Kittridge's housewifely reputation was involved,—for it had been a disputed point in the neighborhood whether she or Mrs. Pennel made the best doughnuts; and of course, with this fact before her mind, her efforts in this line had been all but superhuman.

The Captain skipped in and out in high feather,—occasionally pinching Sally's cheek, and asking if she were going as captain or mate upon the vessel after it was launched, for which he got in return a fillip of his sleeve or a sly twitch of his coat-tails, for Sally and her old father were on romping terms with each other from early childhood, a thing which drew frequent lectures from the always exhorting Mrs. Kittridge.

"Such levity!" she said, as she saw Sally in full chase after his retreating figure, in order to be revenged for some sly allusions he had whispered in her ear.

"Sally Kittridge! Sally Kittridge!" she called, "come back this minute. What are you about? I should think your father was old enough to know better."

"Lawful sakes, Polly, it kind o' renews one's youth to get a new ship done," said the Captain, skipping in at another door. "Sort o' puts me in mind o' that *I* went out cap'en in when I was jist beginning to court you, as somebody else is courtin' our Sally here."

"Now, father," said Sally, threateningly, "what did I tell you?"

"It 's really *lemancholy*," said the Captain, "to think how it does distress gals to talk to 'em 'bout the fellers, when they ain't thinkin' o' nothin' else all the time. They can't even laugh without sayin' he-he-he!"

"Now, father, you know I 've told you five hundred times that I don't care a cent for Moses Pennel, — that he 's a hateful creature," said Sally, looking very red and determined.

"Yes, yes," said the Captain, "I take that ar 's the reason you 've ben a-wearin' the ring he gin you and them ribbins you 've got on your neck this blessed minute, and why you 've giggled off to singin'-school, and Lord knows where with him all summer, — that ar 's clear now."

"But, father," said Sally, getting redder and more earnest, "I don't care for him really, and I 've told him so. I keep telling him so, and he will run after me."

"Haw! haw!" laughed the Captain; "he will, will he? Jist so, Sally; that ar 's jist the way your ma there talked to me, and it kind o' 'couraged me along. I knew that gals always has to be read back'ard jist like the writin' in the Barbary States."

"Captain Kittridge, will you stop such ridiculous talk?" said his helpmeet; "and jist carry this 'ere basket of cold chicken down to the landin' agin the Pennels come round in the boat; and you must step spry, for there 's two more baskets a-comin'."

The Captain shouldered the basket and walked toward the sea with it, and Sally retired to her own little room to hold a farewell consultation with her mirror before she went.

You will perhaps think from the conversation that you heard the other night, that Sally now will cease all thought of coquettish allurement in her acquaintance with Moses, and cause him to see by an immediate and marked change her entire indifference. Probably, as she stands thoughtfully before her mirror, she is meditating on the propriety of laying aside the ribbons he gave her—perhaps she will alter that arrangement of her hair which is one that he himself particularly dictated as most becoming to the character of her face. She opens a little drawer, which looks like a flower garden, all full of little knots of pink and blue and red, and various fancies of the toilet, and looks into it reflectively. She looses the ribbon from her hair and chooses another,—but Moses gave her that too, and said, she remembers, that when she wore that "he should know she had been thinking of him." Sally is Sally yet—as full of sly dashes of coquetry as a tulip is of streaks.

"There 's no reason I should make myself look like a fright because I don't care for him," she says; "besides, after all that he has said, he ought to say more,—he ought at least to give me a chance to say no,—he *shall*, too," said the gypsy, winking at the bright, elfish face in the glass.

"Sally Kittridge, Sally Kittridge," called her mother, "how long will you stay prinkin'?—come down this minute."

"Law now, mother," said the Captain, "gals must prink afore such times; it 's as natural as for hens to dress their feathers afore a thunder-storm."

Sally at last appeared, all in a flutter of ribbons and scarfs, whose bright, high colors assorted well with the ultramarine blue of her dress, and the vivid pomegranate hue of her cheeks. The boat with its white sails flapping was balancing and courtesying up and down on the waters, and in the stern sat Mara; her shining white straw hat trimmed with blue ribbons set off her golden hair and pink shell complexion. The dark, even penciling of her eyebrows, and the beauty of the brow above, the brown translucent clearness of her thoughtful eyes, made her face striking even with its extreme delicacy of tone. She was un-usually animated and excited, and her cheeks had a rich bloom of that pure deep rose-color which flushes up in fair complex-ions under excitement, and her eyes had a kind of intense ex-pression, for which they had always been remarkable. All the deep secluded yearning of repressed nature was looking out of them, giving that pathos which every one has felt at times in the silence of eyes.

"Now bless that ar gal," said the Captain, when he saw her. "Our Sally here 's handsome, but she 's got the real New-Jerusalem look, she has—like them in the Revelations that wears the fine linen, clean and white."

"Bless you, Captain Kittridge! don't be a-makin' a fool of yourself about no girl at your time o' life," said Mrs. Kittridge, speaking under her breath in a nipping, energetic tone, for they were coming too near the boat to speak very loud.

"Good mornin', Mis' Pennel; we 've got a good day, and a mercy it is so. 'Member when we launched the North Star, that it rained guns all the mornin', and the water got into the bas-kets when we was a-fetchin' the things over, and made a sight o' pester."

"Yes," said Mrs. Pennel, with an air of placid satisfaction, "ev-erything seems to be going right about this vessel."

Mrs. Kittridge and Sally were soon accommodated with seats, and Zephaniah Pennel and the Captain began trimming sail. The day was one of those perfect gems of days which are to be found only in the jewel-casket of October, a day neither hot nor cold, with an air so clear that every distant pine-tree top stood out in vivid separateness, and every woody point and rocky island seemed cut out in crystalline clearness against the sky. There was so brisk a breeze that the boat slanted quite to the water's edge on one side, and Mara leaned over and pensively drew her little pearly hand through the water, and thought of the days when she and Moses took this sail together—she in her pink sun-bonnet, and he in his round straw hat, with a tin dinner-pail between them; and now, to-day the ship of her childish dreams was to be launched. That launching was something she regarded almost with superstitious awe. The ship, built on one element, but designed to have its life in another, seemed an image of the soul, framed and fashioned with many a weary hammer-stroke in this life, but finding its true element only when it sails out into the ocean of eternity. Such was her thought as she looked down the clear, translucent depths; but would it have been of any use to try to utter it to anybody?—to Sally Kittridge, for example, who sat all in a cheerful rustle of bright ribbons beside her, and who would have shown her white teeth all round at such a suggestion, and said, "Now, Mara, who but you would have thought of that?"

But there are souls sent into this world who seem to have always mysterious affinities for the invisible and the unknown— who see the face of everything beautiful through a thin veil of mystery and sadness. The Germans call this yearning of spirit home-sickness—the dim remembrances of a spirit once affiliated to some higher sphere, of whose lost brightness all things fair are the vague reminders. As Mara looked pensively into the water, it seemed to her that every incident of life came up out of its depths to meet her. Her own face reflected in a wavering image, sometimes shaped itself to her gaze in the likeness of the pale lady of her childhood, who seemed to look up at her from the waters with dark, mysterious eyes of tender longing. Once or twice this dreamy effect grew so vivid that she shivered, and drawing herself up from the water, tried to take an interest in a very minute account which Mrs. Kittridge was giving of the way to make corn-fritters which should taste exactly like oysters. The closing direction about the quantity of mace Mrs. Kittridge felt was too sacred for common ears, and therefore whispered it into Mrs. Pennel's bonnet with a knowing nod and a look from her black spectacles which would not have been bad for a priestess of Dodona in giving out an oracle. In this secret direction about the *mace* lay the whole mystery of corn-oysters; and who can say what consequences might ensue from casting it in an unguarded manner before the world?

And now the boat which has rounded Harpswell Point is skimming across to the head of Middle Bay, where the new ship can distinctly be discerned standing upon her ways, while moving clusters of people were walking up and down her decks or lining the shore in the vicinity. All sorts of gossiping and neighborly chit-chat is being interchanged in the little world assembling there.

"I hain't seen the Pennels nor the Kittridges yet," said Aunt Ruey, whose little roly-poly figure was made illustrious in her best cinnamon-colored dyed silk. "There 's Moses Pennel a-goin' up that ar ladder. Dear me, what a beautiful feller he is! it 's a pity he ain't a-goin' to marry Mara Lincoln, after all."

"Ruey, do hush up," said Miss Roxy, frowning sternly down from under the shadow of a preternatural black straw bonnet, trimmed with huge bows of black ribbon, which head-piece sat above her curls like a helmet. "Don't be a-gettin' sentimental, Ruey, whatever else you get—and talkin' like Miss Emily Sewell about match-makin'; I can't stand it; it rises on my stomach, such talk does. As to that ar Moses Pennel, folks ain't so certain as they thinks what he 'll do. Sally Kittridge may think he 's a-goin' to have her, because he 's been a-foolin' round with her all summer, and Sally Kittridge may jist find she 's mistaken, that 's all."

"Yes," said Miss Ruey, "I 'member when I was a girl my old

aunt, Jerushy Hopkins, used to be always a-dwellin' on this Scripture, and I 've been havin' it brought up to me this mornin': 'There are three things which are too wonderful for me, yea, four, which I know not: the way of an eagle in the air, the way of a serpent upon a rock, the way of a ship in the sea, and the way of a man with a maid.' She used to say it as a kind o' caution to me when she used to think Abram Peters was bein' attentive to me. I 've often reflected what a massy it was that ar never come to nothin', for he 's a poor drunken critter now."

"Well, for my part," said Miss Roxy, fixing her eyes critically on the boat that was just at the landing, "I should say the ways of a maid with a man was full as particular as any of the rest of 'em. Do look at Sally Kittridge now. There 's Tom Hiers a-helpin' her out of the boat; and did you see the look she gin Moses Pennel as she went by him? Wal, Moses has got Mara on his arm anyhow; there 's a gal worth six-and-twenty of the other. Do see them ribbins and scarfs, and the furbelows, and the way that ar Sally Kittridge handles her eyes. She 's one that one feller ain't never enough for."

Mara's heart beat fast when the boat touched the shore, and Moses and one or two other young men came to assist in their landing. Never had he looked more beautiful than at this moment, when flushed with excitement and satisfaction he stood on the shore, his straw hat off, and his black curls blowing in the sea-breeze. He looked at Sally with a look of frank admiration as she stood there dropping her long black lashes over her bright cheeks, and coquettishly looking out from under them, but she stepped forward with a little energy of movement, and took the offered hand of Tom Hiers, who was gazing at her too with undisguised rapture, and Moses, stepping into the boat, helped Mrs. Pennel on shore, and then took Mara on his arm, looking her over as he did so with a glance far less assured and direct than he had given to Sally.

"You won't be afraid to climb the ladders, Mara?" said he.

"Not if you help me," she said.

Sally and Tom Hiers had already walked on toward the vessel, she ostentatiously chatting and laughing with him. Moses's brow clouded a little, and Mara noticed it. Moses thought he did not care for Sally; he knew that the little hand that was now lying on his arm was the one he wanted, and yet he felt vexed when he saw Sally walk off triumphantly with another. It was the dog-in-the-manger feeling which possesses coquettes of both sexes. Sally, on all former occasions, had shown a marked preference for him, and professed supreme indifference to Tom Hiers.

"It 's all well enough," he said to himself, and he helped Mara up the ladders with the greatest deference and tenderness. "This little woman is worth ten such girls as Sally, if one only could get her heart. . . . Here we are on our ship, Mara," he said, as he lifted her over the last barrier and set her down on the deck. "Look over there, do you see Eagle Island? Did you dream when we used to go over there and spend the day that you ever would be on *my* ship, as you are to-day? You won't be afraid, will you, when the ship starts?"

"I am too much of a sea-girl to fear on anything that sails in water," said Mara with enthusiasm. "What a splendid ship! how nicely it all looks!"

"Come, let me take you over it," said Moses, "and show you my cabin."

Meanwhile the graceful little vessel was the subject of various comments by the crowd of spectators below, and the clatter of workmen's hammers busy in some of the last preparations could yet be heard like a shower of hail-stones under her.

"I hope the ways are well greased," said old Captain Eldritch. "'Member how the John Peters stuck in her ways for want of their being greased?"

"Don't you remember the Grand Turk, that keeled over five minutes after she was launched?" said the quavering voice of Miss Ruey; "there was jist such a company of thoughtless young creatures aboard as there is now."

"Well, there was n't nobody hurt," said Captain Kittridge. "If Mis' Kittridge would let me, I 'd be glad to go aboard this 'ere, and be launched with 'em."

"I tell the Cap'n he 's too old to be climbin' round and mixin' with young folks' frolics," said Mrs. Kittridge.

"I suppose, Cap'n Pennel, you 've seen that the ways is all right," said Captain Broad, returning to the old subject.

"Oh yes, it 's all done as well as hands can do it," said Zephaniah. "Moses has been here since starlight this morning, and Moses has pretty good faculty about such matters."

"Where 's Mr. Sewell and Miss Emily?" said Miss Ruey. "Oh, there they are over on that pile of rocks; they get a pretty fair view there."

Mr. Sewell and Miss Emily were sitting under a cedar-tree, with two or three others, on a projecting point whence they could have a clear view of the launching. They were so near that they could distinguish clearly the figures on deck, and see Moses standing with his hat off, the wind blowing his curls back, talking earnestly to the golden-haired little woman on his arm.

"It is a launch into life for him," said Mr. Sewell, with suppressed feeling.

"Yes, and he has Mara on his arm," said Miss Emily; "that 's as it should be. Who is that that Sally Kittridge is flirting with now? Oh, Tom Hiers. Well! he 's good enough for her. Why don't she take him?" said Miss Emily, in her zeal jogging her brother's elbow.

"I 'm sure, Emily, I don't know," said Mr. Sewell dryly; "perhaps he won't be taken."

"Don't you think Moses looks handsome?" said Miss Emily. "I declare there is something quite romantic and Spanish about him; don't you think so, Theophilus?"

"Yes, I think so," said her brother, quietly looking, externally, the meekest and most matter-of-fact of persons, but deep within him a voice sighed, "Poor Dolores, be comforted, your boy is beautiful and prosperous!"

"There, there!" said Miss Emily, "I believe she is starting."

All eyes of the crowd were now fixed on the ship; the sound of hammers stopped; the workmen were seen flying in every direction to gain good positions to see her go,—that sight so often seen on those shores, yet to which use cannot dull the most insensible.

First came a slight, almost imperceptible, movement, then a swift exultant rush, a dash into the hissing water, and the air was rent with hurrahs as the beautiful ship went floating far out on the blue seas, where her fairer life was henceforth to be.

Mara was leaning on Moses's arm at the instant the ship began to move, but in the moment of the last dizzy rush she felt his arm go tightly round her, holding her so close that she could hear the beating of his heart.

"Hurrah!" he said, letting go his hold the moment the ship floated free, and swinging his hat in answer to the hats, scarfs, and handkerchiefs, which fluttered from the crowd on the shore. His eyes sparkled with a proud light as he stretched himself upward, raising his head and throwing back his shoulders with a triumphant movement. He looked like a young sea-king just crowned; and the fact is the less wonderful, therefore, that Mara felt her heart throb as she looked at him, and that a treacherous throb of the same nature shook the breezy ribbons fluttering over the careless heart of Sally. A handsome young sea-captain, treading the deck of his own vessel, is, in his time and place, a prince.

Moses looked haughtily across at Sally, and then passed a half-laughing defiant flash of eyes between them. He looked at Mara, who could certainly not have known what was in her eyes at the moment,—an expression that made his heart give a great throb, and wonder if he saw aright: but it was gone a moment after, as all gathered around in a knot exchanging congratulations on the fortunate way in which the affair had gone off. Then came the launching in boats to go back to the collation on shore, where were high merry-makings for the space of one or two hours: and thus was fulfilled the first part of Moses Pennel's Saturday afternoon prediction.

XXXI

GREEK
MEETS GREEK

Moses was now within a day or two of the time of his sailing, and yet the distance between him and Mara seemed greater than ever. It is astonishing, when two people are once started on a wrong understanding with each other, how near they may live, how intimate they may be, how many things they may have in common, how many words they may speak, how closely they may seem to simulate intimacy, confidence, friendship, while yet there lies a gulf between them that neither crosses,—a reserve that neither explores.

Like most shy girls, Mara became more shy the more really she understood the nature of her own feelings. The conversation with Sally had opened her eyes to the secret of her own heart, and she had a guilty feeling as if what she had discovered must be discovered by every one else. Yes, it was clear she loved Moses in a way that made him, she thought, more necessary to her happiness than she could ever be to his,—in a way that made it impossible to think of him as wholly and for life devoted to another, without a constant inner conflict. In vain had been all her little stratagems practiced upon herself the whole summer long, to prove to herself that she was glad that the choice had fallen upon Sally. She saw clearly enough now that she was not glad,—that there was no woman or girl living, however dear, who could come for life between him and her, without casting on her heart the shuddering sorrow of a dim eclipse.

But now the truth was plain to herself, her whole force was directed toward the keeping of her secret. "I may suffer," she thought, "but I will have strength not to be silly and weak. Nobody shall know,—nobody shall dream it,—and in the long, long time that he is away, I shall have strength given me to overcome."

So Mara put on her most cheerful and matter-of-fact kind of face, and plunged into the making of shirts and knitting of stockings, and talked of the coming voyage with such a total absence of any concern, that Moses began to think, after all, there could be no depth to her feelings, or that the deeper ones were all absorbed by some one else.

"You really seem to enjoy the prospect of my going away," said he to her, one morning, as she was energetically busying herself with her preparations.

"Well, of course; you know your career must begin. You must make your fortune; and it is pleasant to think how favorably everything is shaping for you."

"One likes, however, to be a little regretted," said Moses, in a tone of pique.

"A little regretted!" Mara's heart beat at these words, but her hypocrisy was well practiced. She put down the rebellious throb, and assuming a look of open, sisterly friendliness, said, quite naturally, "Why, we shall all miss you, of course."

"Of course," said Moses,—"one would be glad to be missed some other way than *of course*."

"Oh, as to that, make yourself easy," said Mara. "We shall all be dull enough when you are gone to content the most exacting." Still she spoke, not stopping her stitching, and raising her soft brown eyes with a frank, open look into Moses's—no tremor, not even of an eyelid.

"You men must have everything," she continued, gayly, "the enterprise, the adventure, the novelty, the pleasure of feeling that you are something, and can do something in the world; and besides all this, you want the satisfaction of knowing that we women are following in chains behind your triumphal car!"

There was a dash of bitterness in this, which was a rare ingredient in Mara's conversation.

Moses took the word. "And you women sit easy at home, sewing and singing, and forming romantic pictures of our life as like its homely reality as romances generally are to reality; and while we are off in the hard struggle for position and the means of life, you hold your hearts ready for the first rich man that offers a fortune ready made."

"The first!" said Mara. "Oh, you naughty! sometimes we try two or three."

"Well, then, I suppose this is from one of them," said Moses, flapping down a letter from Boston, directed in a masculine hand, which he had got at the post-office that morning.

Now Mara knew that this letter was nothing in particular, but she was taken by surprise, and her skin was delicate as peach-blossom, and so she could not help a sudden blush, which rose even to her golden hair, vexed as she was to feel it coming. She put the letter quietly in her pocket, and for a moment seemed too discomposed to answer.

"You do well to keep your own counsel," said Moses. "No friend so near as one's self, is a good maxim. One does not expect young girls to learn it so early, but it seems they do."

"And why should n't they as well as young men?" said Mara. "Confidence begets confidence, they say."

"I have no ambition to play confidant," said Moses; "although as one who stands to you in the relation of older brother and guardian, and just on the verge of a long voyage, I might be supposed anxious to know."

"And I have no ambition to be confidant," said Mara, all her spirit sparkling in her eyes; "although when one stands to you in the relation of an only sister, I might be supposed perhaps to feel some interest to be in your confidence."

The words "older brother" and "only sister" grated on the ears of both the combatants as a decisive sentence. Mara never looked so pretty in her life, for the whole force of her being was awake, glowing and watchful, to guard passage, door, and window of her soul, that no treacherous hint might escape. Had he not just reminded her that he was only an older brother? and what would he think if he knew the truth?—and Moses thought the words *only sister* unequivocal declaration of how the matter stood in her view, and so he rose, and saying, "I won't detain you longer from your letter," took his hat and went out.

"Are you going down to Sally's?" said Mara, coming to the door and looking out after him.

"Yes."

"Well, ask her to come home with you and spend the evening. I have ever so many things to tell her."

"I will," said Moses, as he lounged away.

"The thing is clear enough," said Moses to himself. "Why should I make a fool of myself any further? What possesses us men always to set our hearts precisely on what is n't to be had? There 's Sally Kittridge likes me; I can see that plainly enough, for all her mincing; and why could n't I have had the sense to fall in love with her? She will make a splendid, showy woman. She has talent and tact enough to rise to any position I may rise to, let me rise as high as I will. She will always have skill and energy in the conduct of life; and when all the froth and foam of youth has subsided, she will make a noble woman. Why, then, do I cling to this fancy? I feel that this little flossy cloud, this delicate, quiet little puff of thistle-down, on which I have set my heart, is the only thing for me, and that without her my life will always be incomplete. I remember all our early life. It was she who sought me, and ran after me, and where has all that love gone to? Gone to this fellow; that 's plain enough. When a girl like her is so comfortably cool and easy, it 's because her heart is off somewhere else."

This conversation took place about four o'clock in as fine an October afternoon as you could wish to see. The sun, sloping westward, turned to gold the thousand blue scales of the ever-heaving sea, and soft, pine-scented winds were breathing everywhere through the forests, waving the long, swaying films of heavy moss, and twinkling the leaves of the silver birches that fluttered through the leafy gloom. The moon, already in the sky, gave promise of a fine moonlight night; and the wild and lonely stillness of the island, and the thoughts of leaving in a few days, all conspired to foster the restless excitement in our hero's mind into a kind of romantic unrest.

Now, in some such states, a man disappointed in one woman will turn to another, because, in a certain way and measure, her presence stills the craving and fills the void. It is a sort of supposititious courtship,—a saying to one woman, who is sympathetic and receptive, the words of longing and love that another will not receive. To be sure it is a game unworthy of any true man,—a piece of sheer, reckless, inconsiderate selfishness. But men do it, as they do many other unworthy things, from the mere promptings of present impulse, and let consequences take care of themselves. Moses met Sally that afternoon in just the frame to play the lover in this hypothetical, supposititious way, with words and looks and tones that came from feelings given to another. And as to Sally? Well, for once, Greek met Greek; for although Sally, as we showed her, was a girl of generous impulses, she was yet in no danger of immediate translation on account of superhuman goodness. In short, Sally had made up her mind that Moses should give her a chance to say that precious and golden *No,* which should enable her to count him as one of her captives,—and then he might go where he liked for all her.

So said the wicked elf, as she looked into her own great eyes in the little square of mirror shaded by a misty asparagus bush; and to this end there were various braidings and adornings of the lustrous black hair, and coquettish earrings were mounted that hung glancing and twinkling just by the smooth outline of her glowing cheek,—and then Sally looked at herself in a friendly way of approbation, and nodded at the bright dimpled shadow with a look of secret understanding. The real Sally and the Sally of the looking-glass were on admirable terms with each other, and both of one mind about the plan of campaign against the common enemy. Sally thought of him as he stood kingly and triumphant on the deck of his vessel, his great black eyes flashing confident glances into hers, and she felt a rebellious rustle of all her plumage. "No, sir," she said to herself, "you don't do it. You shall never find me among your slaves,"—"that you know of," added a doubtful voice within her. "Never to your knowledge," she said, as she turned away. "I wonder if he will come here this evening," she said, as she began to work upon a pillow-case,—one of a set which Mrs. Kittridge had confided to her nimble fingers. The seam was long, straight, and monotonous, and Sally was restless and fidgety; her thread would catch in knots, and when she tried to loosen it, would break, and the needle had to be threaded over. Somehow the work was terribly irksome to her, and the house looked so still and dim and lonesome, and the tick-tock of the kitchen-clock

was insufferable, and Sally let her work fall in her lap and
looked out of the open window, far to the open ocean, where a
fresh breeze was blowing toward her, and her eyes grew deep
and dreamy following the gliding ship sails. Sally was getting romantic. Had she been reading novels? Novels! What can a
pretty woman find in a novel equal to the romance that is all
the while weaving and unweaving about her, and of which no
human foresight can tell her the catastrophe? It is *novels* that
give false views of life. Is there not an eternal novel, with all
these false, cheating views, written in the breast of every beautiful and attractive girl whose witcheries make every man that
comes near her talk like a fool? Like a sovereign princess, she
never hears the truth, unless it be from the one manly man in a
thousand, who understands both himself and her. From all the
rest she hears only flatteries more or less ingenious, according
to the ability of the framer. Compare, for instance, what Tom
Brown says to little Seraphina at the party to-night, with what
Tom Brown sober says to sober sister Maria *about* her to-morrow. Tom remembers that he was a fool last night, and knows
what he thinks and always has thought to-day; but pretty
Seraphina thinks he adores her, so that no matter what she does
he will never see a flaw, she is sure of that,—poor little puss! She
does not know that philosophic Tom looks at her as he does at
a glass of champagne, or a dose of exhilarating gas, and calcu-
lates how much it will do for him to take of the stimulus without interfering with his serious and settled plans of life, which,
of course, he does n't mean to give up for her. The one-thousand-and-first man in creation is he that can feel the fascina-
tion but will not flatter, and that tries to tell to the little tyrant
the rare word of truth that may save her; he is, as we say, the
one-thousand-and-first. Well, as Sally sat with her great dark
eyes dreamily following the ship, she mentally thought over all
the compliments Moses had paid her, expressed or understood,

and those of all her other admirers, who had built up a sort of cloud-world around her, so that her little feet never rested on the soil of reality. Sally was shrewd and keen, and had a native mother-wit in the discernment of spirits, that made her feel that somehow this was all false coin; but still she counted it over, and it looked so pretty and bright that she sighed to think it was not real.

"If it only had been," she thought; "if there were only any truth to the creature; he is so handsome,—it 's a pity. But I do believe in his secret heart he is in love with Mara; he is in love with some one, I know. I have seen looks that must come from something real; but they were not for me. I have a kind of power over him, though," she said, resuming her old wicked look, "and I 'll puzzle him a little, and torment him. He shall find his match in me," and Sally nodded to a cat-bird that sat perched on a pine-tree, as if she had a secret understanding with him, and the cat-bird went off into a perfect roulade of imitations of all that was going on in the late bird-operas of the season.

Sally was roused from her revery by a spray of goldenrod that was thrown into her lap by an invisible hand, and Moses soon appeared at the window.

"There 's a plume that would be becoming to your hair," he said; "stay, let me arrange it."

"No, no; you 'll tumble my hair,—what can you know of such things?"

Moses held the spray aloft, and leaned toward her with a sort of quiet, determined insistance.

"By your leave, fair lady," he said, wreathing it in her hair, and then drawing back a little, he looked at her with so much admiration that Sally felt herself blush.

"Come, now, I dare say you 've made a fright of me," she said, rising and instinctively turning to the looking-glass; but she had too much coquetry not to see how admirably the golden plume suited her black hair, and the brilliant eyes and cheeks; she turned to Moses again, and courtesied, saying "Thank you, sir," dropping her eyelashes with a mock humility.

"Come, now," said Moses; "I am sent after you to come and spend the evening; let 's walk along the seashore, and get there by degrees."

And so they set out; but the path was circuitous, for Moses was always stopping, now at this point and now at that, and enacting some of those thousand little by-plays which a man can get up with a pretty woman. They searched for smooth pebbles where the waves had left them,—many-colored, pink and crimson and yellow and brown, all smooth and rounded by the eternal tossings of the old sea that had made playthings of them for centuries, and with every pebble given and taken were things said which should have meant more and more, had the play been earnest. Had Moses any idea of offering himself to Sally? No; but he was in one of those fluctuating, unresisting moods of mind in which he was willing to lie like a chip on the tide of present emotion, and let it rise and fall and dash him when it liked; and Sally never had seemed more beautiful and attractive to him than that afternoon, because there was a shade of reality and depth about her that he had never seen before.

"Come on, and let me show you my hermitage," said Moses, guiding her along the slippery projecting rocks, all covered with yellow tresses of seaweed. Sally often slipped on this treacherous footing, and Moses was obliged to hold her up, and instinctively he threw a meaning into his manner so much more than ever he had before, that by the time they had gained the little cove both were really agitated and excited. He felt that temporary delirium which is often the mesmeric effect of a strong womanly presence, and she felt that agitation which every woman must when a determined hand is striking on the great vital chord of her being. When they had stepped round the last point of rock they found themselves driven by the advancing tide up into the little lonely grotto,—and there they were with no lookout but the wide blue sea, all spread out in rose and gold under the twilight skies, with a silver moon looking down upon them.

"Sally," said Moses, in a low, earnest whisper, "you love me,—do you not?" and he tried to pass his arm around her.

She turned and flashed at him a look of mingled terror and defiance, and struck out her hands at him; then impetuously turning away and retreating to the other end of the grotto, she sat down on a rock and began to cry.

Moses came toward her, and kneeling, tried to take her hand. She raised her head angrily, and again repulsed him.

"Go!" she said. "What right had you to say that? What right had you even to think it?"

"Sally, you do love me. It cannot but be. You are a woman; you could not have been with me as we have and not feel more than friendship."

"Oh, you men!—your conceit passes understanding," said Sally. "You think we are born to be your bond slaves,—but for once you are mistaken, sir. I *don't* love you; and what's more, you don't love me,—you know you don't; you know that you love somebody else. You love Mara,—you know you do; there's no truth in you," she said, rising indignantly.

Moses felt himself color. There was an embarrassed pause, and then he answered,—

"Sally, why should I love Mara? Her heart is all given to another,—you yourself know it."

"I don't know it either," said Sally; "I know it is n't so."

"But you gave me to understand so."

"Well, sir, you put prying questions about what you ought to have asked her, and so what was I to do? Besides, I did want to show you how much better Mara could do than to take you; besides, I did n't know till lately. I never thought she could care much for any man more than I could."

"And you think she loves me?" said Moses, eagerly, a flash of joy illuminating his face; "do you, really?"

"There you are," said Sally; "it 's a shame I have let you know! Yes, Moses Pennel, she loves you like an angel, as none of you men deserve to be loved,—as you in particular don't."

Moses sat down on a point of rock, and looked on the ground discountenanced. Sally stood up glowing and triumphant, as if she had her foot on the neck of her oppressor and meant to make the most of it.

"Now what do you think of yourself for all this summer's work?—for what you have just said, asking me if I did n't love you? Supposing, now, I had done as other girls would, played the fool and blushed, and said yes? Why, to-morrow you would have been thinking how to be rid of me! I shall save you all that trouble, sir."

"Sally, I own I have been acting like a fool," said Moses, humbly.

"You have done more than that,—you have acted wickedly," said Sally.

"And am I the only one to blame?" said Moses, lifting his head with a show of resistance.

"Listen, sir!" said Sally, energetically; "I have played the fool and acted wrong too, but there is just this difference between you and me: you had nothing to lose, and I a great deal; your heart, such as it was, was safely disposed of. But supposing you had won mine, what would you have done with it? That was the last thing you considered."

"Go on, Sally, don't spare; I 'm a vile dog, unworthy of either of you," said Moses.

Sally looked down on her handsome penitent with some relenting, as he sat quite dejected, his strong arms drooping, and his long eyelashes cast down.

"I 'll be friends with you," she said, "because, after all, I 'm not so very much better than you. We have both done wrong, and made dear Mara very unhappy. But after all, I was not so much to blame as you; because, if there had been any reality in your love, I could have paid it honestly. I had a heart to give, — I have it now, and hope long to keep it," said Sally.

"Sally, you are a right noble girl. I never knew what you were till now," said Moses, looking at her with admiration.

"It 's the first time for all these six months that we have either of us spoken a word of truth or sense to each other. I never did anything but trifle with you, and you the same. Now we 've come to some plain dry land, we may walk on and be friends. So now help me up these rocks, and I will go home."

"And you 'll not come home with me?"

"Of course not. I think you may now go home and have one talk with Mara without witnesses."

XXXII

THE BETROTHAL

Moses walked slowly home from his interview with Sally, in a sort of maze of confused thought. In general, men understand women only from the outside, and judge them with about as much real comprehension as an eagle might judge a canary-bird. The difficulty of real understanding intensifies in proportion as the man is distinctively manly, and the woman womanly. There are men with a large infusion of the feminine element in their composition who read the female nature with more understanding than commonly falls to the lot of men; but in general, when a man passes beyond the mere outside artifices and unrealities which lie between the two sexes, and really touches his finger to any vital chord in the heart of a fair neighbor, he is astonished at the quality of the vibration.

"I could not have dreamed there was so much in her," thought Moses, as he turned away from Sally Kittridge. He felt humbled as well as astonished by the moral lecture which this frisky elf with whom he had all summer been amusing himself, preached to him from the depths of a real woman's heart. What she said of Mara's loving him filled his eyes with remorseful tears,—and for the moment he asked himself whether this restless, jealous, exacting desire which he felt to appropriate her whole life and heart to himself were as really worthy of the name of love as the generous self-devotion with which she had, all her life, made all his interests her own.

Was he to go to her now and tell her that he loved her, and therefore he had teased and vexed her,—therefore he had seemed to prefer another before her,—therefore he had practiced and experimented upon her nature? A suspicion rather stole upon him that love which expresses itself principally in making exactions and giving pain is not exactly worthy of the name. And yet he had been secretly angry with her all summer for being the very reverse of this; for her apparent cheerful willingness to see him happy with another; for the absence of all signs of jealousy,—all desire of exclusive appropriation. It showed, he said to himself, that there was no love; and now when it dawned on him that this might be the very heroism of self-devotion, he asked himself which was best worthy to be called love.

"She did love him, then!" The thought blazed up through the smouldering embers of thought in his heart like a tongue of flame. She loved him! He felt a sort of triumph in it, for he was sure Sally must know, they were so intimate. Well, he would go to her, and tell her all, confess all his sins, and be forgiven.

When he came back to the house, all was still evening. The moon, which was playing brightly on the distant sea, left one side of the brown house in shadow. Moses saw a light gleaming behind the curtain in the little room on the lower floor, which had been his peculiar sanctum during the summer past. He had made a sort of library of it, keeping there his books and papers. Upon the white curtain flitted, from time to time, a delicate, busy shadow; now it rose and now it stooped, and then it rose again—grew dim and vanished, and then came out again. His heart beat quick.

Mara was in his room, busy, as she always had been before his departures, in cares for him. How many things had she made for him, and done and arranged for him, all his life long! things which he had taken as much as a matter of course as the shining of that moon. His thought went back to the times of his first going to sea,—he a rough, chaotic boy, sensitive and surly, and she the ever thoughtful good angel of a little girl, whose loving-kindness he had felt free to use and to abuse. He remembered that he made her cry there when he should have spoken lovingly and gratefully to her, and that the words of acknowledgement that ought to have been spoken, never had been said,—remained unsaid to that hour. He stooped low, and came quite close to the muslin curtain. All was bright in the room, and shadowy without; he could see her movements as through a thin white haze. She was packing his sea-chest; his things were lying about her, folded or rolled nicely. Now he saw her on her knees writing something with a pencil in a book, and then she enveloped it very carefully in silk paper, and tied it trimly, and hid it away at the bottom of the chest. Then she remained a moment kneeling at the chest, her head resting in her hands. A sort of strange, sacred feeling came over him as he heard a low murmur, and knew that she felt a Presence that he never felt or acknowledged. He felt somehow that he was doing her a wrong thus to be prying upon moments when she thought herself alone with God; a sort of vague remorse filled him; he felt as if she were too good for him. He turned away, and entering the front door of the house, stepped noiselessly along and lifted the latch of the door. He heard a rustle as of one rising hastily as he opened it and stood before Mara. He had made up his mind what to say; but when she stood there before him, with her surprised, inquiring eyes, he felt confused.

"What, home so soon?" she said.

"You did not expect me, then?"

"Of course not,—not for these two hours; so," she said, looking about, "I found some mischief to do among your things. If you had waited as long as I expected, they would all have been quite right again, and you would never have known."

Moses sat down and drew her toward him, as if he were going to say something, and then stopped and began confusedly playing with her work-box.

"Now, please don't," said she, archly. "You know what a little old maid I am about my things!"

"Mara," said Moses, "people have asked you to marry them, have they not?"

"People asked me to marry them!" said Mara. "I hope not. What an odd question!"

"You know what I mean," said Moses; "you have had offers of marriage—from Mr. Adams, for example."

"And what if I have?"

"You did not accept him, Mara?" said Moses.

"No, I did not."

"And yet he was a fine man, I am told, and well fitted to make you happy."

"I believe he was," said Mara, quietly.

"And why were you so foolish?"

Mara was fretted at this question. She supposed Moses had come to tell her of his engagement to Sally, and that this was a kind of preface, and she answered,—

"I don't know why you call it foolish. I was a true friend to Mr. Adams. I saw intellectually that he might have the power of making any reasonable woman happy. I think now that the woman will be fortunate who becomes his wife; but I did not wish to marry him."

"Is there anybody you prefer to him, Mara?" said Moses.

She started up with glowing cheeks and sparkling eyes.

"You have no right to ask me that, though you are my brother."

"I am not your brother, Mara," said Moses, rising and going toward her, "and that is why I ask you. I feel I have a right to ask you."

"I do not understand you," she said, faintly.

"I can speak plainer, then. I wish to put in my poor venture. I love you, Mara—not as a brother. I wish you to be my wife, if you will."

While Moses was saying these words, Mara felt a sort of whirling in her head, and it grew dark before her eyes; but she had a strong, firm will, and she mastered herself and answered, after a moment, in a quiet, sorrowful tone, "How can I believe this, Moses? If it is true, why have you done as you have this summer?"

"Because I was a fool, Mara,—because I was jealous of Mr. Adams,—because I somehow hoped, after all, that you either loved me or that I might make you think more of me through jealousy of another. They say that love always is shown by jealousy."

"Not true love, I should think," said Mara. "How *could* you do so?—it was cruel to her,—cruel to me."

"I admit it,—anything, everything you can say. I have acted like a fool and a knave, if you will; but after all, Mara, I do love you. I know I am not worthy of you—never was—never can be; you are in all things a true, noble woman, and I have been unmanly."

It is not to be supposed that all this was spoken without accompaniments of looks, movements, and expressions of face such as we cannot give, but such as doubled their power to the parties concerned; and the "I love you" had its usual conclusive force as argument, apology, promise,—covering, like charity, a multitude of sins.

Half an hour after, you might have seen a youth and a maiden coming together out of the door of the brown house, and walking arm in arm toward the sea-beach.

It was one of those wonderfully clear moonlight evenings, when the ocean, like a great reflecting mirror, seems to double the brightness of the sky,—and its vast expanse lay all around them in its stillness, like an eternity of waveless peace. Mara remembered that time in her girlhood when she had followed Moses into the woods on just such a night,—how she had sat there under the shadows of the trees, and looked over to Harpswell and noticed the white houses and the meeting-house, all so bright and clear in the moonlight, and then off again on the other side of the island where silent ships were coming and going in the mysterious stillness. They were talking together now with that outflowing fullness which comes when the seal of some great reserve has just been broken,—going back over their lives from day to day, bringing up incidents of childhood, and turning them gleefully like two children.

And then Moses had all the story of his life to relate, and to tell Mara all he had learned of his mother,—going over with all the narrative contained in Mr. Sewell's letter.

"You see, Mara, that it was intended that you should be my fate," he ended; "so the winds and waves took me up and carried me to the lonely island where the magic princess dwelt."

"You are Prince Ferdinand," said Mara.

"And you are Miranda," said he.

"Ah!" she said with fervor, "how plainly we can see that our heavenly Father has been guiding our way! How good He is,— and how we must try to live for Him,—both of us."

A sort of cloud passed over Moses's brow. He looked embarrassed, and there was a pause between them, and then he turned the conversation.

Mara felt pained; it was like a sudden discord; such thoughts and feelings were the very breath of her life; she could not speak in perfect confidence and unreserve, as she then spoke, without uttering them; and her finely organized nature felt a sort of electric consciousness of repulsion and dissent. She grew abstracted, and they walked on in silence.

"I see now, Mara, I have pained you," said Moses, "but there are a class of feelings that you have that I have not and cannot have. No, I cannot feign anything. I can understand what religion is in you, I can admire its results. I can be happy, if it gives you any comfort; but people are differently constituted. I never can feel as you do."

"Oh, don't say never," said Mara, with an intensity that nearly startled him; "it has been the one prayer, the one hope, of my life, that you might have these comforts,—this peace."

"I need no comfort or peace except what I shall find in you," said Moses, drawing her to himself, and looking admiringly at her; "but pray for me still. I always thought that my wife must be one of the sort of women who pray."

"And why?" said Mara, in surprise.

"Because I need to be loved a great deal, and it is only that kind who pray who know how to love really. If you had not prayed for me all this time, you never would have loved me in spite of all my faults, as you did, and do, and will, as I know you will," he said, folding her in his arms, and in his secret heart he said, "Some of this intensity, this devotion, which went upward to heaven, will be mine one day. She will worship me."

"The fact is, Mara," he said, "I am a child of this world. I have no sympathy with things not seen. You are a half-spiritual creature,—a child of air; and but for the great woman's heart in you, I should feel that you were something uncanny and unnatural. I am selfish, I know; I frankly admit, I never disguised it; but I love your religion because it makes you love me. It is an incident to that loving, trusting nature which makes you all and wholly mine, as I want you to be. I want you all and wholly; every thought, every feeling,—the whole strength of your being. I don't care if I say it: I would not wish to be second in your heart even to God himself!"

"Oh, Moses!" said Mara, almost starting away from him, "such words are dreadful; they will surely bring evil upon us."

"I only breathed out my nature, as you did yours. Why should you love an unseen and distant Being more than you do one whom you can feel and see, who holds you in his arms, whose heart beats like your own?"

"Moses," said Mara, stopping and looking at him in the clear moonlight, "God has always been to me not so much like a father as like a dear and tender mother. Perhaps it was because I was a poor orphan, and my father and mother died at my birth, that He has been so loving to me. I never remember the time when I did not feel his presence in my joys and my sorrows. I never had a thought of joy and sorrow that I could not say to Him. I never woke in the night that I did not feel that He was loving and watching me, and that I loved Him in return. Oh, how many, many things I have said to Him about you! My heart would have broken years ago, had it not been for Him; because, though you did not know it, you often seemed unkind; you hurt me very often when you did not mean to. His love is so much a part of my life that I cannot conceive of life without it. It is the very air I breathe."

Moses stood still a moment, for Mara spoke with a fervor that affected him; then he drew her to his heart, and said,—

"Oh, what could ever make you love me?"

"He sent you and gave you to me," she answered, "to be mine in time and eternity."

The words were spoken in a kind of enthusiasm so different from the usual reserve of Mara, that they seemed like a prophecy. That night, for the first time in her life, had she broken the reserve which was her very nature, and spoken of that which was the intimate and hidden history of her soul.

XXXIII

At a Quilting

"And so," said Mrs. Captain Badger to Miss Roxy Toothacre, "it seems that Moses Pennel ain't going to have Sally Kittridge after all,—he's engaged to Mara Lincoln."

"More shame for him," said Miss Roxy, with a frown that made her mohair curls look really tremendous.

Miss Roxy and Mrs. Badger were the advance party at a quilting, to be holden at the house of Mr. Sewell, and had come at one o'clock to do the marking upon the quilt, which was to be filled up by the busy fingers of all the women in the parish. Said quilt was to have a bordering of a pattern commonly denominated in those parts clam-shell, and this Miss Roxy was diligently marking with indigo.

"What makes you say so, now?" said Mrs. Badger, a fat, comfortable, motherly matron, who always patronized the last matrimonial venture that put forth among the young people.

"What business had he to flirt and gallivant all summer with Sally Kittridge, and make everybody think he was going to have her, and then turn round to Mara Lincoln at the last minute? I wish I'd been in Mara's place."

In Miss Roxy's martial enthusiasm, she gave a sudden poke to her frisette, giving to it a diagonal bristle which extremely increased its usually severe expression; and any one contemplating her at the moment would have thought that for Moses Pennel, or any other young man, to come with tender propositions in that direction would have been indeed a venturesome enterprise.

"I tell you what 't is, Mis' Badger," she said, "I 've known Mara since she was born, — I may say I fetched her up myself, for if I had n't trotted and tended her them first four weeks of her life, Mis' Pennel 'd never have got her through; and I 've watched her every year since; and havin' Moses Pennel is the only silly thing I ever knew her to do; but you never can tell what a girl will do when it comes to marryin', — never!"

"But he 's a real stirrin', likely young man, and captain of a fine ship," said Mrs. Badger.

"Don't care if he 's captain of twenty ships," said Miss Roxy, obdurately; "he ain't a professor of religion, and I believe he 's an infidel, and she 's one of the Lord's people."

"Well," said Mrs. Badger, "you know the unbelievin' husband shall be sanctified by the believin' wife."

"Much sanctifyin' he 'll get," said Miss Roxy, contemptuously. "I don't believe he loves her any more than fancy; she 's the last plaything, and when he 's got her, he 'll be tired of her, as he always was with anything he got ever since. I tell you, Moses Pennel is all for pride and ambition and the world; and his wife, when he gets used to her, 'll be only a circumstance, — that 's all."

"Come, now, Miss Roxy," said Miss Emily, who in her best silk and smoothly-brushed hair had just come in, "we must *not* let you talk so. Moses Pennel has had long talks with brother, and he thinks him in a very hopeful way, and we are all delighted; and as to Mara, she is as fresh and happy as a little rose."

"So I tell Roxy," said Miss Ruey, who had been absent from the room to hold private consultations with Miss Emily concerning the biscuits and sponge-cake for tea, and who now sat down to the quilt and began to unroll a capacious and very limp calico thread-case; and placing her spectacles awry on her little pug nose, she began a series of ingenious dodges with her thread, designed to hit the eye of her needle.

"The old folks," she continued, "are e'en a'most tickled to pieces,—'cause they think it 'll jist be the salvation of him to get Mara."

"I ain't one of the sort that wants to be a-usin' up girls for the salvation of fellers," said Miss Roxy, severely. "Ever since he nearly like to have got her eat up by sharks, by giggiting her off in the boat out to sea when she wa'n't more 'n three years old, I always have thought he was a misfortin' in that family, and I think so now."

Here broke in Mrs. Eaton, a thrifty energetic widow of a deceased sea-captain, who had been left with a tidy little fortune which commanded the respect of the neighborhood. Mrs. Eaton had entered silently during the discussion, but of course had come, as every other woman had that afternoon, with views to be expressed upon the subject.

"For my part," she said, as she stuck a decisive needle into the first clam-shell pattern, "I ain't so sure that all the advantage in this match is on Moses Pennel's part. Mara Lincoln is a good little thing, but she ain't fitted to help a man along,—she 'll always be wantin' somebody to help her. Why, I 'member goin' a voyage with Cap'n Eaton, when I saved the ship, if anybody did,— it was allowed on all hands. Cap'n Eaton was n't hearty at that time, he was jist gettin' up from a fever,—it was when Marthy

Ann was a baby, and I jist took her and went to sea and took care of him. I used to work the longitude for him and help him lay the ship's course when his head was bad,—and when we came on the coast, we were kept out of harbor beatin' about nearly three weeks, and all the ship's tacklin' was stiff with ice, and I tell you the men never would have stood it through and got the ship in, if it had n't been for me. I kept their mittens and stockings all the while a-dryin' at my stove in the cabin, and hot coffee all the while a-boilin' for 'em, or I believe they 'd a-frozen their hands and feet, and never been able to work the ship in. That 's the way *I* did. Now Sally Kittridge is a great deal more like that than Mara."

"There 's no doubt that Sally is smart," said Mrs. Badger, "but then it ain't every one can do like you, Mrs. Eaton."

"Oh no, oh no," was murmured from mouth to mouth; "Mrs. Eaton must n't think she 's any rule for others,—everybody knows she can do more than most people;" whereat the pacified Mrs. Eaton said "she didn't know as it was anything remarkable,—it showed what anybody might do, if they 'd only *try* and have resolution; but that Mara never had been brought up to have resolution, and her mother never had resolution before her, it wasn't in any of Mary Pennel's family; she knew their grandmother and all their aunts, and they were all a weakly set, and not fitted to get along in life,—they were a kind of people that somehow did n't seem to know how to take hold of things."

At this moment the consultation was hushed up by the entrance of Sally Kittridge and Mara, evidently on the closest terms of intimacy, and more than usually demonstrative and affectionate; they would sit together and use each other's needles, scissors, thread, and thimbles interchangeably, as if anxious to express every minute the most overflowing confidence. Sly winks and didactic nods were covertly exchanged among the elderly people, and when Mrs. Kittridge entered with more than usual airs of impressive solemnity, several of these were covertly directed toward her, as a matron whose views in life must have been considerably darkened by the recent event.

Mrs. Kittridge, however, found an opportunity to whisper under her breath to Miss Ruey what a relief to her it was that the affair had taken such a turn. She had felt uneasy all summer for fear of what might come. Sally was so thoughtless and worldly, she felt afraid that he would lead her astray. She did n't see, for her part, how a professor of religion like Mara could make up her mind to such an unsettled kind of fellow, even if he did seem to be rich and well-to-do. But then she had done looking for consistency; and she sighed and vigorously applied herself to quilting like one who has done with the world.

In return, Miss Ruey sighed and took snuff, and related for the hundredth time to Mrs. Kittridge the great escape she once had from the addresses of Abraham Peters, who had turned out a "poor drunken creetur." But then it was only natural that Mara should be interested in Moses; and the good soul went off into her favorite verse:—

> "The fondness of a creature's love,
>   How strong it strikes the sense!
> Thither the warm affections move,
>   Nor can we drive them thence."

In fact, Miss Ruey's sentimental vein was in quite a gushing state, for she more than once extracted from the dark corners of the limp calico thread-case we have spoken of certain long-treasured *morceaux* of newspaper poetry, of a tender and sentimental cast, which she had laid up with true Yankee economy, in case any one should ever be in a situation to need them. They related principally to the union of kindred hearts, and the joys of reciprocated feeling and the pains of absence. Good Miss Ruey occasionally passed these to Mara, with glances full of meaning, which caused the poor old thing to resemble a sentimental goblin, keeping Sally Kittridge in a perfect hysterical tempest of suppressed laughter, and making it difficult for Mara to preserve the decencies of life toward her well-intending old friend. The trouble with poor Miss Ruey was that, while her body had grown old and crazy, her soul was just as juvenile as ever,—and a simple, juvenile soul disporting itself in a crazy, battered old body, is at great disadvantage. It was lucky for her, however, that she lived in the most sacred unconsciousness of the ludicrous effect of her little indulgences, and the pleasure she took in them was certainly of the most harmless kind. The world would be a far better and more enjoyable place than it is, if all people who are old and uncomely could find amusement as innocent and Christian-like as Miss Ruey's inoffensive thread-case collection of sentimental truisms.

This quilting of which we speak was a solemn, festive occasion of the parish, held a week after Moses had sailed away; and so *piquant* a morsel as a recent engagement could not, of course, fail to be served up for the company in every variety of garnishing which individual tastes might suggest.

It became an ascertained fact, however, in the course of the evening festivities, that the minister was serenely approbative of the event; that Captain Kittridge was at length brought to a sense of the errors of his way in supposing that Sally had ever cared a pin for Moses more than as a mutual friend and confidant; and the great affair was settled without more ripples of discomposure than usually attend similar announcements in more refined society.

XXXIV

♣♣♣♣♣

*F*riends

The quilting broke up at the primitive hour of nine o'clock, at which, in early New England days, all social gatherings always dispersed. Captain Kittridge rowed his helpmeet, with Mara and Sally, across the Bay to the island.

"Come and stay with me to-night, Sally," said Mara.

"I think Sally had best be at home," said Mrs. Kittridge. "There 's no sense in girls talking all night."

"There ain't sense in nothin' else, mother," said the Captain. "Next to sparkin', which is the Christianist thing I knows on, comes gals' talks 'bout their sparks; they 's as natural as crows-foot and red columbines in the spring, and spring don't come but once a year neither,—and so let 'em take the comfort on 't. I warrant now, Polly, you 've laid awake nights and talked about me."

"We 've all been foolish once," said Mrs. Kittridge.

"Well, mother, we want to be foolish too," said Sally.

"Well, you and your father are too much for me," said Mrs. Kittridge, plaintively; "you always get your own way."

"How lucky that my way is always a good one!" said Sally.

"Well, you know, Sally, you are going to make the beer to-morrow," still objected her mother.

"Oh, yes; that 's another reason," said Sally. "Mara and I shall come home through the woods in the morning, and we can get whole apronfuls of young wintergreen, and besides, I know where there 's a lot of sassafras root. We 'll dig it, won't we, Mara?"

"Yes; and I 'll come down and help you brew," said Mara. "Don't you remember the beer I made when Moses came home?"

"Yes, yes, I remember," said the Captain, "you sent us a couple of bottles."

"We can make better yet now," said Mara. "The wintergreen is young, and the green tips on the spruce boughs are so full of strength. Everything is lively and sunny now."

"Yes, yes," said the Captain, "and I 'spect I know why things do look pretty lively to some folks, don't they?"

"I don't know what sort of work you 'll make of the beer among you," said Mrs. Kittridge; "but you must have it your own way."

Mrs. Kittridge, who never did anything else among her tea-drinking acquaintances but laud and magnify Sally's good traits and domestic acquirements, felt constantly bound to keep up a faint show of controversy and authority in her dealings with her,—the fading remains of the strict government of her childhood; but it was, nevertheless, very perfectly understood, in a general way, that Sally was to do as she pleased; and so, when the boat came to shore, she took the arm of Mara and started up toward the brown house.

The air was soft and balmy, and though the moon by which the troth of Mara and Moses had been plighted had waned into the latest hours of the night, still a thousand stars were lying in twinkling brightness, reflected from the undulating waves all around them, and the tide, as it rose and fell, made a sound as gentle and soft as the respiration of a peaceful sleeper.

"Well, Mara," said Sally, after an interval of silence, "all has come out right. You see that it was you whom he loved. What a lucky thing for me that I am made so heartless, or I might not be as glad as I am."

"You are not heartless, Sally," said Mara; "it 's the enchanted princess asleep; the right one has n't come to waken her."

"Maybe so," said Sally, with her old light laugh. "If I only were sure he would make you happy now,—half as happy as you deserve,—I 'd forgive him his share of this summer's mischief. The fault was just half mine, you see, for I witched with him. I confess it. I have my own little spider-webs for these great lordly flies, and I like to hear them buzz."

"Take care, Sally; never do it again, or the spider-web may get round you," said Mara.

"Never fear me," said Sally. "But, Mara, I wish I felt sure that Moses could make you happy. Do you really, now, when you think seriously, feel as if he would?"

"I never thought seriously about it," said Mara; "but I know he needs me; that I can do for him what no one else can. I have always felt all my life that he was to be mine; that he was sent to me, ordained for me to care for and to love."

"You are well mated," said Sally. "He wants to be loved very much, and you want to love. There 's the active and passive voice, as they used to say at Miss Plucher's. But yet in your natures you are opposite as any two could well be."

Mara felt that there was in these chance words of Sally more than she perceived. No one could feel as intensely as she could that the mind and heart so dear to her were yet, as to all that was most vital and real in her inner life, unsympathizing. To her the spiritual world was a reality; God an ever-present consciousness; and the line of this present life seemed so to melt and lose itself in the anticipation of a future and brighter one, that it was impossible for her to speak intimately and not unconsciously to betray the fact. To him there was only the life of this world: there was no present God; and from all thought of a future life he shrank with a shuddering aversion, as from something ghastly and unnatural. She had realized this difference more in the few days that followed her betrothal than all her life before, for now first the barrier of mutual constraint and misunderstanding having melted away, each spoke with an *abandon* and unreserve which made the acquaintance more vitally intimate than ever it had been before. It was then that Mara felt that while her sympathies could follow him through all his plans and interests, there was a whole world of thought and feeling in her heart where his could not follow her; and she asked herself, Would it be so always? Must she walk at his side forever repressing the utterance of that which was most sacred and intimate, living in a nominal and external communion only? How could it be that what was so lovely and clear in its reality to her, that which was to her as life-blood, that which was the vital air in which she lived and moved and had her being, could be absolutely nothing to him? Was it really possible, as he said, that God had no existence for him except in a nominal cold belief; that the spiritual world was to him only a land of pale shades and doubtful glooms, from which he shrank with dread, and the least allusion to which was distasteful? and would this always be so? and if so, could she be happy?

But Mara said the truth in saying that the question of personal happiness never entered her thoughts. She loved Moses in a way that made it necessary to her happiness to devote herself to him, to watch over and care for him; and though she knew not how, she felt a sort of presentiment that it was through her that he must be brought into sympathy with a spiritual and immortal life.

All this passed through Mara's mind in the reverie into which Sally's last words threw her, as she sat on the doorsill and looked off into the starry distance and heard the weird murmur of the sea.

"How lonesome the sea at night always is," said Sally. "I declare, Mara, I don't wonder you miss that creature, for, to tell the truth, I do a little bit. It was something, you know, to have somebody to come in, and to joke with, and to say how he liked one's hair and one's ribbons, and all that. I quite got up a friendship for Moses, so that I can feel how dull you must be;" and Sally gave a half sigh, and then whistled a tune as adroitly as a blackbird.

"Yes," said Mara, "we two girls down on this lonely island need some one to connect us with the great world; and he was so full of life, and so certain and confident, he seemed to open a way before one out into life."

"Well, of course, while he is gone there will be plenty to do getting ready to be married," said Sally. "By the by, when I was over to Portland the other day, Maria Potter showed me a new pattern for a bed-quilt, the sweetest thing you can imagine,—it is called the morning star. There is a great star in the centre, and little stars all around,—white on a blue ground. I mean to begin one for you."

"I am going to begin spinning some very fine flax next week," said Mara; "and have I shown you the new pattern I drew for a counterpane? it is to be morning-glories, leaves and flowers, you know,—a pretty idea, is n't it?"

And so, the conversation falling from the region of the sentimental to the practical, the two girls went in and spent an hour in discussions so purely feminine that we will not enlighten the reader further therewith. Sally seemed to be investing all her energies in the preparation of the wedding outfit of her friend, about which she talked with a constant and restless activity, and for which she formed a thousand plans, and projected shopping tours to Portland, Brunswick, and even to Boston,—this last being about as far off a venture at that time as Paris now seems to a Boston belle.

"When you are married," said Sally, "you 'll have to take me to live with you; that creature sha'n't have you *all* to himself. I hate men, they are so exorbitant,—they spoil all our playmates; and what shall I do when *you* are gone?"

"You will go with Mr.—what 's his name?" said Mara.

"Pshaw, I don't know him. I shall be an old maid," said Sally; "and really there is n't much harm in that, if one could have company,—if somebody or other would n't marry all one's friends,—that 's lonesome," she said, winking a tear out of her black eyes and laughing. "If I were only a young fellow now, Mara, I 'd have you myself, and that would be just the thing; and I 'd shoot Moses, if he said a word; and I 'd have money, and I 'd have honors, and I 'd carry you off to Europe, and take you to Paris and Rome, and nobody knows where; and we 'd live in peace, as the story-books say."

"Come, Sally, how wild you are talking," said Mara, "and the clock has just struck one; let 's try to go to sleep."

Sally put her face to Mara's and kissed her, and Mara felt a moist spot on her cheek,—could it be a tear?

XXXV

THE TOOTHACRE COTTAGE

Aunt Roxy and Aunt Ruey Toothacre lived in a little one-story gambrel-roofed cottage, on the side of Harpswell Bay, just at the head of the long cove which we have already described. The windows on two sides commanded the beautiful bay and the opposite shores, and on the other they looked out into the dense forest, through whose deep shadows of white birch and pine the silver rise and fall of the sea daily revealed itself.

The house itself was a miracle of neatness within, for the two thrifty sisters were worshipers of soap and sand, and these two tutelary deities had kept every board of the house-floor white and smooth, and also every table and bench and tub of household use. There was a sacred care over each article, however small and insignificant, which composed their slender household stock. The loss or breakage of one of them would have made a visible crack in the hearts of the worthy sisters,—for every plate, knife, fork, spoon, cup, or glass was as intimate with them, as instinct with home feeling, as if it had a soul; each defect or spot had its history, and a cracked dish or article of furniture received as tender and considerate medical treatment as if it were capable of understanding and feeling the attention.

It was now a warm, spicy day in June,—one of those which bring out the pineapple fragrance from the fir-shoots, and cause the spruce and hemlocks to exude a warm, resinous perfume. The two sisters, for a wonder, were having a day to themselves, free from the numerous calls of the vicinity for twelve miles round. The room in which they were sitting was bestrewn with fragments of dresses and bonnets, which were being torn to pieces in a most wholesale way, with a view to a general rejuvenescence. A person of unsympathetic temperament, and disposed to take sarcastic views of life, might perhaps wonder what possible object these two battered and weather-beaten old bodies proposed to themselves in this process,—whether Miss Roxy's gaunt black-straw helmet, which she had worn defiantly all winter, was likely to receive much lustre from being pressed over and trimmed with an old green ribbon which that energetic female had colored black by a domestic recipe; and whether Miss Roxy's rusty bombazette would really seem to the world any fresher for being ripped, and washed, and turned, for the second or third time, and made over with every breadth in a different situation. Probably after a week of efficient labor, busily expended in bleaching, dyeing, pressing, sewing, and ripping, an unenlightened spectator, seeing them come into the meeting-house, would simply think, "There are those two old frights with the same old things on they have worn these fifty years." Happily the weird sisters were contentedly ignorant of any such remarks, for no duchesses could have enjoyed a more quiet belief in their own social position, and their semi-annual spring and fall rehabilitation was therefore entered into with the most simple-hearted satisfaction.

"I 'm a-thinkin', Roxy," said Aunt Ruey, considerately turning and turning on her hand an old straw bonnet, on which were streaked all the marks of the former trimming in lighter lines, which revealed too clearly the effects of wind and weather,—

"I 'm a-thinkin' whether or no this 'ere might n't as well be dyed and done with it as try to bleach it out. I 've had it ten years last May, and it 's kind o' losin' its freshness, you know. I don't believe these 'ere streaks will bleach out."

"Never mind, Ruey," said Miss Roxy, authoritatively, "I 'm goin' to do Mis' Badger's leg'orn, and it won't cost nothin'; so hang your'n in the barrel along with it,—the same smoke 'll do 'em both. Mis' Badger she finds the brimstone, and next fall you can put it in the dye when we do the yarn."

"That ar straw is a beautiful straw!" said Miss Ruey, in a plaintive tone, tenderly examining the battered old head-piece,—"I braided every stroke on it myself, and I don't know as I could do it ag'in. My fingers ain't quite so limber as they was! I don't think I shall put green ribbon on it ag'in; 'cause green is such a color to ruin, if a body gets caught out in a shower! There 's these green streaks come that day I left my amberil at Captain Broad's, and went to meetin'. Mis' Broad she says to me, 'Aunt Ruey, it won't rain.' And says I to her, 'Well, Mis' Broad, I 'll try it; though I never did leave my amberil at home but what it rained.' And so I went, and sure enough it rained cats and dogs, and streaked my bonnet all up; and them ar streaks won't bleach out, I 'm feared."

"How long is it Mis' Badger has had that ar leg'orn?"

"Why, you know, the Cap'n he brought it home when he came from his voyage from Marseilles. That ar was when Phebe Ann was born, and she 's fifteen year old. It was a most elegant thing when he brought it; but I think it kind o' led Mis' Badger on to extravagant ways,—for gettin' new trimmin' spring and fall so uses up money as fast as new bonnets; but Mis' Badger's got the money, and she 's got a right to use it if she pleases; but if I 'd a-had new trimmin's spring and fall, I should n't a-put away what I have in the bank."

"Have you seen the straw Sally Kittridge is braidin' for Mara

Lincoln's weddin' bonnet?" said Miss Ruey. "It's jist the finest thing ever you did see,—and the whitest. I was a-tellin' Sally that I could do as well once myself, but my mantle was a-fallin' on her. Sally don't seem to act a bit like a disap'inted gal. She is as chipper as she can be about Mara's weddin', and seems like she could n't do too much. But laws, everybody seems to want to be a-doin' for her. Miss Emily was a-showin' me a fine double damask tablecloth that she was goin' to give her; and Mis' Pennel she 's been a-spinnin' and layin' up sheets and towels and tablecloths all her life,—and then she has all Naomi's things. Mis' Pennel was talkin' to me the other day about bleachin' 'em out 'cause they 'd got yellow a-lyin'. I kind o' felt as if 't was unlucky to be a-fittin' out a bride with her dead mother's things, but I did n't like to say nothin'."

"Ruey," said Miss Roxy impressively, "I hain't never had but jist one mind about Mara Lincoln's weddin',—it 's to be,—but it won't be the way people think. I hain't nussed and watched and sot up nights sixty years for nothin'. I can see beyond what most folks can,—her weddin' garments is bought and paid for, and she 'll wear 'em, but she won't be Moses Pennel's wife,— now you see."

"Why, whose wife will she be then?" said Miss Ruey; " 'cause that ar Mr. Adams is married. I saw it in the paper last week when I was up to Mis' Badger's."

Miss Roxy shut her lips with oracular sternness and went on with her sewing.

"Who 's that comin' in the back door?" said Miss Ruey, as the sound of a footstep fell upon her ear. "Bless me," she added, as she started up to look, "if folks ain't always nearest when you 're talkin' about 'em. Why, Mara; you come down here and catched us in all our dirt! Well now, we 're glad to see you, if we be," said Miss Ruey.

343

XXXVI

THE SHADOW
OF DEATH

It was in truth Mara herself who came and stood in the door-way. She appeared overwearied with her walk, for her cheeks had a vivid brightness unlike their usual tender pink. Her eyes had, too, a brilliancy almost painful to look upon. They seemed like ardent fires, in which the life was slowly burning away.

"Sit down, sit down, little Mara," said Aunt Ruey. "Why, how like a picture you look this mornin', — one need n't ask you how you do, — it 's plain enough that you are pretty well."

"Yes, I am, Aunt Ruey," she answered, sinking into a chair; "only it is warm to-day, and the sun is so hot, that 's all, I believe; but I am very tired."

"So you are now, poor thing," said Miss Ruey. "Roxy, where 's my turkey-feather fan? Oh, here 't is; there, take it, and fan you, child; and maybe you 'll have a glass of our spruce beer?"

"Thank you, Aunt Roxy. I brought you some young winter-green," said Mara, unrolling from her handkerchief a small knot of those fragrant leaves, which were wilted by the heat.

"Thank you, I 'm sure," said Miss Ruey, in delight; "you always fetch something, Mara, — always would, ever since you could toddle. Roxy and I was jist talkin' about your weddin'. I s'pose you 're gettin' things well along down to your house. Well, here 's the beer. I don't hardly know whether you 'll think it worked enough, though. I set it Saturday afternoon, for all Mis' Twitchel said it was wicked for beer to work Sundays," said Miss Ruey, with a feeble cackle at her own joke.

"Thank you, Aunt Ruey; it is excellent, as your things always are. I was very thirsty."

"I s'pose you hear from Moses pretty often now," said Aunt Ruey. "How kind o' providential it happened about his getting that property; he 'll be a rich man now; and Mara, you 'll come to grandeur, won't you? Well, I don't know anybody deserves it more,—I r'ally don't. Mis' Badger was a-sayin' so a-Sunday, and Cap'n Kittridge and all on 'em. I s'pose though we 've got to lose you,—you 'll be goin' off to Boston, or New York, or some-where."

"We can't tell what may happen, Aunt Ruey," said Mara, and there was a slight tremor in her voice as she spoke.

Miss Roxy, who beyond the first salutations had taken no part in this conversation, had from time to time regarded Mara over the tops of her spectacles with looks of grave apprehen-sion; and Mara, looking up, now encountered one of these glances.

"Have you taken the dock and dandelion tea I told you about?" said the wise woman, rather abruptly.

"Yes, Aunt Roxy, I have taken them faithfully for two weeks past."

"And do they seem to set you up any?" said Miss Roxy.

"No, I don't think they do. Grandma thinks I 'm better, and grandpa, and I let them think so; but Miss Roxy, *can't* you think of something else?"

Miss Roxy laid aside the straw bonnet which she was ripping, and motioned Mara into the outer room,—the sink-room, as the sisters called it. It was the scullery of their little establishment,—the place where all dish-washing and clothes-washing was generally performed,—but the boards of the floor were white as snow, and the place had the odor of neatness. The open door looked out pleasantly into the deep forest, where the waters of the cove, now at high tide, could be seen glittering through the trees. Soft moving spots of sunlight fell, checkering the feathery ferns and small piney tribes of evergreen which ran in ruffling wreaths of green through the dry, brown matting of fallen pine needles. Birds were singing and calling to each other merrily from the green shadows of the forest,—everything had a sylvan fullness and freshness of life. There are moods of mind when the sight of the bloom and freshness of nature affects us painfully, like the want of sympathy in a dear friend. Mara had been all her days a child of the woods; her delicate life had grown up in them like one of their own cool shaded flowers; and there was not a moss, not a fern, not an upspringing thing that waved a leaf or threw forth a flower-bell, that was not a well-known friend to her; she had watched for years its haunts, known the time of its coming and its going, studied its shy and veiled habits, and interwoven with its life each year a portion of her own; and now she looked out into the old mossy woods, with their wavering spots of sun and shadow, with a yearning pain, as if she wanted help or sympathy to come from their silent recesses.

She sat down on the clean, scoured door-sill, and took off her straw hat. Her golden-brown hair was moist with the damps of fatigue, which made it curl and wave in darker little rings about her forehead; her eyes,—those longing, wistful eyes,—had a deeper pathos of sadness than ever they had worn before; and her delicate lips trembled with some strong suppressed emotion.

"Aunt Roxy," she said suddenly, "I *must* speak to somebody. I can't go on and keep up without telling some one, and it had better be you, because you have skill and experience, and can help me if anybody can. I 've been going on for six months now, taking this and taking that, and trying to get better, but it 's of no use. Aunt Roxy, I feel my life going,—going just as steadily and as quietly every day as the sand goes out of your hour-glass. I want to live,—oh, I never wanted to live so much, and I can't,—oh, I know I can't. Can I now,—do you think I can?"

Mara looked imploringly at Miss Roxy. The hard-visaged woman sat down on the wash-bench, and, covering her worn, stony visage with her checked apron, sobbed aloud.

Mara was confounded. This implacably withered, sensible, dry woman, beneficently impassive in sickness and sorrow, weeping!—it was awful, as if one of the Fates had laid down her fatal distaff to weep.

Mara sprung up impulsively and threw her arms round her neck.

"Now don't, Aunt Roxy, don't. I did n't think you would feel bad, or I would n't have told you; but oh, you don't know how hard it is to keep such a secret all to one's self. I have to make believe all the time that I am feeling well and getting better. I really say what is n't true every day, because, poor grand-mamma, how could I bear to see her distress? and grandpapa,—oh, I wish people did n't love me so! Why cannot they let me go? And oh, Aunt Roxy, I had a letter only yesterday, and he is so sure we shall be married this fall,—and I know it cannot be." Mara's voice gave way in sobs, and the two wept together,—the old grim, gray woman holding the soft golden head against her breast with a convulsive grasp. "Oh, Aunt Roxy, do you love me, too?" said Mara. "I did n't know you did."

"Love ye, child?" said Miss Roxy; "yes, I love ye like my life. I ain't one that makes talk about things, but I do; you come into my arms fust of anybody's in this world,—and except poor little Hitty, I never loved nobody as I have you."

"Ah! that was your sister, whose grave I have seen," said Mara, speaking in a soothing, caressing tone, and putting her little thin hand against the grim, wasted cheek, which was now moist with tears.

"Jes' so, child, she died when she was a year younger than you be; she was not lost, for God took her. Poor Hitty! her life jest dried up like a brook in August,—jest so. Well, she was hopefully pious, and it was better for her."

"Did she go like me, Aunt Roxy?" said Mara.

"Well, yes, dear; she did begin jest so, and I gave her everything I could think of; and we had doctors for her far and near; but *'t was n't to be,*—that 's all we could say; she was called, and her time was come."

"Well, now, Aunt Roxy," said Mara, "at any rate, it 's a relief to speak out to some one. It 's more than two months that I have felt every day more and more that there was no hope,—life has hung on me like a weight. I have had to *make* myself keep up, and make myself do everything, and no one knows how it has tried me. I am so tired all the time, I could cry; and yet when I go to bed nights I can't sleep, I lie in such a hot, restless way; and then before morning I am drenched with cold sweat, and feel so weak and wretched. I force myself to eat, and I force myself to talk and laugh, and it 's all pretense; and it wears me out,—it would be better if I stopped trying,—it would be better to give up and act as weak as I feel; but how can I let them know?"

"My dear child," said Aunt Roxy, "the truth is the kindest thing we can give folks in the end. When folks know jest where they are, why they can walk; you 'll all be supported; you must trust in the Lord. I have been more'n forty years with sick rooms and dyin' beds, and I never knew it fail that those that trusted in the Lord was brought through."

"Oh, Aunt Roxy, it is so hard for me to give up,—to give up hoping to live. There were a good many years when I thought I should love to depart,—not that I was really unhappy, but I longed to go to heaven, though I knew it was selfish, when I knew how lonesome I should leave my friends. But now, oh, life has looked so bright; I have clung to it so; I do now. I lie awake nights and pray, and try to give it up and be resigned, and I can't. Is it wicked?"

"Well, it 's natur' to want to live," said Miss Roxy. "Life is sweet, and in a gen'l way we was made to live. Don't worry; the Lord 'll bring you right when His time comes. Folks is n't always supported jest when they want to be, nor *as* they want to be; but yet they 're supported fust and last. Ef I was to tell you how as I has hope in your case, I should n't be a-tellin' you the truth. I has n't much of any; only all things is possible with God. If you could kind o' give it all up and rest easy in his hands, and keep a-doin' what you can,—why, while there 's life there 's hope, you know; and if you are to be made well, you will be all the sooner."

"Aunt Roxy, it 's all right; I know it 's all right. God knows best; He will do what is best; I know that; but my heart bleeds, and is sore. And when I get his letters,—I got one yesterday,—it brings it all back again. Everything is going on so well; he says he has done more than all he ever hoped; his letters are full of jokes, full of spirit. Ah, he little knows,—and how can I tell him?"

"Child, you need n't yet. You can jest kind o' prepare his mind a little."

"Aunt Roxy, have you spoken of my case to any one,—have you told what you know of me?"

"No, child, I hain't said nothin' more than that you was a little weakly now and then."

"I have such a color every afternoon," said Mara. "Grandpapa talks about my roses, and Captain Kittridge jokes me about growing so handsome; nobody seems to realize how I feel. I have kept up with all the strength I had. I have tried to shake it off, and to feel that nothing was the matter,—really there is nothing much, only this weakness. This morning I thought it would do me good to walk down here. I remember times when I could ramble whole days in the woods, but I was so tired before I got half way here that I had to stop a long while and rest. Aunt Roxy, if you would only tell grandpapa and grandmamma just how things are, and what the danger is, and let them stop talking to me about wedding things,—for really and truly I am too unwell to keep up any longer."

"Well, child, I will," said Miss Roxy. "Your grandfather will be supported, and hold you up, for he's one of the sort as has the secret of the Lord,—I remember him of old. Why, the day your father and mother was buried he stood up and sung old China, and his face was wonderful to see. He seemed to be standin' with the world under his feet and heaven opening. He's a master Christian, your grandfather is; and now you jest go and lie down in the little bedroom, and rest you a bit, and by and by, in the cool of the afternoon, I'll walk along home with you."

Miss Roxy opened the door of a little room, whose white fringy window-curtains were blown inward by breezes from the blue sea, and laid the child down to rest on a clean sweet-smelling bed with as deft and tender care as if she were not a bony, hard-visaged, angular female, in a black mohair frisette.

She stopped a moment wistfully before a little profile head, of a kind which resembles a black shadow on a white ground. "That was Hitty!" she said.

Mara had often seen in the graveyard a mound inscribed to this young person, and heard traditionally of a young and pretty sister of Miss Roxy who had died very many years before. But the grave was overgrown with blackberry-vines, and gray moss had grown into the crevices of the slab which served for a tomb-stone, and never before that day had she heard Miss Roxy speak of her. Miss Roxy took down the little black object and handed it to Mara. "You can't tell much by that, but she was a most beautiful creatur'. Well, it's all best as it is." Mara saw nothing but a little black shadow cast on white paper, yet she was affected by the perception of how bright, how beautiful, was the image in the memory of that seemingly stern, commonplace woman, and how of all that in her mind's eye she saw and remembered, she could find no outward witness but this black block. "So some day my friends will speak of me as a distant shadow," she said, as with a sigh she turned her head on the pillow.

Miss Roxy shut the door gently as she went out, and betrayed the unwonted rush of softer feelings which had come over her only by being more dictatorial and commanding than usual in her treatment of her sister, who was sitting in fidgety curiosity to know what could have been the subject of the private con-ference.

"I s'pose Mara wanted to get some advice about makin' up her weddin' things," said Miss Ruey, with a sort of humble quiver, as Miss Roxy began ripping and tearing fiercely at her old straw bonnet, as if she really purposed its utter and immedi-ate demolition.

"No she did n't, neither," said Miss Roxy, fiercely. "I declare, Ruey, you are silly; your head is always full of weddin's, weddin's, weddin's—nothin' else—from mornin' till night, and night till mornin'. I tell you there's other things have got to be thought of in this world besides weddin' clothes, and it would be well, if people would think more o' gettin' their weddin' garments ready for the kingdom of heaven. That 's what Mara's got to think of; for, mark my words, Ruey, there is no marryin' and givin' in marriage for her in this world."

"Why, bless me, Roxy, now you don't say so!" said Miss Ruey; "why I knew she was kind o' weakly and ailin', but"—

"Kind o' weakly and ailin'!" said Miss Roxy, taking up Miss Ruey's words in a tone of high disgust, "I should rather think she was; and more 'n that, too: she 's marked for death, and that before long, too. It may be that Moses Pennel 'll never see her again—he never half knew what she was worth—maybe he 'll know when he 's lost her, that 's one comfort!"

"But," said Miss Ruey, "everybody has been a-sayin' what a beautiful color she was a-gettin' in her cheeks."

"Color in her cheeks!" snorted Miss Roxy; "so does a rock-maple get color in September and turn all scarlet, and what for? why, the frost has been at it, and its time is out. That 's what your bright colors stand for. Hain't you noticed that little grave-stone cough, jest the faintest in the world, and it don't come from a cold, and it hangs on. I tell you you can't cheat me, she 's goin' jest as Mehitabel went, jest as Sally Ann Smith went, jest as Louisa Pearson went. I could count now on my fingers twenty girls that have gone that way. Nobody saw 'em goin' till they was gone."

"Well, now, I don't think the old folks have the least idea on 't," said Miss Ruey. "Only last Saturday Mis' Pennel was a-talkin' to me about the sheets and tablecloths she 's got out a-bleachin'; and she said that the weddin' dress was to be made over to Mis' Mosely's in Portland, 'cause Moses he 's so particular about havin' things genteel."

"Well, Master Moses 'll jest have to give up his particular notions," said Miss Roxy, "and come down in the dust, like all the rest on us, when the Lord sends an east wind and withers our gourds. Moses Pennel's one of the sort that expects to drive all before him with the strong arm, and sech has to learn that things ain't to go as they please in the Lord's world. Sech always has to come to spots that they can't get over nor under nor round, to have their own way, but jest has to give right up square."

"Well, Roxy," said Miss Ruey, "how does the poor little thing take it? Has she got reconciled?"

"Reconciled! Ruey, how you do ask questions!" said Miss Roxy, fiercely pulling a bandanna silk handkerchief out of her pocket, with which she wiped her eyes in a defiant manner. "Reconciled! It's easy enough to talk, Ruey, but how would you like it, when everything was goin' smooth and playin' into your hands, and all the world smooth and shiny, to be took short up? I guess you would n't be reconciled. That's what I guess."

"Dear me, Roxy, who said I should?" said Miss Ruey. "I wa'n't blamin' the poor child, not a grain."

"Well, who said you was, Ruey?" answered Miss Roxy, in the same high key.

"You need n't take my head off," said Aunt Ruey, roused as much as her adipose, comfortable nature could be. "You 've been a-talkin' at me ever since you came in from the sink-room, as if I was to blame; and snappin' at me as if I had n't a right to ask civil questions; and I won't stan' it," said Miss Ruey. "And while I 'm about it, I 'll say that you always have snubbed me and contradicted and ordered me round. I won't bear it no longer."

"Come, Ruey, don't make a fool of yourself at your time of life," said Miss Roxy. "Things is bad enough in this world without out two lone sisters and church-members turnin' agin each other. You must take me as I am, Ruey; my bark 's worse than my bite, as you know."

Miss Ruey sank back pacified into her usual state of pillowy

353

dependence; it was so much easier to be good-natured than to contend. As for Miss Roxy, if you have ever carefully examined a chestnut-burr, you will remember that, hard as it is to handle, no plush of downiest texture can exceed the satin smoothness of the fibres which line its heart. There are a class of people in New England who betray the uprising of the softer feelings of our nature only by an increase of outward asperity—a sort of bashfulness and shyness leaves them no power of expression for these unwonted guests of the heart—they hurry them into inner chambers and slam the doors upon them, as if they were vexed at their appearance.

Now if poor Miss Roxy had been like you, my dear young lady—if her soul had been encased in a round, rosy, and comely body, and looked out of tender blue eyes shaded by golden hair, probably the grief and love she felt would have shown themselves only in bursts of feeling most graceful to see, and engaging the sympathy of all; but this same soul, imprisoned in a dry, angular body, stiff and old, and looking out under beetling eyebrows, over withered high cheek-bones, could only utter itself by a passionate tempest—unlovely utterance of a lovely impulse—dear only to Him who sees with a Father's heart the real beauty of spirits. It is our firm faith that bright solemn angels in celestial watchings were frequent guests in the homely room of the two sisters, and that passing by all accidents of age and poverty, withered skins, bony features, and grotesque movements and shabby clothing, they saw more real beauty there than in many a scented boudoir where seeming angels smile in lace and satin.

"Ruey," said Miss Roxy, in a more composed voice, while her hard, bony hands still trembled with excitement, "this 'ere 's been on my mind a good while. I hain't said nothin' to nobody, but I 've seen it a-comin'. I always thought that child wa'n't for a long life. Lives is run in different lengths, and nobody can say what's the matter with some folks, only that their thread's run out; there's more on one spool and less on another. I thought, when we laid Hitty in the grave, that I should n't never set my heart on nothin' else—but we can't jest say we will or we won't. Ef we are to be sorely afflicted at any time, the Lord lets us set our hearts before we know it. This 'ere's a great affliction to me, Ruey, but I must jest shoulder my cross and go through with it. I'm goin' down to-night to tell the old folks, and to make arrangements so that the poor little lamb may have the care she needs. She's been a-keepin' up so long, 'cause she dreaded to let 'em know, but this 'ere has got to be looked right in the face, and I hope there'll be grace given to do it."

XXXVII

THE VICTORY

Meanwhile Mara had been lying in the passive calm of fatigue and exhaustion, her eyes fixed on the window, where, as the white curtain drew inward, she could catch glimpses of the bay. Gradually her eyelids fell, and she dropped into that kind of half-waking doze, when the outer senses are at rest, and the mind is all the more calm and clear for their repose. In such hours a spiritual clairvoyance often seems to lift for a while the whole stifling cloud that lies like a confusing mist over the problem of life, and the soul has sudden glimpses of things un-utterable which lie beyond. Then the narrow straits, that look so full of rocks and quicksands, widen into a broad, clear pas-sage, and one after another, rosy with a celestial dawn, and ring-ing silver bells of gladness, the isles of the blessed lift them-selves up on the horizon, and the soul is flooded with an atmosphere of light and joy. As the burden of Christian fell off at the cross and was lost in the sepulchre, so in these hours of celestial vision the whole weight of life's anguish is lifted, and passes away like a dream; and the soul, seeing the boundless ocean of Divine love, wherein all human hopes and joys and sorrows lie so tenderly upholden, comes and casts the one little drop of its personal will and personal existence with gladness into that Fatherly depth. Henceforth, with it, God and Saviour is no more word of mine and thine, for in that hour the child of earth feels himself heir of all things: "All things are yours, and ye are Christ's, and Christ is God's."

†††††

"The child is asleep," said Miss Roxy, as she stole on tiptoe into the room when their noon meal was prepared. A plate and knife had been laid for her, and they had placed for her a tumbler of quaint old engraved glass, reputed to have been brought over from foreign parts, and which had been given to Miss Roxy as her share in the effects of the mysterious Mr. Swadkins. Tea also was served in some egg-like India china cups, which saw the light only on the most high and festive occasions.

"Had n't you better wake her?" said Miss Ruey; "a cup of hot tea would do her so much good."

Miss Ruey could conceive of few sorrows or ailments which would not be materially better for a cup of hot tea. If not the very elixir of life, it was indeed the next thing to it.

"Well," said Miss Roxy, after laying her hand for a moment with great gentleness on that of the sleeping girl, "she don't wake easy, and she 's tired; and she seems to be enjoying it so. The Bible says, 'He giveth his beloved sleep,' and I won't interfere. I 've seen more good come of sleep than most things in my nursin' experience," said Miss Roxy, and she shut the door gently, and the two sisters sat down to their noontide meal.

"How long the child does sleep!" said Miss Ruey as the old clock struck four.

"It was too much for her, this walk down here," said Aunt Roxy. "She 's been doin' too much for a long time. I 'm a-goin' to put an end to that. Well, nobody need n't say Mara hain't got resolution. I never see a little thing have more. She always did have, when she was the leastest little thing. She was always quiet and white and still, but she did whatever she sot out to."

At this moment, to their surprise, the door opened, and Mara came in, and both sisters were struck with a change that had passed over her. It was more than the result of mere physical repose. Not only had every sign of weariness and bodily languor vanished, but there was about her an air of solemn serenity and high repose that made her seem, as Miss Ruey afterwards said, "like an angel jest walked out of the big Bible."

"Why, dear child, how you have slept, and how bright and rested you look," said Miss Ruey.

"I am rested," said Mara; "oh how much! And happy," she added, laying her little hand on Miss Roxy's shoulder. "I thank you, dear friend, for all your kindness to me. I am sorry I made you feel so sadly; but now you must n't feel so any more, for all is well—yes, all is well. I see now that it is so. I have passed beyond sorrow—yes, forever."

Soft-hearted Miss Ruey here broke into audible sobbing, hiding her face in her hands, and looking like a tumbled heap of old faded calico in a state of convulsion.

"Dear Aunt Ruey, you must n't," said Mara, with a voice of gentle authority. "We must n't any of us feel so any more. There is no harm done, no real evil is coming, only a good which we do not understand. I am perfectly satisfied—perfectly at rest now. I was foolish and weak to feel as I did this morning, but I shall not feel so any more. I shall comfort you all. Is it anything so dreadful for me to go to heaven? How little while it will be before you all come to me! Oh, how little—little while!"

"I told you, Mara, that you 'd be supported in the Lord's time," said Miss Roxy, who watched her with an air of grave and solemn attention. "First and last, folks allers is supported; but sometimes there is a long wrestlin'. The Lord's give you the victory early."

"Victory!" said the girl, speaking as in a deep muse, and with a mysterious brightness in her eyes; "yes, that is the word—it *is* a victory—no other word expresses it. Come, Aunt Roxy, we will go home. I am not afraid now to tell grandpapa and grandmamma. God will care for them; He will wipe away all tears."

"Well, though, you mus' n't think of goin' till you 've had a cup of tea," said Aunt Ruey, wiping her eyes. "I 've kep' the teapot hot by the fire, and you must eat a little somethin', for it 's long past dinner-time."

"Is it?" said Mara. "I had no idea I had slept so long—how thoughtful and kind you are!"

"I do wish I could only do more for you," said Miss Ruey. "I don't seem to get reconciled no ways; it seems dreffle hard—dreffle; but I 'm glad you *can* feel so;" and the good old soul proceeded to press upon the child not only the tea, which she drank with feverish relish, but every hoarded dainty which their limited housekeeping commanded.

It was toward sunset before Miss Roxy and Mara started on their walk homeward. Their way lay over the high stony ridge which forms the central part of the island. On one side, through the pines, they looked out into the boundless blue of the ocean, and on the other caught glimpses of Harpswell Bay as it lay glorified in the evening light. The fresh cool breeze blowing landward brought with it an invigorating influence, which Mara felt through all her feverish frame. She walked with an energy to which she had long been a stranger. She said little, but there was a sweetness, a repose, in her manner contrasting singularly with the passionate melancholy which she had that morning expressed.

Miss Roxy did not interrupt her meditations. The nature of

her profession had rendered her familiar with all the changing mental and physical phenomena that attend the development of disease and the gradual loosening of the silver cords of a present life. Certain well-understood phrases everywhere current among the mass of the people in New England, strikingly tell of the deep foundations of religious earnestness on which its daily life is built. "A triumphant death" was a matter often casually spoken of among the records of the neighborhood; and Miss Roxy felt that there was a vague and solemn charm about its approach. Yet the soul of the gray, dry woman was hot within her, for the conversation of the morning had probed depths in her own nature of whose existence she had never before been so conscious. The roughest and most matter-of-fact minds have a craving for the ideal somewhere; and often this craving, forbidden by uncomeliness and ungenial surroundings from having any personal history of its own, attaches itself to the fortune of some other one in a kind of strange disinterestedness. Some one young and beautiful is to live the life denied to them—to be the poem and the romance; it is the young mistress of the poor black slave—the pretty sister of the homely old spinster—or the clever son of the consciously ill-educated father. Something of this unconscious personal investment had there been on the part of Miss Roxy in the nursling whose singular loveliness she had watched for so many years, and on whose fair virgin orb she had marked the growing shadow of a fatal eclipse, and as she saw her glowing and serene, with that peculiar brightness that she felt came from no earthly presence or influence, she could scarcely keep the tears from her honest gray eyes.

When they arrived at the door of the house, Zephaniah Pennel was sitting in it, looking toward the sunset.

"Why, reely," he said, "Miss Roxy, we thought you must a-run away with Mara; she's been gone a'most all day."

"I expect she 's had enough to talk with Aunt Roxy about," said Mrs. Pennel. "Girls goin' to get married have a deal to talk about, what with patterns and contrivin' and makin' up. But come in, Miss Roxy; we 're glad to see you."

Mara turned to Miss Roxy, and gave her a look of peculiar meaning. "Aunt Roxy," she said, "you must tell them what we have been talking about to-day;" and then she went up to her room and shut the door.

Miss Roxy accomplished her task with a matter-of-fact distinctness to which her business-like habits of dealing with sickness and death had accustomed her, yet with a sympathetic tremor in her voice which softened the hard directness of her words. "You can take her over to Portland, if you say so, and get Dr. Wilson's opinion," she said, in conclusion. "It 's best to have all done that can be, though in my mind the case is decided."

The silence that fell between the three was broken at last by the sound of a light footstep descending the stairs, and Mara entered among them.

She came forward and threw her arms round Mrs. Pennel's neck, and kissed her; and then turning, she nestled down in the arms of her old grandfather, as she had often done in the old days of childhood, and laid her hand upon his shoulder. There was no sound for a few moments but one of suppressed weeping; but *she* did not weep—she lay with bright calm eyes, as if looking upon some celestial vision.

"It is not so very sad," she said at last, in a gentle voice, "that I should go there; you are going, too, and grandmamma; we are all going; and we shall be forever with the Lord. Think of it! think of it!"

Many were the words spoken in that strange communing; and before Miss Roxy went away, a calmness of solemn rest had settled down on all. The old family Bible was brought forth, and Zephaniah Pennel read from it those strange words of strong consolation, which take the sting from death and the victory from the grave: —

"And I heard a great voice out of heaven, Behold the tabernacle of God is with men, and he will dwell with them, and they shall be his people; and God himself shall be with them and be their God. And God shall wipe away all tears from their eyes; and there shall be no more death, neither sorrow nor crying, for the former things are passed away."

XXXVIII

OPEN VISION

As Miss Roxy was leaving the dwelling of the Pennels, she met Sally Kittridge coming toward the house, laughing and singing, as was her wont. She raised her long, lean forefinger with a gesture of warning.

"What's the matter now, Aunt Roxy? You look as solemn as a hearse."

"None o' your jokin' now, Miss Sally; there *is* such a thing as serious things in this 'ere world of our'n, for all you girls never seems to know it."

"What is the matter, Aunt Roxy?—has anything happened?—is anything the matter with Mara?"

"Matter enough. I 've known it a long time," said Miss Roxy. "She 's been goin' down for three months now; and she 's got that on her that will carry her off before the year's out."

"Pshaw, Aunt Roxy! how lugubriously you old nurses always talk! I hope now you have n't been filling Mara's head with any such notions—people can be frightened into anything."

"Sally Kittridge, don't be a-talkin' of what you don't know nothin' about! It stands to reason that a body that was bearin' the heat and burden of the day long before you was born or thought on in this world *should* know a thing or two more'n you. Why, I 've laid you on your stomach and trotted you to trot up the wind many a day, and I was pretty experienced then, and it ain't likely that I 'm a-goin' to take sa'ce from you. Mara Pennel is a gal as has every bit and grain as much resolution and ambition as you have, for all you flap your wings and crow so much louder, and she 's one of the close-mouthed sort, that don't make no talk, and she 's been a-bearin' up and bearin' up, and comin' to me on the sly for strengthenin' things. She 's took camomile and orange-peel, and snake-root and boneset, and dash-root and dandelion—and there hain't nothin' done her no good. She told me to-day she could n't keep up no longer, and I 've been a-tellin' Mis' Pennel and her gran'ther. I tell you it has been a solemn time; and if you 're goin' in, don't go in with none o' your light triflin' ways, 'cause 'as vinegar upon nitre is he that singeth songs on a heavy heart,' the Scriptur' says."

"Oh, Miss Roxy, do tell me truly," said Sally, much moved. "What do you think is the matter with Mara? I 've noticed myself that she got tired easy, and that she was short-breathed—but she seemed so cheerful. Can anything really be the matter?"

"It 's consumption, Sally Kittridge," said Miss Roxy, "neither more nor less; that ar is the long and the short. They 're going to take her over to Portland to see Dr. Wilson—it won't do no harm, and it won't do no good."

"You seem to be determined she shall die," said Sally in a tone of pique.

"Determined, am I? Is it I that determines that the maple leaves shall fall next October? Yet I know they will—folks can't help knowin' what they know, and shuttin' one's eyes won't alter one's road. I s'pose you think 'cause you 're young and middlin' good-lookin' that you have feelin's and I has n't; well, you 're mistaken, that 's all. I don't believe there 's one person in the world that would go farther or do more to save Mara Pennel than I would,—and yet I 've been in the world long enough to see that livin' ain't no great shakes neither. Ef one is hopefully prepared in the days of their youth, why they escape a good deal, ef they get took cross-lots into heaven."

Sally turned away thoughtfully into the house; there was no one in the kitchen, and the tick of the old clock sounded lonely and sepulchral. She went upstairs to Mara's room; the door was ajar. Mara was sitting at the open window that looked forth toward the ocean, busily engaged in writing. The glow of evening shone on the golden waves of her hair, and tinged the pearly outline of her cheek. Sally noticed the translucent clearness of her complexion, and the deep burning color and the transparency of the little hands, which seemed as if they might transmit the light like Sèvres porcelain. She was writing with an expression of tender calm, and sometimes stopping to consult an open letter that Sally knew came from Moses.

So fair and sweet and serene she looked that a painter might have chosen her for an embodiment of twilight, and one might not be surprised to see a clear star shining out over her forehead. Yet in the tender serenity of the face there dwelt a pathos of expression that spoke of struggles and sufferings past, like the traces of tears on the face of a restful infant that has grieved itself to sleep.

Sally came softly in on tiptoe, threw her arms around her, and kissed her, with a half laugh, then bursting into tears, sobbed upon her shoulder.

"Dear Sally, what is the matter?" said Mara, looking up.

"Oh, Mara, I just met Miss Roxy, and she told me"—

Sally only sobbed passionately.

"It is very sad to make all one's friends so unhappy," said

Mara, in a soothing voice, stroking Sally's hair. "You don't know how much I have suffered dreading it. Sally, it is a long time since I began to expect and dread and fear. My time of anguish was then—then when I first felt that it could be possible that I should not live after all. There was a long time I dared not even think of it; I could not even tell such a fear to myself; and I did far more than I felt able to do to convince myself that I was not weak and failing. I have been often to Miss Roxy, and once, when nobody knew it, I went to a doctor in Brunswick, but then I was afraid to tell him half, lest he should say something about me, and it should get out; and so I went on getting worse and worse, and feeling every day as if I could not keep up, and yet afraid to lie down for fear grandmamma would suspect me. But this morning it was pleasant and bright, and something came over me that said I *must* tell somebody, and so, as it was cool and pleasant, I walked up to Aunt Roxy's and told her. I thought, you know, that she knew the most, and would feel it the least; but oh, Sally, she has such a feeling heart, and loves me so; it is strange she should."

"Is it?" said Sally, tightening her clasp around Mara's neck; and then with a hysterical shadow of gayety she said, "I suppose you think that you are such a hobgoblin that nobody could be expected to do that. After all, though, I should have as soon expected roses to bloom in a juniper clump as love from Aunt Roxy."

"Well, she does love me," said Mara. "No mother could be kinder. Poor thing, she really sobbed and cried when I told her. I was very tired, and she told me she would take care of me, and tell grandpapa and grandmamma,—*that* had been lying on my heart as such a dreadful thing to do,—and she laid me down to rest on her bed, and spoke so lovingly to me! I wish you could have seen her. And while I lay there, I fell into a strange, sweet sort of rest. I can't describe it; but since then everything has been changed. I wish I could tell any one how I saw things then."

"Do try to tell me, Mara," said Sally, "for I need comfort too, if there is any to be had."

"Well, then, I lay on the bed, and the wind drew in from the sea and just lifted the window-curtain, and I could see the sea shining and hear the waves making a pleasant little dash, and then my head seemed to swim. I thought I was walking out by the pleasant shore, and everything seemed so strangely beautiful, and grandpapa and grandmamma were there, and Moses had come home, and you were there, and we were all so happy. And then I felt a sort of strange sense that something was coming—some great trial or affliction—and I groaned and clung to Moses, and asked him to put his arm around me and hold me.

"Then it seemed to be not by our sea-shore that this was happening, but by the Sea of Galilee, just as it tells about it in the Bible, and there were fishermen mending their nets, and men sitting counting their money, and I saw Jesus come walking along, and heard him say to this one and that one, 'Leave all and follow me,' and it seemed that the moment he spoke they did it, and then he came to me, and I felt his eyes in my very soul, and he said, 'Wilt *thou* leave *all* and follow me?' I cannot tell now what a pain I felt—what an anguish. I wanted to leave all, but my heart felt as if it were tied and woven with a thousand threads, and while I waited he seemed to fade away, and I found myself then alone and unhappy, wishing that I could, and mourning that I had not; and then something shone out warm like the sun, and I looked up, and he stood there looking pitifully, and he said again just as he did before, 'Wilt thou leave all and follow me?' Every word was so gentle and full of pity, and I looked into his eyes and could not look away; they drew me, they warmed me, and I felt a strange, wonderful sense of his greatness and sweetness. It seemed as if I felt within me cord after cord breaking, I felt so free, so happy; and I said, 'I will, I will, with all my heart;' and I woke then, so happy, so sure of God's love.

"I saw so clearly how his love is in everything, and these words came into my mind as if an angel had spoken them, 'God shall wipe away all tears from their eyes.' Since then I cannot be unhappy. I was so myself only this morning, and now I wonder that any one can have a grief when God is so loving and good, and cares so sweetly for us all. Why, Sally, if I could see Christ and hear him speak, I could not be more certain that he will make this sorrow such a blessing to us all that we shall never be able to thank him enough for it."

"Oh Mara," said Sally, sighing deeply, while her cheek was wet with tears, "it is beautiful to hear you talk; but there is one that I am sure will not and cannot feel so."

"God will care for him," said Mara; "oh, I am sure of it; He is love itself, and He values his love in us, and He never, never would have brought such a trial, if it had not been the true and only way to our best good. We shall not shed one needless tear. Yes, if God loved us so that he spared not his own Son, he will surely give us all the good here that we possibly can have without risking our eternal happiness."

"You are writing to Moses, now?" said Sally.

"Yes, I am answering his letter; it is so full of spirit and life and hope—but all hope in this world—all, all earthly, as much as if there was no God and no world to come. Sally, perhaps our Father saw that I could not have strength to live with him and keep my faith. I should be drawn by him earthward instead of drawing him heavenward; and so this is in mercy to us both."

"And are you telling him the whole truth, Mara?"

"Not all, no," said Mara; "he could not bear it at once. I only tell him that my health is failing, and that my friends are seriously alarmed, and then I speak as if it were doubtful, in my mind, what the result might be."

"I don't think you can make him feel as you do. Moses Pennel has a tremendous will, and he never yielded to any one. You bend, Mara, like the little blue harebells, and so the storm goes over you; but he will stand up against it, and it will wrench and shatter him. I am afraid, instead of making him better, it will only make him bitter and rebellious."

"He has a Father in heaven who knows how to care for him," said Mara. "I am persuaded—I feel certain that he will be blessed in the end; not perhaps in the time and way I should have chosen, but in the end. I have always felt that he was mine, ever since he came a little ship-wrecked boy to me—a little girl. And now I have given him up to his Saviour and my Saviour—to his God and my God—and I am perfectly at peace. All will be well."

Mara spoke with a look of such solemn, bright assurance as made her, in the dusky, golden twilight, seem like some serene angel sent down to comfort, rather than a hapless mortal just wrenched from life and hope.

Sally rose up and kissed her silently. "Mara," she said, "I shall come to-morrow to see what I can do for you. I will not interrupt you now. Good-by, dear."

There are no doubt many, who have followed this history so long as it danced like a gay little boat over sunny waters, and who would have followed it gayly to the end, had it closed with ringing of marriage-bells, who turn from it indignantly, when they see that its course runs through the dark valley. This, they say, is an imposition, a trick upon our feelings. We want to read only stories which end in joy and prosperity.

But have we then settled it in our own mind that there is no such thing as a fortunate issue in a history which does not terminate in the way of earthly success and good fortune? Are we Christians or heathen? It is now eighteen centuries since, as we hold, the "highly favored among women" was pronounced to be one whose earthly hopes were all cut off in the blossom,—whose noblest and dearest in the morning of his days went down into the shadows of death.

Was Mary the highly-favored among women, and was Jesus indeed the blessed,—or was the angel mistaken? If they were these, if we are Christians, it ought to be a settled and established habit of our souls to regard something else as prosperity than worldly success and happy marriages. That life is a success which, like the life of Jesus, in its beginning, middle, and close, has borne a perfect witness to the truth and the highest form of truth. It is true that God has given to us, and inwoven in our nature a desire for a perfection and completeness made manifest to our senses in this mortal life. To see the daughter bloom into youth and womanhood, the son into manhood, to see them marry and become themselves parents, and gradually ripen and develop in the maturities of middle life, gradually wear into a sunny autumn, and so be gathered in fullness of time to their fathers,—such, one says, is the programme which God has made us to desire; such the ideal of happiness which he has interwoven with our nerves, and for which our heart and our flesh crieth out; to which every stroke of a knell is a violence, and every thought of an early death is an abhorrence.

But the life of Christ and his mother sets the foot on this lower ideal of happiness, and teaches us that there is something higher. His ministry began with declaring, "Blessed are they that mourn." It has been well said that prosperity was the blessing of the Old Testament, and adversity of the New. Christ came to show us a nobler style of living and bearing; and so far as he had a personal and earthly life, he buried it as a corner-stone on which to erect a new immortal style of architecture.

Of his own, he had nothing, neither houses, nor lands, nor family ties, nor human hopes, nor earthly sphere of success; and as a human life, it was all a sacrifice and a defeat. He was re-jected by his countrymen, whom the passionate anguish of his love and the unwearied devotion of his life could not save from an awful doom. He was betrayed by weak friends, prevailed against by slanderers, overwhelmed with an ignominious death in the morning of youth, and his mother stood by his cross, and she was the only woman whom God ever called highly favored in this world.

This, then, is the great and perfect ideal of what God honors. Christ speaks of himself as bread to be eaten,—bread, simple, humble, unpretending, vitally necessary to human life, made by the bruising and grinding of the grain, unostentatiously having no life or worth of its own except as it is absorbed into the life of others and lives in them. We wished in this history to speak of a class of lives formed on the model of Christ, and like his, obscure and unpretending, like his, seeming to end in darkness and defeat, but which yet have this preciousness and value that the dear saints who live them come nearest in their mission to the mission of Jesus. They are made, not for a career and his-tory of their own, but to be bread of life to others. In every household or house have been some of these, and if we look on their lives and deaths with the unbaptized eyes of nature, we shall see only most mournful and unaccountable failure, when, if we could look with the eye of faith, we should see that their living and dying has been bread of life to those they left behind. Fairest of these, and least developed, are the holy innocents who come into our households to smile with the smile of angels, who sleep in our bosoms, and win us with the softness of tender little hands, and pass away like the lamb that was slain before they have ever learned the speech of mortals. Not vain are even these silent lives of Christ's lambs, whom many an earth-bound heart has been roused to follow when the Shepherd bore them to the higher pastures. And so the daughter who died so early, whose wedding-bells were never rung except in heaven,—the son who had no career of ambition or a manly duty except among the angels,—the patient sufferers, whose only lot on earth seemed to be to endure, whose life bled away drop by drop in the shadows of the sick-room—all these are among those whose life was like Christ's in that they were made, not for themselves, but to become bread to us.

It is expedient for us that they go away. Like their Lord, they come to suffer, and to die; they take part in his sacrifice; their life is incomplete without their death, and not till they are gone away does the Comforter fully come to us.

It is a beautiful legend which one sees often represented in the churches of Europe, that when the grave of the mother of Jesus was opened, it was found full of blossoming lilies,—fit emblem of the thousand flowers of holy thought and purpose which spring up in our hearts from the memory of our sainted dead.

Cannot many, who read these lines, bethink them of such rooms that have been the most cheerful places in the family,—when the heart of the smitten one seemed the band that bound all the rest together,—and have there not been dying hours which shed such a joy and radiance on all around, that it was long before the mourners remembered to mourn? Is it not a misuse of words to call such a heavenly translation *death?* and to call most things that are lived out on this earth *life?*

XXXIX

THE LAND OF
BEULAH

It is now about a month after the conversation which we have recorded, and during that time the process which was to loose from this present life had been going on in Mara with a soft, insensible, but steady power. When she ceased to make efforts beyond her strength, and allowed herself that languor and repose which nature claimed, all around her soon became aware how her strength was failing; and yet a cheerful repose seemed to hallow the atmosphere around her. The sight of her every day in family worship, sitting by in such tender tranquillity, with such a smile on her face, seemed like a present inspiration. And though the aged pair knew that she was no more for this world, yet she was comforting and inspiring to their view as the angel who of old rolled back the stone from the sepulchre and sat upon it. They saw in her eyes, not death, but the solemn victory which Christ gives over death.

Bunyan has no more lovely poem than the image he gives of that land of pleasant waiting which borders the river of death, where the chosen of the Lord repose, while shining messengers, constantly passing and repassing, bear tidings from the celestial shore, opening a way between earth and heaven. It was so, that through the very thought of Mara an influence of tenderness and tranquillity passed through the whole neighborhood, keeping hearts fresh with sympathy, and causing thought and conversation to rest on those bright mysteries of eternal joy which were reflected on her face.

Sally Kittridge was almost a constant inmate of the brown house, ever ready in watching and waiting; and one only needed to mark the expression of her face to feel that a holy charm was silently working upon her higher and spiritual nature. Those great, dark, sparkling eyes that once seemed to express only the brightness of animal vivacity, and glittered like a brook in unsympathetic gayety, had in them now mysterious depths, and tender, fleeting shadows, and the very tone of her voice had a subdued tremor. The capricious elf, the tricksy sprite, was melting away in the immortal soul, and the deep pathetic power of a noble heart was being born. Some influence sprung of sorrow is necessary always to perfect beauty in womanly nature. We feel its absence in many whose sparkling wit and high spirits give grace and vivacity to life, but in whom we vainly seek for some spot of quiet tenderness and sympathetic repose. Sally was, ignorantly to herself, changing in the expression of her face and the tone of her character, as she ministered in the daily wants which sickness brings in a simple household.

For the rest of the neighborhood, the shelves and larder of Mrs. Pennel were constantly crowded with the tributes which one or another sent in for the invalid. There was jelly of Iceland moss sent across by Miss Emily, and brought by Mr. Sewell, whose calls were almost daily. There were custards and preserves, and every form of cake and other confections in which the housekeeping talent of the neighbors delighted, and which were sent in under the old superstition that sick people must be kept eating at all hazards.

At church, Sunday after Sunday, the simple note requested the prayers of the church and congregation for Mara Lincoln, who was, as the note phrased it, drawing near her end, that she and all concerned might be prepared for the great and last change. One familiar with New England customs must have remembered with what a plaintive power the reading of such a note, from Sunday to Sunday, has drawn the thoughts and sympathies of a congregation to some chamber of sickness; and in a village church, where every individual is known from childhood to every other, the power of this simple custom is still greater.

Then the prayers of the minister would dwell on the case, and thanks would be rendered to God for the great light and peace with which he had deigned to visit his young handmaid; and then would follow a prayer that when these sad tidings should reach a distant friend who had gone down to do business on the great waters, they might be sanctified to his spiritual and everlasting good. Then on Sunday noons, as the people ate their dinners together in a room adjoining the church, all that she said and did was talked over and over,—how quickly she had gained the victory of submission, the peace of a will united with God's, mixed with harmless gossip of the sick chamber,—as to what she ate and how she slept, and who had sent her gruel with raisins in it, and who jelly with wine, and how she had praised this and eaten that twice with a relish, but how the other had seemed to disagree with her. Thereafter would come scraps of nursing information, recipes against coughing, specifics against short breath, speculations about watchers, how soon she would need them, and long legends of other death-beds where the fear of death had been slain by the power of an endless life.

Yet through all the gossip, and through much that might have been called at other times commonplace cant of religion, there was spread a tender earnestness, and the whole air seemed to be enchanted with the fragrance of that fading rose. Each one spoke more gently, more lovingly to each, for the thought of her.

It was now a bright September morning, and the early frosts had changed the maples in the pine-woods to scarlet, and touched the white birches with gold, when one morning Miss Roxy presented herself at an early hour at Captain Kittridge's.

They were at breakfast, and Sally was dispensing the tea at the head of the table, Mrs. Kittridge having been prevailed on to abdicate in her favor.

"It is such a fine morning," she said, looking out at the window, which showed a waveless expanse of ocean. "I do hope Mara has had a good night."

"I 'm a-goin' to make her some jelly this very forenoon," said Mrs. Kittridge. "Aunt Roxy was a-tellin' me yesterday that she was a-goin' down to stay at the house regular, for she needed so much done now."

"It 's 'most an amazin' thing we don't hear from Moses Pennel," said Captain Kittridge. "If he don't make haste, he may never see her."

"There 's Aunt Roxy at this minute," said Sally.

In truth, the door opened at this moment, and Aunt Roxy entered with a little blue bandbox and a bundle tied up in a checked handkerchief.

"Oh, Aunt Roxy," said Mrs. Kittridge, "you are on your way, are you? Do sit down, right here, and get a cup of strong tea."

"Thank you," said Aunt Roxy, "but Ruey gave me a humming cup before I came away."

"Aunt Roxy, have they heard anything from Moses?" said the Captain.

"No, father, I know they have n't," said Sally. "Mara has written to him, and so has Mr. Sewell, but it is very uncertain whether he ever got the letters."

"It 's most time to be a-lookin' for him home," said the Captain. "I should n't be surprised to see him any day."

At this moment Sally, who sat where she could see from the window, gave a sudden start and a half scream, and rising from the table, darted first to the window and then to the door, whence she rushed out eagerly.

"Well, what now?" said the Captain.

"I am sure I don't know what 's come over her," said Mrs. Kittridge, rising to look out.

"Why, Aunt Roxy, do look; I believe to my soul that ar 's Moses Pennel!"

And so it was. He met Sally, as she ran out, with a gloomy brow and scarcely a look even of recognition; but he seized her hand and wrung it in the stress of his emotion so that she almost screamed with the pain.

"Tell me, Sally," he said, "tell me the truth. I dared not go home without I knew. Those gossiping, lying reports are always exaggerated. They are dreadful exaggerations,—they frighten a sick person into the grave; but you have good sense and a hopeful, cheerful temper,—you must see and know how things are. Mara is not so very—very"— He held Sally's hand and looked at her with a burning eagerness. "Say, what do you think of her?"

"We all think that we cannot long keep her with us," said Sally. "And oh, Moses, I am so glad you have come."

"It 's false,—it must be false," he said, violently; "nothing is more deceptive than these ideas that doctors and nurses pile on when a sensitive person is going down a little. I know Mara; everything depends on the mind with her. I shall wake her up out of this dream. She is not to die. She shall not die,—I come to save her."

"Oh, if you could!" said Sally, mournfully.

"It cannot be; it is not to be," he said again, as if to convince himself. "No such thing is to be thought of. Tell me, Sally, have you tried to keep up the cheerful side of things to her,—have you?"

"Oh, you cannot tell, Moses, how it is, unless you see her. She is cheerful, happy; the only really joyous one among us."

"Cheerful! joyous! happy! She does not believe, then, these frightful things? I thought she would keep up; she is a brave little thing."

"No, Moses, she does believe. She has given up all hope of life,—all wish to live; and oh, she is so lovely,—so sweet,—so dear."

Sally covered her face with her hands and sobbed. Moses stood still, looking at her a moment in a confused way, and then he answered,—

"Come, get your bonnet, Sally, and go with me. You must go in and tell them; tell her that I am come, you know."

"Yes, I will," said Sally, as she ran quickly back to the house.

Moses stood listlessly looking after her. A moment after she came out of the door again, and Miss Roxy behind. Sally hurried up to Moses.

"Where 's that black old raven going?" said Moses, in a low voice, looking back on Miss Roxy, who stood on the steps.

"What, Aunt Roxy?" said Sally; "why, she 's going up to nurse Mara, and take care of her. Mrs. Pennel is so old and infirm she needs somebody to depend on."

"I can't bear her," said Moses. "I always think of sick-rooms and coffins and a stifling smell of camphor when I see her. I never could endure her. She 's an old harpy going to carry off my dove."

"Now, Moses, you must *not* talk so. She loves Mara dearly, the poor old soul, and Mara loves her, and there is no earthly thing she would not do for her. And she knows what to do for sickness better than you or I. I have found out one thing, that it is n't mere love and good-will that is needed in a sick-room; it needs knowledge and experience."

Moses assented in gloomy silence, and they walked on together the way that they had so often taken laughing and chatting. When they came within sight of the house, Moses said,—

"Here she came running to meet us; do you remember?"

"Yes," said Sally.

"I was never half worthy of her. I never said half what I ought to," he added. "She *must* live! I must have one more chance."

When they came up to the house, Zephaniah Pennel was sitting in the door, with his gray head bent over the leaves of the great family Bible.

He rose up at their coming, and with that suppression of all external signs of feeling for which the New Englander is remarkable, simply shook the hand of Moses, saying,—

"Well, my boy, we are glad you have come."

Mrs. Pennel, who was busied in some domestic work in the back part of the kitchen, turned away and hid her face in her apron when she saw him. There fell a great silence among them, in the midst of which the old clock ticked loudly and importunately, like the inevitable approach of fate.

"I will go up and see her, and get her ready," said Sally, in a whisper to Moses. "I 'll come and call you."

Moses sat down and looked around on the old familiar scene; there was the great fireplace where, in their childish days, they had sat together winter nights,—her fair, spiritual face enlivened by the blaze, while she knit and looked thoughtfully into the coals; there she had played checkers, or fox and geese, with him; or studied with him the Latin lessons; or sat by, grave and thoughtful, hemming his toy-ship sails, while he cut the moulds for his anchors, or tried experiments on pulleys; and in all these years he could not remember one selfish action,—one unlovely word,—and he thought to himself, "I hoped to possess this angel as a mortal wife! God forgive my presumption."

XL

THE MEETING

Sally found Mara sitting in an easy-chair that had been sent to her by the provident love of Miss Emily. It was wheeled in front of her room window, from whence she could look out upon the wide expanse of the ocean. It was a gloriously bright, calm morning, and the water lay clear and still, with scarce a ripple, to the far distant pearly horizon. She seemed to be looking at it in a kind of calm ecstasy, and murmuring the words of a hymn: —

> "Nor wreck nor ruin there is seen,
>   There not a wave of trouble rolls,
> But the bright rainbow round the throne
>   Peals endless peace to all their souls."

Sally came softly behind her on tiptoe to kiss her. "Good-morning, dear, how do you find yourself?"

"Quite well," was the answer.

"Mara, is not there anything you want?"

"There might be many things; but His will is mine."

"You want to see Moses?"

"Very much; but I shall see him as soon as it is best for us both."

"Mara,—he is come."

The quick blood flushed over the pale, transparent face as a virgin glacier flushes at sunrise, and she looked up eagerly. "Come!"

"Yes, he is below-stairs wanting to see you."

She seemed about to speak eagerly, and then checked herself and mused a moment. "Poor, poor boy!" she said. "Yes, Sally, let him come at once."

There were a few dazzling, dreamy minutes when Moses first held that frail form in his arms, which but for its tender, mortal warmth, might have seemed to him a spirit. It was no spirit, but a woman whose heart he could feel thrilling against his own; who seemed to him like some frail, fluttering bird; but somehow, as he looked into her clear, transparent face, and pressed her thin little hands in his, the conviction stole over him overpoweringly that she was indeed fading away and going from him,—drawn from him by that mysterious, irresistible power against which human strength, even in the strongest, has no chance.

It is dreadful to a strong man who has felt the influence of his strength,—who has always been ready with a resource for every emergency, and a weapon for every battle,—when first he meets that mighty invisible power by which a beloved life—a life he would give his own blood to save—melts and dissolves like smoke before his eyes.

"Oh, Mara, Mara," he groaned, "this is too dreadful, too cruel; it is cruel."

"You will think so at first, but not always," she said, soothingly. "You will live to see a joy come out of this sorrow."

"Never, Mara, never. I cannot believe that kind of talk. I see no love, no mercy in it. Of course, if there is any life after death you will be happy; if there is a heaven you will be there; but can this dim, unsubstantial, cloudy prospect make you happy in leaving me and giving up one's lover? Oh, Mara, you cannot love as I do, or you could not"—

"Moses, I have suffered,—oh, very, very much. It was many months ago when I first thought that I must give everything up,—when I thought that we must part; but Christ helped me; he showed me his wonderful love,—the love that surrounds us all our life, that follows us in all our wanderings, and sustains us in all our weaknesses,—and then I felt that whatever He wills for us is in love; oh, believe it,—believe it for my sake, for your own."

"Oh, I cannot, I cannot," said Moses; but as he looked at the bright, pale face, and felt how the tempest of his feelings shook the frail form, he checked himself. "I do wrong to agitate you so, Mara. I will try to be calm."

"And to pray?" she said, beseechingly.

He shut his lips in gloomy silence.

"Promise me," she said.

"I have prayed ever since I got your first letter, and I see it does no good," he answered. "Our prayers cannot alter fate."

"Fate! there is no fate," she answered; "there is a strong and loving Father who guides the way, though we know it not. We cannot resist His will; but it is all love,—pure, pure love."

At this moment Sally came softly into the room. A gentle air of womanly authority seemed to express itself in that once gay and giddy face, at which Moses, in the midst of his misery, marveled.

"You must not stay any longer now," she said; "it would be too much for her strength; this is enough for this morning."

Moses turned away, and silently left the room, and Sally said to Mara,—

"You must lie down now, and rest."

"Sally," said Mara, "promise me one thing."

"Well, Mara; of course I will."

"Promise to love him and care for him when I am gone; he will be so lonely."

"I will do all I can, Mara," said Sally, soothingly; "so now you must take a little wine and lie down. You know what you have so often said, that all will yet be well with him."

"Oh, I know it, I am sure," said Mara, "but oh, his sorrow shook my very heart."

"You must not talk another word about it," said Sally, peremptorily. "Do you know Aunt Roxy is coming to see you? I see her out of the window this very moment."

And Sally assisted to lay her friend on the bed, and then, administering a stimulant, she drew down the curtains, and, sitting beside her, began repeating, in a soft monotonous tone, the words of a favorite hymn:—

> "The Lord my shepherd is,
> I shall be well supplied;
> Since He is mine, and I am His,
> What can I want beside?"

Before she had finished, Mara was asleep.

XLI

CONSOLATION

Moses came down from the chamber of Mara in a tempest of contending emotions. He had all that constitutional horror of death and the spiritual world which is an attribute of some particularly strong and well-endowed physical natures, and he had all that instinctive resistance of the will which such natures offer to anything which strikes athwart their cherished hopes and plans. To be wrenched suddenly from the sphere of an earthly life and made to confront the unclosed doors of a spiritual world on the behalf of the one dearest to him, was to him a dreary horror uncheered by one filial belief in God. He felt, furthermore, that blind animal irritation which assails one under a sudden blow, whether of the body or of the soul,—an anguish of resistance, a vague blind anger.

Mr. Sewell was sitting in the kitchen,—he had called to see Mara, and waited for the close of the interview above. He rose and offered his hand to Moses, who took it in gloomy silence, without a smile or word.

"'My son, despise not thou the chastening of the Lord,'" said Mr. Sewell.

"I cannot bear that sort of thing," said Moses abruptly, and almost fiercely. "I beg your pardon, sir, but it irritates me."

"Do you not believe that afflictions are sent for our improvement?" said Mr. Sewell.

"No! how can I? What improvement will there be to me in taking from me the angel who guided me to all good, and kept me from all evil; the one pure motive and holy influence of my life? If you call this the chastening of a loving father, I must say it looks more to me like the caprice of an evil spirit."

"Had you ever thanked the God of your life for this gift, or felt your dependence on him to keep it? Have you not blindly idolized the creature and forgotten Him who gave it?" said Mr. Sewell.

Moses was silent a moment.

"I cannot believe there is a God," he said. "Since this fear came on me I have prayed,—yes, and humbled myself; for I know I have not always been what I ought. I promised if he would grant me this one thing, I would seek him in future; but it did no good,—it 's of no use to pray. I would have been good in this way, if she might be spared, and I cannot in any other."

"My son, our Lord and Master will have no such conditions from us," said Mr. Sewell. "We must submit unconditionally. *She* has done it, and her peace is as firm as the everlasting hills. God's will is a great current that flows in spite of us; if we go with it, it carries us to endless rest,—if we resist, we only wear our lives out in useless struggles."

Moses stood a moment in silence, and then, turning away without a word, hurried from the house. He strode along the high rocky bluff, through tangled junipers and pine thickets, till he came above the rocky cove which had been his favorite retreat on so many occasions. He swung himself down over the cliffs into the grotto, where, shut in by the high tide, he felt himself alone. There he had read Mr. Sewell's letter, and dreamed vain dreams of wealth and worldly success, now all to him so void. He felt today, as he sat there and watched the ships go by, how utterly nothing all the wealth in the world was, in the loss of that one heart. Unconsciously, even to himself, sorrow was doing her ennobling ministry within him, melting off in her fierce fires trivial ambitions and low desires, and making him feel the sole worth and value of love. That which in other days had seemed only as one good thing among many now seemed the *only* thing in life. And he who has learned the paramount value of love has taken one step from an earthly to a spiritual existence.

But as he lay there on the pebbly shore, hour after hour glided by, his whole past life lived itself over to his eye; he saw a thousand actions, he heard a thousand words, whose beauty and significance never came to him till now. And alas! he saw so many when, on his part, the responsive word that should have been spoken, and the deed that should have been done, was forever wanting. He had all his life carried within him a vague consciousness that he had not been to Mara what he should have been, but he had hoped to make amends for all in that future which lay before him,—that future now, alas! dissolving and fading away like the white cloud-islands which the wind was drifting from the sky. A voice seemed saying in his ears, "Ye know that when he would have inherited a blessing he was rejected; for he found no place for repentance, though he sought it carefully with tears." Something that he had never felt before struck him as appalling in the awful fixedness of all past deeds and words,—the unkind words once said, which no tears could unsay,—the kind ones suppressed, to which no agony of wishfulness could give a past reality. There were particular times in their past history that he remembered so vividly, when he saw her so clearly,—doing some little thing for him, and shyly watching for the word of acknowledgment, which he did not give. Some willful wayward demon withheld him at the moment, and the light on the little wishful face slowly faded. True, all had been a thousand times forgiven and forgotten between them, but it is the ministry of these great vital hours of sorrow to teach us that nothing in the soul's history ever dies or is forgotten, and when the beloved one lies stricken and ready to pass away, comes the judgment-day of love, and all the dead moments of the past arise and live again.

He lay there musing and dreaming till the sun grew low in the afternoon sky, and the tide that isolated the little grotto had gone far out into the ocean, leaving long, low reefs of sunken rocks, all matted and tangled with the yellow hair of the seaweed, with little crystal pools of salt water between. He heard the sound of approaching footsteps, and Captain Kittridge came slowly picking his way round among the shingle and pebbles.

"Wal', now, I thought I 'd find ye here!" he said. "I kind o' thought I wanted to see ye,—ye see."

Moses looked up half moody, half astonished, while the Captain seated himself upon a fragment of rock and began brushing the knees of his trousers industriously, until soon the tears rained down from his eyes upon his dry withered hands.

"Wal', now ye see, I can't help it, darned if I can; knowed her ever since she 's that high. She 's done me good, she has. Mis' Kittridge has been pretty faithful. I 've had folks here and there talk to me consid'able, but Lord bless you, I never had nothin' go to my heart like this 'ere—Why to look on her there could n't nobody doubt but what there was somethin' in religion. You never knew half what she did for you, Moses Pennel, you did n't know that the night you was off down to the long cove with

Skipper Atkinson, that 'ere blessed child was a-follerin' you, but she was, and she come to me next day to get me to do somethin' for you. That was how your grand'ther and I got ye off to sea so quick, and she such a little thing then; that ar child was the savin' of ye, Moses Pennel."

Moses hid his head in his hands with a sort of groan.

"Wal', wal'," said the Captain, "I don't wonder now ye feel so,—I don't see how ye can stan' it no ways—only by thinkin' o' where she 's goin' to— Them ar bells in the Celestial City must all be a-ringin' for her,—there 'll be joy that side o' the river I reckon, when she gets acrost. If she 'd jest leave me a hem o' her garment to get in by, I 'd be glad; but she was one o' the sort that was jest *made* to go to heaven. She only stopped a few days in our world, like the robins when they 's goin' south; but there 'll be a good many fust and last that 'll get into the kingdom for love of her. She never said much to me, but she kind o' drew me. Ef ever I should get in there, it 'll be *she* led me. But come, now, Moses, ye ought n't fur to be a-settin' here catchin' cold—jest come round to our house and let Sally gin you a warm cup o' tea—do come, now."

"Thank you, Captain," said Moses, "but I will go home; I must see her again to-night."

"Wal', don't let her see you grieve too much, ye know; we must be a little sort o' manly, ye know, 'cause her body's weak, if her heart is strong."

Now Moses was in a mood of dry, proud, fierce, self-consuming sorrow, least likely to open his heart or seek sympathy from any one; and no friend or acquaintance would probably have dared to intrude on his grief. But there are moods of the mind which cannot be touched or handled by one on an equal level with us that yield at once to the sympathy of something below. A dog who comes with his great honest, sorrowful face and lays his mute paw of inquiry on your knee, will sometimes open floodgates of sober feeling, that have remained closed to every human touch;—the dumb simplicity and ignorance of his sympathy makes it irresistible. In like manner the downright grief of the good-natured old Captain, and the child-like ignorance with which he ventured upon a ministry of consolation from which a more cultivated person would have shrunk away, were irresistibly touching. Moses grasped the dry, withered hand and said, "Thank you, thank you, Captain Kittridge; you 're a true friend."

"Wal', I be, that 's a fact, Moses. Lord bless me, I ain't no great—I ain't nobody—I 'm jest an old last-year's mullein-stalk in the Lord's vineyard; but that 'ere blessed little thing allers had a good word for me. She gave me a hymn-book and marked some hymns in it, and read 'em to me herself, and her voice was jest as sweet as the sea of a warm evening. Them hymns come to me kind o' powerful when I 'm at my work planin' and sawin'. Mis' Kittridge, she allers talks to me as ef I was a terrible sinner; and I suppose I be, but this 'ere blessed child, she 's so kind o' good and innocent, she thinks I 'm good; kind o' takes it for granted I 'm one o' the Lord's people, ye know. It kind o' makes me want to be, ye know."

The Captain here produced from his coat-pocket a much worn hymn-book, and showed Moses where leaves were folded down. "Now here 's this 'ere," he said; "you get her to say it to you," he added, pointing to the well-known sacred idyl which has refreshed so many hearts:—

> "There is a land of pure delight
>   Where saints immortal reign;
> Eternal day excludes the night,
>   And pleasures banish pain.

"There everlasting spring abides,
And never-fading flowers;
Death like a narrow sea divides
This happy land from ours."

"Now that ar beats everything," said the Captain, "and we must kind o' think of it for her, 'cause she 's goin' to see all that, and ef it 's our loss it 's her gain, ye know."

"I know," said Moses; "our grief is selfish."

"Jest so. Wal', we 're selfish critters, we be," said the Captain; "but arter all, 't ain't as ef we was heathen and did n't know where they was a-goin' to. We jest ought to be a-lookin' about and tryin' to foller 'em, ye know."

"Yes, yes, I do know," said Moses; "it 's easy to say, but hard to do."

"But law, man, she prays for you; she did years and years ago, when you was a boy and she a girl. You know it tells in the Revelations how the angels has golden vials full of odors which are the prayers of saints. I tell ye Moses, you ought to get into heaven, if no one else does. I expect you are pretty well known among the angels by this time. I tell ye what 't is, Moses, fellers think it a mighty pretty thing to be a-steppin' high, and a-sayin' they don't believe the Bible, and all that ar, so long as the world goes well. This 'ere old Bible—why it 's jest like yer mother,—ye rove and ramble, and cut up round the world without her a spell, and mebbe think the old woman ain't so fashionable as some; but when sickness and sorrow comes, why, there ain't nothin' else to go back to. Is there, now?"

Moses did not answer, but he shook the hand of the Captain and turned away.

XLII

LAST WORDS

The setting sun gleamed in at the window of Mara's chamber, tinted with rose and violet hues from a great cloud-castle that lay upon the smooth ocean over against the window. Mara was lying upon the bed, but she raised herself upon her elbow to look out.

"Dear Aunt Roxy," she said, "raise me up and put the pillows behind me, so that I can see out—it is splendid."

Aunt Roxy came and arranged the pillows, and lifted the girl with her long, strong arms, then stooping over her a moment she finished her arrangements by softly smoothing the hair from her forehead with a caressing movement most unlike her usual precise business-like proceedings.

"I love you, Aunt Roxy," said Mara, looking up with a smile.

Aunt Roxy made a strange wry face, which caused her to look harder than usual. She was choked with tenderness, and had only this uncomely way of showing it.

"Law now, Mara, I don't see how ye can; I ain't nothin' but an old burdock-bush; love ain't for me."

"Yes it is too," said Mara, drawing her down and kissing her withered cheek, "and you sha'n't call yourself an old burdock.

God sees that you are beautiful, and in the resurrection everybody will see it."

"I was always homely as an owl," said Miss Roxy, unconsciously speaking out what had lain like a stone at the bottom
of even her sensible heart. "I always had sense to know it, and
knew my sphere. Homely folks would like to say pretty things,
and to have pretty things said to them, but they never do. I
made up my mind pretty early that my part in the vineyard was
to have hard work and no posies."

"Well, you will have all the more in heaven; I love you dearly,
and I like your looks, too. You look kind and true and good, and
that's beauty in the country where we are going."

Miss Roxy sprang up quickly from the bed, and turning her
back began to arrange the bottles on the table with great zeal.

"Has Moses come in yet?" said Mara.

"No, there ain't nobody seen a thing of him since he went out
this morning."

"Poor boy!" said Mara, "it is too hard upon him. Aunt Roxy,
please pick some roses off the bush from under the window and
put in the vases; let's have the room as sweet and cheerful as we
can. I hope God will let me live long enough to comfort him. It
is not so very terrible, if one would only think so, to cross that
river. All looks so bright to me now that I have forgotten how
sorrow seemed. Poor Moses! he will have a hard struggle, but he
will get the victory, too. I am very weak to-night, but to-morrow I shall feel better, and I shall sit up, and perhaps I can paint
a little on that flower I was doing for him. We will not have
things look sickly or deathly. There, Aunt Roxy, he has come in;
I hear his step."

"I did n't hear it," said Miss Roxy, surprised at the acute
senses which sickness had etherealized to an almost spirit-like
intensity. "Shall I call him?"

"Yes, do," said Mara. "He can sit with me a little while to-night."

The light in the room was a strange dusky mingling of gold and gloom, when Moses stole softly in. The great cloud-castle that a little while since had glowed like living gold from turret and battlement, now dim, changed for the most part to a sombre gray, enlivened with a dull glow of crimson; but there was still a golden light where the sun had sunk into the sea. Moses saw the little thin hand stretched out to him.

"Sit down," she said; "it has been such a beautiful sunset. Did you notice it?"

He sat down by the bed, leaning his forehead on his hand, but saying nothing.

She drew her fingers through his dark hair. "I am so glad to see you," she said. "It is such a comfort to me that you have come; and I hope it will be to you. You know I shall be better to-morrow than I am to-night, and I hope we shall have some pleasant days together yet. We must n't reject what little we may have, because it cannot be more."

"Oh, Mara," said Moses, "I would give my life, if I could take back the past. I have never been worthy of you; never knew your worth; never made you happy. You always lived for me, and I lived for myself. I deserve to lose you, but it is none the less bitter."

"Don't say lose. Why must you? I cannot think of losing you. I know I shall not. God has given you to me. You will come to me and be mine at last. I feel sure of it."

"You don't know me," said Moses.

"Christ does, though," she said; "and He has promised to care for you. Yes, you will live to see many flowers grow out of my grave. You cannot think so now; but it will be so—believe me."

"Mara," said Moses, "I never lived through such a day as this. It seems as if every moment of my life had been passing before me, and every moment of yours. I have seen how true and loving in thought and word and deed you have been, and I have been doing nothing but take—take. You have given love as the skies give rain, and I have drunk it up like the hot dusty earth."

Mara knew in her own heart that this was all true, and she was too real to use any of the terms of affected humiliation which many think a kind of spiritual court language. She looked at him and answered, "Moses, I always knew I loved most. It was my nature; God gave it to me, and it was a gift for which I give him thanks—not a merit. I knew you had a larger, wider nature than mine,—a wider sphere to live in, and that you could not live in your heart as I did. Mine was all thought and feeling, and the narrow little duties of this little home. Yours went all round the world."

"But, oh Mara—oh, my angel! to think I should lose you when I am just beginning to know your worth. I always had a sort of superstitious feeling,—a sacred presentiment about you,—that my spiritual life, if ever I had any, would come through you. It seemed if there ever was such a thing as God's providence, which some folks believe in, it was in leading me to you, and giving you to me. And now, to have all lashed—all destroyed— It makes me feel as if all was blind chance; no guiding God; for if he wanted me to be good, he would spare you."

Mara lay with her large eyes fixed on the now faded sky. The dusky shadows had dropped like a black crape veil around her pale face. In a few moments she repeated to herself, as if she were musing upon them, those mysterious words of Him who liveth and was dead, "Except a corn of wheat fall into the ground and die, it abideth alone; if it die, it bringeth forth much fruit."

"Moses," she said, "for all I know you have loved me dearly, yet I have felt that in all that was deepest and dearest to me, I was alone. You did not come near to me, nor touch me where I feel most deeply. If I had lived to be your wife, I cannot say but this distance in our spiritual nature might have widened. You know, what we live with we get used to; it grows an old story. Your love to me might have grown old and worn out. If we lived together in the commonplace toils of life, you would see only a poor threadbare wife. I might have lost what little charm I ever had for you; but I feel that if I die, this will not be. There is something sacred and beautiful in death; and I may have more power over you, when I seem to be gone, than I should have had living."

"Oh, Mara, Mara, don't say that."

"Dear Moses, it is so. Think how many lovers marry, and how few lovers are left in middle life; and how few love and reverence living friends as they do the dead. There are only a very few to whom it is given to do that."

Something in the heart of Moses told him that this was true. In this one day—the sacred revealing light of approaching death—he had seen more of the real spiritual beauty and significance of Mara's life than in years before, and felt upspringing in his heart, from the deep pathetic influence of the approaching spiritual world, a new and stronger power of loving. It may be that it is not merely a perception of love that we were not aware of before, that wakes up when we approach the solemn shadows with a friend. It may be that the soul has compressed and unconscious powers which are stirred and wrought upon as it looks over the borders into its future home,—its loves and its longings so swell and beat, that they astonish itself. We are greater than we know, and dimly feel it with every approach to the great hereafter. "It doth not yet appear what we shall be."

"Now, I 'll tell you what 't is," said Aunt Roxy, opening the door, "all the strength this 'ere girl spends a-talkin' to-night, will be so much taken out o' the whole cloth to-morrow."

Moses started up. "I ought to have thought of that, Mara."

"Ye see," said Miss Roxy, "she 's been through a good deal to-day, and she must be got to sleep at some rate or other to-night. 'Lord, if he sleep he shall do well,' the Bible says, and it 's one of my best nussin' maxims."

"And a good one, too, Aunt Roxy," said Mara. "Good-night, dear boy; you see we must all mind Aunt Roxy."

Moses bent down and kissed her, and felt her arms around his neck.

"Let not your heart be troubled," she whispered. In spite of himself Moses felt the storm that had risen in his bosom that morning soothed by the gentle influences which Mara breathed upon it. There is a sympathetic power in all states of mind, and they who have reached the deep secret of eternal rest have a strange power of imparting calm to others.

It was in the very crisis of the battle that Christ said to his disciples, *"My peace I give unto you,"* and they that are made one with him acquire like precious power of shedding round them repose, as evening flowers shed odors. Moses went to his pillow sorrowful and heart-stricken, but bitter or despairing he could not be with the consciousness of that present angel in the house.

XLIII

✦✦✦✦

THE PEARL

The next morning rose calm and bright with that wonderful and mystical stillness and serenity which glorify autumn days. It was impossible that such skies could smile and such gentle airs blow the sea into one great waving floor of sparkling sapphires without bringing cheerfulness to human hearts. You must be very despairing indeed, when Nature is doing her best, to look her in the face sullen and defiant. So long as there is a drop of good in your cup, a penny in your exchequer of happiness, a bright day reminds you to look at it, and feel that all is not gone yet.

So felt Moses when he stood in the door of the brown house, while Mrs. Pennel was clinking plates and spoons as she set the breakfast-table, and Zephaniah Pennel in his shirt-sleeves was washing in the back-room, while Miss Roxy came downstairs in a business-like fashion, bringing sundry bowls, plates, dishes, and mysterious pitchers from the sick-room.

"Well, Aunt Roxy, you ain't one that lets the grass grow under your feet," said Mrs. Pennel. "How is the dear child, this morning?"

"Well, she had a better night than one could have expected," said Miss Roxy, "and by the time she 's had her breakfast, she expects to sit up a little and see her friends." Miss Roxy said this in a cheerful tone, looking encouragingly at Moses, whom she began to pity and patronize, now she saw how real was his affliction.

After breakfast Moses went to see her; she was sitting up in her white dressing-gown, looking so thin and poorly, and everything in the room was fragrant with the spicy smell of the monthly roses, whose late buds and blossoms Miss Roxy had gathered for the vases. She seemed so natural, so calm and cheerful, so interested in all that went on around her, that one almost forgot that the time of her stay must be so short. She called Moses to come and look at her drawings, and paintings of flowers and birds,—full of reminders they were of old times,—and then she would have her pencils and colors, and work a little on a bunch of red rock-columbine, that she had begun to do for him; and she chatted of all the old familiar places where flowers grew, and of the old talks they had had there, till Moses quite forgot himself; forgot that he was in a sick-room, till Aunt Roxy, warned by the deepening color on Mara's cheeks, interposed her "nussing" authority, that she must do no more that day.

Then Moses laid her down, and arranged her pillows so that she could look out on the sea, and sat and read to her till it was time for her afternoon nap; and when the evening shadows drew on, he marveled with himself how the day had gone.

Many such there were, all that pleasant month of September, and he was with her all the time, watching her wants and doing her bidding,—reading over and over with a softened modulation her favorite hymns and chapters, arranging her flowers, and bringing her home wild bouquets from all her favorite wood-haunts, which made her sick-room seem like some sylvan bower. Sally Kittridge was there too, almost every day, with always some friendly offering or some helpful deed of kindness, and sometimes they two together would keep guard over the invalid while Miss Roxy went home to attend to some of her own more peculiar concerns. Mara seemed to rule all around her with calm sweetness and wisdom, speaking unconsciously only the speech of heaven, talking of spiritual things, not in an excited rapture or wild ecstasy, but with the sober certainty of waking bliss. She seemed like one of the sweet friendly angels one reads of in the Old Testament, so lovingly companionable, walking and talking, eating and drinking, with mortals, yet ready at any unknown moment to ascend with the flame of some sacrifice and be gone. There are those (a few at least) whose blessing it has been to have kept for many days, in bonds of earthly fellowship, a perfected spirit in whom the work of purifying love was wholly done, who lived in calm victory over sin and sorrow and death, ready at any moment to be called to the final mystery of joy.

Yet it must come at last, the moment when heaven claims its own, and it came at last in the cottage on Orr's Island. There came a day when the room so sacredly cheerful was hushed to a breathless stillness; the bed was then all snowy white, and that soft still sealed face, the parted waves of golden hair, the little hands folded over the white robe, all had a sacred and wonderful calm, a rapture of repose that seemed to say "it is done."

They who looked on her wondered; it was a look that sunk deep into every heart; it hushed down the common cant of those who, according to country custom, went to stare blindly at the great mystery of death,—for all that came out of that chamber smote upon their breasts and went away in silence, revolving strangely whence might come that unearthly beauty, that celestial joy.

Once more, in that very room where James and Naomi Lincoln had lain side by side in their coffins, sleeping restfully, there was laid another form, shrouded and coffined, but with such a fairness and tender purity, such a mysterious fullness of joy in its expression, that it seemed more natural to speak of that rest as some higher form of life than of death.

Once more were gathered the neighborhood; all the faces known in this history shone out in one solemn picture, of which that sweet restful form was the centre. Zephaniah Pennel and Mary his wife, Moses and Sally, the dry form of Captain Kittridge and the solemn face of his wife, Aunt Roxy and Aunt Ruey, Miss Emily and Mr. Sewell; but their faces all wore a tender brightness, such as we see falling like a thin celestial veil over all the faces in an old Florentine painting. The room was full of sweet memories, of words of cheer, words of assurance, words of triumph, and the mysterious brightness of that young face forbade them to weep. Solemnly Mr. Sewell read, —

"He will swallow up death in victory; and the Lord God will wipe away tears from off all faces; and the rebuke of his people shall he take away from off all the earth; for the Lord hath spoken it. And it shall be said in that day, Lo this is our God; we have waited for him, and he will save us; this is the Lord; we have waited for him, we will be glad and rejoice in his salvation."

Then the prayer trembled up to heaven with thanksgiving, for the early entrance of that fair young saint into glory, and then the same old funeral hymn, with its mournful triumph: —

> "Why should we mourn departed friends,
>   Or shake at death's alarms,
> 'T is but the voice that Jesus sends
>   To call them to his arms."

Then in a few words Mr. Sewell reminded them how that hymn had been sung in this room so many years ago, when that frail, fluttering orphan soul had been baptized into the love and care of Jesus, and how her whole life, passing before them in its simplicity and beauty, had come to so holy and beautiful a close; and when, pointing to the calm sleeping face he asked, "Would we call her back?" there was not a heart at that moment that dared answer, Yes. Even he that should have been her bridegroom could not at that moment have unsealed the holy charm, and so they bore her away, and laid the calm smiling face beneath the soil, by the side of poor Dolores.

‡‡‡‡

"I had a beautiful dream last night," said Zephaniah Pennel, the next morning after the funeral, as he opened his Bible to conduct family worship.

"What was it?" said Miss Roxy.

"Well, ye see, I thought I was out a-walkin' up and down, and lookin' and lookin' for something that I 'd lost. What it was I could n't quite make out, but my heart felt heavy as if it would break, and I was lookin' all up and down the sands by the seashore, and somebody said I was like the merchantman, seeking goodly pearls. I said I had lost my pearl—my pearl of great price—and then I looked up, and far off on the beach, shining softly on the wet sands, lay my pearl. I thought it was Mara, but it seemed a great pearl with a soft moonlight on it; and I was running for it when some one said 'hush,' and I looked and I saw *Him* a-coming—Jesus of Nazareth, jist as he walked by the sea of Galilee. It was all dark night around Him, but I could see Him by the light that came from his face, and the long hair was hanging down on his shoulders. He came and took up my pearl and put it on his forehead, and it shone out like a star, and shone into my heart, and I felt happy; and he looked at me steadily, and rose and rose in the air, and melted in the clouds, and I awoke so happy, and so calm!"

XLIV

♠♠♠♠♠

FOUR YEARS AFTER

It was a splendid evening in July, and the sky was filled high with gorgeous tabernacles of purple and gold, the remains of a grand thunder-shower which had freshened the air and set a separate jewel on every needle leaf of the old pines.

Four years had passed since the fair Pearl of Orr's Island had been laid beneath the gentle soil, which every year sent monthly tributes of flowers to adorn her rest, great blue violets, and starry flocks of ethereal eye-brights in spring, and fringy asters, and goldenrod in autumn. In those days, the tender sentiment which now makes the burial-place a cultivated garden was excluded by the rigid spiritualism of the Puritan life, which, ever jealous of that which concerned the body, lest it should claim what belonged to the immortal alone, had frowned on all watching of graves, as an earthward tendency, and enjoined the flight of faith with the spirit, rather than the yearning for its cast-off garments.

But Sally Kittridge, being lonely, found something in her heart which could only be comforted by visits to that grave. So she had planted there roses and trailing myrtle, and tended and watered them; a proceeding which was much commented on Sunday noons, when people were eating their dinners and discussing their neighbors.

It is possible good Mrs. Kittridge might have been much scandalized by it, had she been in a condition to think on the matter at all; but a very short time after the funeral she was seized with a paralytic shock, which left her for a while as helpless as an infant; and then she sank away into the grave, leaving Sally the sole care of the old Captain.

A cheerful home she made, too, for his old age, adorning the house with many little tasteful fancies unknown in her mother's days; reading the Bible to him and singing Mara's favorite hymns, with a voice as sweet as the spring blue-bird. The spirit of the departed friend seemed to hallow the dwelling where these two worshiped her memory, in simple-hearted love. Her paintings, framed in quaint woodland frames of moss and pine-cones by Sally's own ingenuity, adorned the walls. Her books were on the table, and among them many that she had given to Moses.

"I am going to be a wanderer for many years," he said in parting, "keep these for me until I come back."

And so from time to time passed long letters between the two friends,—each telling to the other the same story,—that they were lonely, and that their hearts yearned for the communion of one who could no longer be manifest to the senses. And each spoke to the other of a world of hopes and memories buried with her, "Which," each so constantly said, "no one could understand but you." Each, too, was firm in the faith that buried love must have no earthly resurrection. Every letter strenuously insisted that they should call each other brother and sister, and under cover of those names the letters grew longer and more frequent, and with every chance opportunity came presents from the absent brother, which made the little old cottage quaintly suggestive with smell of spice and sandal-wood.

But, as we said, this is a glorious July evening,—and you may discern two figures picking their way over those low sunken rocks, yellowed with seaweed, of which we have often spoken. They are Moses and Sally going on an evening walk to that favorite grotto retreat, which has so often been spoken of in the course of this history.

Moses has come home from long wanderings. It is four years since they parted, and now they meet and have looked into each other's eyes, not as of old, when they met in the first giddy flush of youth, but as fully developed man and woman. Moses and Sally had just risen from the tea-table, where she had presided with a thoughtful housewifery gravity, just pleasantly dashed with quaint streaks of her old merry willfulness, while the old Captain, warmed up like a rheumatic grasshopper in a fine autumn day, chirruped feebly, and told some of his old stories, which now he told every day, forgetting that they had ever been heard before. Somehow all three had been very happy; the more so, from a shadowy sense of some sympathizing presence which was rejoicing to see them together again, and which, stealing soft-footed and noiseless everywhere, touched and lighted up every old familiar object with sweet memories.

And so they had gone out together to walk; to walk towards the grotto where Sally had caused a seat to be made, and where she declared she had passed hours and hours, knitting, sewing, or reading.

"Sally," said Moses, "do you know I am tired of wandering? I am coming home now. I begin to want a home of my own." This he said as they sat together on the rustic seat and looked off on the blue sea.

"Yes, you must," said Sally. "How lovely that ship looks, just coming in there."

"Yes, they are beautiful," said Moses abstractedly; and Sally rattled on about the difference between sloops and brigs; seeming determined that there should be no silence, such as often comes in ominous gaps between two friends who have long been separated, and have each many things to say with which the other is not familiar.

"Sally!" said Moses, breaking in with a deep voice on one of these monologues. "Do you remember some presumptuous things I once said to you, in this place?"

Sally did not answer, and there was a dead silence in which they could hear the tide gently dashing on the weedy rocks.

"You and I are neither of us what we were then, Sally," said Moses. "We are as different as if we were each another person. We have been trained in another life,—educated by a great sorrow,—is it not so?"

"I know it," said Sally.

"And why should we two, who have a world of thoughts and memories which no one can understand but the other,—why should we, each of us, go on alone? If we must, why then, Sally, I must leave you, and I must write and receive no more letters, for I have found that you are becoming so wholly necessary to me, that if any other should claim you, I could not feel as I ought. Must I go?"

Sally's answer is not on record; but one infers what it was from the fact that they sat there very late, and before they knew it, the tide rose up and shut them in, and the moon rose up in full glory out of the water, and still they sat and talked, leaning on each other, till a cracked, feeble voice called down through the pine-trees above, like a hoarse old cricket,—

"Children, be you there?"

"Yes, father," said Sally, blushing and conscious.

"Yes, all right," said the deep bass of Moses. "I 'll bring her back when I 've done with her, Captain."

"Wal',—wal'; I was gettin' consarned; but I see I don't need to. I hope you won't get no colds nor nothin'."

They did not; but in the course of a month there was a wedding at the brown house of the old Captain, which everybody in the parish was glad of, and was voted without dissent to be just the thing.

Miss Roxy, grimly approbative, presided over the preparations, and all the characters of our story appeared, and more, having on their wedding-garments. Nor was the wedding less joyful, that all felt the presence of a heavenly guest, silent and loving, seeing and blessing all, whose voice seemed to say in every heart,—

"He turneth the shadow of death into morning."

HARRIET [ELIZABETH] BEECHER STOWE was born in 1811 and spent her early years living in Connecticut. She was one of thirteen children. Her father, Lyman Beecher, was a popular minister, an abolitionist, and the founder of the American Bible Society. In 1832 Harriet moved with her family to Cincinnati, where she taught at a girls' school and began to write sketches about New England. In 1836 she married Calvin Stowe, a professor and abolitionist. In 1850, she moved with Calvin to Brunswick, Maine, after Calvin accepted a professorship at Bowdoin College. Together they had seven children, four of whom died tragically and at a young age: Charley from cholera, Henry in a drowning accident, Frederick from alcoholism and the emotional wounds he suffered during the battle of Gettysburg, and Georgiana to morphine addiction. Harriet somehow managed to continue to write and support her family despite her hardships. She is the author of *Uncle Tom's Cabin* (1852), *A Key to Uncle Tom's Cabin* (1853), *Sunny Memories of Foreign Lands* (1854), *Dred: A Tale of the Great Dismal Swamp* (1856), *The Ministers Wooing* (1859), *The Pearl of Orr's Island* (1862), *Agnes of Sorrento* (1862), *Religious Poems* (1867), *Oldtown Folks* (1869), *Lady Byron Vindicated* (1870), *Sam Lawson's Oldtown Fireside Stories* (1872), *Poganuc People* (1878), *Pink and White Tyranny* (1871), *My Wife and I* (1871), *We and Our Neighbors* (1875), and *Palmetto Leaves* (1873). During the last fifteen years of her life she lived mainly in Florida. She died in 1896 at the age of eighty-five.